Women Law Enforcers

Investigating

Domestic Terrorists

in

Wyoming Secrets

By

Jonathan McCormick

For Les Wiseman

The Angel of the Night

"Fear not the night. Fear that which walks the night.
And *I* am that which walks the night.
But only evil need fear me ...and gentle souls sleep
safe in their beds...because I walk the night."

Lt. Col Dave Grossman U.S. Army (Ret.)

Revised Edition
2023

Contents

Prologue vii
Chapter One...1
Chapter Two 7
Chapter Three 12
Chapter Four..16
Chapter Five 22
Chapter Six...33
Chapter Seven 44
Chapter Eight...56
Chapter Nine 63
Chapter Ten 66
Chapter Eleven 75
Chapter Twelve..83
Chapter Thirteen..89
Chapter Fourteen 93
Chapter Fifteen..104
Chapter Sixteen 108
Chapter Seventeen 116
Chapter Eighteen 121
Chapter Nineteen 130
Chapter Twenty 139
Chapter Twenty-One...155
Chapter Twenty-Two 161
Chapter Twenty-Three 171
Chapter Twenty-Four..178
Chapter Twenty-Five 186

Chapter Twenty-Six 198
Chapter Twenty-Seven 206
Chapter Twenty-Eight 215
Chapter Twenty-Nine 224
Chapter Thirty 230
Chapter Thirty-One 244
Chapter Thirty-Two 251
Chapter Thirty-Three 260
Chapter Thirty-Four 267
Chapter Thirty-Five 277
Chapter Thirty-Six 286
Chapter Thirty-Seven 293
Chapter Thirty-Eight 299
Chapter Thirty-Nine 313
Chapter Forty 322
Chapter Forty-One 332
Chapter Forty-Two 341
Chapter Forty-Three 348
Chapter Forty-Four 361
Chapter Forty-Five 374
Chapter Forty-Six 391
Chapter Forty-Seven 402
Chapter Forty-Eight 410
Chapter Forty-Nine 415
Chapter Fifty 423
Chapter Fifty-One 430
Chapter Fifty-Two 437
Chapter Fifty-Three 443
Chapter Fifty-Four 450
Chapter Fifty-Five 458
Acknowledgements 465
Prologue 471
Chapter One 475
Jonathan McCormick 479

Prologue

Secret Service Agent Jessica Fukishura had never been in a violent relationship, hadn't been in many relationships of any kind but she knew from the copious University of Berkeley psychology classes, women's studies, and family law courses that the trauma of sexual assault and domestic violence was not only emotional but was a dramatic degradation of a woman's psyche, her physical wellbeing, her interpersonal skills, and financial independence.

She knew what men could do when equipped with a firearm, club, knife, or other deadly weapon. She had witnessed scores of battered women in hospital recovery units and women's resource centers. Saw their battered bodies, their souls on the brink of eternal extinction. She knew early in her law school studies that administering jurisprudence after the fact would not right the wrongs of the past or rectify the present. She knew she had to make a difference…somehow. She just didn't know what course the interception of female humiliation would take…yet.

But she did know that whatever that course might be it would include hurting men and hurting them badly.

Jenewein circled the lake once looking for any sign of his previous visitor who had broken into the main building and ravaged the supply room, destroying bags of rice, flour and making off with cans of meat and prepared food. He concentrated on the plane's movement as his mind wandered back to the incident. Jenewein had wondered at the time why a person in need would have felt the urge to destroy. The kitchen door had not just been broken; it had been smashed beyond repair. He'd seen photos of doors destroyed by SWAT teams; hinges torn from their seats, door jams ripped and hanging loose as though a mini bulldozer had blasted its way through.

Jenewein had to build a new one before returning to Denver. He recalled a strange pungent odor like musky bear stench that permeated the air and hung in his nostrils. And the long brownish hairs caught at the top of the doorway that was certainly not bear...or moose for that matter. Had a lost hunter or prospector been hungry, they would have helped themselves to whatever they needed, which was bush custom, but the wanton destruction was beyond comprehension.

Jenewein had spent hours sweeping just to make the place livable. Now as he made his fly-by, he wondered if his visitor might have been a guy like British Columbia's Allan Schoenborn who fled to the bush to escape police pursuit, wanted for killing three children. Schoenborn lived in the bush animal like for weeks, surviving on grubs when he couldn't find a cabin to trash for food. He was finally spotted by a trapper who made a citizen's arrest, called 9-1-1 and held him until the police arrived. But that wouldn't have explained the damage. He brought his attention back to landing.

Chapter One

"Sheepdogs may be male or female."

Jessica Fukishura

"Her attacker had a weapon, a vicious combat knife, capable of stripping her limbs with one slash. She had no fear; no rapid heart rate, no eyes darting, seeking escape, no scream raging to flee. Nothing but tunnel vision aimed at the person prepared to kill her.

As her attacker advanced with lightning speed, she flowed to her left at a 45 with the grace of a ballerina, just as he lunged the extreme knife at her midsection. As the attacker's forward movement stalled, Fukishura placed all her weight on the ball of her left foot, grabbed his right wrist with her right hand then directed a violent blow to hit his elbow, locking the arm straight. Nano seconds and she had him on the ground and was in the process of breaking bone, oblivious to the screams of pain from stretched tendons and ligaments coming from her "Attacker" clad in the Red Man protective suit and helmet. All she could feel and hear was the vibration of her 60-rate heart, her steady breathing, and the sweat dripping from her underarms.

Within seconds two Secret Service trainers were on her, pulling her off her colleague, yelling, 'Done, Done, Done!'

Jessica released her "Attacker" with a flourish, raised her arms straight in the air, and walked away, bouncing on the balls of her feet, like a fighter. She got him. Son-of-a-bitch, she got him. Dam, she was good. None of these self-centered, narcistic asshole agents could take her down. Never, she gloated to herself.

"God Damn Jessica. What the fuck are you trying to do, kill me? That hurt like hell. You damn nearly broke my arm. What the hell's with you anyway? You still trying to prove you're the baddest agent, able to kick anybody's ass? Fuck this hurts. Fuck," yelled Campbell, the designated agent in the Red Man.

"What! Can't take it Campbell?"

"Shit, no I can't. You are really pissing me off. I'm going to kick your ass when it's your turn in the barrel. Fuck!" he yelled, holding his arm, trying unsuccessfully to move it. "When the fuck are you goin' learn to taper this training? There's not going to be anything left of me at retirement," he said as his anger slowed and he removed his protective helmet and threw it on the floor, pissed and in pain. He rubbed and massaged his arm, walking around in a circle trying to ease the pain.

"Well maybe Sorento will grant your wish someday, or maybe by then you'll be retired to Atlantic City spending your days guarding the one-armed bandits," she smirked, not realizing, as she never did, the torment her cutting remarks made and the alienation they caused.

Sorento had been her boss since her acceptance to the president's protection detail five years previous. He had been reluctant to accept a female agent to the supreme, prestigious Secret Service assignment but he had little choice given her top ranking in all qualifications and her actions during her first offshore protection assignment.

Sorento's apprehension had vanished during a presidential trip to France where President Backus' predecessor, a man many experts thought had an IQ hovering around 80, was entering the

U.S. Embassy for a state function, an element of his European trip set to appease the criticism for America's Middle East policies. It was thought by many administration critics that his lack of academic achievement was the basis for his poor decisions that created hatred for him and Americans worldwide but in fact it was the lack of accurate intelligence and outright deception by his senior staff and CIA senior politicos that bred the illusion of ignorance and regrettably, he did little to refute that image.

There were numerous hecklers waving "America, no friend of France" and "Islam will destroy America." As the president walked by waving to the crowd, moving slowly, trying to make eye contact with those who would prefer to spit on him, two hecklers broke through the barrier and rushed the president trying to sprint the short thirty yards.

Fukishura, who was assigned peripheral detail dressed to blend with the crowd, had attacked both Frenchmen before they were within threatening range. The men had approached abreast of each other planning a united attack. She was innocuous in her drab dark scarf wrapped around her head and the flowing skirt.

The attire covered her ear bud and weapons. She was stationary, for all intense and purposes, enamored with the American's presence. She spotted their movement before they broke the barricade. With one swift, fluid movement she vaulted the four-foot barricade in front and circled to block the protesters' advance.

Fukishura rushed them, stepped to the first assailant's right and lashed with a violent kick to his right knee, breaking it instantly as she simultaneously pulled her Sig Sauer P226 semi-automatic pistol with her left hand and fired two rounds into the second attacker's chest cavity amidst the panicking crowd that had no idea who or what she was, thinking the worse...an attack on the president of the United States.

The incident was over and Fukishura was kneeling beside the fallen attackers as the other agents and French police reacted. The president was sprinted into the embassy while law enforcers converged on Fukishura. French police pushed the crowd back while Fukishura cuffed the live suspect with her Sig still in her left hand, and then checked the shot suspect for signs of life. Finding none, she opened his jacket, revealing a Russian machine pistol-compact and deadly.

The Secret Service detail knew, as did the French police, of her ruse but the reality and magnitude of the incident was momentarily set-back as French agents attempted to grab her, in a hastily made decision to control of the panicking crowd by taking charge of the person the crowd thought was the assailant. Just as Central Directorate of Interior Intelligence-DCRI agents tried to grab Fukishura's arm, her colleagues encircled her, hands extended, warning all to back-off.

Since then she had a lock on her position, emphasized every training day, albeit with animosity from some if not most of her colleagues, male and female alike, due to her arrogance, no holds barred training attitude and as some felt, overall bitchiness.

Back in the changing room, Jessica showered and dressed for her duty day. Since her university graduation and snagging the presidential detail, she'd been partial to Armani clothes. Great pants that hugged her taut frame and jackets cut loose to conceal her Sig.

Fukishura was 5'7" of solid. She'd taken to working out as a kid hangin' at her mom's gym. It was fun to play on the rowing machines and stationary bikes. As a teen, she noticed her body changing as puberty and exercise meshed, producing energy that needed direction. That was what hockey was for, and running, lots of running.

As her teen years evaporated and her hormones meshed with her athleticism, she emerged with a body often cherished and sought by other women, who by their early 20s were already starting to lie about their thigh cheese. Jessica's low estrogen levels kept her bra size around 34 C, and she had no desire for more. She adhered to the seldom coined male phrase of more is less, that it is what a woman does with what she has that is the key to good sexual attraction. Or at least she could fool herself into believing men followed that train of thought.

Today's attire was an Armani's Black Leather Jacket; stand-up collar with an Emerald Cashmere Tank and pinstripe wool/spandex pants $1,700. Ouch!

Worth every dime. Her kicks were Jimmy Choo's Patent Leather Flats in which she had trained and knew her running speed and endurance as well as the shoe's impact on a human knee. She loved the freedom Jimmy gave her, the supple leather that wrapped around her feet like smooth hands, giving her the desired style and the needed practicality.

She figured she had to spend her language bonus on something, why not Armani and Jimmy Choo? Besides, she knew the impression her choice would have at the Ranch. She loved it. Armani screamed "Success".

She keyed her weapons locker, grabbed her Sig with her left hand, released the magazine, checked its contents, replaced it; hit the weapon's butt with the heel of her right hand, seating the magazine. She stopped momentarily in the procedure she had spent years ingraining into her motor skills to fondle her weapon.

The Sig was art, pure and simple. It had a smoothness her hand coveted, a texture her skin glossed over and over, always wanting more.

She brought the piece up to her face, passed the barrel across her left cheek, inhaled the oil fragrance, and recalled the number of times she had this very same semi-automatic shoved in her face, trigger pulled back, her trainer screaming that he was going to blow her brains out...just before she took it away from him and dropped him with her knee ending up in his neck and the Sig pinching his carotid.

During those repeated exercises she was shown the firearm was unloaded but when the adrenalin blasted through her system, there was never time to commiserate on bullets or empty magazine, it was just explode through and take-down.

Continuing to fondle the weapon, she pulled the slide back chambering a round, and then placed the firearm under her right arm pit in a velvety, firm shoulder holster.

She fingered her Spyderco Police Special one hand opening knife clipped inside her belt assuring herself of its placement, acknowledging the affection she had for all blades and the deftness with which she could wield them all.

She closed both lockers, strutted over to the large wall mirror, appraised her look, smiled, feeling the confidence ooze through her soul, fluffed her short black mop and headed out the door.

Chapter Two

"When the wolf comes, you and your loved ones are going
to die if there is not a sheepdog there to protect you."

Lt. Col. Dave Grossman U.S. Army (Ret)

Daniel Jenewein taxied the Otter single engine De Havilland to
the Colorado Leyden Airport's designated runway, his eyes
scanning the vast azure seeking any incoming traffic...this airport
being designated VFR airport-visual flight rules, which equated to
no flight plan or record of his departure.

Satisfied that he owned the skies momentarily, he eased
the throttles slightly and headed toward the Southwest runway.
Absorbing the rising G forces that rose through his lower body
originating in the vibration of the foot controls, gently caressing
each muscle and blood cell as the adrenaline moved to his head.
He accepted the thrill as his own, his to command as the plane
continued its gentle move and acceleration in anticipation of
unleashing its full potential.

Once in position, he advanced the throttle forward and felt the
Pratt and Whitney's 600 horses whisper through his headphones
and catapult two and a half tons of turbo off the 4,800-foot runway.

He allowed the force to push him back into the plush pilot's
seat, feeling the rush through his hands on the throttle. Once

airborne, he banked right and continued his climb, adjusting his heading northwest.

His sole passenger adjusted himself and looked east as Jenewein leveled off at 12,000 feet engaging the autopilot. His passenger continued to be occupied by the spectacular 360 degrees of jagged mountain terrain.

Jenewein closed his eyes absorbing the sun's rays, feeling the warmth spread across his chest and relaxing his muscles.

Pulling himself from his euphoria, he withdrew his 6-inch Tanto knife from its sheath strapped to the front of his seat, reached across the short space and with one fluid motion, thrust the Tanto between Edgar's fourth and fifth ribs, puncturing his atrium, stopping his heart instantly.

Jenewein reached under his seat again and grabbed a large bundle of absorbent terry towel, removed the Tanto and pressed the towel to Edgar's rib cage preventing any blood from hitting the plane's interior. There was none. The heart had to pump blood to move. Edgar's heart stopped in the middle of the pumping process.

Satisfied there was zero blood trace, he wiped the Tanto on the terry cloth still stuck to Edgar, laid the beautiful killing instrument across the victim's lap to retrieve later for disposal and poured himself a coffee from his thermos and opened a Danish he'd purchased from the airport vending machine and enjoyed the rising sun breaking Colorado's eastern horizon.

Jessica was a second generation Japanese American/Canadian whose parents were professionals in Toronto. Her dad Glenn was born and educated in California, taking his doctorate-Ed.D. in education from the University of California at Berkeley, then a job at the University of Toronto where he rose to the College of Education's department head.

Her parents had met during at an anti-Vietnam rally in front of the Toronto city hall years ago. Shelia was from a conservative

Irish Canadian home, graduated from Ecole Polytechnique in Montreal with a Masters in political science and worked for an American think tank in Toronto when she and Glenn met.

Shelia was dedicated to women's empowerment and breaking the cycle of women at the bottom of society's economy and had cemented her commitment to women's rights after the 1989 shootings which left fourteen classmates dead. She never realized that the incident would be the starting point for Jessica's law enforcement interest let alone her daughter's demon and relationship breaker.

The fact that a man could walk into a university classroom with an illegal firearm and open fire on female students, was appalling to the young Fukishura and she decided then and there that she would somehow curb psychopaths.

Little did Jessica realize as a teen that her path would lead to a law degree from her father's alma mater with no job prospects. She decided in her last year that she didn't want to practice law...too boring, but she would complete the degree program, primarily to fend off criticism as being a quitter and avoiding collegial banter during career chitchats. But there was more to her decision than just boredom.

That was a superfluous and superficial reason. Once, during one of her clerkships for a federal judge, she became metaphorically bloodied and disenchanted by the swinging door judicial system.

Numerous times over Friday night pub drinks, her friends and colleagues chastised her for her naivety, blasting her for assuming the law would somehow bring justice to those wronged. It was during those social settings that she began to realize that her motivation all these years was to bring justice to the murdered Montreal women.

The judicial door syndrome was reality and no degree, and no prosecutorial position would bring those women back, give closure to their families or prevent some other lunatic from repeating the slaughter somewhere else. Columbine, Taber, Virginia Tech, and similar school massacres proved her point.

She participated in the campus recruiting machine and interviews with considerable trepidation. Might she be perceived as a quitter if she dumped law?

Besides business, what were her alternatives? She decided to pass on corporate America, shying away from having to defend her leaving law, and chose instead to interview various law enforcement teams bent on increasing their staffs' estrogen level to keep the federal government at bay.

At the time, she wouldn't have been able to articulate the motive. Even today, a decade or so later, she had difficulty acknowledging the motive for her career choice. Primarily, she did the interviews as something to do, something to tell her parents and friends so they'd believe she was still motivated in law but needed another direction. It was also fun to share the interview details with bar friends.

She threw in the CIA and Secret Service just for fun.

And for fun it would be for it was obvious the intelligence community would have no interest in a directionless female law student graduate with an attitude. And she had no intention of giving up the attitude. Turns out, both employers were sufficiently interested but she passed on the CIA, having difficulty getting past their reputation for covertness at all costs...figured they'd keep the women's restroom location a secret.

Both federal authorities wanted more females but not just to fill a requirement. Both agencies wanted Jessica for her straight "A" grade point average, law degree, Japanese and French language skills, and her combat martial arts expertise.

During the Secret Service interview, Jessica asked how they knew of her martial arts skills. The male interviewer refused to elaborate except to say, "We've been following your academic career since your junior year and your personal life was part of that observation."

"So, you are saying that you have been spying on me for two years," she retorted with a haughtiness and arrogance honed at Berkeley.

"Ms. Fukishura, take it as a compliment," retorted the interviewer. "We hire only the best of the best to protect the president of the United States and it takes that long to find out if we wanted to approach you. Your language expertise gives you an automatic twenty-five percent pay boost which would bring you somewhere around $63,000, plus a full medical package, travel, and the prestige. So cut the bull shit and the attitude. You want the job or not?"

And that's how it started. Her first years with the Service were consumed with mundane and boring assignments and the extreme task of keeping her mouth shut. Los Angeles for three years then Vancouver, British Columbia. Why did they need a Secret Service agent in Vancouver? She knew the answer intellectually, but it still didn't make much sense. But she did love the city, the food, and the ethnicity.

She was in Vancouver when she got the call to return to Washington to be considered for the Presidential detail. Always questioning, she asked herself, why me?

The male personnel agent told her it wasn't his idea, but that of congress which felt the president's detail had to reflect the nation's gender and ethnic balance. What? He told her she could take it or leave it. Her choice. Again, this take it or leave it attitude, she thought. Was it her or were these guys just assholes?

What the hell, Jessica thought; this could be a once-in-a-care opportunity. So she took the bait and got sucked into the testosterone world of White House law enforcement.

Chapter Three

After her training session it was almost noon. She decided to grab some lunch before heading back to Bakus' Ranch...The White House.

President Jack Bakus was a former Wyoming senator who rode to the White House on a Democratic ticket that was more, "get the other guys out," than a popular Democratic philosophy and principles.

He had started his first term just two years previously and was riding high on a solid economy, low unemployment and a Democratic controlled senate and house. Baring a major screw up, he was in for the second term. Guaranteed. The Democratic National Party was hoping all politicians kept it in their pants and didn't email underage boys.

Bakus was the fourth or fifth rancher in the White House so that wasn't unique. But this president graduated from Princeton law school, 15th in his class and represented ranchers against the federal government in his Wyoming practice. His Wyoming ranch was a ranch, not an oil field. He raised beef cattle which he marketed to Canada and various EU-European Union countries.

She headed to her favorite deli on Tenth just a few blocks from The Ranch for a cholesterol fix.

Perfect parking right in front of Marg's. These were the times she loved her gecko green Bug. Slick. Slide right into any spot long enough for a corpse.

Jessica was 120 pounds of female who could eat anything and everything. Marg's Deli. Marg's was Brooklyn. Retro-60s theme that offered all the charm of a Kings Highway deli in Brooklyn. Marg's is not for the timid, or faint of heart, which was what drew Jessica. Matzo ball soups, hot pastrami on rye, corned beef, and infinity omelets. Breakfast was 6 am with the yuppie joggers woofing the House Omelet that had more fat than any jogger could lose in a week. The lunch crowd was primarily the Ranch hands who wanted to get out and about for some down time.

Today Jessica's choice was a slim-stacked, New York pastrami, yellow mustard, dried sauerkraut, mayo, and Marg's drizzle concoction on dark rye. Plus the Kosher pickle, dildo size. To die for. Twice!

She ate outside. Jessica needed sweat and testosterone-free air after the last four-hour overload. Round table. One chair. With her back to the brick wall. Her left hand was always resting on her lap. Eating with her right, in Orange, ready to drop, roll and come up with her Sig. Her blood pressure hovering around 160, pounding her arteries with explosiveness bent on tearing their walls.

She forced herself to slow her pace, to enjoy the spring day with the infamous Washington cherry blossoms almost dangling in her hair, dropping from a massive host sharing their fragrance throughout the neighborhood. A couple of deep breaths, a noticeable sigh before she took her fist bite, allowing the pastrami moisture to swish from cheek to cheek before swallowing. Another bite and she leaned back into the chair, feeling the comfort of the wall's support.

Glancing around, she saw several groups of guys grabbing an early lunch watching her intently with the familiar facial expression: a mixture of enquiry and apprehension.

She had come to grips with the numerous times guys had assumed, based on her elusiveness and lack of wedding ring, that she was gay and now it was almost a game she played, eyeing the group, allowing her glance to move from guy to guy, forcing each to wonder if he should approach or if she really was on the other team and not interested in their gender.

She quickly tired of the game, savored Marg's world, downed the rest of her Pepsi, gave one last glace around, smiled coquettishly at the men, cocked her head quickly to the side as though she were throwing shoulder length locks, tossed her trash in door can, then headed for the Bug. Very slow scrutinizing 360 degrees; she glanced over her shoulder to see two tables of males making a mental note of the time so they would program future lunches. She climbed in, locked the doors, pulled out into crowded 1 pm traffic and headed for The Ranch.

She had just pulled into traffic when it dawned on her... she had forgotten to check under the Bug. Damn, she thought. Playing cute games with strangers had resulted in her deviating, the result of which could get her killed. She slammed her fist on the beautifully contoured leather covered Bug wheel, swung to her right into a Shop Night parking area, jumped out, got down on her hands and knees and let her programmed eyes contact the vehicle's undercarriage. Got up and repeated the same at the front, other side, and rear.

Satisfied she hadn't been planted to explode, she got back in the Bug and headed back into traffic, leaving the bystanders scratching their heads at the sight of a lovely brunette crawling around on all fours as though retrieving a child's ball. She made it to the Ranch satisfied she had corrected her major operational blunder.

Jessica always made a statement stopping at The Ranch Guard House. Married or single, every White House male cop and agent peered into the Bug. Skirt? No. Damn! She loved it. Fed her aura. And her ego. Look. Admire. But get close and you are 911 to the ER.

She knew that her attitude reflected her need to control and subconsciously she knew too that it was this predictable behavior that often, if not always, made her an outsider.

This White House officer was unknown to her. He perused her ID, checking it with her facial features, scanned it, and then returned the ID. Next, he had her lean out of the Bug and place her chin on a hand-held iris scanner which chimed twice recognizing her eye anatomy.

Entry scrutiny expanded to a walk around The Bug with a mirror on a stick, looking under the Bug while a second officer maneuvered a golden Labrador in the opposite direction sniffing for explosives. She was relaxed. Standard procedure. No offence given or taken. She passed the scrutiny and was waved on her way.

The Bug parked; she instinctively glanced up at the numerous snipers stationed around the architectural icon's portico and expansive perimeter, never tiring of the pressure that job entailed. Jessica headed for the detail's operation room for the day's duty schedule. Entering the building always took her back somewhat.

Once she walked through the door, she was in Wyoming. Every decorative detail, save for the traditional rooms, was Western. Wagon wheels abound, burgundy leather couches and chairs dominated. Huge coffee tables embedded with horseshoes, and outstanding log lamps seemed to draw visitors into the rural world of America. Monstrous wagon wheel chandeliers adorned entrance ceilings and meeting rooms. The Oval office had an erect mounted Grizzly watching Backus. Each room had a raccoon, fox, wolf or wolverine, scrutinizing politicians.

Bakus had maintained tradition in the state dining room, historic bedrooms, Vermeil and Red Rooms, Entrance Hall and Cross Hall but Backus' living area and political meeting rooms had been John Wayned.

Chapter Four

"Leadership has three essentials;
Humanity, clarity and courage."

Fushan Yuan, Zen Buddhist

S he came first to the interior guard station which required
clearance by everybody.

They passed her ID card through a sophisticate ATM scanner and checked her photo against the real thing. She repeated the iris scanner hearing the familiar acceptance chime. They had her empty her pockets, remove the Sig, put its barrel in a discharge tube's mouth, remove the clip, and remove the chambered shell. Put the Sig, the bullet, the magazine in a tray. Walk through the metal detector. Then, the Wand. A female officer passed the indubitable metal detecting device over every part of her exterior, and then directed Jessica to the body scanner.

She passed, and she mused wondering when a cavity search would be added to the entry protocol. But in fact she was supportive of all scrutiny to prevent the Ft. Hood Trojan Horse incident occurring at The Ranch.

"Nice Armani Jessica. New?" said Elise, the newest member of the Ranch Guard, fresh from a mid-western school (Berkeley graduates had to take shots at the "lesser" schools, if just for fun) and Service Basic Training.

After the scanning, Jessica showed off her Jimmy Choos by executing a few front kicks, a little twirl on one toe while she put her gear back together. Elise was a bit envious of Jessica's fashion, as Elise's duty required a uniform. Wearing a uniform did cut down on the clothing budget even if she looked overweight and unfit with the untailored, baggy butt and 20 pounds of gear.

Passing the other uniformed White House officers and Secret Service agents, Jessica did a little side shuffle/dance, spun around twice as she moved down the hall, giving the boys a taste of her Orange Mind Set, ready to drop, roll and come up Sig ready. Her rep was to toss the formal training when rising from the roll. She knew her antics pissed guys off, and she knew she was rubbing their noses in her superior tactical skills, but she always did it anyway, feeding her anger and distain.

Training was a two-handed Weaver stance with the Sig in her left hand, the right hand cupping her left, with the weapon's butt touching her right palm, all at just about arm's length. Not Jessica. She had too many firearms yanked out of her hands in Combat Martial Arts classes to stay with regulations. Her style was the Weaver but very close to her body, in front of her face. Point Shooting. She'd taken Jim Gregg's class during a Berkeley break and was now a member of his "Hole in One" elite.

Gregg was renowned in law enforcement for his shooting style, having taught U.S. Custom Security and Border Patrol, Canada's Elite RCMP and others, not to use the weapon's sites but to point and pull the trigger. Gregg's "Hole in One" club meant just that, the shooter put five bullets from 15 feet into a small hole in a steel silhouette target.

Jessica never took her qualifier at a range behind a bench at a fixed target per Service regulations. She had to be different. She had an open invitation at the FBI's Hogan's Alley thanks to her 10th degree Black Belt Instructor who was a Hogan's Alley graduate.

The Alley was a variation of Col. Rex Applegate's description of the House of Horrors or Kill House in his *Kill or be Killed*, a manual on hand-to-hand combat and defensive tactics by one of the country's first CIA agents. The Kill House is a building for military and counter terrorism teams to practice urban combat tactics. House details depend on the training objective; counter terrorism plane retake or standard office/house surge. The norm involved live fire at pop-up targets as one moved through a simulated town, office, or other mock scenario. Graduation was executing live fire with a team member in the passenger seat of a jumbo 747 among numerous dummy targets, which the team was retaking from terrorists. The participant had to shoot all the dummies and spare the colleague.

Colonel Applegate had been a world expert on close combat fighting. He served under Major General "Wild Bill" Donovan during the Second World War. Applegate was part of the Office of Strategic Services (OSS), the CIA's predecessor. He was Franklin D. Roosevelt's bodyguard.

Applegate worked in Mexico for the spooks-late 40's. Smith and Wesson' hammerless .38 pistol was the result of Applegate's near death when his revolver stuck in his jacket pocket. Applegate was Jessica's 10th degree Black Belt instructor's mentor. She read Applegate's *Kill or Be Killed* as a requirement for her Yellow Belt promotion which included a multi-page evaluation and demonstration of Applegate's principles and skills.

After her special greeting to the uniforms, she continued to the duty office and saw Sorento leaning against the door jamb shaking his head, but with a huge smile. "Fukishura, you are incorrigible. Do you ever act like a normal woman?"

"Good morning to you too boss. Nope, being normal is boring."

Sorento snorted, "Ya, I guess I should be used to it by now. Campbell is limping around telling everyone he fell off his ladder."

Jessica laughed, recalling kicking Campbell's ass earlier that day and said, "I'm sure all his buds will believe that unless they know with whom he was teamed today. So, what do you have in store for me today?"

"Come in the duty room and let's discuss the schedule."

Sorento let Jessica enter first then followed her past another guard into the heart of the Ranch's protection detail, then into Sorento's office.

The boss' command center was small but comfortable. She took a seat on the burgundy couch-an added touch from Bakus' remodeling. Sorento walked over to the coffee bar and poured them each a mug. Black. "Leanin' Tree" mugs. His logoed with, "You're never too old if you still cock your pistol!" And hers with a cartoon cow with humongous udders logoed with "Udderly Delicious".

Sorento handed Jessica her mug and she laughed, "I don't know how the citizens would react to seeing its top cops drinking from these mugs."

Sorento joined in the humor with a guffaw of his own and raised his mug to clink Jessica's.

She took a sip and relished the strong taste and appreciated Sorento's coffee choice. She figured he must tweak the budget a little to get a monthly delivery of Pinon coffee from New Mexico, his old haunt. Or maybe he bought it himself. Doesn't matter. Today's choice was Manzano Italiano. She recalled it was the namesake of the Manzano Mountains, north of Manzano, New Mexico. Souls? 54

Manzano is 30 plus miles from Albuquerque where Sorento figured he was headed after Estancia High for a Mickey D job. Fortunately, he acquired a sense of survival in Elementary school watching too many kids go nowhere and vowed to get out of town the day after high school graduation.

He developed a taste for Pinon while working summers as a wrangler for local ranchers. Haying and odd jobs with regular hands required him to do as they did and that meant coffee, lots of black coffee.

It was while drinking Pinon during a morning break haying, that his boss, rancher Jim Burroughs put the education bug in his ear and the desire to get it on his own.

Sorento took his advice and graduated from New Mexico State with an agriculture degree, planning on a future in sales with an agricultural chemical supply company.

But being an agriculture representative didn't measure up to his expectations of what life was supposed to be post-graduation. They were suits which didn't fit with his background. To a person, they were all about money, money, and more money. Nothing about the concept of increasing crop production or helping ranchers. Having seen so many ranchers struggle with the limited natural feed supply in barren land, his expectations gained from an ivory tower of naivety were dowsed when corporate recruiters laughed at his ignorance and "small-mindedness."

Knowing he couldn't take his academic skills back to the family ranch and but heads with a New Mexican dynasty and having no engineering skill which he could use to develop more efficient equipment, he turned his back on agriculture entirely and considered police work.

He, like Jessica, found out quickly that law enforcement liked an athletic applicant, which was all he really had to offer since an agricultural degree was worth zip in crime fighting.

But he was wrong on that account as well...all recruiters seemed to value a four-year university education as excellent qualifications for their specific endeavor. Apparently, the parchment reflected an elevated learning ability not represented by others.

He was interviewed extensively by Albuquerque City Police, New Mexico State Police, various county sheriffs' departments and the U.S. Border Patrol. He liked the idea of passing on the big A-Albuquerque, feeling the need to start small, not grapple with a high crime area at the get-go.

It was the Border Patrol to which he gravitated, and which posted him on the Mexican border for five years.

Five years of 115-degree heat, sand, sand and more sand, and the big A started to look appealing. But he had enough of New Mexico's desert and heat and wanted a little culture other than saddle blankets and turquoise. He applied for the Secret Service. He'd been there fifteen years when he brought Jessica to The Ranch.

Chapter Five

Present John "Jack" Bakus was tired. Tired of bullshit politicians. Tired of failing with his campaign promise of non-partisan politics. He was tired of his party members not willing to meet halfway on any issue or legislation. Tired of cabinet secretaries blowing their own horns at every meeting, at every turn of events, each of them feeling they knew the facts for him to decide. They did not and he was tired of them projecting that message. He needed to make a cabinet change and move people out of their comfort zone.

Also, he needed to move federal law enforcers around and get new blood, new ideas into areas of national security. The FBI was out of step with reality and needed to be revamped. The Bureau had to have a huge change starting at the top with their counter terrorism task force if the country was going to make any dint in the increasing threats to the nation.

For years the Bureau had made a cosmetic attempt to cooperate with other agencies with disastrous results. Information either did not flow smoothly between agencies or not at all. The information jam was giving the upper hand to terrorists, particularly those born in America. The bureau had scrambled to recover from the 9/11 disaster.

Investigations revealed agents had ignored obvious preparations being carried out by the suicide bombers on American soil. Eastern Mediterranean loyalists were engaged in flight lessons, internet mapping of airplane seating configurations and flight data recording prior to forcing the planes into the side of the

New York Trade Center and the Pentagon. The underwear bomber being allowed to board an America bound jet with explosives and the Times Square bombers near detonation were all examples of the agency's failure.

A free and democratic society couldn't control citizens, but Bakus knew that with proper leadership...hardcore leadership, by a law enforcer with political protection and the force of his office, the country could be far better protected than it had been and needed to be for the foreseeable future.

Today he was meeting with Cheryl Chapman. Chapman was an anomaly to say the least. Her dossier was classified, not top secret but classified. Classified because if her background and accomplishments were to become public, it would create a military and political firestorm the likes of which the country had never seen or would ever want to experience.

Chapman was a SEAL (Sea, Air and Land) the Navy's special operations force. The United States Navy did not have female SEALs. That was the rule, not policy, the rule. No women. The service offered a litany of reasons to the media; women are too weak, too sensitive to sexy. Yes, they did offer that explanation. But Chapman was a decorated Navy SEAL along with several platoons of other accomplished strong, insensitive sailors who were trained secretly thousands of miles from the male SEAL's training center in California.

The Big Boogy National Wildlife Refuge, 6 hours southwest of Houston, Texas, is home to thousands of migratory birds; geese, ducks, and brown pelicans, in a 4,500 square mile marshland that opens to the Gulf of Mexico. The refuge is closed to the public and closed to the U.S. Fish and Wildlife staff too. The SEAL compound is in the most isolated and remote section which Fish and Wildlife employees were too glad to ignore.

Code named, "Jarc" for Joan of Arc, who led French troops into battle against the English, the SEAL teams were housed in an abandoned farmhouse and outbuildings just east of The Boogy where their firearms, intelligence, counterterrorism, and martial arts training were covertly conducted. The Pentagon had used one of its many Black Accounts; money allotted to a legitimate government account then transferred from one account to another-somewhat like the con shell game where a pea is under one of three cups and the sucker must choose the pea's location-to pay for the cost to reinforce and outfit the various buildings with soundproof shooting rooms and explosives storage. All equipment was barged in under the cover of darkness and completed over an extended period prior to the first trainees' arrival.

After training, the Jarc squads were air lifted by helicopter from Zodiacs five miles offshore in the Gulf of Mexico in a night airlift to Laughlin Air force Base northeast of the refuge. Air Force Base staff was unaware of their covert guests as the SEAL teams landed in a remote section of the base and were transported to their waiting cargo aircraft. The pilots never met their passengers or knew of the squad's mission. In most instances, the pilots landed at a remote and isolated U.S. or American friendly base somewhere on the other side of the world, left the plane and headed for the chow line, their charges waiting out the clock, disembarking during the night for their assignment. The process was reversed with the Jarcs being airlifted by a different flight crew which arrived at night, spent ninety minutes in the officer's mess and returned to their plane having no idea what, if anything, had been loaded in their absence. The new crew reversed their colleague's trip back to Laughlin where the SEAL team was choppered out to sea, dropped from five hundred feet and swam back to their covert base.

Jarc was the back-up team to SEAL Team Six which took out Osama bin Laden. The coalition forces created an interesting diversion for Jarc. The team was aboard the Canadian Destroyer *Athabaskan* patrolling the Gulf of Oman as their normal duty. The team had been choppered aboard the ship during the desert blackness, team members faces covered and were housed in separate quarters for the attack's duration. When one of Team Six's choppers went down, Jarc was mustered and airborne heading to Islamabad for a rescue if needed. Team Six was able to regroup and escape with bin Laden's body so Jarc returned to the ship to await their stand-down orders, which came 24 hours later.

Chapman had risen through the ranks, rejected any of the Navy's attempts to promote her to management and fought fiercely to maintain her qualifications, year after year. But age and nature were catching up to her and Bakus was positive he could make her an offer she couldn't refuse.

The President hadn't met Chapman personally but had followed her career since taking office through weekly reports on the Jarc Squads and their various deployments.

He had originally seen the name Jarc buried in a defense department finance disposition paper he was expected to just browse, initial, and pass back to his staff. But for a reason he still couldn't fathom, the name jumped out at him, and he'd asked a trusted staffer to find out who or what Jarc was.

That effort resulted in a visit by the Joint Chief of Staff who told him of the highly classified program started by Ronald Reagan in his War on Drugs campaign. After their meeting Bakus ordered the general to bury the program even further and instructed that the previous conversation never occurred. For the record they discussed an upcoming NATO meeting in France.

Jarc team success records were impressive, particularly given the political climate of appeasing world leaders who opposed American involvement in foreign politics and highly objected to what is referred to as "Boots on the Ground," a trite phrase referring to having U.S. combat troops involved in ground fighting. The Boogy teams were exceptionally successful...since they did not exist. Jarc teams were often the rolling stone that fueled the opposition to many of the world's dictators and their eventual expulsion from power by rebels armed and trained by Jarc teams.

Their success was equally amazing given their trainees were predominately male Muslims who had a lifetime of ignoring women and often refusing to interact with them.

Bakus often mused that he would love for his administration to take credit for sowing the seed of democracy in developing countries rather than see America's respect be consumed like necrotizing fasciitis, the flesh-eating disease.

Jarc was making that possible.

Chapman and the other squads had made tremendous gains in the political hotspots worldwide. Somalia pirates had been the recipient of the Jarc squads on numerous occasions, Jarc accumulating kill numbers in the double digits.

Jarc did not make arrests. Did not invite media coverage or offer debriefing to the American ship captains who deployed them. Just photographed and fingerprinted the bodies and moved on to the next assignment. Ship captains and crew never knew the SEAL teams were women because there were no conversations. Commanders would receive an encrypted communication advising to expect a SEAL team by chopper. The team would arrive, be housed, and fed in isolation, deplore, return, eat, sleep and be choppered out under the cover of darkness. The crew thought nothing of the secrecy, chalking up the experience to either the CIA spooks or some other cloak and dagger outfit.

Chapman entered the Oval Office drawing Bakus' immediate attention to her statuesque presence in a St. John black Boyfriend blazer; white button-down blouse and light grey Victoria Cropped Pants and 16" boots with 1/3" heel.

Bakus swung around his desk, jumped up and walked briskly toward his guest, extending his hand.

The SEAL personified Bakus' conceived perception; six feet, at least 150 pounds, short curly brunette styled coiffure coupled with the SEAL persona that put the best of men and most women on the defensive, expecting a personality explosion.

"Ms. Chapman, welcome to the White House. I trust my staff has made you welcome."

"My pleasure Mr. President," she said nervously. "Yes sir, your staff was very accommodating. But I really didn't have to wait very long. It is an honor to be asked to the White House, but I must say I'm at a total loss as to why."

"In due time Ms. Chapman, in due time. May I call you Ms. Chapman, or should I refer to your rank?"

"Either is fine sir. But if you like, I'm Chief Petty Officer."

"Okay Chief Petty Officer Chapman, it being so close to noon, how about we have lunch while we chat?"

Bakus led the way through a small hallway past his study to the Oval Office Dining Room, standing aside to let Chapman pass ahead of him. The short walk took them past several Secret Service agents who tensed immediately at her presence, their training and intuition noting her combative aura that was in contrast to her physical presentation.

There were two place settings at the far end of the table. Without thinking Chapman walked to the place furthest from the door, turned and faced Bakus...at attention.

Seeing the rather surprised look on the President's face, she commented, "Sorry sir that was rude of me, just habit," referring to type "A" law enforcers making sure there was a wall behind them when seated...not only publicly, but anywhere.

"No apology necessary Chief, have a seat and we can get started."

Just as the President sat, two white clad servers arrived with silver trays, each carrying a white ceramic tea pot and large white mugs with the White House logo facing outwards. She smiled at the servers and wondered if they used a ruler to center the pot and mug. The two men served Chapman first, which took her aback somewhat, then the President. As the two exited the dining room, two more servers arrived with large white China plates and set each in front of Chapman and Bakus.

"I hope you don't mind my leaving the lunch selection to the White House chef. I believe this is Pan Roasted Rockfish with an Artichoke Barigoule and Salad. I have no idea what the dressing might be. I seem to enjoy the daily surprise. Bon appetite."

"I'm sure it will be delicious Mr. President," comment Chapman.

Bakus nodded and began eating. After French vanilla ice cream and chocolate sauce, he said, "Well, Chief, like the cliché, I know you are wondering why I asked you to lunch."

"Yes sir. I am very confused. I was given orders to appear at the White House, provided military transportation from Laughlin Air force Base and told to dress in my civvies."

"Okay, understood. Let's go to the Green Room where we can be guaranteed privacy."

Bakus advised his secretary not to be interrupted and led the way into the Green Room, which like every other non-public room, was John Wayned. The Green Room was one of three formal state rooms for entertainment, but Bakus felt he needed one for himself and chose the Green Room and had it casualized with deep burgundy walls, realism photos and paintings which brought the outdoors to your soul: bears feeding on Alaska's Kodiak Island, whales breaching off the Hawaiian coast and other breathtaking huge wildlife portraits. And heavy furniture including two oversized black leather armchairs wide enough to kick off your shoes and pull your feet under you.

Once settled in facing armchairs, Bakus said, "I don't need to tell you that the country is in difficulty, both domestically and internationally. We are up to our eyeballs in debt to none other than China, which is bent on taking over the world's economy. Islamist extremists have increased their rhetoric abroad which has incited several American born Muslims to take up arms against their own country...us.

I'm not going to take shots at my predecessors, but Washington has contributed to the mess by directing huge sums and troops to Iraq and Afghanistan to no avail. Both countries will remain forever embroiled in their own tribal conflicts, grow, and distribute drugs and otherwise remain in the Stone Age while exporting terror, attempting to dominate the world with Shariah. The only way they will accomplish that is to destroy from within, not unlike the Holy Roman Empire.

We have become a country of political correctness, ignoring our own founding fathers' contribution to our freedom, straining to make sure we go along to get along. We are no longer 'One Nation, under God, indivisible with liberty and justice for all.' We are a nation of weasels, creepy men and women who have created fiefdoms, nationwide, that are impossible to break. President Reagan attempted to dismantle the food stamp program which, even back then, had matured beyond control eventually defeating his attempts.

I know you are undoubtedly wondering where I'm going with this."

Chapman remained deadpanned with her fingers templed to her chin, elbows on her knees and replied with a slight nod.

"I can handle all of these problems but not those dealing with law enforcement. We've had political appointees and professional law enforcers attempt to manage the rise of militancy without success. They too are afraid of their job security and of offending someone, anyone, up and down the food chain, to the point of inadequacy. The FBI doesn't communicate with the CIA, and each ignores local law enforcement, which is the country's front-line defense against terror. Appointing a so-called Counter Terrorism Czar to co-ordinate has failed because of the political machines.

What I need is someone who will remain under the radar, put together a national counter terrorism system that will include every cop in the nation to share information, from New York's NYPD to Gallup New Mexico's one-man police force and on to LAPD's finest.

I want a woman for several reasons; the first being, and I apologize if this sounds sexist, but a woman can often operate under the radar. Women as a gender, are adept at accomplishment without fanfare and ego enhancing. I believe the right woman can operate from anywhere in the country with a direct line to me and be answerable to only me. She will have some tough nuts to crack... excuse the pun...with some men who are, as I mentioned with the food stamp program, entrenched in their fields, and will feel threatened by not only a White House directive but one delivered by a woman.

Having said that, the right woman will thrive on the challenge and accomplish my goal quickly and entirely covertly. I believe that person, that woman is you Chief."

Watching her wide-eyed expression, Bakus raised a hand as to stop her reply and said, "Whoa, now, before you respond, let me explain my reasoning. There are no other candidates. Your superiors have no idea why you were asked to come here, and I specifically chose not to create a diversion. Neither you nor I owe the military an explanation. Sometimes military personnel forget who their Commanding Officer really is. Be that as it may, my reasoning is this. You have had and are having a remarkable career. Your contributions to your country could fill volumes if any of it could ever reach print. But and I mean no disrespect here, you aren't going to be able to jump from 30,000 feet into the ocean and climb mountains to execute an objective for the rest of your life. I know the Navy has been hounding you to take administrative positions, even offering to send you for a master's degree, all of which you've declined. They will eventually force you to choose and I'm offering you a much better position.

Interested so far?"

Chapman removed her steepled fingers from her chin and stared at the president for a hesitative beat, ran her right hand through her hair while embracing a broad grin.

"Sir, I appreciate your hospitality and candor, but I still don't understand. Are you saying that you want me, a U.S. Navy Chief Petty Officer, to become somewhat of a national crime prevention coordinator? A national cop? If that is the case sir, I think you misunderstand my background and qualifications."

Bakus laughed, shook his head, and said, "No Chief, I'm not mistaken, and I have all the information I need on you and your background. I guess I too am trying to be politically correct and not offend you with any directness, so here goes.

I need an experienced kick-ass, no bull shit military female who will take control of the country's failing law enforcement bureaucracy. I need someone who will shun the media and my inner circle. Someone who will maintain total secrecy while carrying out a combination of covert anti-terrorism activities with your handpicked team and schmoozing various seated law enforcement agencies and either get them on board or isolate them, so they are totally ineffective. We are not trying to create a budget efficiency system but a national law enforcement communicative system that can come down like flies on shit against those who plan to dismantle or otherwise destroy this country.

Is that a better explanation?"

Chapman's grin spread into a laugh as she shook her head in amazement and admiration for a leader who had the balls to come up with such a bombastic plan and with the political severity to pull it off quite possibly...with her help. Chapman knew that to hedge or ask to think on it, would kill the offer immediately, so she replied, "Yes sir, that was a great deal more revealing and yes, I believe I'm the person for the job."

Bakus stood up, clapped his hands together and said, "Great Chief, I was sure you would accept the challenge. How about we seal the deal with a drink and discuss details?"

Chapman rose and followed Bakus over to a mini bar tastefully set up at the end of a full bookcase. The president chose two cut Chrystal high ball glasses, poured three inches of Jack Daniels in each, and offered one to Chapman. "A toast Chief, to our arrangement and to your successful future, and to our country."

Chapman reached out and clinked glasses and drank two mouthfuls before Bakus said, "Let's sit again and start mapping out our plans."

As they walked back to the armchairs, Bakus said, "A couple of housekeeping comments first Chief. As of now your rank is Commander with a pay scale of 05 which puts you around $100,000 with an American Express Black Card for expenses. Openly you will have no connection with either me or the White House. You won't be listed on any personnel file and your pay will be automatically deposited to a bank of your choice personally by me each month. Now, let's get down to business and make some decisions so you can get yourself set up here in Washington with a plausible cover story."

Chapman enjoyed her JD while her head swam with the ramifications of the past hour. Her income had just jumped $30,000 a year, her housing would continue to be covered, albeit somewhat more elaborate than she would expect from her base quarters at Big Boogy. She'd be part of a historic American law enforcement program that had been a desire of cops for generations, and she had to answer to only one person...a military person's dream. She took another draw of the JD and tuned the president in as he laid out his objectives and operating plans.

Chapter Six

"Most people are sheep".

Lt. Col. Dave Grossman

"Jessica, Bakus hasn't been out of the country since he took office," said Sorento. "He's had no real need considering the world economy and his success with his domestic policies. The irony is the world is now coming to us with a G-8 summit scheduled for the Wyoming Ranch and we have no grasp of a domestic threat since he hasn't been back there since taking office.

"Homeland Security, the FBI and even the CIA tried to spin 9/11 in the country's favor, but no one bought it. The evidence is overwhelming that the pilots were here months before the tragedy and there is nothing to indicate there aren't scores or even hundreds more right now. The FBI continues to track down every lead but that doesn't help us. We can't let the president roam around his Wyoming digs without knowing categorically that those we suspect are behind a variety of illegal activities across the country aren't in StoneHead or can get access to the president at the ranch.

"No one would have figured Americans to adopt Al Qaeda's jihad, move to Somalia and plot against their own country. But that's what's happening. You read the briefings about the Minneapolis guys who were Somali refugees as children and left in waves over several years, creating a major geopolitical nightmare.

These men who joined the jihad, their lives resembled European immigrants. They all faced assimilation barriers of race, class, religion, and language.

The Americans, for the most part, had a good shot at success; successful university students or in entry level professions and they gave it up for Al Qaeda. These are the guys who have returned and are out there, blending into our society, preparing to take America down from within, a Trojan Horse if you would.

"I need StoneHead secure and you're it. I want you to select a team of four, put the plan together, and head to Stone whenever you're ready to do the hands on. We need to know everything there is to know about everybody there and everyone who was there. We have no idea who or what's in Wyoming. Bakus may still be cherished by the masses but there's sure to be a nest of anti-Americans that I want rooted. I'm not going to make a team selection suggestion, but you may want to consider our liaison agent working in Arizona. Her name is Rebecca Simpson. There is a strong opinion by federal forces that the reservations are hosting Middle East guests.

"Canada, France, Germany, and the other G country leaders will be here to develop anti-terrorism policies for international application. We'll take care of those arrangements and Backus' staff will be on hand to schmooze the guests. Your team's job is to make sure the Wyoming Ranch is shut tight, no one on that main road, or anywhere near the property that we don't know about. You can't vet the entire community, but you can get a handle on any dissidents, bad guys, or whackos."

"Will do boss. I assume I have some leeway to handle problems with discretion my own way?"

"Yeah, you do Jessica, just don't create so much shit that it flies back and hits me."

She smiled at Sorento, confident he knew her well enough to jest...or sort of. She finished her coffee. Topped up with her dancing card, Jessica left Sorento and his sophisticated China and went to work on the Wyoming Ranch.

She meandered through the various computer workstations until she found one empty, pulled a crappy government issued secretary chair out and plopped herself in front of the Dell.

Entered her password and was immediately brought to the service's main page. Now she had to scan the various databases to find her team. Difficult. She had dropped, kicked, twisted, and otherwise punished every testosterone driven agent in the detail, and she couldn't think of one who would join her team willingly.

Called coming back to bite you in the ass, Jessica thought. She satisfied an aching in her soul by showing her egocentric colleagues that they were full of shit thinking they could outperform a woman, that she didn't think of any future repercussions. Screw it! She'd get a team, even if she pulled them in from hinterland. The emotional release from winning outweighed any repercussions...or at least that is what she had convinced herself...until now.

As she began the process of weaving through scores of files, her mind pondered Sorento's comments and assignment. It wasn't difficult to get her mind around the hate so many Middle Eastern people had for America. During the 2001 invasion of Afghanistan, assisted greatly by local warlord General Abdul Rashid Dostum, who was on the CIA's payroll, hundreds of captured Taliban soldiers were murdered, and their bodies dumped in a mass grave.

For years various American government officials covered up or ignored the incident until the Red Cross and Physicians for Human Rights refused to take "No" for an answer. That attitude, along with eight years of Bush politics, fed the hatred and for many young men, spurred their desire for retaliation.

She regained her concentration and entered key words looking for those agents with street experience like her own. She had trained with two guys years back, one from LAPD with a Bachelor of Science degree in microbiology from UCLA-University of California at Los Angeles. She entered "Spencer".

She found him quickly and read his bio. Apparently, he hadn't given any thought to employment with the science degree and found himself SOL, shit out of luck after graduation. Many of his fellow grads found themselves likewise and ended up taking additional training as lab techs, a program they could have entered out of high school.

Spencer was $50,000 in debt, no job, and no prospects. One of his university lab tech buddies suggested he apply to the LAPD and be their poster boy for higher education. They laughed at the image, but the more Spencer thought of it, the more the idea had merit. Not the put down, but maybe putting his education to work for the community. He applied and was hired before the ink dried on the application.

She scrolled down and saw that he had kept a low profile through the academy as most of the recruits were high school grads with some community college-LAPD didn't want kids applying-and he didn't want to come across as elitist, being one of the only college graduates.

But he came across as a snob anyway which caused him no end of social problems. He wasn't interested in typical "male" chit-chat or testosterone drivel. He sought out like-minded trainees and fell in with them socially, albeit very few.

He excelled in academic and physical challenges and was nicknamed "Micro" for his attention to detail.

Six months on probation after academy graduation, then 18 months in patrol cars, he applied for the sergeant's exam. Was turned down. Had to have five years. But his enthusiasm and intellect were rewarded by taking him out of uniform and putting him undercover.

Jason Spencer had excellent street creds from South Central where the gangsters assumed wrongly that his ethnic background and skin tone grouped him with their limited intellect and home boy demeanor. His arrest and prosecution record were exceptional, which was what eventually attracted the Service.

Spencer had taken a minor in languages from UCLA. He could sound like he'd just arrived from Brussels with a French accent, or similarly from Jamaica or any number of countries.

Tired of hassling gang members who were arrested at breakfast and out for dinner, he transferred to policing illegal weapon's entering Los Angeles.

He'd done his LAPD in-service with the ATF-Bureau of Alcohol, Tobacco, and Firearms, gaining knowledge of a multitude of firearms, particularly those desired by criminals and sold internationally. It was during one of his undercover operations, posing as a Belgium arms dealer that the Secret Service caught wind of his expertise. He'd contacted gang buyers wanting automatic weapons with thirty-round clips. His beard, dreadlocks and accent hid any hint of recognition by the gang members he'd previously busted. Spencer thrived on the adrenalin rush of the ruse, knowing they'd kill him immediately if they had any hint of his real identity.

After six months getting accepted and haggling over the price, a deal was struck for Czechoslovakia made assault rifles with folding buttstock (allowing easy concealment) capable of firing eight hundred rounds a minute for $2,000 a piece, shipped from an undisclosed EU country to the Port of Los Angeles.

The takedown didn't occur at the docks. The enforcement team let them take delivery, pay Spencer his $100,000 for fifty rifles and 10,000 rounds of ammunition, then followed the buyers back to a South Los Angeles warehouse. Spencer took a circuitous route back to the station to log in the money, change clothes and vehicles. He exited the station via the underground secure parking wearing a pulled down ball cap. He was done with the operation.

The LAPD SWAT team was primed for assault. As the buyers arrived at the warehouse, SWAT attacked as the building's automatic doors began to open. Assault vehicles swung in front and back of the buyer's truck with the SWAT team out and surrounding the suspects within seconds. The take-down was choreographed so beautifully it went down in LAPD annuals of great operations. Not only did LAPD retrieve the firearms, arrest the gang member buyers but got intel on rival gangs the guns were to be used to eliminate.

With the intel, LAPD happily eliminated the rivals themselves. The Secret Service heard about the operation through the law enforcement grapevine and approached Spencer. They made him an offer he couldn't refuse.

Since then, Spencer had been stationed out of Morocco with infiltrations into Algeria, Libya, Sudan, and Mauritania assessing threats against the U.S. and the president from Al Qaeda training camps deep within these countries.

One down. Three to go.

She really needed a gender balance, or as close as possible. Stacking the team with men was a prelude to failure. But she needed the best regardless. Perseverance. She found Elisabeth Peltowski working as a liaison with the British Secret Intelligence Service-MI6. Peltowski worked with the BSIS in conjunction with threats of terrorism and espionage, where the threat is expressly against both countries. Jessica assumed Peltowski had been around the world chasing down Al Qaeda members and Jessica banked on her wanting to come back Stateside. Wrong on the first, correct on the second... she'd soon discover.

Peltowski grew up in Nebraska. Corn girl. Masters in criminal justice from the University of Nebraska at Omaha, with a minor in computer science. Not knowing what she wanted to do with the advanced degree, she taught basic computer skills at an Omaha high school but found it too frustrating to teach general skills when she wanted to be involved at a higher level.

She quit and did five years with the State Police-commercial crime, then was picked up by the Secret Service. Jessica wondered what made her cream of the crop. She had to have some skills that set her above the rest. Reading on she found Peltowski did her bones like Jessica, in the hinterland.

For Peltowski it was New Orleans, then Miami where she battled the ongoing influx of threats, perceived or otherwise, from Cuba. Then a transfer to Washington.

Mm, what did she do there, Jessica thought.

Reading on she found that in Miami. Peltowski studied under Ricardo Montabo and his Chilean Jujitsu.

Montabo gained fame by legitimizing the Ultimate Fighter HBO financial phenomenon by winning the first three wins. Jessica had seen several UF fights in pubs with dates. Cage fighting. No rounds. Bare fists. No hits to the throat, groin, or knees, but everything else went until one slapped the canvas.

Uncle.

Booze and UF. Not a good combination. Lots of parking lot fights where testosterone and alcohol got out of hand. After three UF's she passed on dates with cage fighting enthusiasts.

Montabo's skills by themselves weren't sound for law enforcement but combined with the other fighting skills Peltowski earned in New Orleans, Montabo's style added worthy ground fighting techniques. This was good. But what about the intellect?

Down a few more paragraphs she found it. Peltowski wasn't just a computer nerd, she was a hacker. *Son-of-a-bitch, a female hacker,* Jessica thought they were all overweight, male couch potatoes with zip for social skills. So much for stereotyping. From the attached photo Peltowski slid right past the norm with her dark complexion and curly brunette doo.

Outstanding. A license to hack.

Jessica heard the spooks hired hackers, stuffed them in a Maryland basement and let them have at terrorist's bank accounts and track emails. She'd never thought the Service would do likewise. But she understood why they did. They always wanted their own intel on plots against the president and the CIA was infamous for not sharing intelligence.

Peltowski moved from Miami to geek headquarters in

The Ranch's bowels reading all emails from any computer in the world that contained key words that directly or indirectly had an association with violence, firearms distribution and weapons development and Islam or related religions.

She'd organized her filter system to eliminate content that had the feared words or phrases but were in fact harmless. She spent most of her time reading. She found a great deal of Al Qaeda data not directly related to her task, so she logged it and passed it on to the FBI's Anti-Terrorism Team. She'd learn later that her intel was never pursued by the FBI.

She was enjoying her silent attack on terrorism when she was picked to be the Service's liaison with Britain's Secret Service, MI6.

Jessica wanted Peltowski.

Now she needed a cowboy/girl. Someone who'd fit Wyoming. How do you search "Cowboy/cowgirl"? she thought. She hated it when supervisors made suggestions knowing you were almost compelled to follow through with their "suggestion".

Over the years she'd done just the opposite, for spite. But she respected Sorento, and her annoyance was short lived. She figured having an agent who knew her/his way around rednecks would serve her interest. But she wanted to find out if Simpson was in fact the best agent for her needs, so she started with those who graduated from Montana or Wyoming universities. She guessed there weren't too many cowgirls turned Secret Service Agents from Wyoming, Montana, or any other state.

The first name highlighted was Rebecca Simpson. Son-of-a-bitch, she thought. What's this agent got going for her that drew Sorento's attention she wondered. Scrolling through her file she found she'd been a high school rodeo participant, not the Queen but a solid continuous involvement from junior high school onward.

Decent secondary school grades with rodeo as her chosen sport-barrels and something called dobbing. No buckin' broncs or bull riding, so Jessica figured maybe these were limited to male participants.

Simpson graduated from Montana State University with an education degree and spent two years teaching elementary school, then quit. Wonder why, Jessica thought. Boredom? That would have been Jessica's excuse. Jessica loved kids, but friends', not hers and certainly not twenty-five all day long.

Reading along, she saw that Simpson returned to school for a graduate degree in Criminology, then Montana Department of Justice and finally Flathead County Deputy Sheriff.

Where the hell is Flathead County, Jessica wondered. Google. Out in the middle of nowhere. By the Canadian border with towns like Tobacco, Halfmoon, but hey, it was right by Glacier National Park so maybe smokey-the-bear girl had some country smarts the rest of us were lacking.

The next paragraph. Another shock. Simpson was a former Ms. Physique. Holy crap, thought Jessica, this woman is another Cory Everson, former Ms. Olympia with her blond streaked moussed short hair and her 6' 150-pound frame.

Jessica figured boredom hit again at the three-year mark when the Service snagged her. Wonder what her hiring ace was? Reading on she found it. Simpson was some kinda tracker, having led many rescues through mountainous terrain and used those skills to track bad guys through Montana flatlands. Currently Simpson was right where Sorento said she was, assigned to the Phoenix, Arizona FBI office, tracking down leads on the various Indigenous communities and a new movement that could spell attacks against Bakus. She figured she'd swallow her ego of following Sorento's advice and take Simpson.

Assuming these guys would accept a transfer to her unit, she needed one more, making five including herself. The personnel files were rich with agents who might be qualified, but she wanted hunger, not mediocrity. She found it after the second research hour.

Jackson Pennington was former Army Delta Force currently assigned to the Service's Anti-Terrorism unit. Jessica remembered reading Eric Haney's "Inside Delta Force" and wondered how much of that was reality. She went on and read that Pennington had left Delta as a Sergeant, then took an undergraduate degree in History from Northern Michigan University. How does a guy go from Delta Force to History to the FBI to the Secret Service, she wondered.

Reading on she found that Pennington got tired of globetrotting, the shooting house training, and the stress, so he did a 180 and followed a high school dream of a quieter lifestyle, planning to teach high school.

He left Delta for his hometown of Detroit, then entered Northern Michigan University where he was a defenseman on NMU's *Wildcats* hockey team. Jessica Googled the school and found Marquette, Mich. eight hours north of Detroit on the shores of Lake Superior. Well, that's doing a 180 for sure, get away from it all in the boonies, she thought.

Pennington's teaching practicum didn't go well. Notes in his file indicated Pennington questioned who'd die of boredom first, the kids or him. Curiosity took him to a career day during his senior year, probably looking for an alternative to 250 kids daily. He was interviewed by two male FBI agents. Suits. They hired him immediately, convincing him teaching kids would be boring compared to saving them from terrorists.

Five years with the bureau and he was sequestered to the Service's anti-terrorist squad to investigate white supremist groups. Demonstrating outstanding investigative techniques and arrest record, the Service offered him permanence. He took it. He was stationed at the Seattle office.

Jessica figured she'd have something in common with Pennington as she too was involved in ice sports during her Toronto high school years. She'd played hockey at the Ice Gardens at York University where her aggressiveness as center on a forward line won her both honors and criticism.

Chapter Seven

Finishing his coffee, Jenewein disengaged the autopilot, checked his heading, and corrected to 40 degrees North and 106 West which he'd plotted previously on his topographical map laying to his right. He had made this trip so many times; he often thought he could fly it using landmarks alone. Nevertheless, experience taught him years ago to use his instruments, particularly as he headed into the Routt National Forest's many canyons and fiords.

He was currently over Rocky Mountain National Park close to his destination distance of under 300 miles to Little Big Creek Lake in the northwestern section of Routt and the Christians for a Better America lodge and retreat. He was maxing the Otter's 8,000-pound payload of several experimental explosives. Most of the ingredients were harmless until combined, but the new liquid components made his stomach churn with each air current bump. Even trucking them from the Denver warehouse was scary. They told him at the Center there was no danger given their separation, but he had the willies just the same. He was carrying hundreds of vials of hydrogen peroxide, hexamine and powdered citric acid and from what he had overheard in the Center's lab, these compounds, when combined, produced an unstable explosive hexamethylene triperoxide diamine.

His trip's objective was to stock the retreat's lab and its kitchen for a prolonged winter work session by the chosen ten grad students who would be experimenting with several compounds and choosing the one most likely to be used in the following fall's campaign against Congress and President Backus.

The delivery system was the main hurdle and the winter's target. He had numerous cases of vegetables, meats, and dehydrated foods that he would unload from the retreat's dock. Wiping his sweaty palms on his pant leg, he shook his head to refocus his attention on the flight and not his impending doom. He did find it an interesting intellectual exercise though, wondering how American born citizens could turn on their country, its heritage, and constitution with plans to assassinate its president and congressional leaders.

He had no difficulty with his loyalty. As an Al Qaeda sleeper, he was quite comfortable with killing the president and anyone else his handlers requested he eliminate. Growing up in Harlem and home schooled by his Iranian mother, he was convinced the only true believer's role in life was to bring down those who opposed his chosen homeland and its ideology. He learned at his father's hand that life was a chosen path as was death and that a person moved from one medium to another like a star extinguished by humanity's light.

His father graduated from Shahid Beheshti University (formerly The National University of Iran) with advanced degrees in physics and chemistry and took responsibility for Daniel's science education while his mother handled languages, religion, and philosophy.

His father's meager earnings as a cab driver were far from sufficient to maintain their side-by-side apartments, the second of which was leased to an absentee international wholesaler who sent periodic FedEx packages containing more than enough cash to sustain the family's lifestyle. The two dwellings afforded the senior Jenewein a high-tech chemistry lab in which he taught his son chemistry elements and bomb making techniques. In hindsight, he knew his deceased father was more an academic than a practical jihadist, for the elder's formulas were concentrated on complex methods and ingredients, which for all practical purposes were unattainable.

He brought his attention back to the task and prepared to land on Little Big Creek Lake.

Jessica sent Sorento an email giving him details on her decisions, asked him to send the transfer requests to personnel and affect the changes. The team was directed to report to the James Rowley Training Center at Laurel, Maryland within two weeks, allowing them time to make personal transfer arrangements. Jessica would use the time to prepare for their upgrading with defensive tactics, physical fitness, and firearms enhancement at the Center's Physical Training Unit. While at the training facility they'd develop their team unity and lay preliminary Wyoming plans.

The Center in Laurel, Maryland, just outside Washington, was five-hundred acres of specialized tactical and theoretical facilities, making it ideal for Jessica's team upgrading.

Jessica closed the computer and left The Ranch. She stopped to chat with Elise and watched with amusement when none of the male agents joined them.

After a couple of minutes she excused herself and left the building for the parking lot and The Bug-impossible to miss in a sea of vehicles. Approaching her vehicle she clicked the key fob, checked the back seat, 360'd, crouched down, checked underneath, then opened the door, sat down, locked the doors, and keyed the ignition.

Putting on Diana Krall's newest CD she geared up and headed for the security kiosk, showed her ID, and headed back to her flat to pack and transfer to Rowley for the next few weeks.

When she arrived in D.C., she had snagged a spacious two bedroom, two baths at Sedgwick House, a quaint historical mansion transformed into 2 spacious, modern flats, ten minutes from The Ranch. She'd enjoyed decorating quietly with furnishings from

West Elm Furniture in Washington. Not as expensive as she had anticipated so she was able to spend a little extra on the window trimmings and bathroom accessories. It was her hideaway from the hectic Washington pace where she could hold up for days, reading and pigging on Domino's pizza, one her favorites.

The Wyoming gig was Bakus' first biggy requiring her to create policies/procedures from the bottom rung, ferreting out dissidents-if in fact Wyoming had any-and locking down the community so future visits could follow her blueprint. But first she had to get her team to meet her qualifications; physically, mentally, and defensively.

Big job.

Little time.

It was past 6 when she pulled into Sedgwick's covered car park. Her parking slot was the most exposed, per her request, so she had an unobstructed view entering and exiting. She parked, scanned her surroundings, exited The Bug, locked it, and headed for Sedgwick's back door, constantly 360ing with her left-hand twitching somewhat, her entire being in Orange.

There were no bushes or hedges by the back door. Just low planters which added attractiveness without creating a hiding place. She keyed this month's security code with her right hand, entered and closed the door, assuring herself it clicked into place. She'd convinced the owner and other tenant to change the lock from a key system to a code when she moved in. Everyone was pleased with the change and delighted to have a Secret Service Agent in residence.

As she approached her flat's door, she pulled the key from her right-hand jacket pocket, keyed the lock, and entered the flat. Closing and locking the door while turned slightly so she could see the living room and the hall, she deactivated the alarm with her right hand while her left cupped her Sig in its holster.

She stood there silently for what always seemed an eternity, listening for anything out of the ordinary. Satisfied, she proceeded with her routine, checking each room, each closet, under each bed until she was satisfied she was alone. She knew this wasn't paranoia. She'd spent too many years training to take her safety for granted. This was routine.

She headed to her bedroom, took off her jacket, placing it over the valet, kicked off her shoes, removed the Sig from its holster and placed it on the night stand, took off her pants, underwear and headed to the closet for her sweats-an old Berkely sweatshirt and U of Toronto sweatpants and a pair of handmade moccasins.

Next, she headed for the living room, opened the liquor cabinet, and retrieved a bottle of Chianti, uncorked it, left it to breath and headed for the kitchen and a batch of humus she'd made the previous weekend.

Organic tortilla chips, Chianti, and her current novel-Lee Child's latest Jack Reacher-she flopped on the burgundy couch from Skylar.

She was set for the evening.

Her flat looked more masculine than most women would enjoy but she bathed in the leather's fragrance, the red hue walls, and paintings of east coast landscapes. She contrasted this with silk and frills in the bedroom and master bath. She kept the guest bath, bedroom/office neutral, offering herself and guests an enjoyable balance.

She'd just settled in with the first chapter when her encrypted Blackberry went off. Shit, now what, she thought. She wondered to herself if she would have ulcers by 40 with this type of pressure.

She coded the Blackberry and answered, "Yo."

"What the hell kind of greeting is that for one of the nation's top cops Jessica?" spouted her boss.

"Sorry about that, just got my feet up with a glass of red. What's up?"

"I got your email and have sent out the request to personnel. Since then I received a classified email regarding you from the White House. There is someone you need to meet before you head to Rowley. You are meeting her at Starbucks on "M" Street Northwest right across from the Park Hyatt Tea Cellar at 0800 hours tomorrow. The content of your conversation with her is classified. Don't be late. Reflects badly on me," he quipped. Then hung up.

What the hell was that all about she thought. I hardly get going on a project and someone is on my ass already.

Too tired to fix dinner, wine and chips would have to do. She put the novel aside and watched the geek show about the boys trapped in men's bodies while enjoying her less than nutritious dinner. At 8 she threw her sweats on the floor and hit the sheets. She was out immediately.

5 am. Up. Rested. Sweats back on and to the kitchen for coffee, remembering she had to order Sorento's Pinon coffee. Hers was weak by comparison.

Thinking of Sorento, she wondered again about this meeting. What the hell, she'd put on her best complying face, say "Yes Ma'am", and go about her business with the new team.

Yoga first. Up dog. Down dog. Flat dog. Geez she felt good. Fanny pack strapped. Sig inside. Runners on. She stuck her suite key in the pack and headed out the door.

Exiting the building in Orange. 360's until she was satisfied. Right leg against a tree, her head down to meet the knee. Left leg ditto. Off to Constitutional Gardens for 30 minutes of cardio. She loved the morning before vehicle exhaust stifled her breathing, inhibiting her enjoyment.

As she ran, enjoying the feeling of muscle movement, she scrutinized each vehicle and pedestrian and often wondered if in their perusal of her, they considered what she did for a living. Whenever she passed men, or women for that matter, she knew her Orange Aura was projected to them by their concerned facial expression.

In Washington, handgun ownership had been illegal until a Supreme Court ruling declared the legislation unconstitutional. But the fight was not over as local officials vowed to make hand-gun regulations very strict. Jessica often chuckled about this since Washington had one of the highest crime rates in the country. Her dad's hand-gun ownership in Toronto was a breeze by comparison.

Americans, and Canadians for that matter, thought firearms laws in Canada were strict. Not necessarily so. One safety test, a background check and a five-year license was the norm for long guns. Handguns were somewhat more restricted with zero concealed carrying rights except for timber cruisers and trappers, but any citizen could belong to a shooting range and own any number of legal handguns.

Here she was running with a powerful weapon within nanoseconds of her grasp. She knew hundreds of other citizens did likewise in violation of the law. Their philosophy? They'd rather be tried by twelve than carried by six.

She stretched her legs, maximizing each movement, breathing in the fragrance of the Garden's huge floral selection, Amazon Lilies, and Florida Anise Trees. She always smiled running here, was it a hard "A" or soft on the Anise? Her circuit brought her back to Sedgwick's front door. A few more 360's. Coded the door. Entered. Closed the door pushing till she heard the click. Bounded up the stairs to her second floor, another 360 and in the flat.

Off with the sweats and a hot shower. Toweling off she wandered over to her walk-in closet for today's choice. Armani's Three-Button Jacket & Classic Two-Button Pant in black with black riding boots by Marc Jacobs. She loved this jacket as it was generously cut to cover her Sig but still slimming.

Dressed, she did a mirror 360, spinning on her raised right toe. Satisfied with her look, she shrugged into her shoulder holster, removed the Sig from the fanny-pack, pulled the slide slightly to view the chambered round and slid the firearm into the holster.

Breakfast. She often had left over pasta and eggs but today was yogurt on raisin bran. Big bowl with strawberries from the local bodega, two tablespoons protein powder. She added an orange and her vitamin regimen. She sat at her kitchen nook that overlooked Constitutional Gardens in the distance while she ate.

Thinking of nothing, she ate with her right upper arm brushing her Sig under her right armpit, she smiled at the comfort the weapon brought and acknowledged that she would never truly be able to relax, allowing her mind to rest and her body to follow. She didn't dwell on the thought, knowing that to do so would bring on too much self-evaluation which she didn't need now.

Teeth brushed and gargled, she headed to her office/guest room and called Rowley to arrange for housing. She called the secure line at the Center from her encrypted Blackberry. Dallas Romain.

"Hey, Dallas, Jessica Fukishura. How you makin' out at the testosterone factory?"

"Hi Jessica. You still kickin' ass around the Service?"

"But of course, what else would they expect from me? Speaking of kicking ass, I've a new team coming to rattle your chain over the next few days. Can you set us up in a group?"

Jessica was going to say she'd be out today but quickly reformatted and said she'd be out in a few days.

"Sure Jessica, I'm looking at the board and I can put you in the grouping off Powder Mill. Will that work?"

"You bet, thanks Dallas. I'll call in a few and give you an exact time of arrival."

While speaking with Romain, Jessica realized she could take some time off, get to the center before the first agent arrived, and still be ready. She made a quick call to Sorento, asked for the time off to visit her folks, got it, and set her mind to choosing what clothes to pack before she could rethink it and sight work as a reason not to go.

Jessica didn't know what to expect from a White House messenger, if in fact that was who this woman was. She sighed deeply and headed to Starbucks, completing her instinctive flat exiting strategy quickly and efficiently and made it to the Tea Cellar area in record time...credit given to The Bug and her expert driving skills she noted, as she patted the car's dash and squeezed into a parking spot on the street a block from the cafe.

Jessica carried no purse, or handbag as some progressive upscale women chose to call the cumbersome baggage, so her vehicle exit was quick and efficient, like much if not all her life's maneuvers.

She walked into the bistro opening the door with a quick right hand movement and stepped to her immediate left to scan the interior. She spotted a 40ish, striking brunette, lock eyes with her and nodded. They both knew and acknowledged each other almost telepathically.

Jessica made her way through the morning caffeine deprived crowd and grabbed a chair beside the messenger creating somewhat of an awkward communicating arrangement given both women sat with their backs to the wall and had to turn to converse. Jessica looked at her appointment and grinned, both knowing what the other was thinking.

Chapman, sensing Jessica's hyper alertness, wanting success from this meeting and not wishing this cop's instincts to kick in said, "Agent Fukishura, I'm going to reach inside my jacket for my ID." Then proceeded to extract and open a 6" x 6" black leather carrier with the flick of her wrist and showed it to Jessica. The ID showed the appointment's photo, the White House logo and a signature that was quite obviously that of Jack Bakus. That was it, nothing to designate her status, position, or rank, if in fact she had one.

Jessica nodded and Chapman returned the ID to her jacket then started the conversation.

"I'm here at the request of President Bakus to share some critical information that must remain classified and not go beyond the two of us," she said, in a hushed tone one would use in an intimate social setting in a meet and greet tavern.

"The team you've just put together and mustering to Wyoming is one of the first in the nation that will have access to a new information distribution system that was created at the request of the president.

"The system includes every on-going investigation, in every police department, in every community in the nation and it is not maintained by any existing federal bureaucracy.

"My job is to ensure that all federal agencies comply with the mandate and upload their data daily and if they don't, eliminate those who are dragging the system and install staff who will comply with the president's mandate. So that's it. You have access to the system from your encrypted Blackberry, the code of which I will give you before you leave here. You ready for a cappuccino?"

Jessica said nothing.

They made their way to the end of the service line and waited silently, each with her qualms and for Jessica, a growing uneasiness at the return of the distrust she felt when first interviewed by the CIA at Berkeley.

She loved her job, loved the fact that she protected the President of the United States. She basked in her defensive and offensive tactics, her investigative skills, and yes, the fact that she took a back seat to no male. But the Secret Service wasn't the CIA and Jessica suspected Chapman was a spook. Jessica was in Orange while moving slowly toward latte land, but her gut reaction was working overtime with an array of thoughts, taxing her brain, juggling Orange with personal evaluation.

What was in store for her career with this message? Will she be sidetracked for the elusive political agenda of a Washington Machiavellian? Was this messenger cop or politician? Did she really have an aversion to men?

She shook her head at the last thought, smiled to herself and dropped the self-analysis with the intent to ask this Joan Voss attired courier in her spearmint chiffon cardigan and flutter ruffled tank.

They finally progressed to the front of the line, and each ordered black in a mug from a female teen-banger complete with lip rings, nose clips and an eyebrow dagger.

Heading back to their seat Chapman said, "Aren't you glad you missed that vogue?"

Not responding, Jessica straddled her seat watching the front door with her peripheral and said, "Chapman, is it? Look Chapman, I've grown distrustful of everyone, and I mean everyone. I don't know who you are, what you think you know of me, where I work or what I do, for you to make such a presentation. The entire thought is absurd. There is no way federal, state, and local law enforcers will cooperate. They never have and never will.

There are too many egos involved and too many career politicians for your system, whatever it is, to work. You don't look or sound like a White House flunky, but I've never seen or heard of you before and I've been in its inner circles for a long time. Standing outside Bakus' doors I've never seen you pass by, or your name mentioned on the President's visitor list.

So I have every reason to believe you are here to jerk my chain. I don't know who, what or why and I really don't give a shit. I've come too far and invested too much of myself for too long to jeopardize my career by some crazy bull shit plan devised by whom did you say, the President? Give me a break."

She took one last sip of her now cold black and made a move to get up to leave.

Chapman said, "Please, give me a few more minutes of your time. I can give you verifiable information that I think will prove that what I offer is not, what you call bull shit, but reality."

Jessica sat back down, folded her arms, the left hand just inside her jacket and leaned against the back of the chair and said, "Okay, give."

"First of all, I am no threat to you personally or professionally, so you won't have to use your left hand," said Chapman.

That drew a crooked smile from Jessica, but her hand remained in place.

"Second, there is no way you can check me out other than speak with Mr. Bakus, assuming you trust him. There is no one in the Secret Service, FBI or CIA or any other agency who knows me or my background other than what I give them. But I can tell you, in total confidence because I know you fought your way through the male bureaucracy too, I spent over twenty as a SEAL, have been deployed in every friend and foe country in the world and have survived by the same skills you employ. I have no secret handshake, no ring, no resume, nothing to prove what I'm sharing, but you are sufficiently astute to know that what I say is true.

My team and I qualified for SEAL the same as the men. We had our legs and arms tied and jumped into a pool; we did push-ups until our arms were so sore, we ate with our mouths right on the mess plate. We shot for ten hours straight, slept little and shot some more till our fingers and shoulders were chaffed. I'm a SEAL and I think you intuitively know it."

Jessica sat unmoved. No facial expression, no body movement at all as she mulled Chapman's comments. Jessica had fine-tuned her bull shit meter over years of being lied to by so-called colleagues trying to outflank her professionally and she knew, now that Chapman had expanded her proposal, she was genuine. Call it years of instinct, or yuk, women's intuition, but her gut spoke. No one could lie about being a female SEAL. Unless.

Chapter Eight

"Most People are sheep. They are kind, gentle, productive creatures who would only hurt one another by accident."

Lt. Col. Dave Grossman

Quick call to Air Canada at the Ronald Reagan Airport and Fukishura had a flight at 6 that evening. 90 minutes to Toronto, easy, cheap, and enjoyable. She called her mom and planned for her to be picked up at Lester B. Pearson, then called the airport service and returned to packing.

She'd used the air porter numerous times. Convenient. A bargain at $50. She'd spend $100 in frustration and being pissed off, driving, parking, and waiting.

A few days in Toronto, Holt Renfrew, lunch with Mom, visit dad at the U.

Would be good.

She spent the rest of the day cleaning the flat, doing laundry, and then pulled her luggage from the closet.

She packed lightly. A carry-on. Just jeans, a few blouses, sweatshirts, boots, and her running gear. No dress clothes. They'd come later. She'd just closed her leather carry-on when she got a text that the service was downstairs.

She approached Air Canada's Express check-in. She pulled her wallet from inside her jacket and extracted her Air Canada Frequent Flier card. Quick. Simple. Within minutes she was walking to security.

Security. Always a problem. She refused to be without her weapon. She knew the security clerks would have a shit-fit if she walked through the detector, so she diverted to an unmarked door. Knocked and entered.

Buster was Reagan's security chief and just walking out of his office as Jessica entered.

"Hey, Jessica. How're you doin'? Haven't seen you in what, a few months anyway. You here on business?"

"Hi Buster, nope, heading to Toronto for a shopping break with my mom. Just want to be cleared for my Sig."

"Sure, no problem, I'll walk you through myself. What time's your flight? You got time for a coffee?"

"Oh, I've about an hour before boarding. You buying?"

"Same old same old, Jessica, you're a hoot. You kick a cop's ass then want him to buy you coffee." Buster was referring to a joint training session a few years ago on counterterrorism where he'd been unfortunate to be the *Attacker* against Jessica.

"No, just kidding Buster, my turn to buy. You ready now?"

"Yup. Let's go."

Out the door and across the wide security parquet, Buster flashed his ID to the clerk, and they walked around the detector and that was it.

It's certainly who you know, Jessica thought.

They hung around the Starbucks for about forty-five; Jessica ate two muffins in place of dinner, and then headed to boarding after her flight was called.

Buster introduced her to the flight attendant and Jessica flashed her ID and badge for assurances. Good-bye to Buster, down the ramp to business class.

She badged the first attendant and said she was cleared to carry. The male attendant blinked several times, swallowed, wiped his lips, and looked like he was going to have a coronary.

"Hey, it's okay sir. This is all okay. Your pilots know I'm here. I'm Secret Service. Please introduce me to your Air Marshal."

Ma'am, I'm sorry. I've just never been through this before," he said, flustered and trying to regain his professional composure. "I'll get the Marshal."

Jessica found her own seat on. Left side, aisle seat allowed her to have her left arm free as she turned sideways, able to glance over her right shoulder.

Air Canada Embraer's 175 business class had one row of three single seats on the left and three sets of doubles on the right. Empty so far. Air Canada has fifteen Embraer 175s in its fleet manufactured by one the world's top aircraft manufacturers based in Brazil.

As she placed her carry-on in the overhead, she reflected on the recent British court decision which gave forty-year sentences to three men convicted of plotting to smuggle liquid explosives aboard American Airlines, United and Air Canada international flights.

She'd just settled in when an attractive thirty something woman approached her. She opened her jacket revealing her Buffalo (RCMP emblazoned on their badge) clipped to her waistband.

"Hi, I'm Karen Winthrop, RCMP Air Marshal. And you are?"

As Winthrop leaned against the bulkhead, Jessica noted her physique, 5'7" or so, much like a swimmers with broad shoulders, narrow hips. Well dressed, Bloomingdales maybe, Holt Renfrew possibly. Muscular legs. Nice pant material. Lightweight. Jacket loose around her waist and across her chest. Unbuttoned. Blonde. Short style. Like her own. Jessica kept hers short so there wasn't much for a person to grab. This officer is experienced analyzed Jessica.

Jessica stood and extended her right hand of introduction, gave her name and service connection. Pulled her creds from her inside jacket pocket and noted that she'd been cleared by Reagan's security chief.

"Jessica, I understand you've a weapon? Where?"

Jessica said, "My Sig is under my right arm in a shoulder holster."

She opened her jacket to reveal her badge clipped to her waist band and the Sig.

"What do you have in there?" Referring to the bullets in the Sig.

Jessica said, "Winchester Ranger SXT's 9mm."

"Those hollow points have an impressive penetration capability but bad news for airplanes. How about I give you low velocity rounds? Load your spare Sig magazine, switch it with what's in there now, and then go back to your Rangers when you reach Toronto?

"You also have a knife in your waistband."

"Yes," replied Jessica.

"It's a Spyderco. You need to see it?'

"Good choice. Not necessary."

"Let's make the round exchange," Winthrop said.

Jessica got up and followed the Mountie to the plane's business/ first class mess area behind the cockpit just as other business class passengers arrived. Winthrop stepped into the galley, slid aside for Jessica then pulled the curtain closed. She turned, reached down to a drawer, spun a combination, and retrieved a box of the special bullets and handed it to Jessica.

Jessica took a moment to eyeball the rounds. Reading the box, Jessica recalled using this particular round in training. They release less than 1,000 fps-feet per second. The speed at which a projectile must travel to penetrate skin is 163 fps and to break bone 213 fps. Quite low. The fps must increase as the target distance increases. These bullets, called wad cutters, were designed for low velocity encounters such as discharge in an airplane. If a bullet penetrated a plane's fuselage at 30,000 feet, the plane would immediately lose pressure requiring a rapid descent so passengers could breathe.

Jessica removed her spare magazine from the mag holder on her shoulder holster strap and used her thumb to remove all 15 rounds which she slipped into her right jacket pocket.

"How about we put those in the locker here for the flight?" said Winthrop holding out her hand.

Jessica complied, then took the ammo box and loaded her spare mag, took out her Sig, removed the mag and the chambered round, then switched mags, putting the issued one in her shoulder holster pouch. She was about to pull the slide to chamber a round when Winthrop put up her hand.

"Don't mean to sound pushy, but we need to be on the same page. One in the chamber and safety on?"

"You got it," said Jessica.

Winthrop smiled. She thought she'd like this presidential agent. She exited the area first and they took the first two seats up front on the right, Winthrop leaving her assigned seat empty and Jessica abandoning her assigned single.

"So, what are you carrying? May I call you Karen?"

Winthrop said, "You bet. What am I carrying? All members were issued Smith and Wesson's 9 mm 5946 a number of years ago and it works well for me. I can group two rounds in 2" at 3 meters and about the same at twenty. The weapon can be little heavy for some and those with small hands often have a problem adjusting to the large magazine, but otherwise it has been a good duty piece."

'Nice," said Jessica. About the same with the Sig. Do you do any point shooting? I've read that Jim Gregg taught at your training center in Regina and has a 'Hole in One Club' there."

"Yeah, I was fortunate to study with Jim, although I never made the Club. I love his modified Weaver stance. I just can't understand why so many officers extend their arms. It's so easy to have your weapon jerked away."

As both women settled in for the take-off they instinctively turned in their seats to face back toward the rest of the plane, Jessica looking over her right shoulder and Karen over her left, raising smiles from both, knowing they were in sync-Yellow.

Jessica thought this Mountie would be a good partner.

They buckled in, having to flip open their jackets revealing their weapons in the shoulder holsters. A flight attendant walked by, glanced at both women, and took a double take at their weapons. His facial expression was immediately one of fear, her emotions overtaking her brain cells. It took him a few seconds to regain his composure, nervously nodded and scurried away wishing he'd opted for coach. The male attendant never returned.

After the plane was airborne and flattened at 30,000 feet, Karen excused herself, saying she had to get to work and wandered off.

Jessica used the alone time to check with Sorento. She headed to the restroom, closed the door, and retrieved her encrypted Blackberry from the small of her back. This was always a lengthy process away from The Ranch or other secure Secret Service facility.

She accessed her assigned encrypted message system and received confirmation that the agents' supervisors had been contacted and she'd be advised when the process had been completed. Pennington was the easiest to transfer, or so she thought, and he'd be there in two days. Ditto Simpson and Spencer. Peltowski would take longer, so she tentatively lined up training to start in a week. Jessica figured Peltowski would be the least fit and would take additional time to get to speed. After three years of London cabs and globetrotting, she'd be Jell-O.

She secured the unit and exited the restroom and returned to her seat. Pulled her personal Blackberry from her inside jacket pocket, just as the attendant arrived with refreshments. She accepted a ginger ale then flipped the Berry to the lighted face showing her in a martial arts kicking pose. She also had a kick ass phone ring, Toby Keith/Willy Nelson's *Beer for My Horses*.

Their redneck approach to justice, "Round up all them bad boys and hang em high in the street," was Jessica's mantra. An attitude that would surely get her a severe reprimand had Sorento known. Although she had a reputation as a rebel, she was known to follow procedure...most of the time. She sent her mom a text telling her she'd cab it with a friend to the Sheridan and not to come to Pearson. She'd just closed the Berry when Karen appeared.

Karen returned periodically throughout the 90 minute flight but never to sit for long. She had a technique for making herself look inconspicuous while scrutinizing every passenger.

She plopped herself into the curved Embraer seat and Jessica asked her how it went.

"Pretty uneventful. Every guy 20-50 eyeballing me wondering what I'm up to or what I look like naked. Gets boring at times but goes with the job. I used to get it a lot when I started with the force and was on general duty, in uniform."

"How did you manage the come-ons?" asked Jessica.

"Took me a while, I was young and foolishly thought every good-looking guy I stopped for a traffic violation would be a marriage prospect. Not!" After a few in-service courses I got my act together, changed my demeanor and learned the Color Code of Awareness, which you obviously practice as well."

Jessica laughed, "That noticeable huh?"

"Not really, just from law enforcement. We'd have a lot fewer victims if every citizen practiced it, being aware of his/her surroundings and prepared to act rather than react."

"Oh, I agree. I don't know why my colleagues haven't figured out that I take them down constantly in training sessions because I act while they react."

Chapter Nine

Jenewein circled the lake once looking for any sign of his previous visitor who had broken into the main building and ravaged the supply room, destroying bags of rice, flour and making off with cans of meat and prepared food. Jenewein had wondered at the time why a person in need would have felt the urge to destroy.

The kitchen door hadn't just been broken; it had been smashed beyond repair, Jenewein having to build a new one before returning to Denver. He recalled a strange pungent odor like musky bear stench that permeated the air and hung in his nostrils. And the long brownish hairs caught at the top of the doorway that was certainly not bear, or moose for that matter. Had a lost hunter or prospector been hungry, they would have helped themselves to whatever they needed, which was bush custom, but the wonton destruction was beyond comprehension.

Jenewein had spent hours sweeping just to make the place livable. Now as he made his fly-by he wondered if his visitor might have been a guy like British Columbia's Allan Schoenborn who fled to the bush to escape a police pursuit, wanting him for killing his three children. But that wouldn't have explained the damage.

He brought his attention back to landing.

Seeing no obvious signs of an intruder, Jenewein circled again, observing the lakeside aspens for leaf movement, picked up on the westerly direction and maneuvered to land into the wind, dropped altitude, eased back on the throttle then made a perfect pontoon landing. He taxied slowly toward the dock, cut the engine, bringing the Otter alongside the twenty-foot platform.

As the left pontoon hit the dock bumpers, he was on the left brace grabbing the first available tether and snapped it to a hook-eye on the pontoon as the plane glided to a stop. He jumped out and tethered the remaining two hooks, giving the Otter a three-point restraint.

He walked quickly along the wharf and up the dirt incline to the boathouse where he retrieved a large wheel barrel. Returning to the Otter, Jenewein positioned the wheel barrel next to the plane, stepped up to the pilot's seat leaning on one knee as he reached under the seat for a roll of duct tape. He stretched across the console and taped the blood-soaked cloth to Edgar's side to prevent leakage and then threw the tape roll into the cargo area. He grabbed his passenger and pulled him out the door and settled him in to the wheel barrel.

Jenewein worked the cargo to balance the weight then pushed him along the dock and up the incline, finding the task easy given Jenewein's massive chest, arm, and quad muscles, thanks to the center's gym during his downtime.

At the boathouse he transferred the cargo to the carry bucket at the rear of the Kubota all-terrain vehicle then motored the quad behind the main buildings and out into the woods, following a well-used trail as it meandered through the foothills.

Forty-five later he entered a clearing, circled to his left, stopped at a series of human skeletons bleached white from the elements and void of all flesh thanks to the wolves, bears and other predators. Getting out of the vehicle he walked back to the cargo area, grabbed his passenger, and pulled him off the machine then dragged him to the bone piles. He stripped the body of all identification, watch, and jewelry then removed all clothing. He carried these over to the remains of previous fires and tossed them on the ashes. He returned to the Kaput for a can of kerosene which he splashed on the clothes and jewelry. He ignited the pile with his Zippo then carried the fuel back to the machine.

Jenewein reached behind the driver's seat, lifted the lid off a cooler and retrieved a can of beer. He walked around to the vehicle's cargo area, popped the beer, reached into his jacket pocket for a small cigar, lighted it with his Zippo, leaned against the Kubota and watched Edgar's existence disappear.

Periodically he stirred the fire with a stick making sure everything was burning. An hour and three beers later he was assured his passenger's existence was burned beyond recognition so he motored back to the Otter, satisfied that by the morning all the flesh would be gone leaving Ravens to pick the remains.

Within forty-eight the head would be transported miles into the bush by a coyote and all dental remains scattered. In a few days he'd remove the jewelry remains from the burn pile and scatter them in the lake from the fifteen-foot ski boat that the center kept for their summer students' break from their research.

Chapter Ten

After touchdown and as they taxied, Jessica asked where Karen was staying. Turns out she lived at the Colonnade on Bloor just down from the University of Toronto and within walking distance of Sheridan House where the senior Fukishura's lived.

"You know the Rosedale Golf Club?" asked Jessica.

"Sure, just up the street a bit from my place," said Karen.

"How about something totally crazy? Let's meet at the East gate and run the cart paths?"

"Sounds good to me," laughed Karen.

"I have to exit first so let's meet up this side of customs."

"Okay, see you in a few," said Jessica.

Karen got up and was at the exit just as the attendant broke the seal and opened the door to the tube. Moments later she was out of sight. Jessica waited until the other six business passengers had exited. She grabbed her overnight from the overhead, slung it over her right shoulder and headed for the exit.

She caught site of the male attendant watching her with his mouth open, half awe, half hormones. She gave a quick nod in his direction with her right arm up, purposely swinging her jacket up and out, revealing her Sig. She was sure he was going to have a bladder incident. She thought she really shouldn't do things like that to people. She didn't think too long. She loved the reaction. She wondered why. If she allowed herself the time, she'd have realized it was Ecole Polytechnique.

Once in the terminal she spotted Karen leaning against a wall, left leg up and foot against the wall, with her hands clasped in front at her waistband, allowing her quick access to the Smith on her right under the smart looking leather jacket. Jessica wandered over, admiring the Mountie's alertness yet casual demeanor.

"How do customs usually treat you on these home visits?"

"Not too bad but I always have a hassle with my Sig. Seems everyone wants to take it," replied Jessica.

"Let's do a quick tour of the security office and see if we can short circuit the regulations."

"Lead on. I'm game for anything to cut the bull shit. Geez, you'd think I was the terrorist. Some of these guys don't even look at my credentials," said Jessica.

They walked over to an unmarked door, entered, and met an officious looking nerdy-thirty something male with a badge and uniform. Airport Security.

Karen produced her badge and asked for Wally. The two women followed Uniform down a hallway. Uniform knocked on another unmarked door. A muffled, "Enter" groaned from behind the door.

They did. Uniform left.

"Hi Wally, how's your day going?" said Karen as she gave him her $300 smile.

Jessica had to glance away; sure she'd give away the ruse with a huge laughter snort.

"Hi Karen, fairly good, how about yours? You just in on that Reagan flight?"

"Yup, pretty uneventful, thankfully."

"This is Secret Service agent Jessica Fukishura, here for a few days to visit her folks in Toronto. She's carrying her duty weapon, a Sig 229, and wants to bypass security so the guys on duty don't have a fit."

"No can-do Karen. You know the rules; she's not on duty, no unauthorized weapon in the country."

Jessica had been through this before.

"Hi Wally, nice to meet you. Let me show you my credentials."

She brought out her ID wallet containing the Service's issued photo ID and badge and handed them to the security officer.

"Okay, thanks Agent Fukishura. I don't have any problem with them, but the Sig stays here until you board a return flight."

"I understand Wally. I have another ID here for you too."

Jessica reached into her jacket's inside pocket and retrieved another folder. This one was of soft looking dark tan leather with the seal of the Canadian Senate emblazoned across the front in gold script. She handed it to Wally who reached for it with skepticism.

Inside was a Canadian Firearm's Carry Permit, signed by the ranking firearms inspector and countersigned by Senator Art Eagleman. Eagleman had been Canada's Defense Minister for several years before taking the Senate seat. He'd also been a Toronto City Counselor for two decades and had attended Jessica's Secret Service graduation with her parents.

Jessica hated using this influence but guys like Wally pissed her off. How much more qualified did he think someone had to be, over and above being a member of the U.S. Presidential Protection Detail?

Being a Canadian, it was quite easy to obtain a firearms license. All a citizen needed was a safety test and no police record to qualify to purchase any legal firearm anywhere in the country. There was a little redder tape for the carry. Trappers and timber cruisers, those who were air lifted to forests to mark trees chosen for harvest, and of course armored car employees qualified, but the average citizen didn't.

Jessica was a proponent for all women having carry permits. She knew violence against women would be minimized when violent men knew their potential victims were armed. Miami proved that concept when the police department trained several thousand women in firearm's tactics and issued carry permits.

Violence against women dropped dramatically when the story appeared in the Miami press.

"She's been processed before Wally. There isn't anything different," said Karen as she cranked the smile to $500.

Wally appeared apprehensive to give up his authority but was smart enough not to rattle any cages, less the next one ended up being his.

He handed both creds back to Jessica, forced a smile and said he'd take them through security personally, his body language sending the message loud and clear that he wasn't happy being forced to counter policy.

The guide wasn't necessary as Karen passed through countless times without using the metal detector, but she gave him a chance to show off in front of Jessica.

Before they left Wally's office, Karen drew Jessica aside and gave her back her issued rounds and told her to keep the low velocity for the return trip. Jessica excused herself and used the restroom where she made the switch.

The three headed out of the office, the women allowing Wally to leave first and Karen pulling up the rear. Wally walked up to the security kiosk, spoke with the duty manager, came back, nodded, and walked the two around the barrier and to the exit doors.

The women thanked him for his efficiency, shook hands and walked out the double doors grinning hard enough to break blood vessels.

They hailed a cab with surprising ease and headed into Toronto.

Jessica's parents' place came up first. As the cab pulled in front of Sheridan House, she opened her wallet to pay her share.

"Not this time Jessica, this one's on the Mounties. It's been a real pleasure meeting you. See you tomorrow when we trespass at the golf club."

Jessica laughed and said thanks, then offered breakfast on her after the run. "6 am then. Or is it 0600 hrs.?"

They both laughed at the RCMP's penance for the military. Jessica exited. Cabby retrieved her carry-on.

Headed into Sheridan House.

Jessica approached the main door, stopped at the first step and 360'd, pushed through the attractive bronze double doors with *Sheridan House* boldly welcoming all who crossed through the hallowed doors, in gold and silver swirled script then stepped over to the intercom and keyed her folk's flat. Shelia answered, "Hello."

"Hey, you got any booze?" replied Jessica.

Her Mom let out a hoot and said, "Depends on how much you're drinking agent Fukishura."

The Sheridan was part of a huge residential complex on Bloor that encompassed several square miles, including the university. The area had gone through transformation several years ago with investors tearing down the old and erecting the new with rents hovering in the $1500.00 to $2,000.00 range for minimum. Many of the condos were owned outright, selling for millions. She didn't know if her folks owned or rented. Interesting lack of knowledge Jessica thought.

Before Jessica could think of anything cute to rebut, she heard the buzzer, did another 360, opened Sheridan's door, stepped through, closed it, looked intently toward the street, and headed to the elevator.

The elevator doors were open. In. She moved to the controls offside corner so she could attack anyone rushing in attempting to capture the controls.

Uneventful. Off at the fifteenth floor. She stepped out. Hard look left, then right. Walk twenty meters to 1525.

She'd taught her mom years before not to open the door until she knocked so she could use the door viewer. Three viewers actually. Prevents an attacker shooting through the viewfinder into the tenant's eye. She knocked once and the door opened with flourish and Jessica stepped in. Close. Lock. Hugs.

Shelia and Glenn. Her support. Her cheer squad. Her anchor.

"Hi Mom, Dad, thanks for having me."

Shelia grabbed Jessica and gave her another hug then stepped aside for Glenn.

Hugging his daughter, Glenn said," You know sweetheart, I thought I'd be nervous about you being a police officer but every time I hug you and I feel that firearm I am just so proud."

"Thanks Dad. Your support means everything. Sets off a lot of dates too," she added with a nervous laugh.

"Never can figure out how you get by the airport security with that thing though," questioned Glenn.

"Very easy this time, I met an RCMP Air Marshal on board and she walked me through security. We double teamed the security supervisor and had him whimpering in the corner when we left."

Shelia let out a hoot, clapped her hands together, "That's my girl."

Glenn grabbed a bottle of Chardonnay from the fridge, three glasses, and returned to the living room.

"This is so excellent Jessica. We like spontaneous visits. How was the flight?"

"Really quite fun actually. Air Canada's flight attendants were taken aback; particularly a guy who I thought was particularly uncomfortable when he saw my Sig."

"I can imagine," said Shelia. "And of course you accentuated the incident just for fun."

"But of course," replied Jessica with a tilt of her head. "Just after that I met the Air Marshal. Actually she met me. She stood in front of me and asked for clarification on my weapon. She was genuinely nice and understanding. Had me swap ammo for some of her low velocity rounds that wouldn't penetrate the fuselage."

Glenn poured the wine and commented, "Pretty exciting and a great way to extend your networking. This is a new white from the Kelowna region of S.E. British Columbia. They are now producing wines that compete on the international scene with France, Italy, and California. Exceptionally smooth and fruity."

Swirling the chardonnay, sniffing then sipping, Jessica said, "Very nice Dad. Thanks. Karen lives at the Colonnade on Bloor so we're running at 6 tomorrow morning, then coffee at the *Nine to Five*. Mom, why don't you join us at the *Nine* around seven and you can meet Karen?"

"Sounds like a plan. Too bad you have to work dear," she gestured to Glenn, "But maybe the estrogen level would be too overwhelming."

Glenn laughed and said he agreed. He'd be much better off getting ready for his graduate students at that time of the morning.

"And Mom, how about lunch somewhere? And then, are you ready? Holt? Are you up for it? I need a new outfit, this Armani all the time gets boring."

"You bet," said Shelia, and then laughed at the Armani joke, knowing Jessica loved her designer wardrobe.

They caught up on each other's happenings, discussed politics till ten then headed to bed, Glenn saying he'd see his ladies the next night and Shelia confirming 7 am at the *Nine*.

Bakus sat alone in the Oval office at his desk with his back to the three twelve foot, fourteen paned, firebrick red draped windows, reflecting on Chapman's system of keeping her back to a solid wall. He figured a sniper could get a solid shot away but considering even a .50 caliber bullet wouldn't penetrate the glass behind him; he was relatively safe...or was he.

It was on nights like this with rain beating against the 9 mm thick glass that he commiserated on his loneliness and hence his safety. He had no one to worry about him, wonder about his health, his stress or whether he was coming to bed soon. Tonight, with at least twenty people clustered outside his doors, he had turned most of the lights off, angled one of the beige couches to face the fireplace, poured himself a generous four fingers of JD and sat with his feet on the coffee table.

Chapman's task was highest on his agenda, and he always ended his day with her reports. He was pleased with her progress and was comfortable setting her update aside and like many similar nights, he thought back to Lois' long and painful illness.

They had been married for twenty years, twenty fun filled years enjoying rural Wyoming while each pursued separate careers; she as a back-country MD and he represented friends and fellow ranchers in legal battles with the federal government over a myriad of issues from export regulations to the BSE (bovine spongiform encephalopathy or mad-cow disease), then as a U.S. Senator.

Lois had noticed the lump during her own routine breast examination and immediately had it biopsied and, like most, if not all women, feared the results. Days later she received the results... malignant.

Her aggressive treatment put the cancer in remission for seven years but then it came back with a vengeance and there was no hope for a second treatment. Her health declined rapidly, succumbing on a beautiful spring Sunday on the deck of their ranch house.

Bakus' sadness stemmed from his guilt. He felt that he had abandoned her in her time of need, traveling back and forth to Washington during her treatment trauma and only putting the Senate on hold when the disease accelerated, and he knew he had to be with her. He stopped his anguish, pinched between his eyes with his right hand, relieving the tension and noticed when he removed his hand that his fingers were wet.

He took another pull on the JD and felt the comfortable burn as it made its way past the ache in his chest. He glanced at the sound of the rain beating against the windows and noticed how the drops joined with the security lights' brightness to create a sparkle as they bounced off the windows. He shook his head, realizing the beauty would have been welcomed under different circumstances and then went back to his musing.

Could he have made a difference had he tempered his work schedule earlier? Probably not, he thought, but the doubt lingered, particularly on nights like this when he missed her terribly, missed her warmth, her caressing his neck as she curled up next to him in front of their stone fireplace at the Stone Hedge ranch house.

He'd not dated anyone for five years after Lois was gone, always thinking he was betraying her and their marriage by even looking at another woman, but life's doubts and second guessing brought him eventually in to the realm of single females during his extended Washington lifestyle and as the years moved on, he found himself asking the occasional new acquaintance out for dinner and after a number of no second dates, he finally succumbed to the physical and slept with a forty-five year old California lobbyist.

After several more dates and an equal number of unbelievably aggressive sexual encounters, he told her he couldn't provide the commitment she was seeking, and they parted company.

Since then he went for the second date to get sex but never called for the third. He had created a string of pissed off Washington women and his reputation as an insensitive asshole spread quickly. Finding it difficult to date casually, he put his time and energy into his work and the eventual presidential nomination and ultimately the presidency.

He sighed loudly, downed the last of his JD, went to his desk and put the rest of the evening's reading material in to his briefcase and headed upstairs to the living quarters.

Chapter Eleven

Jessica headed for the spare bedroom/office with her overnight, closed the door, put her case on the floor, placed the Sig and secure Blackberry on the nightstand, stripped, hung her outfit in the closet, did her nightly bathroom routine and crawled into bed.

She was asleep instantly.

5:30 am. She bounced out of bed, grabbed a glass of water, and did 15 minutes of up/down dogs then snagged her sweats, fanny pack and keys. She slipped the Sig, credentials and both Blackberrys into the pack along with the keys and tip toed to the front door.

A quick glance left and right as she exited and walked to the elevator. Down button. Stood back against the far wall, right leg up on the wall for balance and her left hand on her pack. Instinct.

Elevator arrived. Empty. She walked on, turned, pushed for the lobby, and moved to the opposite corner. Foot up, hand on pack.

First floor arrival. Door open. Eyes left and right. Walk to the front door and out. I stretched stretching then off for the golf course at a steady pace.

She spotted Karen jogging in place, waiting by the course's main gate.

"Hey good morning, Serge-referring to the red serge dress/ceremonial RCMP uniform. How you makin' out this morning?"

"Pretty good Washington. You?"

"Fabulous! Ready for a new outfit from Holt & Renfrew? How about joining my mom and me for lunch, then shopping?"

"Yeah, a new outfit! I'm always on the prowl for something new. You got it. What time?"

"Let's do it straight up. You know Badali's on Front Street?"

"Sure. Meet you guys there. Can't believe you've been in the neighborhood, and we've never met."

"Yeah, weird huh?"

"Okay, let's get some serious exercise going."

They took off through the golf course, enjoying the rolling hills, ponds, lakes, and various fauna for about forty-five and ended back at the front gate. They cooled down on their way to "Nine to Five" and got there about seven and spotted Shelia at a table for four.

"Hi Mom, been waiting long?"

"Nine to Five" was a homey local joint, not fancy décor but comfortable, obviously catering to the professional thirties crowd. Walls were a muted tangerine with scores of framed retro photos and local dignitaries, politicians and U of Toronto educators who'd made it on the world stage with innovative research or political commentary. Booths were scattered willy-nilly, creating a unique ambiance.

"Nope, just got here. Been yuppie watching; just relaxing."

The two women stood beside the booth while Jessica made the introductions.

"Mom, this is Karen Winthrop. Karen, my mom, Shelia Fukishura."

Karen eyeballed Shelia out of habit. Carbon copy of Jessica, albeit without the Japanese allure, given Shelia was Irish. Older obviously. But Karen would have pegged her in her forties. Longer brunette than Jessica. But then she doesn't have to worry about hair grabs. Jessica's height. Flawless complexion. Her outfit spelled success. Black cashmere turtleneck down over her hips over black tights. A single-breasted red wool reefer hung on a hook next to the booth. Stylish. Money. Success.

"Hi Karen, nice meeting you. First Mountie I've met, and I must say my pleasure."

"Nice meeting you too Shelia."

"So, what's good here?" asked Karen

"They have a breakfast burrito to die for," replied Shelia.

"Okay, I'm in. Do we order or?"

Jessica said, "The server will be over in a minute. Coffees?"

She got up and wandered to the coffee bar. Three large plain white ceramic. Back to the table. She got the usual male glances. Her response was her, 'I'm hot and sweaty and love lathering together' look. Then she noticed several thirtyish women glancing her way. Not paying much attention she sat down with the brew with the female glances bouncing around her frontal lobe.

"Hey, Jessica, you notice those women eyeing you?" Karen asked.

"Yeah, I did, but didn't know if they wanted me or smelled my athleticism."

"Well maybe a little of both," replied her mom.

"Why Shelia, you are naughty," said Karen with a snorting laugh causing coffee to spurt through her nostrils.

The waiter arrived.

Young.

Cute.

Student.

Burritos all around.

"Jessica tells me you live just around the corner. How long have you been there?" Shelia asked.

"About since I took the airline job, three years or so. I moved from the West coast where I was a member, general duty officer, at the UBC-University of British Columbia campus for a while after transferring from hinterland and my first assignment," replied Karen.

"I would have thought the UBC job would have been perfect, all those young graduate students in need," sighed Jessica, fluttering her eyes dramatically.

"I didn't have any expectations when I took this position. I just had to find a post more challenging than arresting drunk students.

The Force (RCMP) tends to assign Depot grads to the remote areas across the country and I was a city girl, graduated from the University of Ottawa in Poly-Sci and fell for the first job offer that paid good money. I never thought I'd be sent to the boonies. But hey, I survived and I'm now The Sheriff at 30,000 feet."

"Where are you from originally? The Ottawa area?" asked Shelia.

"My ancestry is Cree and Irish, the Cree being my mom. She and Dad met when Mom came to Ottawa to lobby **Hydro-Québec** from flooding our ancestral lands for a dam project. Mom loved Ottawa, loved the hustle, the human interaction and she loved the challenge of knocking heads with politicians. I've got the political bug in my genes. Dad works as assistant to a Member of Parliament (MP). Dick Joseph, have you hear of him? Been an MP since forever, representing western Ontario."

"No, never heard of him," replied Shelia, "Jessica?"

"No, never heard of him, but you see we have something else in common. Remember the credentials I flashed at the airport? Well Senator Art Eagleman helped me get the carry permit and gave me the fancy leather card holder with the Senate insignia. He's been a family friend for, how long Mom?"

"At least twenty years dear," said Shelia.

Their breakfasts arrived and the kid filled their mugs with more brew. Karen flashed him her, "You don't have a chance kid" smile and he trotted off heart pounding, glancing over his shoulder several times and almost bumping into another table. All three women laughed. Shelia said, "You girls are incorrigible. And I love it. This is so much fun. Go on Karen, tell us more."

Karen continued her narrative while the three women enjoyed their urban burrito...not Mexican but delicious none the less.

"Let's see," she started, "After winning against Hydro, Mom was really jazzed with politics but didn't want to run for office, so she applied for a job with a newly elected MP from Nunavut just after it was made a territory. She's worked for Leona Aglukkaq for about four years now. Leona is now the Health Cabinet Minister and is working on First Nations northern development to improve living standards, plus bringing down health care costs country wide.

"I've been extremely fortunate. I obtained a great education and spoke fluent Cree and French and passable English. I thought the force would give me a bonus for being trilingual. Not. But they did fast track me. I'm a corporal and should make sergeant before I'm 35. Pisses off a lot of guys who stopped with their high school diploma or a little college."

"There you go Karen, we're so in synch," replied Jessica.

"I used to get so tired, didn't I Mom, of listening to men whine about how they were so discriminated. Really? White men in the States and Canada discriminated? Give me a break. Now I just kick their ass in training and love every minute of it. I beat many of them on the job too."

"Forgot to tell you Mom, Karen trained with Jim Gregg at depot. Hey, Karen, we can do the range while we're here?"

"You bet. I'm off for four then go back on for four so, yeah, I can do the range. Between shopping I mean."

"Shelia, do you shoot?"

"Geez, no, I leave that to my Gregg and Jessica. He gave her the bug. Or maybe I did inadvertently, from my days at Ecole Polytechnique. Gregg and Jessica used to spend hours at the range near our home. I thought she'd either be a cop or figure skater.

Glad she chose the former. I love knowing my girl is out there bustin' bad guys, giving them pain and jail time."

"Wow, Shelia, sounds like you could do some ass kicking yourself with that attitude," replied Karen.

"Well you know Karen that tragedy at the university was so terrible, and I still think that if any one of those women was carrying, that bastard would have been dead before he could raise the rifle."

"Okay girls, enough heavy stuff. Let's talk shopping," said Jessica. "What time's it now? Shit, it's almost 9."

She put her nose under her armpit and smelled. "I'm gettin' ripe. We gotta get a shower and get to gettin'."

"Okay Karen, Badali's straight up. Mom and I'll meet you there and have Badali's red in a glass ready when you arrive."

Jessica got up first, 180'd and stepped to the side for Karen and Shelia.

"Karen, do you do that twirling thing too?"

"What's that Shelia, some kinda figure skating thing?"

"No, I mean that turning around like she does," pointing to Jessica and twirling her index finger.

Karen laughed as they made their way to the front to pay.

"Yes, I do it too Shelia, it's part of what we call the Color Code of Awareness, constantly being aware of our surroundings, being able to spot trouble before it hits us, right Jessica?"

"That's it. You need to do it too Mom. I taught you that a long time ago along with several defensive moves."

"I know dear. I just forget. I become complacent living in such a safe neighborhood."

"You're forgiven." said Jessica.

"But you have to pay for breakfast. Thanks Mom. Let's get out of here Karen before she can come up with an excuse," laughed Jessica.

Shelia paid and left a generous tip to compensate for her daughter and Karen's harassing the poor kid. *He'll have wet dreams for a week after today*, she thought.

She joined Karen and Jessica on the street. She watched briefly in amazement, as both women lined themselves up, one watching left and the other watching right. This was habit for Jessica, but she didn't realize Mounties would have the same training or instincts as a Presidential Detail Agent. Interesting. She'd have to ask Karen at lunch.

"Okay ladies, all done, and I paid the kid a little extra for your shameless behavior."

All three laughed and said they'd meet up in a few hours.

Karen walked the ten blocks to her flat. Not much traffic, foot, or vehicle for this time of day. Interesting morning she thought. Wonder what Shelia does for a living. Need to ask. Don't think she's a homemaker. Not the temperament. Very weird that she and Glenn live so close, and Jessica has been visiting for years and we never ran into each other. And to think I was prepared for a confrontation with her on the flight. Live and learn Karen.

Karen did 360's continually while walking the ten. She passed a number of Toronto's finest either walking a beat or in PCs (police cars). As she eyed them peripherally, she wondered their level of awareness.

"Bill" was a Vancouver City cop assigned to the G-8 Conference in Vancouver. They'd met at an anti-terrorism in-service. Over muffins at break he commented that he never took his weapon out except to qualify yearly. *Oh, my god,* thought Karen. And this guy is protecting the likes of the U.S. President, Canada's Prime Minister, and British politicians?

Just being around Jessica for the short time, her own instincts and Fukishura's aura, told her Jessica was no "Bill." She wanted to learn more about this fed.

At her apartment's front door, she headed to the elevators keeping her mind on her surroundings but wondering about this new relationship.

Chapter Twelve

"Then there are wolves. Wolves feed on sheep.
They have a capacity for violence, and no
feelings for their fellow citizens."

Lt. Col. Dave Grossman

Jessica and Shelia walked briskly back to Sheridan House, sometimes chatting but otherwise just enjoying the morning and each other's company. Jessica saw the guy before he knew she existed.

Jeans, hoodie with a jean jacket. 5' 10" Young. Eighteen or so. White. Unshaven. Day old beard. The neglect look or just lazy. He had zeroed in on Shelia's handbag on her left shoulder.

Jessica was auto Orange. Kept the guy in her vision while letting her vision wander.

Fifteen feet. 10. 6.

Hoodie reached for Shelia's purse just as Jessica stepped to her left at a 45-degree angle. She grabbed Hoodie around his waist. She pivoted on her left toe, swinging her hips and brought her right knee up into his chest with such force bystanders heard the crack. She grabbed him as he started to fall and gently moved him over to her left, so he landed resting against a light pole.

Shelia freaked out.

"Shit, what the hell's going on?"

"It's okay Mom, he just had an accident."

Two senior women had been walking behind them.

"June, did you see that? That asshole tried to steal that lady's handbag and that girl laid him out."

"Good for you sweetie. Nice going. You want us to call the cops?" June's friend asked.

"No, that's okay ladies; he's going to be okay."

Jessica leaned down to the attacker and whispered in his ear.

"Asshole, If I see you again, your broken bones will be the least of your concerns. Understand?"

Hoodie stared at her wild-eyed, holding one arm across his chest. He just nodded.

"Okay Mom, time to go," Jessica said as she got up from Hoodie and walked over to Shelia.

Both women continued, Jessica's heart rate barely above 60.

"Should we call 911?" June asked her friend.

"Why bother. This little shit isn't hurt too badly. No blood. Maybe a few broken limbs. Let's just go."

They did. Little Shit was left sitting against the lamp post wondering what the hell just happened to him and how many of his ribs were broken.

Jessica and Shelia made it back to Sheridan House in about 15 minutes.

Shelia asked as they approached the front door, "Jessica, don't you ever get tired of being in this Yellow all the time? And you didn't seem phased at all about hurting that guy."

"Not at all mom, it just means I'm aware of my surroundings. I actually get more out of life by observing everything going on, compared to everyone else who lives in White. Those people are zoning out. And that guy doesn't deserve anyone's sympathy. Don't get me started on the number of people wearing ear buds."

"Yeah, I guess I do forget sometimes. By the way, what did you say to the thief?"

"Oh that? Not much. Suggested he find another line of work, or something to that affect."

Shelia shook her head and laughed, still finding it difficult to understand that the daughter of a university professor and political staff member had the skills to do so much damage and not raise a sweat or have any remorse.

While Jessica showered, Shelia sat at her desk and booted her Dell to check accounts and emails. She'd worked for MP Cathy McDougal for about five years, acting as her liaison between the politician and various government agencies. She had a number of emails to return so she concentrated on that while Jessica was getting ready.

Jessica came out of the bathroom wearing a robe and her hair in a towel and wandered out into the living room. Glenn and Shelia's flat was about 1200 sq. feet with a nice south view over the harbor and Lake Ontario through huge bay windows across the length of the living room.

They'd decorated in a contemporary/realist style with paintings and photos of various nature scenes, a number of Shelia's quilts on walls and laid over the chairs and the piano bench. Two couches sat in the middle of the living room facing the harbor with occasional chairs set in a semi-circle to make a comfortable socializing area with everyone being able to enjoy the view.

They hadn't used Japanese culture in any rooms but the offices. Glenn loved his ancestry but wasn't immersed in it as one might expect. He spoke the language fluently but didn't use it at home unless it was just Jessica and him and then not that often anymore. He just didn't see the need. Jessica knew the language and culture and that was all he wanted or expected. Anything more would be obtuse, he figured. He did make killer spring rolls though.

Jessica hit the kitchen for a coffee, some her dad had left from his early rise. Then over to the window to marvel at the gorgeous seascape. She looked down at the busy Toronto lifestyle and commiserated over the difference between this city and New York, Chicago, Washington, or a dozen other American cities. Toronto was incredibly clean by comparison. Folks interacted on streets, in shops and eateries without fear of offending or being attacked for communicating with another human being. But this wasn't her life. Toronto didn't need the likes of her. Washington did and she'd already begun to feel anxious to get back in the saddle.

Couple of deep breaths. Relax. Drink coffee. That will relax me; Jessica thought and laughed at herself. She plopped on the couch, brought her legs up under herself and leaned back into the light patterned chintz overstuffed cushion and enjoyed the sailboats readying for a blustery day and her coffee.

After what seemed like forever, Shelia exited her office, grabbed a coffee, and joined Jessica on the couch. "I never tire of this view," she commented.

"I can see why. It is breathtaking. And all for $1,200.00 a month," replied Jessica.

Shelia laughed. "In your dreams dear, I think you'd pay that much for 600 square feet, a four-hour commute from here."

"Any news on the man front Jessica?"

"Same ol', same ol' Mom. I go out with a guy from work and it's cop talk all night. I need a diversion on my down time, not more of what I've dealt with all day. I've tried dating hockey players, thinking there would be a natural connection, but every one of them dumps me after they find out what I do for a living. I'm proud of my career and will not lie just to get laid."

"Well, neither would I dear, but don't you miss male companionship, just to feel a hard body, smell their difference?"

"True, that is divine, but the cost just seems to be too great sometimes. Or maybe I'm gay." Jessica knew there wasn't anything she couldn't talk to her mom about, given their history of openness. She did shock her a few times as a teenager asking questions about sex positions, but Shelia had surprised her by laughing then giving her as much information as she had, and the safe sex speech about a dozen times.

"We've chatted about this before dear and you've always wondered if you have a penchant for women. Any thoughts lately?"

"Not really. It's not like I find myself obsessing about women I see at work or socially. I do wonder though if I have an unresolved or underlying dislike for men. You know, there isn't a day that goes by that I don't think of those poor women at Ecole Polytechnique and my anger is directed toward the men who Lépine ordered out of the classroom so he could murder the women. Those men were spineless, despicable human beings and I often wonder if I subconsciously group all men with them."

"There is probably a degree of truth there Jessica. That massacre affected you more than I ever imagined. You undoubtedly credit your law enforcement career choice to that incident."

"That I do Mom, that I do, every day and particularly when I am either taking down a suspect or training with my male colleagues. I know I react with more force than is necessary and have been called on it many times by my superiors. But you know, I don't really want to temper that enthusiasm, anger or whatever it is. I always feel good after a takedown and the accompanying adrenaline rush. I won't give that up, even if it means being single forever."

"That's good dear, very healthy attitude. I agree that you would be miserable if you had to temper your aggressiveness. Or is it more politically correct to call it assertiveness?" Shelia replied with a wry grin.

"So, since I have my mom's blessing to be either aggressively heterosexual or passively homosexual, let's get on with our day. Thanks for listening Mom."

"Always here for you sweetheart, gay or straight," Shelia said with a laugh, getting up and hugging Jessica.

They sat there a while enjoying the view and each other's company when all of a sudden Shelia jumped up, "Okay gotta get going. I'm hungry already. Let's get ready. What are you wearing?"

"Actually I didn't bring anything but sweats, jeans, and boots. Nothing dressy, but hey, why not. I've got those Wrangler Boot Cut jeans and ruffled shirt and hiking boots. My leather jacket will cover my Sig. I'm good. What about you?"

"You think you'll outdo your mom? I have a jean shirt by Wrangler, Jag jeans and Tony Lama boots.

Will that do? He Haw."

Jessica laughed at her mom. "Okay, let's do it."

30 minutes. Arrived at front door together. Shelia did a little spin to show off her outfit. "What do you think dear?"

"Fabulous Mom, does Dad know how lucky he is?"

"I know he does. I remind him of it constantly."

Shelia stopped moving and stared at Jessica in her white shirt, jeans, and shoulder holster with the large semi-automatic handgun under her right arm pit. "I'm always amazed the local cops allow you to carry that when the government has such restrictions on citizens carrying."

"I know Mom, it may change some day, but you have to remind yourself that we have a much lower crime rate than Americans, so there isn't a great push for the legislation. I do believe however that a lot of Canadian women carry concealed firearms regardless of the law."

"Okay enough of the heavy chat. Let's get to Badali's, I'm ready for pasta," said Shelia.

"Let's do it girlfriend," laughed Jessica. And the two of them headed out the door. Jessica first. 360's. Shelia. 360's and laughing, Jessica shaking her head and smiling heading to the elevator.

Chapter Thirteen

As they exited Sheridan House, Jessica turned to Shelia and said, "It's only a few blocks, should we walk?"

"No way. I've had enough excitement for one morning. The next guy will get a broken leg, nose, and arm."

"Probably," grinned Jessica.

Hailed a cab.

Badali's in three minutes. Twenty bucks minimum.

Joe Badali. Everything natural and homemade. Badali's wasn't just a restaurant. A Brasserie, but more cosmopolitan than simply French. 100-years old. 17,000-square-foot brick and stone. Two-story. Separate dining rooms. High ceilings and three-meter-high windows. White tablecloths. Casual almost a west coast bar setting. Front and center fireplace. Pizza. Pasta, Pasta, and more Pasta.

House special is Penne al Arrabiatta-spicy red sauce of sun-dried tomatoes, fresh mushrooms in an olive oil, garlic, and herbs. Dessert? Tiramisu-Italian ladyfingers, Savoiardi-dipped in espresso, then topped with mascarpone, triple-cream cheese made from crème fraîche/sour cream, and cocoa.

Jessica and Shelia entered the brasserie and were hit immediately by tantalizing aromas. Garlic, vino, yeast, cheese, and fireplace warmth. Karen was in the bar/holding area working on an Italian margarita, Amaretto, Triple Sec, Gold Tequila, Sour Mix, and orange juice.

Karen saw them making their way through the lunch crowd. She put her arm up with three fingers to the bartender.

Drinks were on the table when Fukishuras finished wending their way through the upscale crowd.

"Hey! Hi girls. Great place, eh? Love the aroma," said Karen as the other two arrived.

Jessica and Shelia mounted bar stools. Wiggle into comfort. One leg over and sipped their drinks. "Oh, my, the Italians really know how to make a margarita. Be a tough call between them and Puerto Vallarta bartenders," claimed Jessica.

"Here, here," replied Karen, raising her glass.

"How was your morning ladies?" asked Karen.

Shelia glanced at Jessica. Questioning. Wide eyed.

"Go ahead Mom, you're dying to tell her, "Encouraged Jessica.

"Well Karen, you will appreciate this being an ass kicker yourself," started Shelia excitedly.

Karen looked perplexed, wondering where this was going.

"We were walking back from breakfast, me of course in what you call White. Bam! Some guy is sliding toward the light post with Jessica's help."

"What happened? Did the guy have a heart attack or something?"

"Shit no," said Shelia, moving forward in her seat, her voice rising.

"Jessica kicked the crap out of him before anyone could blink. Of all those on the sidewalk, only two women walking behind us saw anything."

"Come on, you're bullshitting me Shelia," said Karen, turning to Jessica for confirmation.

Jessica just smiled and nodded.

"Really? What prompted the ass kicking Jessica?" Karen asked.

"Mom should really finish this as she has such a flourish with hyperbole," smiled Jessica.

"Oh, I'll tell you for sure. That little turd deserved every bit of pain you gave him and more. The jackass tried to take my handbag. The son-of-a-bitch. I didn't even notice, but Jessica did. Get this Karen, apparently as Turdy was walking toward us, Jessica's, what do you call it, antenna? came up and knew what he was up to. I felt his hand on my bag, then not. The next thing I saw was Jessica helping the guy lay down against the lamp post. Then the two women behind us started applauding whatever Jessica did-I later found out she kneed him in the chest. Oh, I just love my cop daughter! You think it will be on You Tube?" Shelia exclaimed.

"Well cheers to you agent Fukishura," Karen saluted with her drink and a huge grin.

"Another one down. 911 or leave him to rot in the gutter?" Karen asked.

"The gutter," replied Jessica.

"I also told him that if I ever saw him in the neighborhood again, I'd break every bone in his body. When we left, he seemed to be commiserating his options, if he could figure out what commiserating was."

"Fabulous!" cheered Karen.

"Drinks are on me after that marvelous display of defensive tactics," announced Karen.

Just then their server bounced over, all 38 DD of her, and announced in a high-pitched whiny voice, that their table was ready. Drinks grabbed; they marched after "Double D" to a balcony table overlooking the main dining room.

The aroma was even more powerful here as they settled into their seats. Their server handed them menus. 14" long. Heavy taupe paper, double sided printing.

"Double D" left them to select and said she would return with drink refills.

"Man, look at this menu!" said Karen in amazement.

"Too many choices for me, I'm going to have their famous." added Karen.

"Let's make that three. You okay with that Jessica?" suggested Shelia.

"You bet. The portions are huge here, so we really need this second drink to help our digestion," encouraged Jessica.

"Here, Here," cheered Karen as they all emptied their glasses just as their server came by with fresh drinks.

"Here we go ladies. All freshened up," announced Double D.

"Are we ready to order?"

"Yes, we are dear. We're all having the Penne Polo Al Olio," announced Shelia in her best Italian.

"Wow, Shelia, you're a woman of many talents. I'll assume you speak French too?" Karen asked.

Chapter Fourteen

Peltowski, although assigned to liaison with MI6, wasn't allowed to carry a firearm. No knife either since they'd been outlawed throughout the UK due to the increase in street attacks with blades. Being female, she wasn't allowed to interview male Islamic suspects or travel to Muslim countries. Job restrictions which she had never anticipated.

The irony in Britain was that the government had banned firearm ownership pretty much outright and their crime rate, including those committed with firearms, continued to climb. And they wouldn't allow a highly trained Secret Service Agent to carry. Absurd complained Peltowski to herself and anyone who would listen...the latter usually at the local pub, much to the local drinkers' chagrin and annoyance.

She didn't miss the hypocrisy since Britain's monarchy is protected by armed officers in Her Majesty's Body Guard what she felt was the equivalent to the Secret Service.

She was a secretary. Pissed her off the first day when Sir Edward Barton, MI6's Senior, advised her of her duties. Pompous asshole. She mused daily that she was ready to bail from this country.

Pillar of justice, Magna Carta, my ass, she thought. MI6 had teams of hackers world-wide but few women. As a female, she was a minority in what should be a non-gender job. She did enjoy the hacking though. She'd participated in President George W's "scary memos," which were his warrant-less eavesdropping activities justified as threat assessments against the United States.

The fact that she was *listening* in on Americans when she wasn't on American soil, justified any illegalities, the argument being she wasn't physically in the United States. She tapped emails from every corner of the world, routing bank transfer data to her CIA counterparts at Langley and any suspicious communications that didn't deal directly with the president, to the FBI's Counter Terrorism unit in New York.

Peltowski took a long lunch, walked around Buckingham Palace to bring things into perspective. As much as she hated her London job, she relished the British megalopolis experience.

She ate at the Cavendish in the Victoria Shopping Centre and was on her third coffee when her encrypted Blackberry went off. She made her way to the restroom, locked herself in a stall, flipped open the Berry, and entered her codes. Checking the message, she found the news she'd been wanting for months, a transfer back to the states.

She was ecstatic. She whipped open the stall door, scaring the hell out of three women freshening their make-up. She hustled out of the Cavendish and did a quick walk back to MI6 headquarters at Vauxhall Cross.

She'd just settled into her desk when her supervisor approached with a grim expression, "Ms. Peltowski, I received disturbing news," he said in his clipped Oxford English. "It appears your country requests your immediate return to America. We've been asked to expedite your departure enabling you to arrive in Washington soonest."

"Thank you for the news, sir, I appreciate your assistance. Thank you also for the opportunity to serve my country with MI6," replied Peltowski, holding in a grin and her delight.

"I suggest you hasten your departure. We've completed all the necessary paperwork and you can be on your way immediately."

"Thank you, sir. I'll just clean out my desk and be on my way," she added as she stood and shook his hand.

The desk took five minutes then she grabbed her coat and walked out, putting several years of misery behind. Her flat had traditionally been sub-leased to the newbie, and she did likewise. Could be out and on the way to James Rowley in less than a week. Yowzer! Peltowski was one happy woman, refusing to wonder what it would be like to work for a female agent.

The Penne Polo Al Olio arrived. They dug in. No talking. Just lip smacking and groans.

Tiramisu? Divine. They were ready to chat now over coffee. Chat was limited, as all three had the next item on the day's agenda in mind.

"Okay ladies let's see what Holt has to offer the young and restless," offered Karen.

Jessica picked up the tab, leaving a generous tip for Double D, given the levity they had at her expense, and the trio headed to Holt Renfrew. As they exited Baladi's, Shelia asked, "Okay, are we going to take our chances with Toronto civilization or take a cab?"

"Let's walk. I need the air and my brain needs defogging from the margaritas," replied Karen.

"One block east, then north two, not too far from the University of Toronto," Jessica laughed, "Maybe we should give Dad a call and ask him to join us."

"Now that would be a hoot, watching Glenn wander around nervously in Holt, alternating between worrying about the financial damage and being nervous around women in and out of change rooms," added Shelia.

They made it in 10 minutes. No handbag snatches.

First stop was cosmetics for a complimentary hand massage and make-up by Estee Lauder, then up two flights to the vast women's section. Today Donna Karan's Pre-Spring Preview was scheduled and the place was packed. They found seats off to one side, still with a good view of the runway and settled in. Servers began passing champagne flutes among guest. "Just what we needed girls, more booze," laughed Shelia as they toasted each other.

After the show they meandered through the various designers' displays, grabbing this and that. In and out of the change rooms for four hours, showing each other their outfits, yes-ing and no-ing, adding suggestions on what each outfit would match with what they had in their closets.

Day's end, Karen had chosen Roberto Cavalli's white stitched-sleeve blouse & printed stretch jeans. Jessica had a Gucci striped buckle caban & brown halter top with wide leg off-white cuffed pants, nicely fitted at the hips. Shelia had chosen a belted sand color long sleeve safari jacket, with flap patch pockets along with a shell-print off-white shirt and off-white wide leg cuffed pants. All Gucci.

Satisfied with their wardrobe additions, they headed up to Holt's Café on the mezzanine for coffee.

Seated, Jessica said, "Well girls, that was the most fun I've had in ages. The most I've probably spent in ages too. But who's counting except Dad...for you Mom."

"Not him sweetheart. We each contribute to the household budget, and he's never questioned how much I spend on clothes," replied Shelia.

"Of course that's probably because when we first hooked up, I told him I was worth every dime I spend on myself." she added.

Karen and Jessica smiled at the pleasure of Jessica's Mom being blessed with a partner with whom she was an equal.

"So, what are everyone's plans for the rest of the day?" asked Jessica.

"Well, I've a date," replied Karen.

"Not much for me. Dinner with Glenn and get ready for tomorrow. I've a big day. My boss has several pieces of legislation pending, so I have a lot of research scheduled," responded Shelia.

"May I join you and Dad for dinner? Then I can check on my team's progress and hit the sack early," asked Jessica.

"Of course. Let's cook together and pamper your dad," added Shelia.

"Okay then. Karen, you interested in training tomorrow morning at the Toronto Police Academy? If we can get in," asked Jessica.

"Can do. So happens I graduated with a guy, Tom Hortonn, who joined the police service here. I'll call him and set it up. You know where it is? 9 am?" replied Karen.

"Yup sounds good. We can compare techniques. You ready for guns, guns, and more guns? asked Jessica.

"Bring them on," said Karen with a smile.

"Oh, my god girls, unleash you two on Toronto citizens and the rest of law enforcement can take holidays," quipped Shelia.

They all laughed. Karen headed home and Shelia and Jessica did likewise in the opposite direction.

Jessica turned toward the retreating Karen and yelled, "Hey Canuck, all the details tomorrow about your date."

"Wolves are aggressive sociopaths".

Lt. Col. Dave Grossman

Once back at the Otter, Jenewein used the Kubota to unload the cargo and transport the food to the kitchen storeroom and the chemicals to the lab. The process took the longest with the explosives as he handled each chemical case gingerly, easing it out of the Otter and on to the terrain vehicle's trailer.

It was dark when he completed the unloading and refueled the Otter from the wharf's main fuel supply. Exhausted, he walked slowly up to the main building, grabbed a couple of beers from the kitchen and settled in front of the satellite television to recuperate.

There were times like this, when after a long day, he could enjoy urban amenities while basking in rural solitude. The retreat was totally self-sufficient with back-up generators used only when there were a series of cloudy days which limited the solar panels efficiency.

He got a kick out of watching national networks cover the latest terrorist plot. He raised his can and toasted an FBI spokesperson who rambled on about how their integrated investigation had uncovered several Afghanistan immigrants who were planning explosions in various American cities.

These were sweet observations, times that he had tremendous respect for his Al Qaeda leaders who pulled the strings with impunity. American law enforcement were chasing their tails thinking they were making progress in their so called "fight against terrorism" by arresting the likes of Najibullah Zazi when in fact the latest arrestees were among the hundreds who were sacrificing themselves for the likes of Daniel who, after his plan to join Christians for a Better America was approved, his handlers put all their resources in to the diversionary tactics to ensure his efforts went undetected.

Watching an advertisement for female hygiene products he found his mind wandering back to the Center's decision to eliminate Edgar. Edgar had spent four years at the Colorado Fundamentalist University when he showed promise in his senior philosophy classes, producing research papers which pondered the wisdom of many of the West's Middle Eastern decisions, questioning the existence of Israel and their war with Egypt in 1968, asking the reader if Israel would have been successful had they not had America's financial backing.

Edgar was interviewed numerous times during his senior year and was gradually brought within the inner circle while he continued to show interest in Christians for a Better America's national objectives. But a week ago Edgar questioned the morality of disrupting governments with demonstrations and incendiary devices. He was never advanced to the position to know of the assassination plots, but the mere questioning of the group's goals and motives brought a unanimous decision for his elimination.

After Jenewein was airborne earlier that day, one of the inner circle directors impersonated Edgar at the Denver Airport, boarding a flight to Edgar's home town of Los Angeles. Once in L.A. the impostor disappeared and would rejoin the Denver campus weeks later. As far as anyone knew, Edgar went home for a visit and was never seen again.

Jenewein made himself a couple of sandwiches from lunch meat he found in the freezer, had another beer then went to bed early, planning a seven am departure.

Once home, he'd refuel then head to Cow Springs, Arizona where he'd pick up six "Navajo" religious leaders and deliver them to the Denver campus where they would participate in seminars over several weeks and evaluate the graduating students for their inclusion in the winter's chemistry research at the lake. His passengers were Al Qaeda chemists and ideologists who would make the final decision for the winter retreat's participants.

He knew one of their main objectives was to produce TATP, triacetone triperoxide and make it stable to inject into plastic bottles. Jenewein would return the Al Qaeda operatives to the isolated air strip at Cow Springs in two weeks and then retrieve them once winter set in at Routt.

Glenn was home by the time Shelia and Jessica arrived. He had antipasto on the bar, brochette- proscuitto con melone, carciofi ripieni-stuffed artichokes and three wine glasses of red.

"Hey Dad, what a nice surprise, thanks," said Jessica as she and Shelia put their coats over the hall tree.

Glenn was on a stool looking over the city's nightscape as Shelia rushed over to him, planting a passionate kiss. "Thank you, sweetheart. This is very thoughtful. I assume you had just as great a day as we did."

Jessica was next with a hug and kiss for Glenn, who seemed to be getting a little embarrassed, blushing somewhat with a sheepish grin. He slid off the stool, gave each of his girls a hug, and each their goblet.

"You're welcome. So, tell me where you lunched, what you bought, and fill me in on this kick ass Mountie." said Glenn.

"Okay Dad, first, you ready for a fashion show?" Jessica asked.

"You bet."

Shelia and Jessica trotted to the office excited to share their day. Jessica removed her Sig, holster and placed them on the night stand, changed and came out swinging and swaying. Runway models. "So, Glenn, what do you think? Do we impress?" Shelia asked.

"Wow. You girls are spectacular. Truly, I'm stunned. Fabulous outfits. Nice."

They all took their drinks and antipasto into the living room, plunked themselves onto the chintz and marveled at Toronto's nightline through the bay windows.

Shortly, Jessica got up and wandered into the kitchen. "Okay guys, what should we make for dinner?"

"I picked up frozen Atlantic salmon fillets at the market. Let's do sushi. I started the rice about 40 minutes ago just before you got home," suggested Glenn.

"Sounds good Dad. Will you do a salad? Mom and I'll do the sushi."

"You bet. But I'll let you guys get your stuff moving before I invade your space. I'll stay here, have another glass of wine, and enjoy the view."

Shelia came into the kitchen as Jessica peeked at the rice and noted it was just about done. She made a vinegar syrup for the rice; sugar and white vinegar, rested for ten then scooped out the rice into a wooden bowl with a salted bottom then poured the syrup over the rice. Yum. She loved this recipe.

Shelia placed a large section of parchment paper out on the counter; laid Nori-dried seaweed sheets-down to make a large rectangle, then added rice. Rolled the two flat with a rolling pin. Jessica cut the fillet into wafer thin slices. Laid them on the rice. Shelia then rolled the mixture and the paper tightly into a jelly roll shape. She let this sit while Glenn made the salad.

Glenn scooted around Shelia and Jessica and retrieved salad makings from the fridge and located himself at the counter's end and put the salad together with spinach leaves, red and yellow peppers, mushrooms, real bacon bits and an assortment of scrounged goodies from the fridge, then added balsamic and olive oil. He was done as Jessica cut the sushi into bite-sizers, removed the filo paper, and placed them on a serving platter.

"How about we take our dinner and wine back into the living room and you guys can fill me in on your Mountie?" suggested Glenn.

"Sounds good," chorused Shelia and Jessica.

They loaded their plates, refilled their goblets, and headed back into the now darkened living room and took up residence where they had departed, lapping their plates, and tabling their goblets. Dug in.

Between mouthfuls, Glenn asked, "So, tell me about your Mountie."

"Well, let's see." And Jessica recounted her meeting Karen on the plane, the ammo exchange and the customs attempt to confiscate her Sig. Glenn got a kick out of the exchange with customs, given his firearms background and knowledge of Jessica obtaining the coveted carry permit.

Both women then filled him in on their luncheon and the shopping spree. And Shelia was right, he never questioned the cost, much to his credit, thought Jessica.

Around 9 Jessica excused herself, letting her folks know she and Karen were training in the morning and she was beat, and then headed to the office to crash. Filled her goblet in route. Shutting the door she headed for the bed, stripped, hung her clothes in the closet, hit the TV remote, grabbed her glass of red and got under the covers. Naked. Too tired to do teeth.

Surfing, she came across a romantic comedy in progress and settled back, goblet in hand. Every guy she'd dated never called her after they learned her occupation. One guy even said he didn't date chicks with guns. What a moron, thought Jessica.

She dated often after joining the service, mostly other agents, but quickly found those relationships extremely boring as conversations always centered on work. She tried dating professional hockey players, figuring she'd have something in common with them given her teen years on the rinks. A New York Islanders National Hockey League center took her out to a Broadway play in New York, but left her during intermission when he saw the butt of her Sig. Not to be put off from hockey players, she dated a Washington Capitals defenseman when he played home games and enjoyed their six-month relationship until she mistakenly answered his cell instead of her own, during a night over and found his wife on the other end.

She figured she needed to stick with law enforcers but would narrow the field to guys who had broader interests than just work.

She'd met many guys who would come to work on their days off, hoping for action to fill their adrenaline fix. Maybe a cop who liked to garden, or maybe long-distance biking, I could get into that she thought. Or better yet, how about a veterinarian, given her decision to get a cat. Mumm that sounded like a good action plan, so she made a mental note to start asking around when she got home...which vets are single.

Chapter Fifteen

"Then there are sheepdogs.
They are warriors.
They walk toward gunfire, not away."

Lt. Col. Dave Grossman

S impson got her transfer info when she returned from chasing down leads in Tuba City, Arizona. These small dissident groups who believe they've been hard done by and felt the government and particularly the president was responsible for their fate were grating her.

She was investigating the resurgence of Indigenous dissidents who believe they could revive late 60's "Red Power". These domestic terrorists were convinced they could improve their lifestyle and political position by waging war against the American government.

They'd started with small attacks on their own communities, blowing up this and that with impunity. Then they graduated to neighboring states doing office buildings and businesses. The FBI was leading the investigation, but the Service wanted in because intelligence indicated their ultimate goal was to take their objectives to the White House.

None of the investigators believed these desert hoods could put together the sophisticated C4 explosive devices themselves. They were getting outside help, quite possibly offshore.

There was no evidence...yet. but law enforcements' collective opinion was foreign involvement was prevalent.

The joint investigation had some success busting individuals for weapons or explosive charges, but they weren't able to connect the dots to the organizers. The FBI believed the leaders were holed up in the boonies, similar to bandits of the Wild West or Afghan Taliban insurgents. And it was the latter terrain similarities that propelled the belief that the bombings and recon ventures to neighboring states were Al Qaeda.

Blending in simple; grow the hair long, speak English and have a rudimentary knowledge of local aboriginal lore and presto, a Middle Eastern male was Native American.

It was difficult to identify the imposters because locals protected participants believing they were heroes, regardless of their origin.

She had a great deal of tracking experience; the reason she was chosen as the Service's contribution to the investigation. No FBI agent had her skills. On one occasion she'd tracked John Redfoot, believed to be one of the lieutenants, to Diablo Canyon East of Flagstaff.

The team found a shack with food, firearms, ammunition, and explosives, but nothing to tie the equipment to a person or group.

All the equipment was American made, even the military MRE-meal ready to eat-rations, those disgusting canned meals even the most ravished soldier rejected.

She had just missed them.

The stove still warm. Horse tracks led up a steep incline to a plateau, and then disappeared in rocky terrain, making it impossible to track. A chopper from Phoenix was equally unsuccessful as was a satellite pass by NSA-National Security Agency's bird.

The deep rocky fiords that crisscrossed the Arizona landscape held hundreds of hiding spots, and sniper locations, which Simpson had pointed out numerous times to her less knowledgeable federal employees to no avail.

Simpson's plan was for her to enter the area on horseback, but she was shouted down by the FBI who felt it too dangerous for a single agent without back-up.

Simpson responded with, "We have horses for everyone. We can go in as a posse." That too was shouted down with vigor by agents who expressed horror at even the thought of being on a horse and more so of having to abandon their wingtips.

So they advanced in Jeep CJs, Chrysler's small, terrain friendly outback vehicle. The caravan's dust was seen for miles in the clear air and flat desert approach.

She was delighted for the transfer even though she questioned her ability to work with a woman supervisor. Her experience had been that these agents all had an axe to grind. It usually meant trying to be better than a man and that was often at the cost of the project or assignment.

Hopefully this Fukishura will be different.

Since all her investigations had been north and east of Phoenix, the Service allowed her to live in Flagstaff, about 90 minutes north of Phoenix and home to Northern Arizona University and the Grand Canyon. She loved the small-town atmosphere of Flagstaff. Cooler in all seasons, particularly summer, than the rest of Arizona. Snow in December when Phoenix was one-hundred degrees Fahrenheit.

She'd spent many a summer day fishing just south of Flagstaff at Oak Creek Canyon. Sort of organized fishing in the wilderness where catching your limit depended more on your prompt 11 am arrival to coincide with the hatchery release upstream, than any wilderness lore or expertise.

So, it was either a transfer, or continue to chase the elusive terrorist and to hide in Oak Creek Canyon or the bottom of the Grand Canyon on her days off.

But she was ready for a change.

Her apartment was a rented furnished, so not much to pack. She gave her landlady notice immediately, apologized for any inconvenience, sited duty calling as her excuse and paid a full two month's rent, just to get out. Simpson planned to be on a plane out of Phoenix within two days of her orders.

Chapter Sixteen

Jessica woke. Looked at the clock. 6 am. No! Oh, my head, she thought. Too much vino. She fell back asleep. Or tried to. Shit, she said out loud. 9 am with Karen. Up and out of bed. Stretch. Jog in place. Up dog, down dog. Warriors 1,2,3. Coffee.

She threw on Shelia's robe and meandered out into the kitchen. First one up. Coffee going. Sniff the grounds. Sure not Pinon but it would have to do. While coffee brewed, she toasted a thick piece of the local market's high density multi-grain bread.

Coffee done, she poured a huge mug, buttered the toast plus peanut butter, and headed for the living room. Just dawn and the south facing view gave her an impressive sunrise.

Fifteen minutes. Coffee and toast down. Head to her mom's office computer to check on her team's ETA.

Surprise!

Dallas Romain advised that Peltowski and Simpson would arrive in two days. Spencer was being notified ASAP. ETA unknown. Jackson had not heard from yet. Were these guys eager for a new assignment or anxious to leave their present? I'll know pretty soon, thought Jessica.

Change of plans obviously. She'd have to head to Rowley herself tomorrow. That was okay. She'd relaxed for a couple of days. Visited her folks. Met a great colleague and was ready for the saddle. She headed for the shower. Then to the academy. She was anxious to see the Mountie's skills. Quite a few, she predicted.

She fondly recalled one of her early trainers taking her aside and telling her to use her looks and femininity to visually disarm bad guys, and then hit them with everything she had. She did. It worked every time. No matter how tall or how heavy, she smiled as she turned on the water. She suspected Karen did likewise.

Jessica acknowledged Romain's message and advised she'd be on tomorrow's flight back to Reagan and would be at Rowley that afternoon. She jumped into the luxurious steam.

"Sheep generally do not like sheepdogs. They look like
a wolf. They have a capacity for violence. But they
differ from wolves in that they care about others."

Lt. Col. Dave Grossman

Spencer was warming himself with a fire of dried camel shit outside Timimoun, Algeria with members of France's Foreign Legion and Berber locals with whom he'd been working the past two years.

France's participation in the war against terrorism was to dispatch its elite Foreign Legion troops to work with America's covert units-Delta, CIA, and Secret Service.

The Berbers and other local tribesmen often volunteered, intending to rid their country of distasteful foreigners. Others fought for money.

Their assignment? Locate and either infiltrate Al Qaeda and Taliban training camps that were scattered throughout Africa's deserts or eliminate incoming or exiting personnel.

Al Qaeda and the Taliban were constantly re-supplying their forces, but they couldn't rely totally on disenchanted villagers and ideological fanatics; they needed trained fighters.

Pakistan's ongoing dispute with India had the bulk of Pakistan troops on their southern border, leaving the remote border with Afghanistan open to the Taliban and Al Qaeda to set up training camps.

The coalition strikes into Pakistan were sporadically successful. The Pakistan attacks had killed senior Qaeda figures including Abu Jihad al-Masri and Usama al-Kini, who was believed to be a key component in the 1998 American Embassy bombings in East Africa and the Marriott Hotel in Islamabad. And of course Anwar al-Awlaki, considered by many Americans to be behind the Fort Hood, Texas shootings.

President Bakus threatened to cut military aid to Islamabad unless the country increased its attacks against Al Qaeda and the Taliban, but he held little hope that his threat would produce results given Pakistan's inability to break the back of the insurgents in the Baluchistan province.

Al Qaeda graduates moved covertly through northern Africa and Libya disguised as herders. They were met by Egypt's al-Gama'a al-islamiyya who moved them in produce trucks into Jordan with ready access to Iraq where they'd fight for Al Qaeda or be sent to Afghanistan through Iran.

Spencer's group had considerable success. They'd identify the target or targets then track them physically and with satellite imagery, and then have them intercepted by CIA contractors for elimination.

During Spencer's time in North Africa he'd seen a surge in militant attacks in Mali, Algeria, and Mauritania

A British hostage murder and a Malian Army patrol attack in Mali, an aid worker in Mauritania murdered, a bus bombing in Algeria killing American oil workers and European tourists kidnapped in Niger and held in Mali were draining Spencer's limited personnel and he saw no relief. Although he felt positive America's presence in North Africa was making a difference, he could often hear his soul scream for relief from the continuous maiming/killing.

Spencer was shocked from his revere by, "يدلب بحرن بلدي المساسفرين الصحارء زميل-Welcome fellow desert travelers," emitted a quiet voice from the dark.

Jason, the Berbers, and French soldiers grabbed their Chinese made Type 74 automatic rifles and rolled into the darkness from their fire's heat just as their guests opened fire. "يدلب بحرن المساسفرين الصحارء زميل You Americans will not escape," shouted a voice from the other side of the camp.

The French and Berbers waited for Jason's lead. Quickly Jason yelled,"وقف الطالق اللنار. راننا. نحن خاوة. نحن البرربر.Stop shooting. We are brothers. We are Berber."

There was a split second of silence, broken by increased strafing by their attackers. Jason gave his signal button two clicks and opened fire with his suppressed rifle. The team followed his lead. Immediately Jason ceased fire and crawled away from the camp making his way into the surrounding rocks in total darkness, his silence guaranteed by his filthy thobe-hooded robe.

As his team continued to return fire, Jason crawled above the fray and positioned himself over a smooth boulder giving him a vantage point over the attackers. He flipped his night goggles over his eyes and immediately saw the ten attackers encircling the camp, each man moving slowly toward the clearing: creeping, slithering toward their kill.

With no hesitation, Jason slipped the auto on single fire, scoped out the attacker closest to the clearing and squeezed. A head shot. No screams. Nothing. The attackers had no idea one of theirs took a hit. Buoyed by his success, he pivoted the weapon to the next attacker. Pfft. Another down. He repeated this procedure for ten minutes; then the shooting stopped. Jason scanned the perimeter for another five minutes, none of his men moving or speaking. Finally Jason slithered over the boulder and slinked up to each of the dead attackers. He frisked each but found nothing but their Kalashnikov-AK-47 rifles. No identification. No clothing markings.

Convinced the threat was terminated, he crawled his way over the bloody remains of two attackers, feeling blood and brain matter cling to his thobe and cover his hands and face. He triple clicked his communications button and received one in return as he came in to the clearing. He stood as his men returned to the campfire and one of them said, "لكل أن انعد ة. نحن نجاح. ةديج نحن نحن." We are good. We are successful. Let us eat."

The men took their positions around the fire, sitting just outside the circle of light with their weapons across their laps as they passed around the مال موحللل واو زرأل rice with lamb meat and gahwa saada and Arabic coffee.

Spencer felt the secure satellite phone vibrate. He got up to take a leak. A ruse for privacy. Headed away from the fire and into darkness. When out of earshot, he accessed the system and received his orders. He was delighted. Three years of heat, camel shit and months in the same clothes was enough. He had the clothes on his back and one change. No flat to rent.

He was back in Morocco in two days and on a plane to Rowley.

Or so he thought. He'd lived on the edge for so long he forgot that city folks might not take too kindly to his appearance or smell. Back in Morocco, he stopped by the CIA's detention center located in a steel-beam structure in an innocuous area of the city.

He chatted briefly with the operative regarding a prisoner he'd transported previously with the expectation of some means of information extraction.

The CIA interrogator, who fashioned himself a water-boarding expert, advised Spencer there was little the Al Qaeda graduate had to offer and therefore he was being transferred to Guantanamo the next day.

Spencer asked about the other secret American terrorist prisons in Bucharest, Romania, and Sicily. Kyle Fuego said, "Much better than we've done Jason. Your shipping those guys through Tunisia was brilliant. I still can't fathom how you got them on board the container ship, let alone how our guys off loaded them in Sicily. I suspect you had some help from *silent* friendships."

Ignoring the reference to the Sicilian underworld with whom Spencer had collaborated for years, he said, "Glad it's all worked out. I'm out of here today so it may be a while before we'll be in contact again. Don't know who my replacement will be. Take care of yourself Kyle."

They shook hands and grabbed each other's shoulders in a mock embrace as Spencer made his way outside and through Morocco's slums to retrieve his ID and one credit card from his secret stash, left there when he hit the desert.

He found a cheap motel where he showered and changed. His time was limited so he kept the beard, now three years in the growing. His change was clean two weeks ago but sitting in a duffle had not bestowed freshness. His shirt was tan with several rips in the arms. Wrinkled. His pants were similarly crunched with numerous stains. No Tide in the desert. He was a little less offensive after the shower, but not by much.

He got to the airport and without thinking; credit carded a one-way ticket to Washington. He found an espresso kiosk and treated himself to the tang of Moroccan black, found a chair with his back to the wall and slowly sipped while awaiting his flight.

His mind was wandering over the last couple of days when he all of a sudden, he jolted, his instinct kicking in, albeit too late.

Red Flag, red flag. One way ticket! Shit, how could I be so stupid, he thought. Hardly any luggage. Still smelly. Beard. Worse than the Christmas Day bomber over eastern Canada and Detroit, Michigan.

He sighed to himself realizing he was compounding the problem with his shoulder holstered semi-automatic which he had planned to declare upon entering security, but now it was too late. Here it comes. Too late.

Six Moroccan soldiers spotted him and quickly descended, surrounded him, removed his firearm, checked him for other weapons and politely directed him to accompany them. He knew better than to question the process and followed them willingly.

Everyone in a secure room off the main corridor. Spencer recalled his early training about these experienced troops, their history after Morocco's independence from France and Spain.

Five troopers levelled their M16 rifles at Spencer while the sixth asked him for his identification.

"Sir, you are American Secret Service?" asked the Major.

"Yes, sir. I am. You can verify my identity with Col. Tahar Ben Jelloun", referring to his White House assigned local contact.

"Please excuse me then sir while I do just that. Please remain as you are and appreciate the company of my men."

Ten minutes later the Major returned.

"You Americans are a very strange people, Agent Spencer. You are an elite law enforcement officer and yet you smell like camel shit and look like a Tamazirt," referring to a small town in north Algeria.

"I'm sorry for the inconvenience Major. I apologize. May I catch my flight sir?"

"Yes, go on Agent Spencer. And please, for the sake of your fellow Americans, take many showers. Soon."

"I will Major," Spencer said with a slight smile. "May I ask that you pass me through your security and flight attendants, so they are not alarmed by my odiferous presence?"

"Certainly. But be assured that my men have removed the magazine from your pistol and the bullets and will give the firearm and bullets to the pilot. Please come with me."

With that, Spencer picked up his battered carry-on, left their detention and headed for his flight. The Major, good at his word, guided him right to the airlines boarding tunnel, advising the quizzical attendant of their charge.

Chapter Seventeen

Spencer arrived at Reagan at midnight. Not tired. Jazzed with his new assignment. Had no idea what it was. He was out of Africa and that said it all. He retrieved his firearm from the captain, reassembled, holstered, and left the airport with a renewed effervescence for his job. Grabbed a cab and headed to Rowley.

The trip took him about 30 minutes given the lack of traffic. He spent the time gazing out at what he'd grown up to know as civilization. He knew the intellectual answers but emotionally he couldn't get around the fact that so much of his last three years had been spent in an area where life and death was a daily tossup. He knew much of that world hated America. Hated any developed country.

For not sharing their wealth?

Their expertise?

Knowledge?

He'd heard it all, living with dissidents. He could never figure out why they ignored the millions sent to the Sudan, Ethiopia, and other impoverished areas only to have the war lords take the money and the thousands of tons of food. Even the hand water pumps Canadian volunteers help install were often either stolen or broken.

His useless commiseration was interrupted by their arrival at Rowley.

Spencer grabbed his one small carry-on and walked quickly to the gate and was greeted immediately by the night guard standing behind the fourteen-foot-high fence with an M16 leveled at his mid-section.

Spencer stopped abruptly and stared in disbelief.

"Stop right there Sir. This is a secure government area," barked the MP, Military Police, as his partner leveled his weapon at Spencer as well.

"Whoa soldier, easy on the weapon my man. I got it. I'm going to withdraw my Secret Service ID slowly from my inside pocket, don't fuck up and shoot my ass," replied Spencer as the MPs shifted their stance aggressively behind the high wire fencing, high intensity lighting, cameras and shit knows what other security devices observed Spencer.

"Slowly Sir!"

Spencer followed directions. Retrieved his ID and tossed it gently toward the guards.

"That won't cut it Sir. Pick it up and bring it to the fence and hand it through the slot, then step back five paces," ordered the Cpl. MP.

Spencer did.

"Sir, face down, arms and legs spread. Do it now Sir.

Spencer did.

"Don't move Sir."

He didn't.

The first MP came through the gate within fifteen feet of Spencer, never varying his M 16's muzzle direction from Spencer. The second guard approached, kicked Spencer's legs wider. The MP placed his M16's strap over his head so the firearm was across his back. He stepped through Spencer's legs and put his left knee directly into the small of Spencer's back with all his weight on that knee.

"Do not move Sir. If you move, my partner will shoot you in the head. Do you understand? Sir!"

"Yes, I do soldier," grunted Spencer as he felt all the wind blasted out and the back pain set in.

The MP grabbed Spencer's right wrist and forcefully pulled it up and behind Spencer. Grabbed his left arm and did the same, then handcuffed both wrists with the backs of his hands facing each other. Once Spencer was cuffed, the guard patted him down for weapons. Finding none, he grabbed Spencer's duffle and emptied it on the ground. Found the Sig. Removed the clip, then the chambered round. Put all separately in his thigh pocket.

"Sir! Your ID looks nothing like you. You are going to be detained. I'm going to step back and level my rifle at your head. If you move before being directed to do so, I will shoot you in the head. Do you understand? Sir!"

"Yes," replied Spencer.

The MP rose off his left knee, stepped back as he swung his rifle off his back around his shoulder and in the ready position.

"Sir, stand straight up and continue to face outward. Sir!" The last word shouted as though the soldier were answering to a command himself.

Spencer did as instructed.

"Sir, turn and face us."

Spencer did.

The second MP was still fifteen feet off to Spencer's side while the other MP was directly in front about twelve feet away.

"Sir, you are going to take small steps forward. You are going to enter the gate behind us, walk ten feet then stop. Do you understand these instructions Sir?"

"Yes."

"Do it now. Sir!"

Spencer began walking very slowly, taking small steps, placing one foot carefully after the other thinking what a dumb shit he'd been, not taking the time to regain some physical respectability by shaving and deodorizing.

He'd spent so much time being his own boss, Spencer thought to himself as he walked slowly forward, caring not about his appearance, he'd left Africa with his head up his ass. Once through the gate, he heard the gate close and lock just as he reached the 10' distance. He stopped.

"Sir, my partner is going to open the guard house door. You will step inside five feet and stop. Do you understand these instructions Sir?"

"Yes."

"Walk. Sir!"

Spencer did as instructed. One MP opened the guard house door and Spencer looked inside as he walked and saw what looked like a ten-foot by ten-foot room with bars across the front. Oh, fuck, what have I done? Thought Spencer.

Spencer entered the guard house and stopped at the five-foot mark and heard the guard house door shut. Then the second guard walked around him, maintaining his rifle muzzle at Spencer. Walked over to the barred room and opened the jail door.

"Sir, you will step inside the jail and stop. Do not turn around. Do you understand these instructions Sir?"

"Yes."

"Walk. Sir!"

Spencer did, stopped inside the jail door. Immediately he heard the door slam closed and lock.

"Sir, back up and put your hands through the bars. I will unlock the handcuffs. Sir!"

Spencer did as instructed, and the handcuffs were removed.

"Sir, if I may ask. What the hell are you doing coming here at this time of the morning? Sir!"

"Good question soldier," replied Spencer, as he turned toward the guards as he rubbed his wrist.

"Plain and simple, I fucked up. I just got into Reagan and figured the way I looked no hotel would have me. No wheels. Limited luggage. The airline almost didn't board me."

"This was a pretty big fuck up Sir. Whatever your assignment, it isn't going to be a welcome home Agent Spencer now, Sir. A hotel is probably looking pretty inviting, even smelling like shit."

"You are right there soldier. My supervisor is going to be rightly pissed. What happens now?"

"You'll remain here until 0800 hours Sir. At which time I will contact the training center's director for instructions. Your weapon will be locked in our safe. Good night, Sir."

With that both soldiers walked over to desks and immersed themselves in paper work with their rifles at the ready leaned up against their respective desks.

Spencer flopped on the bed, put his arm over his eyes and was asleep instantly.

"Sir! Rise and shine Sir! Seems like you have a reputation that tells our director that you may be a little crazy but not a threat to national security, Sir. The director will be here momentarily and escort you to your quarters where toiletries have been laid out for you to return your body odor to that of a U.S. Secret Service Agent. Sir!" Laughed one MP as he unlocked the jail door.

"Coffee Sir?"

Chapter Eighteen

Jessica hit the shower, grabbed the sweats from the previous day, shrugged into her shoulder holster, retrieved the Sig, then headed into the living room to almost run into Shelia.

"Good morning Jessica. You about ready to head out?"

"Yes, Mom. I have to head back tomorrow. Sorry to cut my visit short, but my team is arriving early, and I have to be there before they arrive."

"Of course sweetheart. I understand," replied Shelia.

"Your dad's still sleeping, but I'll let him know when he gets up. He'll understand."

"Great. Then I'm off to meet Karen."

With that she left the flat and headed to the elevator in Yellow, slipping Shelia's shell jacket on as she moved.

She hailed a cab and was at the Training Centre by 8:45. Entered the massive building. Then stood in awe at the impressive foyer that was a total one eighty and a contrast to the building's activities. The thirty-foot walls were glass on three sides with the back wall painted a mulberry with Richard Brown's Legend Series spaced asymmetrically.

Ten of entertainment's icons were emblazoned with Brown's pen and ink mastery and framed three by four feet. Visitors repeatedly stopped and spent a moment with Bing Crosby, Louis Armstrong, Marlon Brando, Shirley Temple, Clark Gable, Ray Charles, Katherine Hepburn, Humphrey Bogart, W.C. Fields, and Jack Nichols. The reflective nostalgia was impressive.

There was a waiting area in one corner with several couches, matching occasional chairs, the ubiquitous magazines and coffee machine. She took a seat and people watched while she waited for Karen.

The TPS Center was impressive. It boasted a 65-million-dollar 300,000 sq. foot facility on 16 acres, two 30 position firing ranges, a close-quarter area, and a tactical village, it was the tactical village Jessica hoped they'd get access to this morning. Very similar to the FBI's Hogan's Alley, the Village was just that, a mock community with stores, playgrounds, and schools in which any number of tactic responses were created.

8:50 Karen came through the main doors dressed similarly to Jessica and shouted, "Good Morning. You been waiting long?"

"Nope, just got here. You wanna get some coffee at their cafeteria before we find your friend?"

"Better yet, I called Tom last night and he's meeting us at 9:00 there."

They walked over to the security kiosk and presented their identification and told the officer about meeting Hortonn. The guard looked at Jessica with raised eyebrows and a smirk but didn't say anything as he picked up the phone and hit a button.

"Tom, Jack here at the main desk. I have two female cops here: a Horseman and a Secret Service Agent, looking for you."

"Okay, I'll give them their temporary passes and send them to the cafeteria."

"Tom will meet you at the cafeteria. He said you are to be given the VIP treatment along with these Visitor badges. The cafeteria is through the main door, then signage will get you the rest of the way. I apologize for what may have sounded like a sexist remark but we're still mostly male at Toronto Police Services and you took me aback quite a bit. I'm sorry if I offended you."

"No apology necessary Jack. We take it as a compliment assuming you weren't questioning our abilities," said Jessica, projecting her offensive, aggressive mood, defending her gender, her skills and what many of her former dates called, "PMS mode."

"We're both armed," added Karen. "Do you want us to leave them somewhere?"

"Yes, as you go in the main door, the locker room is on the right. As you enter, there is a firearm locker and civilian staffer who will store them for you."

Gym bags over their shoulders, the two headed for the interior main door, thanking Jack as they left. Inside they found the weapon storage cage and presented their ID to the staffer.

"Good morning officers. I'm Susan. Please step inside and stabilize your weapons per regulations, then give the firearm, magazine and chambered bullet to me and I'll log them in."

The staffer was referring to a four-foot-long tube, about six-inches in diameter set at an angle facing the user called a Firearm Unloading Station. The firearm's muzzle was placed into the tube while the magazine and chambered round were removed. If there was an accidental discharge, the bullet would be captured by the safety tube.

Having done so with both firearms, they gave them to the staffer who had already prepared the paperwork from their ID's, had them sign in and placed the Smith and Sig in the same locker located on the cage's back wall.

Relieved of their weapons and their responsibility, Karen and Jessica walked back through the locker room and made a right in the main hallway and followed the signs for the cafeteria.

"What was that about Horsemen?" asked Jessica.

Karen laughed. "That refers to the horse and rider with the lance we have on the rear fenders of our PC's-police cars. Our badges, or tins as we call them, have a buffalo head front and center, but we don't get any verbal reference to the animal. Thank goodness."

"That's kinda weird, but really significantly different. Very Canadian I suspect," added Jessica.

The cafeteria wasn't what either of them expected. Cafeteria. Schools. Hospitals. Durable chairs and tables. Food distribution line. Not here.

First impression was of fine dining. Avocado tile floor. Tiles set diagonally. Dark Oak dining tables seating 4 each with flower arrangements. Total seating had to be eighty. One wall was an enormous fish tank, at least 10,000 gallons with tropical inhabitants.

Asymmetrically spaced on light oak walls were a number of David Crighton's ink and water-color paintings. Noticeable immediately was his "Toronto City Halls" which includes a classic "Red Rocket" streetcar, as well as a couple of brightly colored neighborhood collages "Bloor West Village" and "The Junction". "King's College Circle" and "Hart House" from Crighton's "University of Toronto" were similarly huge in size, at least ten feet by six feet.

This collection had to have been specially commissioned, as the artist's typical size is of a more modest scale. The walls and art complimented each other, blending what the eye saw, creating calm and uplifting ambiance not usually seen in a public facility.

Off to one corner was a self-service coffee bar under a ten-foot carved *Kicking Horse Coffee* sign sitting out about six inches from the wall. Underneath and to the side was a large plaque giving details of the coffee's origin. First thought was that the coffee had cowboy origins. The name. Not so. From Invermere, British Columbia and named for Kicking Horse Pass which stretched Alberta to British Columbia across the Continental Divide of the Rockies. The Canadian Pacific Railway was constructed through this pass in the 1800s.

They grabbed large white mugs and helped themselves to today's roast, *Grizzly Paw*, and meandered over to one of the empty foursome settings. Nine was past coffee time and the beginning of various training sessions either at the range behind the weapons cage and locker area, the drill hall, or one of twenty-six classrooms. There were a few men gathered in small groups. No women. Every male did a fast forty-five-degree eyeball at Karen and Jessica.

Hard to miss.

The women smiled as they sat down and did a hair flip, unsuccessfully, given their short crops, but they both laughed at their junior high behavior.

Neither thought of their attire.

"Make you feel a little like a tenth grader?" asked Jessica.

"Yeah, kinda cute really. Guys are the same if they're 15, 55 or 95."

"So, how're we going to work this?" asked Karen.

"Well, besides take downs, I have a fetish for handguns and shotguns. I guess fetish is the wrong term. What I mean is I'm constantly aware of the possibility of a handgun being stuffed in my face, or a shotgun. Of course the latter wouldn't leave much left of me, but my attack works perfectly, and I just thought we could share techniques, perfecting our individual styles," said Jessica.

"Sounds good to me," replied Karen. "I have a knife fetish and have nearly broken wrists and arms because I react so violently against one being, as you say, stuffed in my face."

"Okay then, let's see what Tom has to say about us being here and if we get the go ahead, let's practice those. I have training semi-autos in my bag, knives too. No shotgun though. Too big to snag away from the Service's training area unnoticed."

"Don't tell me a federal agent stole government property?" asked Karen.

Jessica laughed. "No, just procured for personal training sessions."

"Meant to tell you, I have to head back tomorrow. I got info from my boss that my team is arriving sooner than I expected.

That means they're either keen or ready for a transfer or both. I just hope it doesn't mean they're doing such a piss poor job their current supervisor is glad to get rid of them.

Their present assignments were classified, so I don't know the ins and outs of their performances, but their bios are impressive. If anyone doesn't work out, I'll just have to go with a smaller team. I've no time to get a replacement."

"Sounds exciting. Obviously classified, so I won't go there. I can head back either on time or before my four. Why don't we go back together? I'll be assigned a jump seat in the galley, but can come up and visit periodically," replied Karen.

Just then a guy walked up. Six foot or so. Dark, blonde, short wavy hair. About 200 and compact. Not bad looking. He introduced himself. Tom. Intros all around and Karen's classmate sat down.

"So, what brings you guys to Trana, colloquialism for Toronto,` besides Holt, that is?"

"Well, Jessica is visiting her folks, taking a couple of days between assignments and I'm on my four-day rotation. And yes, we actually did Holt yesterday with Jessica's Mom and we had a blast, didn't we Jessica?"

"You bet. Gave a boost to the local economy while we were at it."

"Glad you're having a good time. I take it your present outfits were not a part of your Holt experience," he quipped with a wide grin.

He continued on before the agents could retort, "So, you want to give our new facilities a go while here?"

"Yes, if we could, commented Karen, moving the conversation on quickly before Jessica could respond to Tom's sexist remark, albeit in jest to get a rise from the women. "To get some training in and just hang out. We're both heading back in the am," replied Karen.

"Okay. I've cleared it with the Academy Director, and you have the run of the place. You have a few minutes to catch up before you kick butt?"

"Sure," replied Karen.

"Jessica, Karen tells me you're with the Secret Service. Are you able to tell me what you do?"

"Sure, Tom, I can say that much. I'm with the Presidential Protection Detail."

"No shit. Well, I'm impressed. How did you get a gig like that? Were you in law enforcement before that?"

"Nope, I graduated from Berkeley with a law degree, and I guess I had skills they needed," replied Jessica.

"Makes me feel like a lowly civil servant, next to an Air Marshall and a Secret Service Agent," replied Tom smiling.

Both women put their heads together, smiled and said in unisons. "What can we say?"

Tom shook his head and laughed. Jessica was first to speak to quell the awkwardness of the women's boldness.

"Tell me how you two met and ended up in law enforcement," asked Jessica.

Tom replied first. "Like everyone else, I didn't know what I wanted to do when I entered the U of Ottawa, so I took general studies the first year and fell in love with Poly Sci, political science, and that's where Karen and I met. Just friends, but we seemed to hit it off. Did a lot of parties together and shared some dicey political rhetoric too, eh Karen?"

"Yeah, we did Tom. You remember the *Blue Goose Pub* near the campus where we hung out on Free Pitcher night?"

"I sure do. What was that bartender's nickname?"

"Soul Train. You ever know his real name? asked Karen.

"Craig Stevenson, if I recall correctly. But everyone knew him as Soul Train, Tom Cruise's double from *Cocktail*," said Tom.

"Jessica, this guy Soul Train was incredible. You remember Cruise in *Cocktail*? Well Soul Train could do the bottle tossing and more. He was the night's entertainment and I'm sure made more in tips than any server could. Women loved him. They would get on the bar, lay down and Soul Train would pour booze in their mouths, down their blouses and elsewhere.

Customer favorites were *Orgasm* and *Orgasm on the Beach*. I don't think the ingredients were as important as the show."

"Sounds like an interesting guy. Don't know that I would have been brave enough for the bar, but the show sounds like it would have been fun to watch."

"What got you into law enforcement Tom?" asked Jessica.

"I loved Political Science and thought about grad school but there was a glut of people in government and nothing on the horizon for employment. I didn't want to leave the East so I went to a Head Hunter, took a battery of tests, and found I had some skills in which Toronto Police Services would be interested."

"Now that's bullshit for sure," said Karen.

"Tom is very modest, even for a man. He's Toronto Police Service's supervisor for Transit Security. After 9/11, Toronto went into high gear with community security. Considering the London Transit bombings, Toronto's progressiveness and aggressiveness paid off. Toronto's Subway system and the entire transit security program have averted a number of dissident attacks. So, Tom here is a honcho, even though he wouldn't tell you himself," said Karen.

"Thanks Karen," Tom said, bowing his head in acknowledgement and waving her comments aside, as his face flushing.

Karen quickly changed the subject to decrease her friend's crimson glow.

She said, "Do you remember the bandoliers Soul Train had? Jessica, this guy would take off his shirt, put on a huge cowboy hat, don two Mexican bandoliers-ammunition belts-strung criss-cross across his chest, filled with empty shooters. He had double holsters on a gun belt, carrying a fifth of Jose Cuero in one holster and Jack Daniels in the other, or he'd carry Baileys and Sambuca and give one shot of each in open mouths for a *Shoot and Load* favorite. Guy was a legend. I know he made many a girl sweat and wet, for sure."

"Geez, now I'm really sorry I missed him," said a wide-eyed Jessica.

"Well if you get to Ottawa, maybe with the president, pick the best steak house and you'll find Soul Train. Married to a great woman, two kids. Did well for himself. Don't think he's doing orgasmic shooters though. The seen and wanna be seen from government, favor whatever he's managing," added Karen.

They chatted a little more, and then Tom glanced at his watch and said he had to get back to work, a finance meeting. He got up and said sarcastically about the meeting, "Very thrilling. Lots of joy for an adrenaline junkie like me."

He made his exit and Jessica and Karen left too, thanked him again and headed to the gym.

Chapter Nineteen

The gym was a typical college facility at first glance but with huge sliding doors that separated the massive room into a basketball/tennis court. One wall housed specialty rooms; defensive tactics, meeting rooms with media bells and whistles, rooms for surveillance and traffic instruction, and then one large classroom, not unlike a high school or college class with adult size desks and a complete wall of chalkboard. At the gym's far end were the lockers and showers. His and Hers.

Karen and Jessica put their clothes, holsters, and shoes in lockers, and then dressed in their workout gear. Jessica put on her sports bra then strapped on an unusual holster to the small of her back with black webbed one-inch strapping and plastic snap closure.

The holster was similar to what patrol officer's use for handcuffs with a closure flap. Inside she placed a large Blackberry-looking device that she had retrieved from her Sig holster cross straps. The little holster was fastened to the shoulder holsters cross strap just above the double magazine holder under her left armpit.

"What's that thing?" asked Karen.

"Oh this? It's the Service's secure satellite device. We needed something that would work anywhere in the world with encryption capabilities and there was nothing available, so the federal government commissioned a firm to design one. And this is it." As she pulled it out of the holster and showed Karen.

It was indeed just like many of the handheld devices on the public market.

"Who made it?"

"Well that's classified. But what I can tell you is there were no American firms interested in the challenge. The feds didn't want to give the classified business to an offshore company, so they chose a company in North America. Enough said?"

"Enough said." Karen knew immediately to which company Jessica was referring. It was Canadian. The company controlled the professional wireless handheld device market on and off depending on their technical offerings.

They headed to the defensive tactics room.

Upon entering both women were impressed with the designer's foresight. The majority of the floor was 3" padding similar to a martial arts dojo (training room), with just a two-foot wood floor perimeter around the mats. The walls housed cabinets with Plexiglas doors so you could see the training rifles, shotguns, pistols, and knives.

Karen said, "What do you want to start with?"

How about some running and calisthenics, so we don't sprain something?"

With that they took off there runners and started jogging the room's perimeter. Both women bounced on their toes, boxer like, alternating powerful front kicks at imaginary knees and groins as they started their running regimen.

"We should jog on the mats. It will do wonders for our calves," said Jessica with a laugh knowing her new friend wasn't interested in body shaping.

Karen laughed but didn't respond, concentrating on her breathing, moving her arms in circles, and practicing elbow smashes and groin kneeing as she gained speed around the gym's perimeter.

Ten minutes later they were warmed. They stopped and did ten minutes of squats, lunges, and push-ups, finishing off with three sets of 50 crunches.

"Knives?" asked Jessica.

"Sure."

Jessica walked over to the equipment cabinet and chose a couple of red training knives, identical to the one she took from her fellow agent in training several days ago in Washington. She withdrew a bottle of red dye from the cabinet and applied a generous portion to the knife tip.

Karen took the knife, did several diagonal slashes, a few front jabs, and overhead downward stabs, then indicated she was ready.

The women were veterans and knew that training had to be as realistic as they could get with or without a Red Man padded training suit.

Jessica stood still while Karen attacked her by grabbing Jessica's sweatshirt with her left hand and jammed the knife under Jessica's chin, the blade at an angle to slice her throat. Jessica was in Orange without telegraphing her body language.

"Okay bitch, this is your day. I'm gonna give you something you've always wanted but never found a guy big enough to feed you the real thing," yelled Karen, spittle flying into Jessica's face.

"Oh, please, please, don't hurt me." Jessica pleaded as she thrust both arms out and up, complying, showing submission.

"I'll do whatever you want, just don't hurt me."

"Shut..."

Just as Karen got the first word out, Jessica moved.

Jessica's hands swung up with incredible force as she grabbed Karen's wrist pinning it to Jessica's chest. Simultaneously Jessica stepped forward at a forty-five-degree angle with her right leg and hip, behind Karen's right leg. Still pinning Karen's hand, Jessica twisted her upper body to her right and threw Karen over Jessica's right hip. As Karen went down, Jessica followed her to the ground, ending up on top of Karen with the knife touching Karen's sternum. The red dye mark startlingly obvious.

"Yowzer!" Karen yelled. That was incredible. I love it. Your force would have plunged that motherfucker right into my chest." Karen was known to be vocal while training, realistic.

Jessica let Karen up. They tried it again and again, altering between attacker and victim. Even though each knew what was coming, they were helpless to intercept the move, action being faster than reaction.

Before they knew it, forty-five minutes had passed. They put the knife back in the cabinet and Karen chose a red training semi-automatic handgun.

Many civilians are often confused between semi-auto and full auto. Full auto firearms simply mean they fire continuously as long as the trigger is depressed. They are illegal in most of North America, with the exception of Kansas where a civilian may purchase a fully automatic firearm provided, she/he qualifies for a permit; a background check, local law enforcement approval, fingerprints, photographs, pay a $200 fee and adhere to tight federal regulations.

Semi-automatics like those Karen and Jessica carry, means the firearm discharges a round every time the user pulls the trigger, until the magazine is empty. The slide moves back and forth, propelled by expelled gases from the discharged round.

This time they started with Jessica being the attacker. She turned her back on Karen. Took a moment to psych up. Spun around so quickly it took Karen by surprise.

Jessica held the firearm with both hands and pushed the semi right into Karen's face. Muzzle right up against her nose and started pushing Karen back.

"I told you that I'd find you alone one day and blow a hole muthawfucker through your ugly fuckin' face," yelled Jessica.

"Oh, god, please. Why are you doing this? What do you want, pleaded Karen, as she put her arms up in compliance.

"Oh, you..." was all Jessica got out.

Karen simultaneously dropped her head to remove the target, stepped to her left at a forty-five degree angle, grabbed Jessica's firearm with both hands around the slide preventing it from firing then and forced the firearm violently back into Jessica's face, brought the gun down to her midsection, pivoted on her left foot forcing Jessica to the floor, then kneed her repeatedly in the groin. The later move was completed with about twenty percent force to prevent injury.

"Son-of-a-bitch!" That is the defensive move I learned. Where the hell did you learn that?"

"My first posting was in an urban/rural area and being from the city I was quickly bored. I learned of a defensive tactics instructor I told you about. He studied in Seattle under an American Society of Law Enforcement Trainers' Washington Director. A lot of my tactics are from him but not RCMP approved. My attitude is, "Tough Shit. I'll use whatever works to save my ass," replied Karen.

"This is very weird," said Jessica.

"My trainer was in California. They have to be from the same discipline."

"Could be for sure. It's nice to know we have something else in common and for me, I know you would have my back any time."

"Ditto," said Jessica.

With that they high fived each other and went back to training, using various attack moves countered by effective defensive tactics. One they both excelled in was a firearm from behind-at the head, lower, middle back. They dropped each other repeatedly even though each knew what was coming.

About ninety minutes into their training the door opened and a guy, 6-2, 230 pounds, shaved head, weight lifters build, burst through.

"What the fuck are you two doing in here? You're not TPS. Who gave you permission to be here?" he yelled.

Karen said quietly, "And you are?"

"None of your fuckin' business! You have no right here. Now get the hell out."

"Easy my man," said Jessica, wondering where the steroid freak came from.

"We have clearance from the academy's director. Now if you need to, shuffle off and ask her yourself."

"Fuck you bitch. Are either of you even cops?"

"Now, never you mind junior. Go now and tell the director you found a couple of females in your tactics room," said Karen.

With that the guy turned and stormed out of the room, slamming the door in the process.

"What was that all about?" asked Jessica.

"Oh, we have a few dinosaurs still prowling law enforcement that feel women are incapable of doing the job. And of course we have juicers like him.

Some Mounties actually go out of their way to make life difficult for women, but fortunately rookies are young, progressive, and come into the service knowing women are equals, so they tend to ignore guys like him and the assholes either change or transfer out.

Usually the latter. But recently there have been a number of harassment suits against the force by women.

"There have been over a thousand sexual harassment suits settled by the RCMP over the past few years with millions paid out to women who endured the disgusting behavior. And yet the perpetrators remain on the job."

Jessica and Karen were just grabbing their gear when the door flew open again and the juicer entered with who they assumed was the director.

The woman was fifty's with short, blonde-streaked brunette locks wearing white summer slacks and royal blue satin blouse with bouffant sleeves.

"Hello officers. I'm Academy Director Margaret. Jake here is with our patrol unit and was a little confused, so I wanted to make sure he understood you had clearance."

"Jake, meet Karen Winthrop of the RCMP's Air Marshall Service and Jessica Fukishura with the U.S. Secret Service."

Karen extended her hand to shake, "Sorry for any misunderstanding Jake."

Jessica did likewise but said nothing.

Jake refused to shake.

Reminded Karen of a time when she was invited to a defensive tactics seminar in a neighboring police district put on by their trainers. She and seventy other Mounties were invited and had all arranged their work schedules to attend. No one thought to ask permission. Skills were skills. Your own time. Taught by qualified law enforcement defensive tactics instructors.

But she figured the RCMP exercised their territorialism when they heard another police department had something to offer which they didn't offer members. Now here was Jake who felt threatened by outsiders using the TPS facilities. Strange.

"So, what have you ladies been doing in the defensive tactics room? Anything you care to share?" Jake asked arrogantly, hands on his hips, smirking. All three women knew he was baiting them, wanting a show and tell so he could trounce the guests.

Karen looked at Jessica, Karen gave a little nod.

"Sure, be glad to Jake. How about you grabbing the Red Man and we can show you what we practiced. You okay with that Margaret?"

Margaret had many law enforcement years under her belt and intuitively knew what the two female officers planned and figured it was time some of these apes on testosterone overdrive were taught a lesson.

Margaret didn't leave, but leaned against the wall by the door, arms crossed at her chest, failing in her effort to suppress a smirk.

Without responding, Jake walked over to one of the larger cabinets wearing a wicked grin, pulled out and donned the Red Man fully padded suit and helmet with plexiglass face mask.

Jake took no time in getting ready and grabbed a training knife and bounced onto the mat, dancing around, indicating he was ready.

Under the muffled protection he asked, "Okay which of you ladies want to take me down?"

Karen looked at Jessica and they did rock, paper, scissors, and Jessica won. She stepped into the middle of the mat and faced Jake.

Jake immediately ran at Jessica with a slashing motion, which, had it connected, would have sliced through her left shoulder. Theoretically.

But Jessica wasn't where Jake thought she'd be.

As Jake made his move, Jessica had already stepped to a forward forty-five-degree angle, and as Jake moved passed her, she grabbed his right wrist then wrapped her left arm over, around his upper right arm, grabbed her own wrist, pivoted on her left foot, and locked his arm straight forcing him to the floor. As she swung Jake, she put more pressure on her hold and dropped to her right knee. As Jake hit the mat, face first, she put her left knee in the small of his back and pulled back with both her arms, cranking his shoulder almost out of its socket, his screaming from under the helmet sounding somewhat muffled.

Jessica kept the pressure on for a few seconds longer than necessary, then let him go, jumped up and punched the air.

"Fukin' A. asshole."

Jessica knew that comment was very unprofessional, but she had one hyper testosterone experience once that week and a second one was a bit much.

Karen walked over and gave Jessica a high five.

Margaret was still by the door, the smirk now a wide grin. She turned and left.

Chapter Twenty

"The corrupt are treacherous,
and deceitful, proud of
themselves, flaunting their
abilities."

Fushan Yuan, Zen Buddhist

Jake was trying unsuccessfully to remove the Red Man helmet with his left hand, his right arm hanging useless by his side.

As Jessica and Karen entered the locker room Jessica said, "I forgot to ask you how your date went last night?'

"Shitty. You know the older I get the more distrusting I am of guys. When I was twenty-five I wouldn't date guys under 30 as every one of them wanted to get into my pants. Now that I'm over 30, they still do it.

Last night, this guy Brett, I met at a Starbucks; asshole wouldn't even pick me up. I should've taken that as a hint. He had me meet him at some East Indian restaurant on Young. I had no idea how to dress so I did the middle of the road thing with a skirt and blouse.

It should have been jeans and sweatshirt. The guy was already seated with a beer. Wouldn't get up when I arrived. Had to order for myself. Then half way through fire hot curry, he says, "So, you okay with us going back to your place. Mine's kind of a dump."

"What a prick. I was so pissed, I got up and walked out and hailed a cab. The jerk probably had no idea why I left.

Sorry about the tantrum. I should have said the date was fine and be done with it. But I'm so tired of dealing with men, a love life and dating, I could scream. I guess I just did. Jake just set me off I guess."

They'd arrived at the lockers and were getting their street clothes, when Karen continued her dissertation on men.

"Sure did my bones good to see you teach that smart-ass a lesson. I used to get that crap all the time, in depot and on the street. Some guys wouldn't partner with me, thinking I couldn't hold up my end. Every new assignment, I had to prove myself and it got tiring.

Air Marshal is just me and I really love it. Can't figure out why the force has such a large turn over with this position. Maybe the travel and away from home four days at a time gets to members after a while."

"Glad you got that off your chest. I often feel the same way, so I hear you," replied Jessica.

"Let's hit the showers," added Jessica. They peeled off their sweaty pants, tops and underwear and walked side by side to the showers, towels over their shoulders, exhibiting none of the normal girl, girl behavior in locker rooms.

"Geez, this reminds me of dorm living, sharing showers. I often wondered how many gay experiences were started or wondered about in those times," asked Karen.

"Me too," said Jessica. "Berkeley was the home of the free spirit, suburb to gay San Francisco, as you recall, so gayness, so to speak, was everywhere and everyone probably tried it at one time or another."

They entered the shower area, each in separate stalls, and turned on the water, stepped under the spray, wet down, and lathered up, hair and all. Both took their time, luxuriating in the warmth and freedom, knowing the other had her back. Pretty hard to shower in Yellow.

Jessica stole a glance at Karen washing her hair under the spray. Jessica's feelings flipped back and forth wondering if in fact she had a physical attraction to Karen. Moments later the feeling slipped underneath her psyche radar as Karen lathered. Jessica sighed and finished showering.

They were drying off when Karen said, "What time do you head out tomorrow."

"Don't know yet, haven't checked the flight schedule yet. You?"

"The 8 am flight is usually the busiest and the one on which we expect trouble, if it's going to come. Guys who haven't left themselves enough time for check in, boarding etc. tend to get a little out of hand. How about I make a reservation for you for that flight and tell them you'll pay with, what did you call it, The Ranch's credit card, at boarding?"

"Sounds good to me," laughed Jessica.

"So you have plans for tonight or do want to get together for dinner?" Karen asked.

"Nothing."

Jessica thought for a minute as she ran the towel over her chest and neck area.

"I've an idea. You really need to meet Glenn. He was quite fascinated by Mom's tales of your job, and he'd love the opportunity to chat and get to know you. Why not let him make a reservation somewhere. You come to their place for drinks and us all head to where ever, from there."

"Great. Will give me this afternoon to do laundry before I hit the road again. Ugh! I'll go from Reagan to Miami, then to Los Angeles, then Vancouver and back here."

"Here's another idea," Jessica added. "What time is it?"

She glanced at her watch sitting on the locker room bench.

"A little after 11. Why don't we shoot up to the university and surprise Dad for lunch. You can meet him, and then carry on at his place later?" said Jessica.

"Great. Give him a call."

Jessica dug her personal cell phone out of her bag and called the university.

"Hi Dad, it's me. You free to take two beauties to lunch in about forty-five minutes?"

"Okay, we're just finishing up at the academy and we'll grab a cab and be there."

Karen heard the one-sided conversation and when Jessica hung up, she said, "Good. Let's get to gettin' then," she said, both of them seemingly not too upset at forgoing the shooting range.

They dressed, did their hair, makeup and were out the door in thirty.

They stopped by the weapons cage and retrieved their firearms, using the Firearm Unloading Station in reverse. They put the safety on and placed the firearms in their holsters. Jessica put the secure device into its pouch on the shoulder holster cross straps.

Karen was the last to load and lock. She turned to Jessica. "Okay. I'm ready for Glenn."

Terry Robinson had been agonized by the market's sudden downturn all week and today wasn't bringing any relief. The Toronto Stock Exchange TSX was down, as was the NYSE's Dow and it was only the first hour of trading.

He'd tried to bust through the downward trend of several portfolios he managed. Collectively they'd dropped an average of twenty-seven percent in the last thirty days and his clients were panicking. Not only were hundreds of millions of dollars at stake daily, but many of his clients were retirees who depended on their monthly dividends for their lifestyle.

Robinson's decisions were hurting their bottom line.

Other clients were mega investors such as teachers' retirement groups and huge union financial ventures with members demanding clarification of the downturn. He was under tremendous pressure and this morning's financial reports weren't making his decisions any easier. Then his stress level went into overload.

His head office in Washington called.

"Hi Stacy. Yes, I'm just watching the sales as we speak, and I have no idea what's causing the downturn. No, I don't see any advantage of selling even just a few million.

"There's no data to indicate this is going to level off any time in the near future. Everything is depending on the new governments in Canada and the States. If these leaders don't bail out of the various manufacturing sectors soon, this trend will continue.

"No, I don't see it that way. If we sell off the teachers' portfolio, they will drop us immediately and They're convinced, as I am, that this downturn is just a blimp for the long term. Give it a couple of years and we'll see things turn around.

"Sure, I don't mind. What time is the meeting? Okay, I'll catch the first flight out of Pearson in the morning. Okay, see you then."

"Fuck!" yelled Robinson, as he slammed his fist on his desk. "Fuck, Fuck, Fuck. Shit and god damn to hell. Son of a bitch, if this thing wasn't going sideways fast enough, I have to go to Washington and explain myself." He looked around his office wondering who was listening to his tirade.

He called his secretary and asked her to book him a flight the next morning on Air Canada and to run off all the latest activity on the teachers' and auto workers' portfolios advising her he would give her additional directions as the day proceeded so he would have the negative figures for tomorrow's meeting. He put the phone down, opened his drawer and took out a bottle, grabbed a few capsules, swallowed dry and went back to analyzing the latest disaster.

The University of Toronto was a huge institution located on Bloor St. and covered 100 acres. They boasted 9,000 staff members, 50,000 undergraduates with 840 programs and 11,000 graduate students with 520 programs. Contrasted with Jessica's alma mater, Berkeley had 100 grad programs.

Glenn was a tenured professor and finding him in the campus maze was easy, given the taxi ride from the training academy. The cabby let them out at the main entrance. Paid. Quickly headed through the main entrance, across a large foyer to a bank of elevators, both women did 360's as they walked.

In the first elevator. Both moved to the far corner. Turned to face the doors. Training. Instinct. In the corner where, if an altercation were to occur they would have an excellent attack position. Two steps to the door, front kick to the groin or a side-step and a broken knee.

They entered the school of education's main office to have the secretary let Glenn know they were there. Never knew if he had a student in his office. He didn't and came out immediately with his jacket on.

Karen was at once taken aback by how strikingly handsome he was; six feet with salt and pepper short curly hair, Mediterranean complexion complimenting his Japanese heritage on a squared face, trim physique with a definite spring in his step.

"Hi sweetheart and Officer Winthrop, I presume."

Glenn walked over to Karen and extended his arm and shook hands. Karen would have none of it and gave him a hug.

"Wow! That has to be my first Mountie hug," he said with his arms still spread wearing a sheepish grin. "Nice to meet you and welcome to the U of T. Nothing special here I'm sure, given your graduating from the University of Ottawa, in the heart of the heavy hitters."

He stepped to the side and gave Jessica a hug. "Hi honey. Thanks for inviting me to lunch. I assume you're paying."

Everyone laughed as Glenn guided them out the department's door and walked them to the elevator, Jessica knowing there was no way Glenn would let them pay.

"How about the *Yellow Griffin Pub*, just down the street. We can walk."

"Sounds good to me," replied Jessica.

"Okay by me too. Maybe you can tell me a little about yourself Glenn. Jessica said she'd leave your history up to you."

They exited the elevator, out the main door and turned left on Bloor and started walking.

"Oh, by the way Jessica, your mom asked me to make sure my wallet was inside my coat jacket and that I walk in the middle of the sidewalk, looking straight ahead so I don't get pick pocketed and you don't have to kick somebody's ass."

Both women laughed and Jessica promised not to flatten any would be muggers. She hooked her right arm on to her dad's right and Karen taking up Glenn's other side.

Pedestrian traffic was reasonably light given the noon hour and they made good time, arriving at the Pub in ten minutes. Neither Jessica nor Karen had been to the Griffin before, and they suspected it was Glenn's university haunt. Many professors tended to hang out with their graduate students, not only to cement professional relationships, but they were often friends with their senior students, having worked closely for years on one or more academic projects.

Graduate school was 180 degrees different from undergraduate studies. Undergrad students were often treated like second class citizens with barely sufficient brain power to locate the classroom. Professors often used the first and second year to weed out students they felt wouldn't make it to graduation.

Graduate school in contrast was delightful. Smaller classes, one on one with professors who actually asked for student input. In all fairness to professors, entry qualifications to graduate schools were high, giving instructors the crème de la crème.

The pub's exterior was very unassuming. Protruding slightly over two heavy black doors was a simple carved black wooden sign, Yellow Griffin Pub est. 1820. Glenn opened the right double door and allowed Jessica and Karen to enter ahead of him. Jessica thought the exterior very similar to what she'd seen and read about Upper Canada and the British Thirteen Colonies of the 1700's on America's East coast.

Jessica expected the interior to be dark and foreboding as she'd experienced in many other period pubs. Not so. Although the décor was typical English 1820's with heavy dark wooden beams creating a seven-foot ceiling, causing some men to automatically duck from the illusion of lack of height, the walls were a light oak paneling with professionally framed photos of UK castles, hunting scenes with riders decked out in red jackets and brown jodhpurs riding black Standard Bred horses, giving a lighter than expected ambience.

Along one far wall was the bar and at its end was the dart pit where eight boards and score charts dominated the wall. Track lighting followed the wall's length, allowing each board and chart to be lit separately. Part of another wall was set aside for a raised ten by ten entertainment stage. The rest of the interior housed about fifty heavy dark tables with four-inch square legs, each table hosting four matching chairs sans cushions.

The three found a seat and while Glenn went to the bar for their beer, Jessica and Karen glanced at the menu written on parchment tacked to eight-inch by eleven-inch black plywood.

Not offering the typical British fare of eggs and bangers, meat stuffed pastry or shepherd's pie, the Griffin featured a selection of over 35 burgers. Patrons had to first select their choice of patty: beef, lamb, bison, salmon, vegetarian, hickory-rubbed chicken breast or pork escalope, French for white meat.

All burgers were served on large Kaiser Rolls accompanied with gigantic garlic dill pickles.

Glenn returned quickly with three pints of British mild ale. It's often assumed Brits drink their brew warm. Not so. British beer is usually served at temps between 10/14°C 50/57F, traditionally cellar temperature carefully controlled by modern pubs. Glenn explained that mild ale is malty beer that originated in the United Kingdom in the 1600s or earlier.

Glenn toasted Jessica and Karen, "To a delicious lunch with charming company."

"Hear ye, hear ye." replied Karen. "Glad to meet a man who appreciates women and expresses it with charm and grace."

Jessica looked at Glenn and smiled, knowing her dad was taken aback by Karen's assertiveness.

"So, what are we eating Glenn, this being your haunt, what do you recommend?" asked Karen.

"I love the chicken breast with mozzarella and garlic."

"Okay by me," said Jessica. "You Karen? Wanna make it three?"

Karen waved a server over and gave Glenn's recommendation times three, not giving it a thought that she might have usurped Glenn's position as host.

After the server left, they each glanced around the pub enjoying the strange warmth of a hideaway in the middle of a megalopolis.

Jackson Pennington had been out of Seattle more than in, during his tenure in the West Coast office. Not that he argued about his absence during the fall, winter, and spring rainy seasons.

He was currently in Orofino, Idaho investigating a white supremacy, Christian group which had a mountain fortress about 2 hours southeast of the small Idaho town in heavily forested terrain. Fly-bys produced zero intel, leaving only ground reconnaissance.

National Security Satellite photos showed nothing, although the satellite's thermal imaging indicated a large substance emitting considerable energy, not produced naturally. Federal technicians calculated the imagery was producing energy equivalent to that of fifty humans. But no physical sign was ever evident.

The Secret Service's Seattle agent in charge had considered a forceful interdiction but given the compound was serviced by one dead-ended road at 6,000 feet, the entry team would be blind without intel.

He chose to send Pennington on a solo recon. Pennington was to truck it to the compound, over forestry roads to within ten crow miles, then up the mountain through thick forest. Instructions were to photograph and return images via satellite and maintain covert.

Pennington had argued with his boss that they should drop him in airborne. Carver replied that the Service didn't have Delta's budget and therefore Pennington would have to hoof it.

Pennington recalled the conversation as he hiked from 2,000 to 4,000 feet through heavily timbered terrain. He checked his GPS-global positioning periodically but otherwise delighted in using his well-honed Delta skills that had transported him many miles in every global terrain possible.

This was very similar to Bosnia where he and his team dropped in to assassinate a Serb leader known to be leading ethnic cleansing. In and out in 24 hours. He was enjoying the physical, having tired of the endless research from an Orofino motel room where he posed as a geologist from the National Geological Center, exploring the area around the Dworshak Dam on the North Fork of the Clearwater River outside Orofino.

He did, however, obtain the intel that produced the upcoming raid. There were rumors of isolated groups of people living off the land who had extreme religious beliefs and kept to themselves. If that proved to be true, then the group was receiving their supplies from a covert source, since there appeared no knowledge of them in Orofino.

The town folk quickly accepted him for who he wasn't. Much of his job was listening to local banter in pubs, coffee shops and the launderette. He found the experience unchangingly similar to his Delta recon activities in small Afghan villages where he'd been sent to gather intel on Taliban insurgents.

Six hours into the hike, on time and on track for a night arrival, he had about two hours to total darkness. Even as dusk approached he was almost invisible with his black recon attire. He circled a large boulder and found a crevice where he stretched out, able to see for miles in the direction he'd just traversed and hear anything moving above.

He carried the Service issued Sig in a shoulder holster under his down jacket. On his right thigh was a Ruger Mark 111, a specially chambered .22 pistol with a six-inch barrel. Light. Silenced. Quiet. Accurate. A comfortable fit in the hand of a combat shooter.

Cradled in his arms with a supportive front sling was the Heckler & Koch PSG1 A1 Semi-Automatic Sniper Rifle in 7.62 mm X 51 caliber, Schmidt & Bender scope, twenty-six-inch heavy polygonal silenced barrel, one twenty round magazine and four in his left thigh pouches. His weapon of choice for more years than he cared to remember with Delta.

Stretched out, he turned his internal clock for two hours, alert to Yellow and was out.

Robinson turned from his monitors and noticed it was after five. He hadn't moved since Washington called. He dialed his secretary, updated her on the data he needed for his meeting and asked her to leave them on her desk and call it a night. Walked to his built-in bar. He loved this office. Corner. Twelfth floor. Eight-hundred square feet of opulence that said, "He'd made it".

And it could all come crashing down on him any day. Maybe sooner if tomorrow's meeting didn't go well. He swung open the cabinet's door and chose Chivas, a cut glass tumbler and two cubes from the hidden fridge and walked over to the sitting area overlooking the city.

He spent the next two hours drinking and recapturing some of his accomplishments of the last twelve months. At seven, he left his empty glass on the end table, grabbed his jacket, threw the printouts and other documents for the meeting into his briefcase and left his office, grabbing the additional paperwork from the secretary's desk.

Walking to the elevator he realized he was half in the bag and decided to take a cab home and leave his car in the sub-garage. Thirty minutes later, he was in his apartment, clothes thrown on the floor and collapsed in bed. What a fucking nightmare today had been, he thought, before he passed out.

Karen asked Glenn a number of questions about the university and his professorship, then the conversation gravitated to politics, Shelia and the governments in the states and Canada. Glenn explained that he had some very definite ideas that he'd learned to keep to himself given Shelia's intense involvement. He commented positively on the changes coming to the states and said he planned to keep abreast of the progress or lack thereof.

The world's problems were solved just as their food arrived along with ale refills.

Glenn waited until Jennifer and Karen took a bite, waiting for a response.

"This is really good Glenn. Thanks for the suggestion," offered Karen.

"Yeah, really good Dad."

"Karen, Shelia filled me in on how you got from the U of Ottawa to the RCMP but how did you get into Air Marshal Service?"

Karen swallowed, took a swig of ale then said, "I was bored. Short answer. As I mentioned to Shelia and Jessica, I transferred out of a small south central B.C. town to the University of British Columbia just to get back to the city. Babysitting drunken overage teenagers proved too much. It seemed as though I was hauling drunks every night, often the same ones as the previous shift. It got to be a bit much. Hardly any investigative involvement.

So I started searching for something more challenging, but still not office bound. And I found the Flying Horsemen. The training was quite intense and of course male dominated. The shooting was phenomenal though. Close quarter combat shooting within ten feet and often less than six. Low velocity bullets that produce more of a loud pop than an ear cracking gunfire blast.

A lot of defensive tactics, take-down procedures that I had to pretend to acknowledge because I don't really believe in most of it. So much of the suspect apprehension techniques are geared for low suspect reverberation, rather than suspect control and officer safety. You see that in the Taser controversy." She took another swig. Bit into her Kaiser, dressing oozing down her chin.

She napkinned her chin, as Jessica picked up the conversation. "The Taser is unbelievably controversial in the states, but getting equally so in Canada," offered Jessica. "A great deal of training is conducted by Taser, but often hotdoggers figure the Taser is a quick solution to apprehension and control; using the impact tool rather than their verbal skills."

They concentrated on their food and ales with the occasional chat, most coming from Jessica and Karen about one female patron or another, what they were wearing and whether the outfit looked good or not.

Glenn was happy to enjoy his meal and let the estrogen level drop peacefully.

Glenn finished his Kaiser, ale and ordered coffees all around. By the time the coffee arrived, Karen and Jessica had finished their burgers and settled back in their seats, as much as one could on the hard surface.

"Great lunch Dad. Thanks. This was nice, just the three of us. Would be good to have Mom here, but this is nice too. You ready for more of today?"

"Sure, what do you have in mind?"

"Well, Karen and I are heading back tomorrow. I got word my team is arriving sooner than I anticipated and I have to be at Rowley before they arrive, so tonight is our last night here for a while. I told Karen you were "The Man" for good eateries. Just look at this place. How about we commission you to make reservations at one of your favorites? Karen will join us for drinks at your place around 6, and then we will head out. Whadaya think?"

Glenn laughed. "I love it. Sure, I'd be honored to take three gorgeous and charming ladies to dinner. And. And," he held up a hand. "And the evening's on me."

Karen had a huge grin but said nothing.

"Well, sir knight, your invitation is overwhelmingly accepted by these two charming and gorgeous ladies, right Karen?"

Karen stood and curtsied graciously and said, "I too would be honored to be one of your dates for this evening sir."

"Okay, then. I'll make a reservation as soon as I get back to the University and I'll call Shelia to give her a heads-up and ask her to check our booze supply."

"Glenn, let me leave the tip. Your generosity is overwhelming, but you must let me participate," asked Karen."

"Okay. Thanks Karen."

Karen retrieved her slim wallet from the right inside of her jacket, removed two twenties and placed them under her empty ale glass. She knew from her university days servers make minimum wage and rely on tips for their real income. Dining protocol was twenty percent, but Karen always felt she owed her success to many others, and she needed to repay by helping someone else. The bill was about $60 so she was leaving about a sixty percent tip. She felt good.

"Okay Dad, we'll let you get back to your ivory tower, a little jab at her dad for his academic career in contrast to being in the trenches. Karen is going home to do housework of all things and I'll go back to your place to make some calls, shower, and get ready for tonight." She gave him a hug and a cheek kiss and walked over to the curb to hail a cab.

"Thank you for a lovely lunch Glenn and charming company. I'm looking forward to this evening," said Karen. Then she too was gone, heading down Bloor toward, what Glenn assumed was her condo.

"You're welcome officers, see you tonight." With that, Glenn headed back to the U to look at his department's proposed budget for the next fiscal year.

Shelia wasn't home so Jessica let herself into the flat and headed to the office to check her emails. As she sat in the office chair she realized she was exhausted. Or was it the two brews she had for lunch? She glanced at the bed and its comfort won out over emails. She took off her jacket, pulled the Sig and laid it and the secure phone on the night stand, removed the shoulder holster, and flopped on the bed, bringing the comforter over her. Eyes closed. Out.

When Glenn got back to his office, he called Shelia on her cell. He found her just after she'd left a meeting with David Kopas, an upper level CSIS agent, Canadian Security Intelligence Service-Canada's CIA. She was having coffee with Kopas and outlining when they'd meet next.

"Hi Sweetheart. Not interrupting anything am I?

"Nope. Just having coffee and going over my notes and planning another meeting. What's up?"

"Jessica and Karen are coming for drinks tonight then dinner out. You interested in The Calgary?"

"Oh, Glenn, I'd love it. It's been years since we were there. Of course I'm game for that. Do the girls know you've picked The Calgary Steak House?"

"Not yet. Let's keep it a surprise. This is their last night here. Jessica has to get back and Karen's cutting her days off so she can go with. How about asking David and Cathy to join us."

"Good idea. This should be a very interesting evening. What a social mix ."

Glenn left Shelia to do the invitation and called The Calgary for reservations. 8 pm for six. Done. Back to work. It was now four. He figured he'd get in another hour to work on the budget proposal, then head home. Whatever happened to the joy of teaching, he wondered as he started in on the figures.

Chapter Twenty-One

"Sheepdogs disturb sheep.
The sheepdog is a constant reminder that there are wolves.
Sheep would prefer that sheepdogs didn't have guns, give traffic
tickets, or be airport security armed with an automatic rifle."

Lt. Col. Dave Grossman

Pennington woke. Dark. Complete. He stretched while still prone. Got the kinks out. Moved his arms around quickly to generate heat. Quietly got to his knees and peered out of his sunk. Perfect. He cupped his watch and hit the glow button, then the one for compass. Got his bearings. Shrugged into his pack. Slung the H & K across his chest. Turned and headed up the mountain. It was hard uphill climbing but nothing he hadn't done countless times previously. If it weren't for his physical conditioning, he'd find it exhausting.

Uneventful. Except the screams of rabbits losing a quick owl encounter. And wolves honing in on a mule deer, signaling back and forth, keeping their bearings. Another scream.

Four hours and he was atop no name mountain. Almost above the tree line. Flora small. Tallest trees maybe six feet. Another bearing check. Off about 5 degrees. Adjust. Continue.

Another hour and he spotted the compound's light glow. Just enough for his ATN Delta PVS 7-night goggles. He'd convinced the Service to purchase this particular unit because of his experience with Delta. He got a kick out of ATN. The manufacturer applying the Delta name, after it had secured the government contract to supply hundreds of them to Delta forces and Delta's Afghanistan military partners.

He retrieved the Deltas from his pack. Strapped them over his wool hat. Pulled the chin strap tight and moved on. No idea if this wacky group had night sentries.

As he got closer, he could make out the compound in an eerie green from the yard lights on various buildings. They were grouped in a bit of a valley. Maybe two-hundred-feet lower than his position. He moved across the valley's ridge. No sign of sentries.

He figured the largest building was their primary for housing and eating. He found another ground indent, removed his H &K, and placed it in direct line with the primary and settled in for sunrise. His assignment was to infiltrate the *Christians for a Better America's* perimeter, confirm intel and photo their operation, sending images via NSA's satellite link to Seattle.

He settled in for the wait, commiserated on how people, and groups in particular, could be so pissed at America as to plot to assassinate its president, thinking chaos would result and their twisted concept of democracy would prevail.

Rejection by mainstream America produced splinter groups like CFBA who felt it their Christian duty to awaken America by whatever extreme measures were necessary. Timothy McVeigh had been a Christian. He was this group's hero. He was just unlucky they believed. They had in mind to follow McVeigh's philosophy but with a more effective target.

The Ranch.

Jessica woke with the sound of rumblings emulating from somewhere in the flat. She ran her hand over her face, glanced around the spare bedroom/office to orient herself, looked at her watch and noted it was 4:30. Geez, am or pm she wondered. She swung her legs out of the bed, glanced at her Sig, took a moment to orientate herself, then made her way out of the room. She found her mom in the kitchen scurrying around with various kitchen implements, concentrating on whatever.

"Hi Mom. When did you get home?"

"Oh, shit Jessica. You scared the crap out of me. What are you going to with that gun?"

"Sorry about that. I got home from lunch with Dad and Karen and saw that quilted bed and couldn't resist," she replied slipping the Sig into her pocket.

"I heard about your lunch. I hope you enjoyed yourself as much as your dad did."

"Absolutely. What's up for tonight?"

"Glen made reservations at a really fabulous place that he's keeping a surprise, given it's your last night here. And I hope you don't mind, but I invited David Kopas. You remember I mentioned him. He's my liaison with CISS. Then I thought about Cathy having another meal by herself and invited her too. You okay with them?"

"Of course! We'll make a Partaaaa," she said, accentuating the last syllable. "You want I should get some booze and munchies?"

"No need. We have everything here. Except that disgusting humus you eat."

Jessica laughed. "Okay, what can I do?"

"Well, we have some time before everyone gets here. I thought I'd putter in the kitchen while you relax."

"Sounds good to me. I have some phone calls to make, and then I'll shower, dress, and join you."

Jessica headed back to the office/guest room, closed the door. Retrieved the secure phone and sat at the desk and called Romain. The connection took a few seconds as she heard the system run through its series of clicks and pauses as the transmission was processed through NSA's satellite system.

The Secret Service used the National Security Agency's SafeNet system, which provides command uplink encryption. The algorithms employed in these units are used as the military satellite system and incorporate technology to provide the highest level of security for U.S. Government satellite links.

"Hi Dallas. Jessica Fukishura here. Any word on my team members' ETA?"

"Hi Jessica. Yup. Spencer arrived with a fanfare. You'll hear all about it later. Peltowski and Simpson are scheduled for tomorrow. Jackson's still in the field. Washington's contacted his supervisor in Seattle, but he has to wait till he hears from Jackson in the next day or so."

"Okay then. Thanks Dallas, see you in a couple." Jessica closed the Blackberry and headed to the shower.

Spencer was on his second cup of military coffee, having waited all day for something to happen, when what appeared to be the World Wrestling Federation current champion slammed open the guard house door with such force it hit the wall and bounced back only to be slammed again as Rowley's Director entered the room.

Kipfensteiner was a little bit of Jessie Ventura, the former wrestler and governor of Minnesota; the grey hair but shorter than Ventura's, but the height and bulk were identical.

"Who the fuck do you think you are Mr. coming to my training center with all the appearances of being hit with flying camel shit, tempting our guards to blow your fuckin' ass away?" yelled Kipfensteiner in a deep, bellowing manner, each word stressed with a deep, intimidating tone.

Spencer jumped to attention with considerable embarrassment. He suspected the director would be unhappy, but not to tear his head off. "My apologies Director. Poor judgment. I received my orders while in the field, got back to Morocco and grabbed the first plane available."

"Damn good thing your reputation precedes you Spencer, otherwise I'd kick your ass outa here so fast you'd be flyin' like a fuckin' NFL football. Get your shit and follow me."

"Good job men. I'll let you know if you need to finish the job on this prick."

"Yes sir. Sir, Agent Spencer had his issued Sig on him when detained. It's in our safe."

"Fine Sgt. Transfer it to the base's main armory. He can sign it out when he leaves, which may be PDQ."

"Yes sir," replied the Sgt. wondering how soon the PDQ, pretty damn quick, might be.

Spencer quickly grabbed his duffle and ran after the director who was already getting into a golf cart.

He threw his duffle in the back and jumped in just as the director hit the pedal. Throwing Spencer back against the seat. No one spoke.

Kipfensteiner hit a main street, hung a fast left causing Spencer to grab hold. A quick stop. Then a right on Agriculture Rd. and full speed, fifteen mph-for about five-hundred yards then a quick left in to a cul-de-sac and four two story townhouses. Kipfensteiner headed for a driveway, up the curb and slammed on the brake inches from the garage door. Childish. But Spencer had to smile. The Director had to do something to exert his control and put Spencer in his place.

"Let's go Agent. These are your digs for your duration. Out."

The director walked quickly up the walk, drew a key out of his pocket and opened the front door and walked in. Left Spencer at the entrance. "What the hell are you waiting for Agent? An invitation to enter?"

"No Sir." Spencer took off his shoes and walked in to the foyer, placed his duffle and shoes down and wandered in, the shoe removal ingrained from his years in the Islamic faith of Africa.

Found the director in the kitchen with his butt hanging out of the fridge. He came up with two beers. Tossed one to Spencer.

"Okay Agent. I believe a detailed explanation is in order for your actions. Drink your beer and let's hear it."

"Yes Sir," replied Spencer as he twisted the cap off the Bud and pocketed the cap. Spencer laid out what he could of his last assignment, knowing the director understood his vagueness in various areas.

"Okay. I buy it. I hope to hell you get your shit together before Fukishura gets here. You guys have a small window to get skilled and teamed.

"She'll be here tomorrow. Hit the shower. I'll have training gear sent over, boots etc. Have them left on the porch. You've got an hour. The mess for dinner and drinks. Out to the main street. Left. Building B. It will be the last drinks you get for a while."

"Yes Sir. And thank you."

"Once Agent. Once."

Chapter Twenty-Two

Jessica showered, dried off and donned Shelia's robe again and came in to the office. She dressed in her new Gucci caba, brown halter top and off-white cuffed pants. She borrowed a pair of Shelia's Marc Jacob's tan Riding Boots. Shoulder holster. Secure phone. Sig. Back to the bathroom for hair and make-up and she was ready. She headed to the living room to find Shelia dressed in her new safari jacket, off-white shirt, and pants.

"Are we hot or what?" remarked Shelia. "I'll bet Karen's wearing her new outfit too."

Jessica did a little twirl then said, "So, where's the booze?"

"No reason we can't start on some margarita's while we wait for your dad. He should be here pretty soon."

They went in to the kitchen and got the margarita's going just as Glenn came through the front door with a flourish. "Well, ladies. Are you ready for this evening?" He sauntered over and gave Jessica and Shelia a hug and cheek kiss. "Shelia, are we all set with our additions to the party?"

"Yup, they'll be here at six."

"Great. I'll head to the shower and be back in thirty," he said over his shoulder as he headed to the master bedroom.

"How do men do it?" asked Jessica.

They busied themselves preparing the drinks and getting the snacks ready.

In thirty Glenn materialized with a three-button plaid silk and linen sport coat, white, button down dress shirt and light tan pleated slacks.

"Oh, my, Dad, you look terrific!"

"I second that," said Shelia, as she came over and gave him a hug and a lip kiss, leaving her latest shade.

"Thanks. You guys look pretty terrific too."

They'd just settled in the living room when the doorbell rang. Glenn jumped up and jogged to the door, glanced through one of the security holes, then opened the door gracefully, stepped to the side and bowed to his guests. Cathy entered first and responded with a curtsy, David following with a huge grin.

"Welcome guys. We were just getting started on some margaritas." Glenn took their coats, hung them on the tree behind the door as Shelia and Jessica came up.

"Glad you guys could make it. Glenn made reservations at The Calgary. Cathy, David, this is Jessica. Jessica, this is the Honorable Cathy McGregor and David Kopas."

"My pleasure. Nice to meet you. Come on in."

Everyone traipsed in to the living room as Glenn handed drinks to Cathy and David. Then the doorbell rang. Again.

"Got it," said Glenn as he headed for the door. Once open, Karen stood in her new outfit, Roberto Cavalli's white stitched-sleeve blouse & printed stretch jeans.

"Karen, what a beautiful outfit. From Holt?"

"Yes. You like?"

"I do. Very becoming. Come on in."

Karen left her jacket on while Glenn led her to the living room, making introductions, and then poured her a drink.

Shelia met Karen as she entered the living room. Gave her a hug and cheek kiss. Took her arm and guided her to Cathy and David. "Karen, I'd like you to meet my boss, The Honorable Cathy McGregor, Member of Parliament for Calgary. And this is David Kopas with CSIS."

Karen shook hands with each, took Glenn's offered margarita and sat in an angled chair facing the others. As she sat, her jacket started to open...which she quickly closed.

MP McGregor said, "Please call me Cathy everyone. So, Jessica and Karen, tell David and me a little about yourselves."

"My folks probably already told you what I do Cathy, but for David's benefit, David, I'm with the Secret Service, assigned to the Presidential Protection Detail. That's all I can offer."

"Well, it's a good thing we're not at a mixer or I'd be SOL here," said David.

"Sorry to say David, but I can't add a lot to the conversation either. I'm with the RCMP's Air Marshal Service and my itinerary is classified. Actually, what I just told you is privileged information. If we were to meet outside this room, you're obligated to not know me."

"Say no more agents. I'm not a clerk with CSIS," replied David with a smile "You're more at risk with these guys, excluding Cathy, than with me."

"I must confess, when Shelia asked me to join you guys tonight, I figured Jessica would be here. And I hoped that Karen would be too. I've an offer, I hope you can't refuse. David and I discussed this at length and came to the mutual conclusion that we can consider this a social and networking evening."

How did you know I'd be here?" asked Jessica.

"I'm minister for public safety. The country's top cop, at least politically. I just happened to be chatting with Tom Hortonn regarding other matters and he casually mentioned a little tiff they had at the Training Academy. Apparently two visiting cops put some arrogant TPS patroller in his place."

"Oh, don't tell me you kicked someone else's ass Jessica," asked Shelia.

"Enough you guys. This is embarrassing," pleaded Jessica waving her arms in mock defeat.

"Okay, so you can see why I figured you two would be here?"

"Sure. So what's your idea Cathy?"

"It may seem irresponsible to discuss this with Shelia and Glenn present, but I believe our history together warrants any breach. David and I need co-operation within both your agencies. We constantly run into either agency red tape or politics and either or both slow our operations considerably. I believe your supervisors would agree.

Operations from the FBI, CIA and the Service are hampered by Canadian law enforcement bureaucrats. Each of the American agencies has civilian politician leaders. The RCMP Commissioner is from the ranks and recently appointed so time will tell of his co-operation.

These guys think of politics first and the operation second. I'm not slamming the need for civilian oversight, hell, that's what I do, but not at the cost of an operation. I believe. No, David and I believe that we can kick up interagency co-operation several notches by having you two on board so we can kick ideas around and get a feel for whatever the incident might be.

You can give us your opinion and insight all below the radar. Nothing classified, but certainly sensitive. This wouldn't be something you'd clear with your supervisors."

"Why hasn't this been proposed before Cathy? It seems to me that interagency co-operation has been lacking for far too long. My experience is that without implementing your proposal, we'll never see a change in my lifetime. Hell, the Service can't seem to decide about what coffee to serve without a committee. Count me in," said Jessica.

"I agree," added Karen. "The RCMP has to be one of the most politically sensitive and politically correct and media shy agencies in the world. Members can't Taser without wondering if they're going to be castigated by Ottawa, or worse, fired.

Inter-agency operations are so complex and paper heavy that time sensitive ops are often lost before they get a chance. So, yes, I'm in. I took this job with the Marshal's Service so I could make a difference with the fight against terrorism and if I can extend that, I'm in."

"Fabulous," said David. "You understand Shelia and Glenn, this conversation never took place?"

"What conversation? Oh, you mean chatting about the Calgary Steak House?"

"Great, I'll be in touch with you both and get contact information," laughed David.

"Better get it tonight David. I won't be available for some time after tonight," said Jessica.

"Okay by me. Let's do it after dinner," said David.

"Speaking of dinner," commented Glenn. "I made reservations at The Calgary Steak House to which the previous conversation referred. I hope that's okay with everyone."

"Oh, now that's more than just a coincidence," said Karen, tilting her head to one side in a questioning manner.

"Why is that?" asked Glenn.

"Tom Hortonn and I graduated from the U of Ottawa. He paved the way for us to use the Academy. He and I were reminiscing and cluing Jessica in on campus life at the O and he mentioned a bartender who was infamous. Craig Stevenson. He is now the general manager for The Calgary Steak House. This is going to be incredible." said Karen. "I have to call and see if he's going to be there tonight. Do you mind? It's not that I don't appreciate the present company, but I might not have this opportunity again for some time," she said as she walked into the foyer pulling out the phone book.

"Not at all," said Cathy. "Tell us about this guy after you make the call."

"Hell, I know all about him," mentioned Jessica. She proceeded to tell the Soul Train story while Karen found The Calgary's phone number and called.

"That's it. Soul Train is in house tonight," cheered Karen.

"So, we're set to go?" asked Glenn. "It's about 7:15. By the time we catch a cab, we should be at The Calgary for our 8 reservation.

Everyone finished their drinks, took their empties to the kitchen, and made their way to the front door. Karen exited first and automatically set herself up to the left of the flat's front door. The party came next with Jessica taking up the rear. All headed to the elevator, with Karen and Jessica the last to enter.

Cab. Twenty-minute ride. Pull up in front of the Calgary among scores of other diners arriving simultaneously. Karen in the door first. Quickly to the maitre'd. Gave him her business card, wrote "U of O Blue Goose", and asked him to give it to the General Manager. The others mingled behind her. Waited. A moment. Stephenson came hurriedly out of the kitchen with a face cracking smile and embraced Karen, swinging her around, her legs bumping in to the hordes waiting for tables.

"Karen, my god, what are you doing here? I mean, what are you doing? Geez it's been what ten years or more? This your dinner party?" He made his way around the group introducing himself. "You guys have a reservation? Come, I have just the table for you." He noted to the maitre'd to cancel the table he had for them and asked everyone to follow him.

Stephenson took them through the foyer and into the main dining room. The bar area was to the right, an area about twenty feet wide and as long as the dining room. Forty feet. Behind the cocktail area was a wall of glass with light mahogany shelves lined with various spirits. The dining room's many supporting beams were likewise paneled, each holding double light sconces.

The dining room to the left was separated from the bar by end-to-end dark leather oval booths backed with a two foot railing and spiral system, providing warmth and a separation from the hustle of the foyer and bar. Tables set for four or six were discreetly placed throughout the dining area with ample space between each for a feeling of privacy.

Stephenson took them to a table set for six with linen table cloth, silver plated flatware and a twelve-inch bronze bucking bronc and rider, the base of which held several small candles which emitted an intimate glow. He pulled chairs out for the women. When the men were seated, he took their drink order himself, returning briefly, served the drinks in cut crystal with one for himself.

Momentarily a server arrived with an additional chair drawn beside Karen. He raised his glass.

"Welcome to The Calgary. May we fulfill your culinary dreams and may your commiserating be enhanced by our spirits and your friendship solidified by our ambiance."

Everyone raised and clinked their glasses with a chorus of, "Here, Here."

"Karen. What have you been up to since Ottawa? And how did you know I was here?"

"Craig. First, this is really great to see you again. I've told everyone how we met and the fun you provided struggling students. I'm also not surprised that The Calgary snagged you. You have incredible talents that shouted success.

As for how? Remember Tom Hortonn? Well, Tom is with TPS, and we met him the other day, had coffee and he got Jessica and me into the academy as guests. As for me, I've been with the RCMP for some time and work here in Toronto. That's the short version. What about you? We heard you married Jamie and have two adorable kids. True?"

"Jamie will be delighted to hear herself referred to as adorable. I love this business and seem to have a flare that The Calgary appreciates.

Jessica. From whence do you hail?"

"Well Craig, for starters, let me say that it is a pleasure to meet the infamous Soul Train. I thought my Berkeley social education was superior but after hearing about the Blue Goose, I realized I've been deprived. I am with the Secret Service's Presidential Protection Detail."

Soul Train went saucer eyes. "Welcome Agent Fukishura, to our humble Calgary.

"You know I have politicians in here constantly, your Honor being among them. Hollywood's sweethearts as well; Arnold, Barbara and Bruce, but Jessica, you are the first Secret Service Agent to honor us." He raised his glass again.

"I think I speak for everyone; we've never had anyone compliment us with such sincerity and flash," said Jessica expressing a sincerity that surprised even her.

"This evening is on me. Not The Calgary. Me. Your Honor, Professor, Shelia, David, and agents, please enjoy your drinks and company and I will return shortly with your appetizers."

After he left, looks were exchanged and Glenn said, "That's never happened to me before. Jessica, you need to come home more often and definitely with Karen."

Everyone laughed, clinked glasses, and chatted while neck craning the atmosphere.

Fifteen minutes later, a chorus of servers descended on their table with trays of sautéed garlic shrimp, fresh oysters, escargot, black and blue smoked Ahi tuna and sockeye salmon. The servers placed the trays as the maître d' appeared with fresh drinks. Conversation slipped away as they enjoyed their appies and drinks. Everyone raved about the salmon with capers, red onion, and herb cream cheese.

Forty-five later, Stephenson led a server entourage each carrying a tray. As they arrived, other servers appeared to clear their appie plates and the empty trays. Servers approached with small portions each of beefsteak tomato and red onion salad with crumbled blue cheese and vinaigrette dressing, butterfly filet mignon topped with asparagus, blue crabmeat covered with hollandaise sauce, prime rib with Yorkshire pudding, lobster tail and Alaskan king crab legs in lemon butter.

Stephenson, having supervised the serving, dismissed the staff, then produced several bottles of Burgundy and Chablis, poured each a glass, placed the bottles on a side board, bowed to his guests. "Enjoy."

Everyone was momentarily too stunned to speak. "I concur with Glenn. We must do this more often", voiced Shelia with a song in her voice.

With that, the conversation ceased, and the thrill of exquisite cuisine was enjoyed.

Sixty minutes later, the dinner party was immersed in tranquility, each guest savoring dinner's tailings when Stephenson returned.

"I sincerely hope you enjoyed our chef's contribution to your evening." With that he turned and gestured to several staff that quickly moved to the table with bottles of Black Stork XO Brandy and snifters.

One server placed several brandy warmers on the table as each diner was poured a generous swirl, another server placed individual snifter heaters in front of each guest. Stevenson did likewise for himself. Everyone heated simultaneously. Craig raised to the group.

"It has been an honor to be your host for this evening. I wish you all the best in your daily ventures and invite you back at your pleasure."

David and Glenn rose simultaneously and walked around the table, shook his hand, and gave him a hug, thanking him for a memorable evening and his overwhelming generosity.

Karen was to have the last word. She raised her brandy and said, "Praise to Soul Train. You done good. You're still The Man."

"My pleasure," he said with a grin. As he approached the women, each rose to give him a hug and expressed their appreciation for his hospitality.

Glenn and David rose to assist the women from their chairs and the party headed to the foyer. Jessica was the last to leave, withdrawing four fifty's from her wallet and placing them under a brandy snifter. The meal would price out at three hundred. The service was remarkable, worth every penny.

Outside, cabs were hailed. As Karen was getting into her cab, she shouted to Jessica, "Pearson, 8 am." Then she was gone.

Chapter Twenty-Three

"If you have a capacity for violence and no empathy
for your fellow citizens, then you are an
aggressive sociopath, a wolf."

Lt. Col. Dave Grossman

They worked feverishly to extract the packages from the
Canadian Pacific Rail cars parked at the switching yard
waiting for the next personnel shift to take the cars to the logging
communities.

Jack Johntree and Billy Sam were Nimíipuu, Real People,
members of the Nez Perce First Nations located near Lewiston,
Idaho. Johntree and Sam were part of a network that downloaded
drugs smuggled from Alberta hidden in steel containers welded to
the railcars' undercarriage.

The Canadian Pacific cars were specifically chosen for their
machinery cargo destined for logging outfits spread throughout the
region southeast of Lewiston. Tonight the cars were parked in a
railyard just north of the Clearwater River and the northern border
of the reservation waiting for the trip south which had to be made
during daylight due to the treacherous terrain.

This drug shipment was marijuana from southern Alberta
known for its potency and top dollar. Although some states
had legalized the drug, the product lacked the quality found in
this illicit marijuana. The men were unloading the large plastic
wrapped packages onto a trailer pulled by a Honda Rancher 500

quad with modified mufflers making it almost undetectable in the total blackness.

They had just completed the removal of the last package, were headed back to the mountain trail that would take them to the clearing where they'd meet a packtrain from Wyoming, when a vehicle made a turn in front of the train engine and caught them in its headlights.

Nez Perce Tribal Police.

Who else would be out here at this time, they thought.

The track between the railcars and structures was too narrow for them to turn around and escape.

Johntree was driving with Sam riding the jump-seat behind him. As the Tribal Police 4 x 4 truck caught them in its headlights, the ATV stopped and waited the officer's arrival. Sam reached behind and pulled out an empty plastic coke bottle and a role of duct tape from the quad's equipment box. He withdrew a Smith and Wesson Model 41 semi-automatic .22 pistol from his inside jacket holster, stuck the coke bottle on the end and taped it to the semi's muzzle, then let his right arm dangle beside him in the darkness. He tapped Johntree once on the shoulder to indicate he was ready if Johntree couldn't talk his way out of the confrontation.

Jorge George was the Nez Perce Tribal Police chief who had caught the graveyard shift because one of his few officers had called in sick with the flu.

George was on autopilot given he'd not had any sleep since the previous night, skipped dinner, and made rounds for the last four hours. He turned in front of the train's engine and proceeded to drive around the rail-yard's storage buildings when his headlights picked up the ATV and trailer.

His instincts told him the presence of an all-terrain vehicle at this time of night meant nothing but trouble, but he had no back-up from his department and the Nez Perce County Sheriff's department would take too long. As he approached, he angled his vehicle, kept the suspects in his headlights and lighted the vehicle with the police car's side halogen spotlight.

George exited and walked slowly toward the ATV and two passengers. "Kinda late at night for a tour through the railyard isn't fellas?"

"Yeah, it is Chief, but this was the only time we could pick up the discarded rail-ties. Didn't mean to cause you any problems. We're just on our way home," said Johntree.

"Well you boys know this is private property. Do you have permission from the rail company to pick these things up?"

"Sure do Chief. Got permission earlier today. My old lady wants me to make her a garden and I thought these would be perfect. And free."

"Let's just check these out so I can list them in my report," said George as he walked forward into the police car's light.

Johntree and Sam knew their chance to talk their way out had gone. As George passed Johntree, Sam swung his right arm up and across his body and fired two .22 rounds into George toppling him away from the ATV. As George struggled to pull his own weapon, Sam swung off the machine, put the small caliber pistol to his head and pulled the trigger three times, killing George instantly. The soft drink company providing the improvised silencer.

Johntree slid off the ATV and both men hauled George to their trailer and placed him on top of the marijuana. Sam pulled on a pair of leather gloves and got in the police cruiser, backed out to the train engine, waited for Johntree, and followed him out of the railyard.

Johntree stopped at the trailhead and decided to pick Sam up later on the highway between Lewiston and Spaulding after Sam had hid the police vehicle in a nearby drainage ditch.

Spencer walked the director to the front door. Watched him golf cart away. Back inside. Lock the door. A little tour of his new digs. The foyer was followed by a short hallway that was interrupted by one step down through an arch to a sunken living room with vaulted knotty pine ceiling. The room was tactfully done with taupe carpet, two chocolate toned couches and matching occasional chairs. Each piece of furniture was fronted with a heavy oblong, pine, glass topped coffee table.

Walking further to the back of the town house, up one step to a dining room where the extension of the pine furniture saw a heavy twelve-foot table and six matching chairs. The dining room was separated from the kitchen by a ten-foot bar and six high back pine bar stools. The kitchen appeared to be fully equipped.

Spencer opened the fridge to find it fully stocked with juices, milk, fruit, and vegetables. This can't all be for me he thought. He wandered out of the kitchen to meet up with the entry hall which took a left turn to the bedrooms, three of them. All furnished in various versions of the living and dining room pine style. He chose what would be the master bedroom with an ensuite and found the bathroom with towels, shampoo, and shaving gear.

All the years he'd been with the Service, he'd never experienced this treatment. Longevity perks, or hazardous duty luxuries? This was very nice for an outfit obviously pissed off at him.

He started the shower. Geez, triple nozzles, he couldn't recall ever basking in such luxury. Peeled his clothes and threw them in the corner. Grabbed the shaving soap, razor and wash cloth off the counter and stepped into the shower. Oh, this feels good, he thought. How long had it been since he'd showered?

Too long he figured. Wondered why his body hadn't protested with body sores. Hair lathered, scrub, rinse. Lather, scrub, rinse. Shave. Then again. Lots of body lather. Rinse. Lather again. Oh, this was wonderful, he thought. He took his time shaving, knowing his skin would be tender and the beard was long. Would have been better to use scissors first to get the bulk off, but he figured he could just work at it slowly, like pealing an orange. Took time but he got it with only a few nicks. Kicked the undrained hair into the shower corner.

After what seemed like forever, he stuck his head under one of the water heads and leaned his hands against the tile shower wall, letting the hot water cascade over his body. Enough. Out. Grabbed a fluffy white towel. Body scrub dry. He was about to tackle his hair when he caught his mirrored image. He stopped and stared at the mirror. A stranger looked back. At least ten years younger than he'd remembered the last time he caught his reflection in a filthy Timimoun gas station's mirror. This might be good for my soul he thought.

He wrapped the towel around his waist and jogged out to the front door. Peep hole. Nothing. Open the door. Ah. Clean clothes and decent boots. "Oh, man, I love it", he said out loud.

Back inside. Lock the door. Jog back to the bedroom and dressed. Did a few knee bends and toe raises to get his body used to the boots newness. He brushed his teeth for the first time in months, grabbed the door key from the foyer side table and out the door.

Real food? Maybe. Or maybe military chow. Either way, it will be better than the desert crap he'd been eating. He wondered if his body would rebel against the richness of tonight's fair. He found Building B easily, a drab rectangle about fifty feet long by forty. Composition shingles, aluminum siding, plain Jane. Then he opened the door. No Jane.

What he found was right from Los Angeles's Restaurant Row. La Cienega, where luxury and opulence were common place for Hollywood's elite. He'd been a car jockey while at UCLA, parking the Jags, Mercedes, Rolls and Bentleys. His heart would race as he held the vehicle door open for one after another of long-legged beauties he'd only encounter in magazines.

Building B's interior wouldn't be classed as opulent. Maybe tastefully decorated. A combination of mahogany railings, extended bar, mirror enhancement, linen table settings and what had to be real silverware. Flowers on each table.

There was no host, so he wandered past the foyer and into the main dining area and noted the Director sitting with three other guys in the far corner. He quickly marched over, body erect, head up, arms swinging. Had to give a better impression than earlier this morning. "Good evening Director. Gentlemen."

"Well, let me live and breathe. Is this really agent Spencer, who just an hour ago the Service was considering having fumigated? Welcome Spit and Polish. Meet your skills upgraders: This is Beat O'Toole who'll check your firearms skills and beside him is Donald Cousins who will work getting you acclimated to our decadent lifestyle. This other gentleman is Noor Hassanali, your PT. instructor. We like to call him our Ball Buster. Agent Fukishura is your defensive tactics instructor. I also want you checked medically. A doc will be by the town house at 0800 tomorrow. Gentlemen, this is Jason Spencer, formerly Camel Dung master of North Africa."

Each agent stood and offered a firm hand shake. O'Toole gestured to the bartender with an open hand for five beers. Momentarily the brew arrived and after each had their pint, O'Toole held his up and toasted. "Here's to our scrubbed and sweet-smelling agent. Welcome back Jason."

"Here, Here." was chorused by the others.

They swapped stories, each man anxious to learn as much as they could about the Camel Dung Master. One beer down and a white clad man of about twenty-five approached the group.

"Excuse me gentlemen, Director," said the man standing at ease with his hands clasped in the small of his back. "This evening, in honor of Agent Spencer's return, I have prepared Southwest oven-roasted chicken, slow-simmered ribs, taquitos, corn tortillas stuffed with guacamole, cheese, salsa and chicken enchiladas, burritos and my famous refries. Sir. If it meets with your pleasure, I will bring platters of each for family style serving."

"Excellent Kent! Bring it on. Gentlemen, I hope I wasn't presumptuous in accepting Kent's suggestion. He will make you whatever you desire."

"Good for me," said Spencer. "I've survived on plants and rodents for so long I'm not sure my body can handle this. But I'm going to go out in style. You said Fukishura's arriving tomorrow?"

Everyone laughed at Jason's reference to how much time he had to fart freely. Everyone returned to drinking, Kent having refreshed their brew.

Their meal arrived shortly on several platters which were passed around, each man heaping Kent's cuisine on massive fourteen-inch white plates. More beer. This time bottles of Mexico's Corona with lime wedges were passed around with more left in a large ice filled metal tub beside Spencer.

The evening passed with general conversation about politics, both federal and international, and women. Sports were ignored, everyone knowing Spencer would have no idea of the happenings in that social arena.

Ten o'clock and the Director bid his good evening. Everyone took his cue and headed out as well. All drillmasters were billeted at the Center during training sessions. Good nights given all around as they headed out.

Spencer let himself into the town house, locked the door and headed to the master. Lying on the bed was several underwear sets, T shirts, socks, cargo pants and sweatshirts. And pajamas. Out of habit, he took dining room chairs and placed one under the door knob of each of the exterior and the bedroom doors. Dumped his new clothes on the floor, got under the covers and was out in minutes.

Chapter Twenty-Four

O nce inside the flat, Glenn suggested Inniskillin Ice wine, retrieved a fridged bottle and poured each a slim, tall liqueur glass, then took them on a tray into the living room and served Jessica and Shelia. He recalled the first time he'd heard of ice wine and the ensuing fascination with the British Columbia winery's process of harvesting the white grapes after they'd frozen at -8 degrees C/17F.

They sat enjoying Toronto twinkle, the white dots from shipping traffic on Lake Ontario, then Jessica said, "I have to get to bed. I'm meeting Karen at Pearson at eight and I want to get a run in first." She kissed her folks and headed to bed. Too tired to brush, she placed her Sig and secure phone on the nightstand, stripped, let everything fall on the floor, then climbed under the duvet and was out.

Karen called Dirk at headquarters the minute she entered her condo. "Hey Dirk. Karen Winthrop here. How's your evening going?"

"Hi Karen, not bad. Lots goin' on as usual. How about you?"

"I'm in need of four of your babies for a black op. Any chance you have some hangin' around you can get to me tomorrow at Pearson?"

"I do. And I can get them to you. How about I deliver them to your condo first thing in the morning?"

"Won't work. I'm at Pearson at seven. Can you get there?"

"You bet. I'll meet you at the main security office with these babies. I'll test them myself."

"Great. And Dirk. This is an interagency operation. We never talked. Can you bury their existence."

"Not to worry. No paperwork. Besides, you remember what my crib looks like. No one could ever inventory it in a million years."

"Thanks Dirk. I owe."

"I'll take you up on that with a martini."

"Sounds good. And Thanks Dirk. Keep your blood sugar up." She was referring to Dirk's geeky habit of working for days on end, surviving on candy, pop tarts and caffeine.

They clicked off and Karen did her nightly routine and slipped beneath the covers, her Smith on the bedside table.

Robinson woke late, too drunk last night to remember to set his alarm. He had a raging headache and knew from past experience; the hair of the dog was all that would get him mobile. He poured himself a tumbler of Absolut, found a frozen enchilada, microwaved it for two minutes, then headed back to the bedroom to pack. Shit, he thought, why the hell didn't he leave himself time? Because my life's being sucked down a toilet and I can't swim, he told himself.

He heard the ding. Retrieved the burrito. Or was it an enchilada. Who the fuck cares? He dribbled on hot sauce then left it to cool and headed for the shower, downing most of the tumbler on the way. Quick shower shave. Back to the kitchen naked. Grab the food. Woof it down. Tumbler empty. Up to the brim again. Woof that down too, then called a cab.

Run back to the bedroom and pack an overnighter-shirt, underwear, and shaving gear. Shit, he wasn't going to make his 9 am flight. No time to brush. Out the door, slam, lock and run to the elevator. Wait. Fuck. He forgot his briefcase. Back to the apartment, fumble for keys. In, grab the case and out again. The elevator. Down. Out the main door to see the cab pulling away. Fuck. Fuck. Fuck. He threw his overnighter on the ground and screamed.

Another cabby saw his predicament and pulled up. In the cab and head for Pearson. Can he make in time? 7:30. Two hours before flight? He didn't think so. He leaned over the front seat urging traffic to move. He figured his blood pressure was pushing two hundred.

Jessica was up at 4 a.m. Up and down dog. Hamstring stretches, sweats, shoes, shoulder holster, Sig, secure phone, Shelia's windbreaker hanging in the hall closet, keys and was out the door by 4:30. Easy run. Out of Sheridan. Run straight to the right 15 minutes and return. Dark, but street lights made it easy. No rapists or muggers at this time. Either that or her aura kept them at bay.

Back in the flat by 5. Coffee on. Pack the new outfit in the overnight. Tight. Tough. Will have to do. Shower and into her arrival outfit. Dress. Hair and makeup. Sig. Phone. Kitchen for toast and coffee. Two coffees. Note for folks and out the door by 6:30.

Traffic was heavier than expected but cab made good time. Air Canada. Right in front. Efficient cabby. Twenty tip. Grabbed her bag. Over her right shoulder. Through the auto doors and head for the main security office. Starbuck's Grande Latte first.

"A sheepdog can walk into the heart of darkness, into the universal human phobia, and walk out unscathed."

Lt. Col. Dave Grossman

Pennington woke with the sun just breaking the horizon, its orange glow spreading along the tree tops. Still dark. Time to move.

He moved slightly. Rose on one hand, just enough to observe the target buildings. Lights on inside. Movement. Breakfast being prepared? He slid out of his nest, the camera held tightly against his chest by a rubber halter that wound around his back and attached to the camera, the H & K at hip level as he rose to a crouch, moving forward, doing 360's, observing his terrain for any sentries not previously detected.

He made his way to the barn at the outskirt of the compound. Circled around behind, coming up on a side window, grimy with barn crap. Clear enough. He placed his nose to the glass. There must have been at least 100 bags of commercial fertilizer. He did the math... Holy shit! Five tons. He craned his neck, pushed his head against the window trying to see beyond the pallets of destruction.

There it was. Twenty fifty-gallon containers of solvent-Nitromethane. He recalled from his briefing, this stuff was used for dry cleaning, degreasing and obviously bombs. It had greater high explosive power than TNT-dynamite. McVeigh had mixed it with ammonium nitrate-commercial fertilizer. Pennington had no idea what these hilltop whackos planned to use as a detonator, but with the intel the FBI already had, plus what he's witnessing, they had probable cause for a search warrant, albeit a heavy-handed delivery system.

He wasn't going to permit or be a part of another Waco where the ATF-Alcohol, Tobacco and Firearm's agents approached the Davidian compound personal pick-ups pulling horse trailers. How dumb could they be, he thought. No, this raid was going down hard and fast. These American traitors, his label, weren't going to rally a firearm attack. They were going down, dirty, hard, and immediately.

The materials he saw were innocent enough on a farm, but these guys had no equipment to degrease, and he didn't see a dry-cleaning store. They farmed squat. He slung his H & K over his left shoulder. Pulled the camera forward, increasing the rubber band's tension across his back, up to the window and clicked off a dozen shots angling the camera to prevent reflection. He allowed the camera to spring back against his chest. He maneuvered around the barn to the front corner, still concealed by darkness and took a variety of shots of the compound covering a full three-hundred-and-sixty-degree view.

Satisfied he had the evidence necessary for a take-down, he retraced his steps. Back around the barn. Stop at the corner. Listen again for any sounds. None. H&K in front. He prepared to sprint across the open area to the bush and up to the nest. He stepped out from the corner. Looked left. Came eyeball to eyeball with six feet and two hundred pounds.

Black beard. Long hair. Surprised. Mouth open to scream. Without hesitation, Jackson lifted his left elbow and whipped it into Black Beard's face, sending his head backwards. Jackson raised the H&K's butt, cocked both arms bringing the rifle barrel over his right shoulder, and then delivered a swift blow to Black Beard's forehead with a popping motion. Down. Check him. Out.

Shit, Pennington thought. He was cutting it pretty close. He dragged Black Beard behind the barn, flipped him over. His pack was in the nest. Something to tie this fucker with. He checked Black Beard again to make sure he was still out. Lifted his head and pulled his eye lid back. Out.

Pennington scooted around the barn's perimeter in a duck walk feeling for any debris left from a hay bale or equipment repair wire. He was around the second side when he felt the end of wire sticking out from lumber piled against the barn. He pulled on it, turned and retraced his steps. Pulling, duck walking, until he felt the wire end release.

He quickly made his way back to Black Beard and bound his wrists back-to-back behind his back. Pulled his legs up and with the extra wire, wrapped his feet and finished up with the wire around Black Beard's neck, pulling his head up, leaving him looking like a Cirque du Soleil contortionist. Pennington pulled a bandana from his own pocket. Finger inside Black Beard's mouth forcing it open. Stuffed the bandana in. Good for as long as he needed him quiet.

Back to the corner. One look, left. No one. He sprinted across the short openness and hit the bush and up to the nest. Back down out of sight. Time was running out. He moved his head slightly to his right, making mike contact. "Vancouver, Washington. Current weather conditions?"

"Morning fog, temperature hovering around +5", answered the FBI's Emergency Response Unit, known as HRT or Hostage Rescue Team, currently deployed at the Lewiston, Idaho airport's secure hangar.

The twenty-person team was in a Cougar Attack helicopter equipped with encrypted radio/satellite communications, capable of 616 km/382 miles with their two turbo Makila engines, waiting for Pennington's recon data.

Lewiston to the compound was 200 kilometers/125 miles. There and back with fuel to spare. The FBI believed the Christian's for a Better America male followers were holding the women and children hostage to their extremist lifestyle. The government planned to do a successful intrusion, bringing the hostages to safety.

Pennington signaled the assault team that he was in position and that detailed transmissions were to follow.

He silently removed his digital camera with telephoto lens from his pack and attached the tripod jamming its legs into the ground overlooking the compound. He proceeded to click off numerous frames showing each building as it related to the whole and to the surrounding terrain. Seconds. He then connected his satellite phone to the camera, entered his restricted codes and transmitted. He repeated the procedure with the hand-held digital.

The images went satellite to Seattle and bounced to the FBI's SAC-Special Agent in Charge, who downloaded them to a laptop opened to the HRT's Team leader in Lewiston and himself. Once satisfied the images provided all the necessary recon data, the HRT leader gave a whirling motion with his right hand and the two choppers were quickly rolled out of the hanger by six wheeled diesel carts. Once outside the choppers cranked to life and within seconds they were airborne East to target.

SAC transmitted a three second squeal over the satellite phone from inside Vancouver Weather One, that told Jackson that his mission was accomplished and to stand-down and backtrack covertly. Pennington repacked his gear and slid out of his natural culvert backwards and was on his way downhill within thirty seconds. Down faster than up. He was at the forestry road in forty minutes just as the choppers raced overhead toward their objective; FBI firearms designates with their machine gun pods, 20mm cannons and 68mm rockets hanging out the ship's sides at the ready.

He was walking toward his concealed battered Chevy pick-up when gunfire erupted. He threw his gear into the passenger's seat, unstrapped the thigh holster, removed the pistol's magazine, and chambered round and slipped them into his jacket pocket, repeated the process for the H&K. He retrieved the weapon bags from the passenger side floor and stowed each firearm, grabbed the keys out of his pocket and blasted out of his bush concealment and headed West.

Thirty minutes from leaving the bush, his satellite phone went off. He pulled over near the ditch, kept his foot on the brake and hit receive. He waited for the customary clicks and silence, then the SAC's voice was clear. "Get back here ASAP. You're moving. Details upon arrival here."

Pennington was somewhat taken aback by the call's abruptness and transfer thirty minutes after completing a mission. No down time. Goes with the territory he thought as he put the truck in gear and continued out of the mountains as the sun started to show over the spruce tops behind him.

Lewiston, Idaho wasn't that far. An hour from Orofino to Lewiston. Good highway. Breakfast in Lewiston, lunch in Ellensburg and Seattle in about seven hours.

Breakfast was on the horizon, then the Red Robin for lunch in Ellensburg. Odd that his interest was so concentrated on food. He remembered the Red Robin from hangin' with some of the Seattle agents at the original Robin under the East Ave. Bridge just south of the University of Washington from which many agents graduated. Good memories.

Chapter Twenty-Five

Simpson had one large bag and a carry-on. She'd dressed in Wranglers, a white button-down shirt, and her beat-up cowboy boots. The boots had been with her since high school and looked like the track record they boasted. The same could be said for her Miller Lubbock style cowboy hat she'd also had since high school. Miller called it *presoiled* which must be marketed to line dancing chicks in Los Angeles, Simpson figured.

She had her over size jean jacket too just in case it rained. Ya, right. In Arizona? It was really to cover her shoulder holster. She suspected a lot of folks carried, particularly since the state recently passed legislation authorizing concealed carry in bars and restaurants. That was a time bomb just waiting detonation she thought.

Two hours to Phoenix so she headed out early and made good time. She dropped the government vehicle at the Phoenix office. Didn't socialize. No one in the office paid much attention given her reputation as a loner living in Flagstaff. She grabbed a taxi and headed for the airport.

She hadn't taken the time to reserve a seat and figured she'd go stand-by if necessary. She told the driver to let her off wherever he found space. And he did. At the beginning of the Terminal Two which she found out served Alaska, Continental, Great Lakes, and United airlines. Great Lake Airline?

In Arizona, she questioned. Weird.

First order of business was to find the airport security office. She spotted a guard and asked him. He looked at her somewhat suspiciously and directed her to an office just ahead to the right. She advanced on the door, dragging her gear with the guard watching and speaking into his shoulder mike.

She pushed open the door to find a typical bureaucratic office but with a tough looking aging supervisor behind the counter. He approached her briskly, obviously already having made up his mind as to what this chick wanted. Simpson introduced herself, "Good morning sir. I'm Secret Service carrying a weapon under my left armpit. May I show you my ID?"

Simpson thought for sure the guy was either going to faint or shit himself given the wide-eyed facial expression. She had to stifle a grin as he stammered and placed his hand on his semi-automatic. "Yes, you may, very slowly ma'am, cause you sure don't look like no cop I've ever seen before."

Simpson reached inside her jean jacket slowly with her left hand and extracted her Service ID and handed it over to the supervisor. "Son-of-a-Bitch! I've sure as hell never seen one of these before and attached to something that looks like you."

She ignored the comment and replied, "I just wanted to check in with your office so you can advise your staff as to my presence. I'm going to try and get a flight out today for Washington. Wish me luck."

"Well agent good luck with gettin' a flight, pretty hard to come by."

Simpson thanked him, turned, and left the office. It took him a matter of seconds to radio his staff. She wondered how he worded it to keep the transmission professional. She had to laugh. Men. Boys really. What a hoot. Most fun I've had in months, she thought.

She walked up to the first counter. Continental. They had several flights leaving that day with some available seats. They wanted a thousand bucks, one way, for a seven-hour flight with my legs up to my boobs, plus having to land in New Jersey first.

Screw that she thought. She knew she could drive it in a day. She had them try flights from Albuquerque, New Mexico, and Tucson but they were identical. Shit.

She wasn't giving in. And the government sure as hell wasn't going to pay for First Class. She checked several other airlines with the same results. It would take the day at least and with the lay-over, add another day. Double Shit.

She headed to the service counter pulling her larger bag and trying to keep the carry-on over her shoulder. She asked the attendant for the driving distance to Washington. 2,300 miles. Next, she asked for Enterprise Car Rental and was pointed to a spot around the corner from the service kiosk. She thanked the attendant and dragged her gear there.

She asked about a Ford F150, one way to Washington. The clerk looked at her like she was going to steal the truck right there and then.

Attitude.

Everyone had one.

Not everyone had a good one.

"Ma'am, I will give you my credit card and identification. Do you have a 150?" With that she purposely pulled her left side jacket back to reveal her Sig while she extracted her ID with her other hand.

I'll give you attitude bitch. You figured I was some dumb chick who couldn't afford shit. The clerk looked like she too was going to either wet herself or have a heart attack. She wouldn't touch the ID. Simpson flipped it open.

"Ma'am, I'm a United States Secret Service Agent. You can confirm this by reading my ID, viewing my badge on my belt and/or calling security."

Simpson figured she opted for the latter as she ran from the counter, threw open a side door and disappeared. Simpson just leaned on the counter waiting for the inevitable, which occurred faster than she'd expected. Two guards rounded the corner from the service desk with hands on their weapons until they saw the subject of the alarm.

Huge grins appeared on their faces as they sauntered over to the Enterprise counter. Each guard extended his hand to shake, and Simpson responded with her killer smile and flirty body language. Gotta use it somewhere, she thought.

As Simpson chatted with one guard while the other went behind the counter, knocked on the door and waited for someone to look through the peep hole and come out. The clerk did. She listened as the guard spoke with her. Simpson saw that her face was turning a good shade of crimson and she felt sorry for the stupid stunt she pulled. The clerk came over and resumed her spot behind the counter.

"Amy is it? I could have handled myself differently. I apologize." She extended her hand to shake, and it was received. "Shall we start over?"

Before the guards left, one said, "So, Agent Simpson, you're going to pass on the plane for a 2,500-mile drive in a pick-up?"

"You bet. I'll be dammed if I'll pay a thousand good ones to sit with my legs around my neck for eight hours, then stay over in New Jersey of all places. Nope, give me a good pick-up with my ID hangin' around my neck and I'm out of here."

The two guards bid her a good trip, smiling, and shaking their heads as they headed back into the bowels of the airport.

Amy completed the paperwork, Simpson passing on the extra insurance stating that her credit card covered it. Amy made a call then instructed her to retrieve the truck right in front of the Continental Airlines counter exit door.

"Amy, may I ask a favor? Might I borrow about four feet of string?"

"Sure Agent Simpson. I'll be right back." She went through the door again, albeit a little slower this time. Momentarily she returned with the string. "Are you really going to hang your badge around your neck?"

"You bet. Thanks Amy. I hope you can enjoy the rest of your day."

"Oh, I will Agent. I guarantee you I will. Nobody will believe this happened to me. Nobody."

Simpson folded the rental papers and slipped them and keys into her outside jacket pocket, grabbed her bags and headed back the way she came. She found a teenager standing beside a new Ford F150 Blue Flame King Ranch 4 X 4 pick-up, short box six feet, four door, with leather interior, sixteen-inch rims with BF Goodrich All-Terrain tires and what appeared to be all the bells and whistles. "Son-of-a-bitch", she hollered, "This is the way to travel."

The teen gave her the keys, thanked her for using Enterprise and disappeared inside trying to glance over his shoulder nonchalantly. Simpson opened the rear passenger door and stored her gear, slammed it, and walked around the hood and got in. She felt at home, comfortable in this type of vehicle.

She used her personal smartphone to access Google Maps and plotted a course; Phoenix to the interstate ten which would take her to Tucson, El Paso, Texas, Fort Worth, Little Rock, Arkansas, Nashville, then a straight shot to Rowley. She took her badge off her belt and looped it into the string and hung it around her neck. One hundred all the way baby, she said to herself.

Before she headed out, she called Rowley per her transfer orders, to let them know her ETA-estimated time of arrival. She didn't tell Dallas Romain her mode of transportation, just that she'd arrive early tomorrow morning. He was fine with that and said he would inform Agent Fukishura.

After she hung up, she yelled, "Giddy up baby", put the F150 in gear and eased her way out into the line of traffic. She was on the interstate within fifteen and heading to a career change, the details of which she had no idea. But she was gonna have fun the next twenty-four hours.

Heavy traffic south out of Phoenix for the first thirty minutes, then it cleared, and she topped it up to 80 mph. Based on the tank size and mileage of friends with F150's she figured she could get around 400 miles per tank. Six or so, fuel stops.

She listened to local country radio and the hours breezed by. Not yet noon. She stopped for fuel at a Circle K service station on I-10 outside of Las Cruces. Headed to store to pay. Did. Found a pay phone and the number for the New Mexico Public Safety Bureau. Dialed. Identified herself and asked that an officer meet her at the Circle K.

Within minutes two patrol cars screeched into the gas station, lights ablaze. Officers out and running into the station. Three officers stood mouths agape for several seconds before one came out of his brain freeze and said, "What the hell's going on here?"

Their first sight was of a six-foot woman in tight jeans, white blouse, beater jean jacket, scruffy cowboy boots, and a battered cowboy hat covering curly blonde hair. She looked to be about 150 pounds of curves and muscle.

Simpson identified herself, showed her ID, but didn't acknowledge her carry status. Assured them no emergency existed. Asked them to chat outside.

"I need your help fellas. I must be in Washington yesterday and I couldn't find a flight that would get me there in time or one that didn't have me pretzelled for ten hours. I think I can drive it faster if I can have your help."

"Hold on a sec. Agent Simpson. I've an idea. Let me check with our watch commander," said the youngest trooper.

He returned quickly with thumbs up. "The watch commander instructed us to take you to the Texas border, New Mexico is giving a pass. He will notify the Texas Rangers of your need and they will have a patrol car waiting outside Juarez to escort you to the

Louisiana border. They in turn will hand you over to the Louisiana boys and so on all the way to Washington." He said with a face breaking grin. "And I will take you to the first hand-off. Will that help you Ma'am?"

"You bet it will Trooper. I really appreciate the help. Let's get to gettin'."

Twenty-three hours to Washington. Six Red Bull's and appreciation to all her law enforcement colleagues, she pulled into Rowley at ten in the morning.

Wired.

Simpson parked the F-150 outside Rowley's main gate, grabbed her gear, chirped, and headed for the guard station. An MP was waiting for her on the inside of the fourteen-foot sliding gate carrying his M-16 across his body.

"Good morning Ma'am, what can I do for you?"

"Good morning Corporal. I'm Secret Service Agent Simpson reporting for training. May I enter and be processed?"

"One moment Ma'am," He keyed his shoulder mike, turned his head slightly, keeping his eyes on Simpson while he spoke. Another MP came from the station carrying his M-16 identically. "ID Ma'am?"

"My ID is in my right inside jacket pocket. I'm armed. May I retrieve it?"

"Yes, Ma'am, very slowly Ma'am," replied the Corporal, very much in Orange. The tension was palpable.

Simpson reached into her jacket and retrieved her ID and handed it through the gate's information slot. The Cpl. flipped it open and dropped his gaze to read while the other MP kept Simpson in his watchful stare. First MP looked back up at Simpson, back to the ID, back to Simpson. "Welcome to Rowley Agent Simpson. Please accompany my partner to the guard station to relieve yourself of your firearm and receive directions."

The gate opened automatically, indicating a third MP was watching and listening via CCT-closed circuit television from the station. Simpson walked through the gate and joined the second MP to the station, Simpson in front and Second MP bringing up the rear.

She entered the station to be met by a Sgt. behind the counter ready with a firearm's relief form and tray. "Good morning Agent, Simpson, welcome to Rowley. Please remove your Sig's mag and chambered round in the discharge tube to your left. Leave the slide open and give the works to me."

Simpson complied. Signed the form and watched the Sgt. take her firearm and deposit it in the safe.

"Sgt. I have a rented F-150 from Enterprise in the outside parking area. Locked. May I leave you the keys and direct Enterprise to retrieve?"

"Certainly Agent," he said as he extended his hand and Simpson deposited the keys and rental contract.

Processing was quick and painless. While in administration she called Enterprise and told them their vehicle's location and that the keys and contract were at the guard station. There was a significant pause from the clerk. "Ma'am, did I understand you correctly, the rental is at a guard station?"

"Yes, you heard correctly." she said pleasantly. "You have the destination address on the rental form. Just tell your driver to show ID at the guard station and she/he will be given the keys."

"Yes Ma'am." The clerk replied somewhat skeptically.

She learned she'd have roommates, an Elisabeth Peltowski and Fukishura. This is really going to be interesting, she thought.

"Please proceed to the administration building for your accommodation assignment."

"Thank you Sgt.," said Simpson as she hauled her gear and herself back out the door. At the curb was a waiting golf cart.

Running from the guard kiosk was the Sgt.

He walked past her and stopped at the cart. "Throw your gear in the back Agent, and we'll proceed to the Admin. Building."

"This isn't necessary Sgt. I can walk."

"Agent, rank has its privileges."

"I'm just an agent Sgt. I have no rank."

"Yes, Agent, but I do," he noted with a mischievous grin as Rebecca stowed her gear in the vehicle.

The trip took thirty seconds. No time for conversation, thank the lord, thought Simpson. The Sgt. dropped her off in the middle of the cul-de-sac and pointed to the assigned building.

Simpson thanked him, grabbed her gear, and headed up the walk, turned and waved her thanks to the Sgt. She knew she'd not see him again until she left if that happened at all. Fraternization was not tolerated, under any circumstances.

Karen arrived at Pearson shortly before seven, having skipped her normal routine in favor of getting more sleep and preparing for her lengthy absence. She stopped at a coffee kiosk for three grandes. Her quick pace put her just outside the security area to find Dirk sitting at a lone table with coffee. Well, she couldn't give him the coffee. She'd keep it for Wally.

"Hi Dirk. Been waiting long?"

"Nope, just got here. Won't keep you. Here are the units. Be Safe"

With that he left. Took all of 15 seconds.

She watched him walk away and noticed Jessica watching her, leaning up against the wall, one foot pulled up behind her resting on the wall. Karen shook her head as she approached the agent wearing a huge smile. "Good morning. You just get here?"

"A little bit ago. Been people watching, wondering where each might be heading. Dirk must be a man of few words."

Karen gave her one of the coffees and gestured they move to tables in a corner. Both sitting with their backs to the concourse wall so they could observe.

"Cheers!" said Karen as they clinked coffees. 'Yeah, Dirk is exceptionally talented but wants little to do with any of us socially or professionally other than what you saw".

"So, what's your procedure before boarding? You check with security to see if there are any alerts?"

"Yup. I'll head over there when we're done our coffee. The experts, those who consider themselves knowledgeable in human behavior, tell us it is not the agitated traveler but the silent one that is most likely to blow. Sort of like in high school when counselors told girls to watch out for the quiet guys, the ones who could be stalkers.

Don't believe it. Everyone is suspect. Our screening system is excellent but not perfect, or else they wouldn't need me. But I check them all. We had a retired couple who were smuggling cocaine in secret baggage compartments. The dogs missed it, but I caught them. The guy was agitated, thinking security would chalk him up to a normal person pissed off at something. I had them stopped one foot off the plane.

You get enough sleep?"

"So, so. I crashed as soon as my head hit the pillow. But I got a run in this morning. Not much to pack so I was on the road quickly."

"I checked and Wally is on duty this morning. I have the units. Destroy the slip that's taped to the back with the email address once you memorize it," Karen said as she slid one across the table to Jessica. "I sound like the tape recording from Mission Impossible," she said with a laugh.

Jessica put her hand over the package and slid it along the tabletop and into her jacket's left inside pocket.

"Let's go see Wally," said Karen.

They threw their empty coffee containers in the nearest trash and headed for the main security office.

Knock. Enter. Uniform guy. Different one. Karen produced her Buffalo and asked for Wally.

Down the hall they went with Uniform guy.

Robinson sprung out of the cab, reached back for his briefcase and carry-on, threw two twenties at the cabbie, and raced through the auto doors. Not opening fast enough. Kicked them.

He ran up to the Air Canada desk. Stood in line. Quickly looked at the clock on the wall. Shit.

Then he caught sight of the Business Class check in counter and realized he was in the wrong line. No line at Business. Not excusing himself, he pushed through the crowd, ducked under the webbed divider, and ran.

He fumbled for his ticket and pushed it at Air Canada's clerk.

After checking his ticket, she said, "I'm sorry sir, your flight has boarded. You'll have to re-ticket for another flight."

"No. No. No. You don't understand. I must be on that flight. I have a business meeting in Washington I can't miss."

"Just a moment sir and I'll check."

She turned and picked up a phone at the far corner of the counter area and turned her back.

Moments later she returned. "Sir, the boarding agent said that he'll hold boarding if you can get through security immediately."

"Okay. Let's go."

She processed his ticket. He grabbed it from her and ran to the security lanes. No wait. He threw his carry-on to the conveyor belt, removed his pocket things, and headed through the metal detector.

Wankkkkkk.

"Sir, please step over here so I can check you with the handheld." asked a security agent.

"What the hell's your problem? I put everything on the conveyor belt."

"Please sir. It will only take a moment."

"Shit. You're going to make me miss my flight."

He stepped to the side; oblivious to the stares he'd attracted particularly the ones from security supervisors.

The agent passed the wand and stopped at his right-hand pocket when the device Wankkkkkk.

"Sir, please remove whatever is in your right-hand pocket."

"There isn't anything there." Robinson said as he jammed his hand into the pocket and felt around. And pulled out a quarter.

"Thank you sir. You're clear to proceed."

Robinson grabbed his carry-on, his jacket and pocket stuff and ran down the concourse. Showed his ticket to the Air Canada agent standing solo by the loading ramp. Ran down the ramp and into the plane.

He ignored the flight attendant's greeting and pushed his way into business class, stuffed his carry-on in the overhead and sat.

First attendant who passed he snarled, "Gimme a double bloody Mary." He figured another drink was the only way to get his head out of the vice.

"Yes sir, right away."

Chapter Twenty-Six

"Wolves feed on sheep without mercy."

Lt. Col. Dave Grossman

Jenewein woke with a start, tossing his head side to side to orientate. The room was pitch-dark. Not a sound. He racked his brain searching for a clue to his sudden alertness. Nothing. No sound. Then he heard it. Waves and what sounded like pounding on hollow metal. He slid out of bed, grabbed his Russian GSh-18 semi-automatic pistol from the nightstand and slipped quickly to the bedroom door, putting his ear to the panel. Nothing.

He placed his back against the wall and reached across to the deadbolt sliding it open then opened the door slowly with his left hand, the GSh-18 across his chest facing the opening. Black. Nothing. He moved down the hallway and to the living room's bay window, peeking around the curtain. It was coming from the plane, but he couldn't see beyond the blackness.

He exited the building through the back door and made his way around the building's corner and in a few quick steps grounded himself at the crest overlooking the lake. He could just make out the shape of a man banging on the Otter's pontoons with his feet; several stomps with one foot then repeating with the other foot.

Getting into a crouch he duck walked down the wharf's gangway, his bare feet quietly carrying him forward. As his vision improved with the closing distance he observed that the guy was huge; well over six feet as his head was above the Otter's wings and the guy had to weigh 300 at least. He slowed his advancement not wanting to spook the guy. The retreat was only accessible by air or horseback and the latter only after several days ride from Big Lake.

Jenewein was about fifty feet from the Otter and its assailant when his left foot hit an empty jerry can with a resounding clanging reverberating across the lake. Behemoth turned to the sound with a start and took off toward land, feet pounding, swaying the dock dramatically.

He was on the wharf's far side as he passed Jenewein blasting a foul pungent odor that almost keeled the pilot over. Jenewein stood, leveled the semi at the fleeing intruder and fired off ten 9 mm rounds.

He heard Behemoth hit land and pound his way up the walkway and into the bush. Too dark to follow him, Jenewein moved to the plane and retrieved a large flashlight from under the back seat and checked the Otter for damage. He scanned the door, windows, windshield, let the beam pass over the propeller then down on the pontoons.

Nothing. Not even a dint. What the hell was the pounding, he wondered? He opened the pilot's door and scanned the interior. Nothing disturbed. What was he after? If he didn't know any better he'd figure it was someone unfamiliar with a plane trying to elicit a response like you would an animal, hitting it seeking a reaction.

Jenewein closed the door and stood back passing the light across the wings and their struts when he noticed a tuff of hair caught on a metal bur at the wing tip. He stood on the wharf's raised edge reaching up for the hair. It felt like the course hair of a moose. He grabbed the wing strut lifting his weight off the dock bringing the wing down. He whiffed the deposit and snapped his head back in recoil. The same pungent odor he got as Behemoth dashed by and the same as he'd found previously on the main house's back door.

"What the fuck is going on," he asked out loud. He took out a hanky and grabbed the hair folding it within the red cloth and stuffed both into his sweatpants pocket and made his way back to the house vowing to return at first light and follow the trail into the bush.

"There is nothing morally superior about being a
sheepdog; it is just what you choose to be."

Lt. Col. Dave Grossman

"Good morning Wally," Karen said as Jessica closed the door after them. "How's your morning so far?"

"Pretty uneventful Karen, thanks for asking. Did you two have some good down time in Trana?"

"We did," said Karen. "I got to meet Jessica's folks, met an old school buddy, and enjoyed great meals. Oh, and we shopped."

"Well I knew that was a given" he laughed. "What can I do for you agents," Wally said, trying to regain his previously lost composure over the firearm issue.

"This coffee is for you. Enjoy. I need to leave this package with you to give to a David Kopas later today. He'll provide ID. Do you mind? Oh, and would you walk us through security? I have my Smith and Jessica has her Sig."

"Sure, no problem on both counts, and thanks for the coffee. No alerts for you. You have your eye on any of our passengers this morning?"

"Nope, just the usual."

Okay, then, let's go. The sooner we get you processed the more time you have to figure out the good guys from bad."

"Wally, do you mind if I change magazines in your discharge tube before we head out?"

"Help yourself Jessica. You know the way." She did and switched the high velocity magazine for Karen's rounds.

All three left the security office and headed to the metal detectors, stepped around them as Wally spoke quietly to an agent who nodded and stepped aside. Jessica and Karen walked through, turned, and shook Wally's hand and headed down the concourse.

Wally would advise the pilots and crew.

The duo walked up to the boarding agent and offered him empty boarding folders for appearances, Karen having arranged for the airline to bill Jessica.

The Air Canada agent pretended to read each, welcomed them aboard and directed them to Business Class on the left at the bottom of the ramp.

Karen having no assigned seat, nodded to Jessica, and headed back to coach and her jump seat. Jessica stored her carry-on and took her assigned seat by the window.

She'd just settled in to wait for take-off when an attendant brought the passenger in the first single seat a drink. Reflectively she glanced at her watch. Must have had a rough night. The attendant asked her if she'd like coffee and said he'd have it to her after take-off.

The plane began to taxi, entered a runway and the *Buckle Seats* sign went on. She settled back and felt the seat's construction envelop her body. Perks. Not bad, she thought. The attendant walked by checking each passenger's belt, ensuring the clip was driven home. He'd just left when Jessica felt the roar and physical rush of the two General Electric under wing engines push forth their massive thrust.

Very short take-off and they were airborne at a thirty-degree angle.

Moments later the coffee arrived in a large white ceramic mug, emblazoned with the Air Canada logo, on a silver tray with cream, sugar, and a silver spoon. Jessica thanked the attendant and declined the additives.

Five minutes later the captain came on the speaker to advise their air speed of five-hundred mph would be reached at a cruising altitude of 30,000 feet with arrival time at Reagan at approximately 10:30.

Weather in Washington was clear with a current temperature of fifty-degrees Fahrenheit, ten-degrees Celsius. The flight attendant did the usual safety presentation to which no one listened. Jessica undid her seatbelt and enjoyed her coffee.

Ten minutes into the flight, the Bloody Mary Guy stopped the attendant and asked for a double. That arrived within a couple of minutes. Jessica could just make out his right hand as it grabbed the drink from the attendant.

No thank you.

Zero social grace.

Downed it.

All.

This was a breakfast flight. Thank goodness thought Jessica. She was starving. The attendant came by and explained the morning breakfast choices: Eggs rancheros. Two poached eggs on half English muffins topped with a mild salsa and grated cheddar cheese and fruit slices.

"Stop." said Jessica. "Say no more. I'll have the rancheros." Rolling the "Rs" Spanish style. California habit.

"Yes, ma'am, excellent choice. We make the dish fresh, and it should be ready in fifteen minutes."

"Thank you. I'm starved."

The attendant went to each passenger asking the same question. Jessica couldn't hear their answers, but it didn't take long for him to finish with Bloody Mary Guy. Loudly.

"I don't give a fuck what you bring me. Just bring me something."

"Yes sir, right away."

Jessica's antenna was working overtime. She moved from Yellow to Orange in a nano second, adjusted herself in the seat, automatically checking her Sig, bouncing a little as she did.

The guy seemed to settle back. Breakfast arrived and she dug in. Making sure she could exit quickly if necessary. She wondered if Karen had been notified of Bloody Mary Guy or whether she too was enjoying breakfast.

The rancheros were excellent, better than she'd expected for airline food. Good go, Air Canada. She woofed the eggs then worked on the fruit and was done by the time Bloody Mary Guy got his order. The attendant took her tray as he walked by and said he'd be back with more coffee.

Just then Bloody Mary Guy started yelling, "This tastes like shit. You call this food? Get this hell out of here."

The attendant rushed down the aisle and was about to remove Bloody Mary Guy's tray when Bloody Mary Guy grabbed the attendant by his lapel. The attendant fell to the carpet.

Instantly Jessica was out of her seat moving the two seats forward in seconds. Bloody Mary Guy still held the attendant with his right hand, the attendant on the carpet, hands up to protect himself, fear seeping from every pore. Jessica reached down and grabbed the back of Bloody Mary Guy's right hand with her left, placing her thumb on the back of his hand and wrapping her fingers under and around his hand. She squeezed her thumb and fingers together twisting Bloody Mary Guy's right hand up and back against the seat.

Bloody Mary Guy screamed in pain and whipped his fork in Jessica's direction with his left hand. Instantly Jessica punched Bloody Mary Guy between the eyes with her right hand, twisting her upper body which put a tremendous force in her delivery. His head flashed backwards, hit the window, bounced forward again from the dual impact.

Instant stop? Not quite out, but close. The attendant was on his feet, back peddling out of reach.

Jessica took her right hand and placed it over her own left increasing the pressure on Bloody Mary Guy's right hand. She maneuvered him out of his seat and walked him toward the front of the plane. Bloody Mary Guy screaming in pain all the way. She stopped and turned to the other passengers, "Federal Agent folks. All is in order. Please confirm that sir," referring to the flight attendant.

"Yes, folks this woman is a U.S. Federal Agent. Thank God."

Before Jessica could get Bloody Mary Guy into the front galley, cheers went up from the other seven passengers. "Shut the drapes," she ordered the flight attendant. "And get me a set of cuffs. Notify the Captain."

The attendant retrieved a set of handcuffs from a side drawer and gave them to Jessica who cuffed Bloody Mary Guy to the jump seat. The guy was obviously drunk, but his facial expression indicated he was so scared she thought he might have messed himself. Tough shit she thought. What an asshole to pull a stunt like that on a plane.

Ten seconds later the captain unlocked the cockpit door and came into the galley. "What the hell's going on here?"

"U.S. Special Agent Fukishura sir, Secret Service. I'm on my way back to Washington on business. You were advised of my presence and weapons."

"Oh, man. Yes I was Agent. I couldn't put the two together at first. Our flight attendant gave me the password to let me know he wasn't speaking under duress, so it was safe to come out. Scared the crap out of me and my co-pilot though. Nice going. Who is this guy?"

"I think he's too drunk to talk right now. I don't think he's going to be any trouble. I took the liberty of checking his ID. He's a securities broker with a Toronto firm. Could be he just got pissed early in the day and made a judgment error. Let's get him some coffee and sober him up. Maybe we can avoid charges. He had no weapons other than the fork with which he tried to stab me."

"You're the expert Agent. Whatever you decide is fine with me. I just have to have it all in my flight report."

Jessica was giving instructions to the attendant; coffee for Bloody Mary Guy, when Karen burst into the galley with her right hand inside her jacket, poised to draw. "What the hell's going on?"

"Hi Cpl. Winthrop, this gentleman got out of hand and physically accosted our flight attendant, then tried to stab me with a fork. He's resting now, being ingested with Air Canada's quality caffeine. Hopefully he'll come out of it and realize he made a complete ass of himself, a poor judgment call, and will be extremely apologetic and humble so we won't have to charge him."

"And I missed all the action. Shit Jessica, I take these flights for weeks on end without an incident and you fly twice and hit the jackpot on number two. I gotta hang around you more often."

Jessica smile, bowed and said, "My pleasure Marshal."

Chapter Twenty-Seven

Peltowski had settled her flat, subleasing quickly, giving all the details to MI6's liaison clerk who would pass it along to Peltowski's replacement. She'd transferred her bank balances to her home account in Nebraska which she'd kept from her university days. Packing was easy as well. The Service would take care of all the arrangements so all she needed to do was take her essentials and clothes for a few days and she was done.

The flat was furnished, so the movers would pack everything and ship it to Rowley, her only known next address. She retrieved her Sig from the MI6 armory, signed for it to be delivered to the airline before her flight. What a bunch of assholes, she thought. They can't even trust a Secret Service agent and they have crazies all over the country carrying unlicensed, illegal firearms.

Finding a flight wasn't as easy as she'd thought. Where the hell did all these people come from? Geez, there must be thousands of travelers 24/7 out of London. She finally found an American Airlines flight to JFK, then to Reagan. No plane changes. Nine hours. Boeing 777. This was doable.

She opted for Business Class for the nine-hour flight. Since the Service paid for Coach, she paid the difference, three thousand. Ouch! But it would be worth it to leave this crappy assignment in style and comfort. She even checked online to see what the three big ones would get her. She found it astounding that she'd leave at Noon London time and arrive at JFK at one that afternoon. She laughed at herself, pretty fast flight, she thought.

On flight day, she chose a simple Water-blue striped jacket with a white shirt, standing collar & wide leg white pants. The jacket fit nicely over her shoulder holster. Felt good to have it back on. Although weird with no weight to it.

Her air porter arrived early so she could spend the majority of her time at Heathrow, sitting in the boarding area waiting to leave London.

The drive was uneventful, the air porter getting her to the American Airline's section efficiently. She checked in and was immediately met by a guy who looked as American as Brad Pitt, but was in fact an MI6 agent tasked with delivering her Sig. He had her sign delivery, and then gave the weapon to an airport security official who told her she could pick it up with her luggage at JFK.

"Fine", she said arrogantly, turned rudely from the Brit and left. Pissed! She went through security with her one carry-on holding a change of clothes and her personals. Uneventful unless one would consider her anger at her former host country.

She bought a novel from one of the kiosks-a love story; a Starbuck's Vanilla Latte Grande and ruminated on why she had so much pent-up anger...not like me she thought.

Settled into one of the comfy chairs in the First-Class Lounge. Forty-five minutes before her flight, she was called with the other First/Business Class passengers to board. She had been pre-boarded, so she headed down the loading tube and was greeted by the first-class attendant. Peltowski showed her flight packet and was led to J-4, a solo window seat, far right-hand corner, as far from the restroom and activity as she could find.

She stowed her carry-on and settled into the plush wrap-around seat and glanced out the window, waiting for the remainder of the passengers. After about thirty minutes, she heard the doors close, lock and the plane begin taxiing. The attendant came by asking for her drink preference. "Margarita", she said.

Her drink arrived just before the seatbelt sign was lit. She belted in, downed her drink, and prepared for take-off.

I've got to rid myself of my negativism about this last assignment, she thought. Won't do my image any good to be seen as a complainer. I'll start with the Margarita and work from there, she decided. No looking back. Her orders were to report to Rowley and an Agent Fukishura. Never heard of her. Hope she's not another onward and upward management types.

Take off was quicker than she'd expected given the size of the 777 and its dual Rolls Royce engines. The plane's take-off angle was considerable, giving it a quick access to its 37,000-foot cruising level.

Once the plane leveled and the seat-belt light extinguished, several attendants circulated presenting the menu. Peltowski chose the Regatta Russian River Valley Chardonnay with an appetizer plate of marinated beef, thin potatoes, smoked sesame salmon and sweet cucumbers. For her entre she chose seared fillet with porcini mushroom butter and bordelaise sauce with assorted grilled veggies. Dessert was light, a fruit and cheese plate.

She was served another Margarita while she relished the ambiance. Seemed like a strange reflection for her, ambiance, on an airplane? But this was her first time out of coach. She was going to savor every morsel, so she figured, yes, ambiance.

Her meal arrived and she waved her face over the plate, taking in the aroma, and picked up her fork.

Savored.

The time went by too quickly. Her tray was retracted, her chair extended to a bed, pillow and blanket and she was out for the duration, waking up shortly before the descent to JFK. She woke refreshed, ready for the time change and adjusting to life in the States.

JFK was uneventful. Coffee and snacks were served while passengers disembarked for New York.

The trip to Reagan was pretty much up and down. She exited Reagan, went to security to retrieve her firearm, and was met by Buster Saborino, Reagan's Security Chief. She presented her passport and Service ID.

One glance and he extended his hand to shake. "Welcome back Agent Peltowski. I'll personally see you through security and customs." He watched her puzzled look and offered no explanation for several seconds. "You've been expected Agent. Your new boss advised you'd be arriving sometime today. I've always paved the way for Agent Fukishura through security and customs for her weapons and I'd be happy to do the same for you and any other Secret Service agent." He gave her back the ID and passport.

"Wow, well, thanks very much Buster. This is an unexpected pleasure. You wouldn't believe the crap I've had to put up with from the Brits regarding my Sig. Assholes wouldn't even let me carry a knife. And let me tell you, the streets of London ain't the safest."

"I can only imagine. Odd, that they have such a short memory of their ass in a ringer and us saving it. Anyway, you're back on solid ground now. They're history." And with that he handed her the Sig, already out of any wrapping. He then gave her the magazine and one round. "You can load it in the discharge tube in my office, just down the hall. Help yourself."

She did. Chambered a round, safety on and placed it in her shoulder holster.

Karen checked Bloody Mary Guy since she didn't hook him. Secure. She headed back to coach to make sure panic hadn't set in. She stopped in Executive. "Hi folks, I'm Cpl. Winthrop with the RCMP." She showed her Buffalo. "There's no reason for alarm. The gentleman is doing fine and there is no threat to you or the airplane. Thank you for understanding and your co-operation."

She was going to give the same speech in coach but in speaking with the attendants, no one knew there was a problem. How could they not have heard the guy screaming she thought?

The remainder of the flight was uneventful. Jessica sat with Bloody Mary Guy for security, allowing Karen to work the rest of the plane, and to keep him quiet until he sobered. Just before beginning the approach to Reagan, the captain returned to advise he had notified airport security of a man in custody and that there was no security breach. "We don't want those ground cowboys scaring my passengers by storming the plane. They know you and Cpl. Winthrop have the suspect in custody. We'll let the passengers disembark first; secure the loading tube, then you can take your guy to security. That work for you agent?"

"Works for me Captain."

With that, he returned to the cockpit and moments later the seatbelt light blinked, and they started their descent. Karen came to join Jessica in the front jump seats, sat, buckled in, and looked at Jessica. "Man you are really something Washington. We need to work on an extended operation."

"Wouldn't that be great? You never know. We're going to be in touch anyway so maybe." She was sharing the captain's security conversation as the Embraer hit tarmac, brakes smoking and slowing to a crawl within minutes.

The attendants stood at the exit doors and thanked everyone for flying Air Canada. No mention of Bloody Mary Guy from the Executive passengers. Coach passengers were oblivious.

Moments after the last passenger left, the airport security team burst through the open Executive door just as Karen and Jessica were un-cuffing Bloody Mary Guy from the seat and re-cuffing his hands behind his back. Karen stepped forward to intercept but was upstaged by the captain.

"Hold it right there," he barked with both hands up, palms forward. "Didn't you get my transmission? These agents have everything under control and will escort the suspect to security. You can take custody there. Now back off and let them do their job."

"Yes, sir, Captain, we received your transmission, but by airport policy, we must come aboard and confirm all is as transmitted, less you were transmitting under duress."

"Someone in your office has his head up his ass then because I transmitted the code for duress free. I'm in command of this airplane. Now get the fuck out of the way and allow these agents to escort the suspect."

Without another word, the officers complied, albeit both sporting scowls, stepped back to allow Karen and Jessica to take their arrestee past them and out the tube. The agents stealing a quick glance at each other with raised eyebrows. Karen had previously retrieved Bloody Mary Guy's carry-on and briefcase and she followed Jessica out the tube.

Jessica draped Bloody Mary Guy's suit jacket over his shoulders to cover the fact that he was handcuffed. They exited the tube to find the lobby empty. All passengers were gone, and no one was paying any attention. Great, thought Jessica. She guided him to the security office, knocked, reached around her prisoner, and opened the door, moved him inside and was about to close the door when the security team and the captain entered with Karen bringing up the rear.

Jurisdiction, Canada, or the U.S.? Technically it was Canada until they left the tube. Jessica took up Bloody Mary's cause with Buster and the security officers. After listening to Jessica, Buster agreed to not process unless he had a history or priors in either country. Jessica agreed and signed him over to Airport Security. She went to the holding cell where the now sober passenger was sitting awaiting his fate. "Mr. Robinson, I don't have to tell you that your behavior was unbelievably stupid that could easily have caused an inflight panic."

"Yes, Agent, I know how stupid I've been. I'm not making excuses but want to explain. I got a call at my Toronto office yesterday summoning me to the head office in Washington to explain why my portfolios have taken a nose-dive. I felt sorry for myself, thinking the bottom was dropping out of my world, then the booze took over my thinking and you saw the results. I apologize to you and the RCMP member, the other passengers and crew. You'll never have to worry about a repeat performance."

"I sincerely hope not sir. Airport Security is checking on your history. If you have no record in either country, you'll be free to go but there will be a record of this incident. You may still make your meeting in time. I encourage you to get some breakfast and another coffee before you leave Reagan."

"Will do Agent and thank you. I'm also sorry about the fork."

"Apology accepted. Good luck at your meeting." And with that she turned and left the secure facilities and went back to the main office.

Karen was sitting in Buster's office waiting. "Turns out our guy has no record in either country so we're going to release him, no charges. I assume you read him the riot act."

"That, plus. He should be good to go. Maybe we can get him out of here pronto so he can make his meeting. He seems like a nice guy."

"Can do. What was that all about with the captain? Not sure what brought it on. Kinda pissed at the security guys. Must be some history there. So, you're off to wherever and I'm on the con-necting flight to Miami. Hopefully an uneventful trip." They both laughed.

"Agreed, we're going to keep in touch, right?" asked Jessica.

"You bet," replied Karen.

"Buster, before I go, may I use your discharge tube?"

"Of course, Oh, and Jessica, one of your agents arrived earlier, Elisabeth Peltowski? I took her through security and immigration myself. She's probably out of Reagan by now."

"Thanks Buster. That was nice of you. We really appreciate the extra you give us. It can be such a pain in the ass having to go through the same routine time and time again with security and airline staff."

"My pleasure."

Jessica reversed her Pearson process and returned to the main foyer to say goodbye. She and Karen hugged, shook Buster's hand, and made their way out of the security office. Karen headed back to the Air Canada boarding area and Jessica to the main entrance to flag a cab.

He woke with a start. Lying in a strange bed, looking up at the ceiling, he instinctively reached for his SIG, then panicked, not finding it. He glanced about, still not recognizing his surroundings but totally in Orange. Seeing the closed bedroom door, the barricading chair and the sunlight peering through a gap in the drapes, reality set in and he relaxed.

Spencer awoke surprisingly refreshed. It took him a moment to associate himself with his surroundings. Wondered when, if ever, he'd awake like a normal man. Rhetorical question.

He threw off the covers, got out of bed and headed to the bathroom. Sweats. Somewhere around here. He found the pile of new clothes in the living room where he'd dropped them, along with the other clothes that had been delivered the evening before.

Sweats.

Plain navy-blue pant and a grey top. Original he thought, somewhat sarcastically, but at least they had the secret service logo. Don't be an ingrate he told himself. These clothes feel like a million bucks compared to what I've been wearing the last few years.

He headed for the kitchen, found coffee, and got a pot going while he located bread, peanut butter, honey, eggs, bacon, and grated cheese. Man, what a life, he told himself. He pulled several slices of bacon from the package, plopped them in a frying pan, put on low heat and headed for a shower and shave.

He luxuriated in the latter two, exiting with a vigor he'd not experienced for some time. Toweled off, he wrapped the towel around his waist and headed for the kitchen for coffee. Poured a cup and sat at the breakfast nook staring out the living room window; at nothing.

He plated the bacon under paper towel and cracked three eggs and let them simmer. Back to coffee in the living room. He wondered how much shit he was in with the Service. Didn't know what he was thinking to come to the Rowley the way he did. No excuse. Just a major fuck up.

Oh, well, he sighed, he'll take whatever ass kicking Fukishura handed out. He hoped his track record helped. Enough of the somber mood he thought. I'm out of the desert. Fuckin' A, he yelled to himself, punching his arms in the air.

He headed back to the kitchen in top spirits, served up his breakfast, refilled his coffee and went out the back door to the deck to eat. A gorgeous East coast morning. Nothing better he thought. Shit happens. Wipe it up and move on. He ate and enjoyed. With no orders, he figured he'd head over to the commissary later and get a pocketbook, come back and chill till the axe dropped when Fukishura arrived.

Chapter Twenty-Eight

"The sheepdog is always sniffing around the perimeter,
checking the breeze, barking at things that go bump
in the night, and yearning for a righteous battle."

Lt. Col. Dave Grossman

Pennington cruised into Lewiston and the Saloon's packed parking lot. Folks stoking up for the day he figured. He was greeted at the front door by a hostess who showed him to a seat at the far end, handed him a menu and asked if he wanted coffee. Looked at him with an odd expression. He said yes to coffee then got up and headed to the restroom. Locking the door behind him, he was shocked by what he saw.

Mad man from the mountains, he thought. Hair, face dirty. Bush clothes. He'd forgotten about that. He washed up as best he could. Removed his jacket, shoulder holster, and shirt and washed his pits. Dried. Ran wet hands through his hair and dried it with the paper towel. Put everything back on, buttoning his jacket at the bottom to keep it from opening and reveling his firearm. Got back to the table just as the server brought his coffee.

"Sorry about my bushman appearance," he said in his most polite manner. "I've been camping and am heading home to Seattle. Hope I don't look too bad."

"No problem sir. What can I get you?"

"Eggs, scrambled, sausage, toast and hash browns will do it. Oh, and could you bring some salsa or hot sauce?"

"Right away. And sir. You really don't look that bad. You should see some of the guys who come in here after hunting." She smiled, turned, and left.

That was nice of her, he thought. Okay. What to expect from the new assignment? Zip. He knew absolutely nothing. He could be sent anywhere given the world's political climate and its distain for the U.S. federal government. Maybe things will be better with the new administration. Well nothing he can do about it now, he thought. He got up, went to the newspaper rack, got the day's Seattle paper, returned to his seat, relaxed, and started with the daily comics.

He finished the comics and just started on the front page when his food arrived. He thanked the server and dove in. Great food and plenty of it. He was on his third coffee and working on the toast when he looked up to see a Nez Perce County deputy sheriff standing beside his table.

"May I help you deputy?" Jackson noted the deputy was wearing an old style .38 caliber pistol, not the 9 mm. semi-auto to which most departments had gravitated. It hung, western style, dangling from a holster low on his right hip.

"As a matter of fact you can son," replied the deputy who took the liberty of sitting down across from him. The deputy motioned for the server to get him coffee, then he took a piece of Jackson's toast, jammed it, and ate. The deputy's coffee came, and he sipped it black.

"Have a seat deputy." Jackson said sardonically. "What can I do for you?"

"Well you see son, the deputy was hovering around fifty or so, I saw you drive up in that piece of shit truck. I rolled my cruiser window down and listened to the engine's rumble and figured you had a lot of money in that engine for a vehicle lookin' like trash. So I got to thinkin' that maybe that vehicle wasn't what it appeared to be. When you came in, I took the liberty of snoopin' around and lookin' underneath. I saw that the undercarriage was beefed up with additional suspension, torque bars and added weight and thickness to the chassis. Pretty odd I thought. So I ran your plates and what do you think I found son?

"I have no idea deputy. But I have a feeling you're going to tell me."

"Well, see, I found the truck registered to a Washington State company called ABC Garbage Disposal. Then I thought, garbage disposal guys wouldn't need a souped-up truck like this. But druggies would.

"What do you say about that son?"

"Do I understand you correctly deputy, you believe I'm a drug smuggler?"

"Could be. I'm just checkin' and havin' a friendly chat.

"You see son, we're not a bunch of hicks across the Washington border like you think we are. I called a buddy of mine in Olympia, and he checked. The ABC Company doesn't do much of a business. So I got to thinkin' again. It would be pretty convenient to bring drugs to the reservation where I have no jurisdiction, and someone like you with a hot vehicle picks the stuff up and distributes. Fast vehicle, might even outrun a trooper."

"What do you think son, any of this makin' any sense?"

"Well deputy, I don't know what to say. I'm just a guy on my way home from camping. Restoring vehicles and souping them up is my hobby."

"We'll see son. The other problem I'm havin' with you and your truck is we got us a chief of police dead just over there on the reservation. Farmer found his body dumped in a drainage ditch, two shots to his upper chest and three to his head. Looks like an execution to us and son cops take a particular dislikin' to one of our own murdered. Just to let you know, I'm passing this info on to the Washington State troopers who are goin' keep an eye on you 'cause I don't believe your bull-shit story for a minute.

If I'm right, I'll come and bring your sorry ass back here myself."

Pennington finished his coffee, put a five tip down and got up to go. "Have a nice day deputy."

He scooped up his check and headed to the till, the deputy close on his heels. As Pennington paid his bill, he turned and noted deputy dog's name plate, 'Jones'. Pennington put his wallet away, making sure to keep his ID out of Jone's sight, nodded to the deputy and thanked the cashier for a great breakfast.

Pennington walked outside into the parking lot and to the truck. Jones stopped outside the Saloon's front door, propped one foot against the iron railing and stared at Jackson. As Jackson left the lot, he did a little wheel chirp, suppressing the desire to flip the deputy the finger.

Jessica went out the main Air Canada doors, hailed a cab and was out of the parking lot as Karen was settling in on her flight to Miami. She must see a lot more action than I, she thought, but it was interesting that I had the encounter and not Karen. Do I draw attacks somehow? That can't be. She knew the bad guys picked up on her aura. She dropped the self-evaluation and had the cabby drop her off at her flat where she would pack another bag and be at Rowley by mid-afternoon.

Back in Washington and her flat, Jessica dumped the overnighter out on the bed and retrieved a larger duffle from the closet. Underwear. She grabbed a handful then thought; woops I can pass on the red lace. Sox, T shirts, sweatshirts, runners, and her Elite Spiders; a pair of well-worn waterproof Magnum Tactical boots into the duffle. No dress clothes.

The Bug was right where she'd left it, albeit a little dirty. She opened it remotely, did her usual inspection, and slid behind the driver's seat. God, she loved this little thing. She fired it up and took off out of the rear parking lot. Stopped at the street. Took a left and was off. First stop was the car wash. She hated a dirty vehicle.

Pearson Airport security's chief, Wally, was well into his day, monitoring various flights in and out of Toronto, supervising his security guards and coordinating their efforts with the RCMP members stationed at Pearson, when a knock came to his outer door. He heard a male voice speaking with reception and got up to enquire. As he rounded the corner hallway and entered the office lobby, he spotted the source.

Male, around thirty-five, five foot ten inches, give or take, sandy blond hair, cut short, stocky athletic build-no excess on this guy, clean shaven, blue/green eyes, prominent cheek bones and chin, probably one hundred and ninety or so. Chocolate brown slacks, tan button down, brown, and white tie and camel sport coat. The man turned as Wally entered the lobby. "Are you the security supervisor sir?"

"Yes, please follow me." Wally knew this guy's identity but wasn't going to ask for ID in a public area. The two walked back to Wally's office. Wally opened the door, stepped aside letting Kopas enter, closed, and locked the door.

"Wally, is it? I'm David Kopas with CISS. I understand you have a package for me?" Kopas reached into his right inside jacket pocket and produced his ID, never revealing the firearm Wally knew was under his left arm pit.

The supervisor read the credentials then said, "I was expecting you, Agent Kopas. I have your package," as he turned, squatted in front of a large safe, dialed the combination, opened the door, and retrieved a brown package, rose, turned, and gave it to Kopas.

"I've been told this meeting never took place," he said with an air of superiority.

"That's right, sir." He took the encrypted cell, turned, unlocked the door and was gone.

Pennington passed on lunch in favor of getting to Seattle as soon as possible. He entered the government lobby and approached the bullet proof glass paneled reception.

"Sorry Agent Pennington, I didn't recognize you right away," she said as he slid by on his way to his supervisor's office. "No problem Susan. Good to be back. The boss in?"

"You bet," she shouted as he made his way down the hall.

Pennington walked through the open door to find his boss already getting up from his desk.

"Good afternoon boss. What's up?"

"Hi Jackson. Nice job. Heard the entry team rounded everyone up and are transporting them to Fort Lewis. Nice touch. The FBI can handle them from here. The SAC was particularly appreciative of your skills and asked that I pass on her thanks."

"My pleasure sir, what does Washington have in store for my transfer?"

"No idea. What I do know is you have twenty-four hours to get to Rowley and report to agent Fukishura. I'll have your personal papers and gear sent. Don't worry about your house either. We'll keep everything as is until you know where you'll land, and then we pack and ship. We'll let your landlord know. The least we can do after giving you such short notice."

"Okay, thanks boss. I appreciate the help." With that, Pennington turned and headed back the way he came. He pulled into his driveway and entered the small house from the rear door.

He grabbed his duffle from the spare bedroom. Filled it hurriedly with the basics, underwear, T shirts, cargo pants, runners, and his Magnum boots. He retrieved his Sig from his floor safe under the boxes in his closet. Slipped a magazine home, pulled the slide which injected one in the chamber.

He took his shoulder holster off the closet hook and struggled into it and inserted the Sig. He called SeaTac and got a seat on a flight out at seven then called for a ride. He slipped on his leather bomber jacket, out the door and met an airporter at the curb.

Pennington was the first out at the airport, grabbed his bag and ran through the door.

Pennington introduced himself to the airline kiosk attendant who had his charge slip ready for a one-way executive class flight. Jackson signed it and produced his ID and slipped it across the counter. "Ma'am, might you advise the captain and crew of my presence and that I'm armed?"

She complied with his request, albeit somewhat intimidated by the request.

He made his way through security simply by producing his identification then to loading. The attendant showed him to an aisle seat, where he could turn slightly to view the plane's rear and still not intrude on the other passengers.

He settled into his seat just as the doors were closed and the 737 began taxing. Nobody in the window seat F. This is going to very relaxing, he thought. As the plane continued its heading to a designated runway, the attendant came by and asked if he wanted anything to drink. "JD with a little ice please", Jack Daniels Black Label.

"Certainly sir, and tonight's cuisine is Ellensburg Angus Fillet, roasted red potatoes with herbs, roasted green beans and red peppers with your choice of Prosser, Washington vineyard's Alexandria Nicole Cellars' Cabernet Sauvignon or Merlot. Dessert is Goat Cheese Cake from Tamara Murphy's Brasa restaurant in Seattle. Which wine would you like sir?"

"Everything sounds fantastic. I'd like the Merlot please." Certain irony here he thought, considering he'd just driven through Prosser a few hours previously.

"Yes sir. I'll get your JD after take-off and your meal will arrive shortly after we settle in at 35,000."

"Excellent. Thank you."

"My pleasure sir." The attendant turned and headed for the front galley just as the seatbelt sign came on. Pennington hooked himself and prepared for the thrust. He settled back into his seat and allowed himself to commiserate regarding the last twelve hours. Here I'll be at thirty some odd thousand miles above terracotta preparing to eat lavishly and twelve hours ago I was preparing for a gun fight.

And what to expect at Rowley? He had no idea. No inkling. No different really than when he was Delta Force where he was deployed any time, any place in the world. But he'd never traveled first class with Delta, usually in the belly of an Air force cargo jet. He was feeling pretty good. Tired, but good. He'd played a key role in taking down the McVeigh followers.

The plane gained altitude quickly then continued at a less exaggerated angle, leveling off at 33,000. He was taken out of his revere as the attendant brought his JD with the captain right behind him.

"Agent Pennington, I'm told. I'm Captain Snyder. Welcome aboard. I trust our crew is treating you well?" Snyder extended her hand.

Pennington took it and said, "Thank you Captain. Yes, the crew is very understanding and treating me royally. I trust there isn't problem with my firearm."

"Not at all. We're proud to host someone with your expertise and unenviable job. If there is anything I can do to assist, please let the attendant know. Enjoy and thanks for flying Alaska Airlines."

"Thank you Captain. Living in Seattle, is there any other airline?"

Snyder laughed, saluted, and returned to the cockpit. Pennington could hear Snyder lock the door and slide the secondary steel reinforced door home. Pennington closed his eyes and felt himself relax. The JD helped. He had just sipped the last when his dinner arrived, served on a tray draped with what looked like real linen, accompanied by flat ware, not plastic, and a rose in a vase. A second attendant stood behind with the Alexandria Merlot and a long stem wine glass. Gotta love executive class, he thought.

They placed his food on the plane's drop tray, poured the wine, left the bottle, and departed, allowing him to savor the aroma of Alaska's cuisine.

Pennington devoured the steak and vegetables, stopping periodically to enjoy the wine. He sighed, smiled, then reached for the Goat Cheese Cake. Ate that in three bites. He had to wait only a few moments before the attendant came by and retrieved his tray. He placed the stowaway tray in the armrest, kicked his seat back to prone and was nuzzling into the seat when the attendant once again appeared with a blanket and pillow.

"Would you like the light out sir?"

"Yes, please."

"Have a good rest sir.

Pennington wiggled into the seat once, closed his eyes and was out.

Chapter Twenty-Nine

Pennington woke with the captain announcing their beginning descent in thirty minutes. The former Delta Agent retrieved his shaving kit from his carry-on and went to the lavatory. He applied deodorant, shaved, combed his hair, replaced his shirt, weapon, and headed back to his seat just as the seatbelt sign lit. He stored his kit and strapped in.

Landing was smooth and uneventful. Just as he was about to rise to retrieve his carry-on after all other passengers had exited, the captain came into executive class. "Agent Pennington, if you'll permit me, I'll take you through security myself. I've notified Reagan's security chief and he will be waiting for us at the end of the tube."

"Certainly Captain, thank you, I appreciate the effort."

Pennington retrieved his luggage and followed the captain up the tube where they were met by a security guard who introduced himself as "Buster." The three moved through the boarding area and into a security office among stares from lingering passengers.

"Agent Pennington, something big must be happening at Rowley. You're the fifth agent I've processed in the last two days. May I confirm your ID for the records?"

"Certainly, and thank you Buster, I appreciate your help." Pennington passed his credentials to Buster who eyeballed them and returned.

"My pleasure Agent. You can thank your new boss, Agent Fukishura. She advised that the group of you would be passing through and asked that I extend the same courtesy to all of you that I have to her for years."

Pennington exited Reagan and flagged a cab and was outside Rowley within an hour.

Jessica made it to the training center in forty-five minutes. She had trained so often at Rowley that she half expected to meet the same guards as previously. No such luck. New guys. She had to wait for a supply truck to pass and be inspected. It took a long time but soon she moved forward and rolled down her window as she drove slowly to the fourteen-foot chain link gate.

Two MP's exited the guard station. One MP greeted her and after Jessica declared her status, the main gate rolled open and she was motioned to drive forward, then stop by the guard house in front of the second gate which, when opened, would allow her entry to Rowley. Once inside, the main gate closed and one guard circled behind her vehicle coming up on her passenger side with his M-16 pointing through her window. Standard procedure. Didn't faze her. She knew the routine.

"Good day Ma'am. What can we do for you?" said the guard approaching her side.

"Good day Sgt. I'm temporarily assigned to Rawley for training."

"You may step out of the vehicle Ma'am."

Jessica did as instructed and left her driver's side door open. She knew they wanted to be able to see inside.

"Please step over here ma'am and stop in front of me."

Jessica did as instructed. She knew the next process was for the other guard to check inside and underneath the vehicle. He did. Then he spoke into his shoulder mike and third guard appeared with a Golden Lab. The second guard stood back keeping his rifle leveled at Jessica while Lab and handler circled The Bug several times. The Lab sniffed the Bug's wheels, under the engine compartment, around the front and under the hood. Satisfied there were no explosives, the Lab and the handler retreated to the guard station.

First MP addressed her. "Ma'am, you may produce your ID. Where is it located Ma'am?"

"In my jacket, inside left pocket. My duty weapon is under my right armpit."

"Use your right-hand index finger and thumb and pull your jacket away from your body. Then slowly reach inside your jacket and retrieve your ID. Do it slowly Ma'am."

Jessica did as instructed, impressed with the efficiency and professionalism of the MP's.

She extended her right hand with the ID and gave it to the guard.

"Ma'am, I'm going to look at your ID while my partner trains his M-16 on you. Please do not move. Do you understand these instructions Ma'am?"

"Yes, Sgt. I do."

The guard held his rifle taut into his right shoulder and flipped the ID open with his left, looked at the photo, then Jessica, then the photo and finally Jessica. "Agent, where's your badge?"

"Clipped on my pants belt, Sgt. May I pull my jacket back further to show you? It's on my right side."

"Do it."

Jessica slowly moved her jacket back to reveal her Secret Service badge. Kept it open and looked at the guard.

"Very well Agent Fukishura, proceed to the guard station where my partner will relieve you of your duty weapon. The weapon will be stored in the armory until you either need it to train or you leave Rawley. Do you understand these instructions Agent?"

"Yes, Sgt. I do."

The third guard, armed with what looked like a Berretta semi-automatic favored by the MP's, stood in the building's foyer. "Agent, you have a weapon you're leaving with us. Please step over to the discharge tube to your left, remove the magazine and chambered round. Once done, give all three items to me."

Jessica did as instructed. Once the guard had her firearm, magazine, and round, he moved behind a counter where he slid a form and pen in her direction. She knew the drill by heart. She stepped over to the counter, read the form and signed her name.

"That'll do it Agent. Welcome to Rawley. Sorry for all the procedures." Referring to the increased security since 9/11. "We're sure you understand. This your first time here?"

"I understand Sgt. and no, this must be my umpteenth time at Rowley. Please take care of my baby. I feel naked without her." After the words were out of her mouth, she realized it was the wrong thing to say to a U.S. Army Sgt. who would be pushing 25 if not younger. She felt a slight facial flush as a huge grin broke across the guard's face. Embarrassed, she turned and quickly left the station, got into the Bug, and headed for the administration building.

Fukishura pulled into the parking area for the main building, parked, got out, chirped the Bug, and headed in. No reception necessary here. The Director's office door was open where he sat at a massive oak desk, at least fourteen feet long and four feet wide, piled high with...whatever. "Walter, good morning! How's my favorite Director this morning?"

Kipfensteiner stood, a smile so wide, it could break his face. "Jessica, how the hell are you? I've been waiting for days wondering when you'd make it. My staff and yours are on pins and needles wondering what's going on."

He stepped from behind his desk, walked around and extended his hand to Jessica, which she took.

"Welcome back to Rowley Jessica. What are you up to this time?"

"I have a team that's heading West to secure the Western Ranch for the upcoming G-8 Summit, to make sure there are no new residents taking flying lessons."

"That's going to be a tough job. Wide open like that."

"We'll set up perimeters and security systems. The Air Force will enforce a no-fly zone and state officers will handle egress and ingress. The agents I don't envy are those screening journalists and politicians' support staff. Behind a desk day after day. No, thank you. Anyway. Can you give me an update on which team members are here and who's straggling?"

"You bet. Spencer arrived at 2 am and was taken down by the MP's and put in lock up till the morning."

"What? You're telling me the guy arrived in the middle of the night?"

"Yup. Looked like shit. Smelled like shit too. Actually camel shit. His clothes were a wreck. Beard. Only a beat-up duffle. He did have his ID though but since the photo didn't match his current face, the MP's thought it wise to hold him until I arrived.

I'm glad they didn't roust me in the middle of the night. I would have been more pissed than I was. Guy cleans up good though. We had dinner the first night and he has his shit together. Not the camel variety either," he chuckled.

"Okay. Since we're talking about men, any word on Pennington?"

"Yup to that too. He's on a flight from Sea-Tac. He should be here first thing tomorrow."

"Okay. What about Peltowski and Simpson? "

"They're here. Checked in earlier. Simpson drove from Flagstaff via Phoenix and Peltowski direct from Heathrow to Reagan. Both agents seem delighted with the new assignment."

"Don't know why. They have no idea what it is. Do you have them set up?"

"I set the guys together and you three in the townhouse right next door. Your trainers have been briefed and are ready to go with your schedule. Otherwise Rowley is at your disposal. All I ask is a copy of your activities so I'm in the loop. You've been here successfully so many times Jessica, I have no problem giving you free rein."

"Thanks Walter. I appreciate the confidence. It makes my job a whole lot easier. So, I'm out of here. Which townhouse is ours?"

Chapter Thirty

Pennington paid the driver and walked up to the MP waiting by the sliding gate. "Good Morning Cpl. I'm Agent Pennington with the Service. May I show you my ID?"

"Yes, Agent, with one hand please."

Pennington complied.

"Agent Pennington, welcome to Rowley Sir. Please proceed to the guard station to relieve yourself of your weapon and receive directions to administration."

Pennington went through the same routine as the others with the exception of the transportation to the admin building. He wasn't offered a ride. He was processed by a clerk who took little notice in him. She gave him instructions to his townhouse, neglecting to say that Spencer was already housed there.

He found the house. Turned the front doorknob. Locked. Strange, they didn't give me a key. He rattled the door a little when it suddenly flew open and he was confronted by a physical carbon copy of himself, save the complexion and dreads.

The reflection scowled.

"Help you?" growled Spencer as he stared at Jackson's six feet, black wavy hair, and dark complexion bronzed by many hours in the sun and a bulky chest as part of at least a two-hundred-pound physique.

"Hi, sorry about that. Administration didn't tell me there was going to be anyone in the house. I'm Jackson Pennington, just transferred from Seattle to Fukishura's team. You are?"

Spencer extended his hand and apologized. "Hi, nice to meet you Jackson, I'm Jason Spencer. Sorry about the attitude. I was couching and fell asleep. Come on it. I'll put on some coffee."

"Learning is the gate, not the house."

Japanese warrior Yagyu Menenori

Simpson sat her luggage on the porch and knocked on the front door, not knowing what to expect. What she got was a thirty something five seven woman with a black Meg Ryan doo dressed in yellow sweatpants, black hoodie, fuzzy leather slippers holding a tubular margarita. "Hi, I'm Rebecca Simpson. You must be Elisabeth."

"Welcome to the group, whatever it may be, Rebecca. Come on in. I just made a pitcher and was sitting on the deck. Throw your gear in the corner over there," she pointed to the end of the hall, "and come on into the kitchen."

Simpson followed her into the hallway, tossed her gear and headed to the kitchen where she found Peltowski pouring her a margarita in a tube usually seen as a beer glass, twelve inches tall and about a three-inch mouth. No handle. Frosted. Salted. Peltowski handed it to her and motioned them into the living room.

"This tastes unbelievable. I've been on the road for the last twenty plus hours from Arizona, going hell bent and this is the first chance I've had to put my feet up. I may just fall asleep right here."

"No flights I take it. Were you in the Phoenix office?"

"Yes and No. I was officially there but I worked out of my apartment in Flagstaff. Kinda neat actually, being away from the city. I grew up country."

"Yeah, I kinda figured that somehow," Peltowski replied with a laugh." You must get a variety of public responses."

"I do. But you know Elisabeth, when the Service approached me eons ago, I sure as hell wasn't going to change the way I dressed, no offense.

I'm sure my size has a lot to do with the public's response."

Elisabeth laughed again, "I know. I have a friend who's license plate holder reads, 'I've PMS and carry a .357.' She gets a lot of responses. We're still in the minority with the Service. There isn't a man on the face of the earth who can relate."

"Hear, Hear," toasted Rebecca. Where were you when Fukishura beckoned?"

"Oh, let me tell you about it. MI6 in London. I was led to believe I was going to be involved in monitoring and tracking terrorist finances. What I got was a prissy snob MI6 liaison who limited my computer access, prohibited my carrying and pretty much shuffled me aside. I was ready to join any new team as long as it was out of Britain.

"What really pissed me off was their attitude, like we were some back country bumpkins who had no idea of analyzing world threats. What I really wanted to do, but figured I'd kiss my career goodbye, was to hack into their system and really fuck them up." She laughed at the joy she'd obviously experienced at the thought.

"Oh, that would have been fantastic. I love the idea" Rebecca replied, laughed, and clapped her hands in the air. "Too bad you couldn't do it. Let me tell you about the characters with whom I've been working, the FBI boys in suits and wing tips. Oh, my god. I was assigned to work with their investigative team tracking what I believe is Al Qaida instructing on reservations.

"Had I been allowed to track on horseback, we'd have had more success and the insurgents would have been down and out. We travelled through the desert in Jeeps for god sake. They knew we were coming hours before our arrival at the various hideouts.

I was able to gain considerable field intel that they completely blew, over and over again. My effectiveness was pretty much gone by the time I heard from Fukishura.

What really pisses me off was, I know these reservation insurgents are amateurs and are receiving professional input from their Middle Eastern cousins, but I could never prove it. An Iranian male with long hair looks very Native American."

"So, Fukishura has a tracker and a hacker. I heard there are two other agents joining the team. Any idea who they are or where?" asked Elisabeth.

Rebecca just got the words out, "No idea," when there was a knock at the front door.

Both agents set down their drinks and headed to answer. Door open. Fukishura.

Jessica extended her hand to shake. Both agents took it enthusiastically and stepped back to allow her entry. "Am I in time for drinks or have you guys polished the pitcher?"

Rebecca and Elisabeth laughed, shaking their shags and closed the door behind their new boss. They led the way into the living room as Jessica dropped her gear in the foyer. Elisabeth retrieved a frosted glass from the freezer and poured a tall one for Jessica.

"It's obvious we don't need introductions so welcome to Team Ranch Wyoming," said Jessica.

"No shit," replied Rebecca. "We're really going to Wyoming to set up a western Ranch. Oh, my god. I think I've died and gone to heaven. I can't believe you chose me for this. I can't believe you got me out of that god forsaken desert with those FBI assholes to join a team with female agents. Oh, my god." She was waving her arms excitedly, spilling her drink, licking up the spill on her arm and hand.

Jessica laughed, "It took me some time to find the agents I wanted on this team. You had what I wanted." She wasn't going to tell Simpson that Sorento had recommended her. No need to stroke this agent's ego.

While Rebecca was continuing her excited utterance, Elisabeth was walking around shaking her head, lifting her eyes to the ceiling thanking whomever for this blessing. "I echo Rebecca, I too can't believe this. How did you know I was ready to transfer? You obviously want and need my skills but how did you know I was ready?"

"That was the easy part. I'm female. I know MI6's reputation. And of course I knew about the FBI's boys' club. I was pretty sure you two would be ready. Sorry I couldn't tell you beforehand about the assignment."

"Well, we did question your being the agent in charge. No offense, but our gender does have a bit of a reputation of being estrogen on steroid instead of excelling at management, particularly managing other females."

Jessica laughed. "No offense taken. I knew you'd question it, and it would take a while before you'd trust me. You can make up your mind in the next few weeks while we hone our skills. You can transfer out if you don't like what you see and experience. Fair?"

"Good for me," said Rebecca.

"Me too," echoed Elisabeth.

"You two have any problem with the MPs at the main gate?" asked Jessica.

Elisabeth said, "No, not really. Just experience I guess. I know they have to keep this facility tight. We can't have anyone knowing our protection plans, filming our presidential limo training, driving under siege etc. So, no, I expected it."

"How about you Rebecca?"

"I too was prepared for it. Even being hit on by the Sgt. I take that back he wasn't really hitting on me 'cause he would know better. Just the flattering comments while he drove me here was kinda surprising, unprofessional."

"You got driven from the administration building to here?" said Elisabeth with raised eyebrows and an open mouth. "How about you Jessica? You get a ride?"

"Nope. No cowboy hat."

All three laughed at Rebecca's expense.

"We heard there were four of us. When do we meet the other agents?" asked Rebecca.

"We've got time before dinner. Let's go find them," Jessica said as he downed her drink and headed for the door.

Rebecca and Elisabeth shared a quizzical look, downed their drinks, and rushed after her. Jessica headed out the door and made a right turn across the grass with the other two running after her. Jessica walked up to the front door of the townhouse next door and rapped. A few seconds later the door opened with two guys standing side-by-side.

"Gentlemen, Jessica Fukishura. The cowgirl is Rebecca Simpson and Hoodie is Elisabeth Peltowski. We're having an impromptu meeting next door over a pitcher of margaritas. Please join us." She extended her hand to shake. The men exchanged facial expressions. A cross between being set up on a once in a lifetime blind date and being double crossed by a friend who wanted to bust their balls.

"Sure. " replied Spencer as he gave a quizzical look to Pennington who shrugged, raised his eyebrows and they trotted after their colleagues.

They settled themselves in the living room. A duplicate of the one Spencer and Jackson shared. Elisabeth took the roll as hostess, came in with a fresh pitcher of margaritas. Poured all around.

Fukishura started with, "I'm glad you all arrived in time. We need to get up to speed quickly so let's begin with a little history of each of you. What were you doing when the transfer came? Let's start with you Elisabeth and work our way around. I'll be last."

"Okay. I was working with MI6 as their Secret Service liaison..." She shared what she had told Rebecca, then continued, "Prior to London, I had been to various national offices. I was successfully decrypting in Washington.

"I'm originally from Nebraska, University at Omaha. I taught high school computer science for a while but got bored with the simplicity. I got my master's in criminology and did five years with the state police in commercial crime, and I've been hacking for the government ever since. I'm very glad to be out of Britain and home. Am looking forward to working with everyone." She gave a nod to Pennington.

"I'm Jackson Pennington, just in from Seattle. I thought I'd be a little late because I didn't get my transfer notice until late yesterday afternoon. These are the clothes I lived in for the past four days. Two days ago I was on an Idaho mountain top reconning an FBI strike against the Christians for a Better America compound.

"They have all the material for a McVeigh bomb. The strike team was landing as I descended the mountain and was driving away.

"I graduated with a degree in History from Northern Michigan University and played hockey. I had planned to teach high school, but my practicum put me to sleep just about the time the FBI was recruiting. Five years with them, then the Service approached and asked if I wanted to cross the street.

"I didn't know the Service tracked law enforcers, university students and the like. Apparently, the powers that be had monitored me since I left Delta and wanted to use my anti-terrorism experience, the degree and FBI training to their advantage. They gave me a hell of a financial incentive, so here I am. My main thrust is domestic terrorism."

"Rebecca Simpson. Cowgirl from Montana. I've been riding horses since I was little. I graduated from Montana State with an education degree. So I guess we have something in common

Jackson, Elisabeth. I taught for two years and thought I'd like it, but I found that caring for twenty-five kids all day long wasn't for me. I went back to school and got a master's in criminology and went with Montana Department of Justice then joined the Flathead County Sheriff's department until the Service came a callin'.

"Flathead is just south of the Canadian Border by Glacier National Park. I spent the rest of my sheriff time tracking bad guys. I ended up with a pretty good record. I either found them alive or dead, but I found every one of them.

"Today I arrived from Phoenix, well actually Flagstaff, where I've been working with the FBI. They sequestered me too, tracking a Native American dissident group which is regenerating the '70's rebellion, only this time with Al Qaeda style bombs.

"I drove from Phoenix overnight. I have about five Red Bulls in my system and feel I'll crash any moment, or after another margarita, whichever comes first."

Jackson interrupted," Sorry to interrupt the flow, but I gotta ask, how did you make a twenty-four-hundred-mile trip in, what, twenty-four hours?"

"A little help from our law enforcement friends along the way." She glanced at Jessica to see if she wanted more info, somewhat hesitant to give more for concern she would get shit on for her stunt. Nothing.

"Before we go one, I have another question," said Jackson. "Did I hear the rumors right that you were a body builder?"

"Oh, boy, talk about something coming back to bite me in the ass," Rebecca said with chagrin. "Yes, I dabbled in the sport, if you want to call it that. And no, I don't do it now and haven't for many years.

"When I was with the sheriff's department, I lived for the job and the adrenaline rush, but they wouldn't let me work seven days straight and I was bored. I took up weightlifting at the local gym and got hooked. I found it very easy and could bulk up quickly.

Anyway, long answer to your short question. Yes, I was a body builder."

"Very cool," acclaimed Jason. "No wonder the bad guys drop so quickly."

Everyone had a little laugh at that comment not realizing Rebecca did in fact use her body weight and muscle mass to drop guys hard. She didn't tell them she still lifted weights three times a week.

Jason offered, "I received my transfer notice while in Northern Africa. I'd been locating Al Qaeda recruits and preventing them from returning to Iraq and Afghanistan.

"I graduated from the University of California in L.A. with a degree in microbiology. I liked the science but couldn't see myself working in a lab as a career.

"I was heavily in debt, and someone suggested LAPD, so I applied. I found I had a knack and was deployed undercover after eighteen months on the job. My minor in languages aided my placement. LAPD wanted someone to infiltrate firearms smugglers' operation importing their wares through Los Angeles Harbor.

"I did that for a while, busted quite a few and was pretty much wearing out my cover when the Service knocked. After training they sent me to Northern Africa where I was able to blend in quickly. Combination of dialect and my handsome complexion I expect," he said with a smirk. "Anyway, good times for a long while," he said sardonically. "Got a lot of Al Qaeda recruits to change their minds."

"Thanks everyone," said Jessica. "You can expound on your experiences as we go along but this will give each of you an idea of your team members. This is essential, given our task. We're going to Wyoming to set up a western Ranch at the President's property. Sorento has directed us to close it up tight.

"As you understood from Rebecca's comments regarding the Arizona insurgents, we suspect we have a great many Middle Eastern illegals whose intentions are questionable to say the least. What we're doing here is regrouping, regenerating our skills so we can arrive in Wyoming as a unified, skilled team. You're bringing valuable skills to the operation, and I'm pleased and enthused by your individuality.

"Jason, I understand you've already seen a doc here and you've been given a clean bill, just a little malnourished. Rowley's chef can take care of that, and you should be back in top form in a few weeks.

"The Director has arranged for our trainers. Beat O'Toole is doing firearms. I want you all to shoot as many rounds as your body can stand. Have fun and take several days. O'Toole will start you with just firing your Sig. Shoot, shoot, shoot. I want hours on that range. O'Toole will then take you through a variety of shooting house experiences. I'll let him explain those. Jackson, this will be a refresher for you.

"After O'Toole is satisfied you're on top of the Sig, he'll go back and do the whole thing over again with a variety of handguns, standard rifles, and automatics such as the one you used in Idaho Jackson. We have no idea what to expect on this assignment and have to cover all bases. Rebecca and Jackson's experiences will be invaluable to us. We will be rousting all the nut cases out of the bush and will deal with them one at a time.

"With satellite internet so readily available, anyone or any group could have set themselves up in the mountains and locals would have no idea of their presence. We may be fortunate and have only a few, but as Rebecca and Jackson will attest, they're out there and are geared to get at Bakus one way or the other. Our job is to destroy them before they get a chance, then close up the president's ranch...tight.

"I'm going to be your defensive tactics trainer. I know it may appear strange and against federal policy, but I think you'll agree when we get going that it has merit. I want us to be one in defensive tactics. I want each of us to know exactly what the other is capable of and to have each other's back. The philosophy I've honed for years with the Service is attack your attacker. I'll clarify that as we go.

"The other trainer is Donald Cousins. He has been laid on us from Washington. We're going to be on our own out there. Washington wants to make sure we remember their policies and procedures before cutting their tether. This won't take long and will be non-confrontational. Not like your first week's orientation when you joined the Service. Sort of like grad school compared to undergraduate. Any questions?"

"Okay. You'll undoubtedly have some as we go along, so don't hesitate to ask. If I don't know the answer, I'll find it. Everyone needs clothing etc. and you're probably wondering about things you left behind. If your personal items are coming courtesy of Uncle Sam, let the administration clerk know where you want them sent. I suggest you have them held by the Service until this assignment is over. If you need clothes right now, let the administration know and they'll outfit you with training duds.

"Anyone with furniture etc.?" No one responded so she continued. "I want you to concentrate on Rowley exclusively. Are any of you in a relationship that will require your attention?" No one responded. This is better than she expected, thought Jessica.

"Good. Well, not good, but you know what I mean. I expect none of you have heard of me before your transfer. I'll give you a little of my background, but you'll have to pick most of it up, as you will of each other, during training. I graduated from the University of California at Berkeley." She smiled and nodded at Jason. "I received my law degree from them as well. After graduation I was like you Jason, heavily in debt and no idea what I wanted to do with the degree.

"I knew I didn't want to be a lawyer after seeing the gong shows in courts during my internship practicums. I found out late in my third year that I needed more, but I loved the law. Go figure. Anyway, I went to the university's recruiting sessions but didn't find anything of interest. There was every law enforcement agency in California represented as well as several federal.

"The FBI was there but I wasn't impressed. Sorry Jackson, no disrespect. I just knew I would never be able to follow their regimen. Then out of the blue, the CIA and the Secrets Service contacted me.

"The CIA recruiters were very strange. Every question I asked was answered with a question, so I passed. The Service was more open and straight forward. They told me they wanted me for my law degree and my languages." She nodded again to Jason. "I spent my early years bouncing around from field office to field office. I was in Vancouver, British Columbia when my transfer came. Sorento was up front with me, saying he was instructed to increase the estrogen level of the Presidential Protection Detail and I jumped at the chance.

"I knew I'd spend a great deal of time proving myself, but I didn't care. I wanted it. Turns out I didn't have to prove myself for very long. The Paris incident sealed my credentials." Not seeing any quizzical looks she continued. "So that's me."

"Tomorrow, we'll get started at 0800 hrs. with a briefing in the communications center, which is right next to the administration building. We have a tentative timeline of two weeks but that can be shortened or lengthened depending on our needs. Our operation takes precedent over any other unit, so nothing else is being scheduled until we're done."

They spent the next hour chatting and getting to know each other. Jessica shared her Toronto experiences...minus CISS.

Jason talked a lot about the Arab culture and how it relates to world terrorism.

Elisabeth tried to explain how the Service tracked international emails, but nobody understood so she gave up.

Jackson told the story of deputy dog in Lewiston where he stopped for breakfast. They all laughed at the confrontation and knew why Jackson hadn't shown his credentials but felt for the life lost. They had seen the classic film *Easy Rider* with Peter Fonda and the encounter with small town law enforcement and the resulting backlash of Fonda confronting that deputy dog.

"Jason, I understand you can lead us to dinner?" said Jessica.

"You bet. Get ready for an unbelievable meal on Uncle Sam. The respect expressed for us by the staff felt good after so many years of being the villain. Follow me agents to a culinary experience to which your taste buds will dance."

Everyone rose in concert and left the townhouse in mass, Jason leading the entourage.

Their meal would have been considered exceptional under any circumstances, but remarkably so considering it was prepared by a government agency. Kent offered roast chicken with rosemary, oregano, sage & thyme served with a bottle of Maryland Cabernet Franc. Dessert was stracciatella, somewhat of a chocolate chip Italian ice cream. Director Kipfensteiner stopped, expressed his support for their training and operation, then excused himself, pleading pressing paperwork.

Jessica said, "I hope everyone is enjoying this evening. I know I am and I'm especially enjoying the opportunity to get to know each of you a little more."

Exhaustion and hunger took over as the agents concentrated on enjoying Kent's presentation, putting socializing on the back burner.

After finishing her meal, Jessica said, "I studied your personnel jackets until I was cross-eyed, and it's been nice to enhance that with your personality. Having said that, this is the last of these we'll have until the night we leave. You're on your own at the academy cafeteria right beside us here.

"I've been up since four, Rebecca you've been up all night so how about we extend our thanks to Kent and his staff and hit the sack?"

The team made their way back to their townhouses. Goodnights all around. Closed doors. Everyone was in bed and out within thirty minutes.

Chapter Thirty-One

8 am everyone was present. Two coffees and scones down, Jessica began their first meeting.

"This operation is classified. You all know how to bracket yourselves under that category. When President Johnson had his Texas White House, the Detail hit the community hard and overtly. The bad guys knew they were coming and went underground. Ditto for both Bush presidents and their Texas compounds. We're doing it differently."

"Rebecca. Horse training. Couple of questions. Can you pass yourself as one? Do you have anyone in Montana who would say you work for them? You'll need a truck registered to them as part of your cover."

"I can and yes, as a matter of fact, I do. A deputy with Flathead County started a training business a few years ago as an aside and retirement plan. His son is a Marine and has a Junker. I think he'll loan it to us. He'll set up a training job in StoneHead," Replied Rebecca.

"Okay. Work the phones between training sessions. Have messages routed through administration. Get something firm. He needs to know the ramifications and secrecy of the operation. If he's receptive, then we'll discuss it here. If we all agree, then we'll give it to Washington to process for the OSA-Official Secrecy Act. If he agrees to their conditions, we're in."

"Jackson and Elisabeth, you guys are teaching." Both agents gave her a blank expression. "Let me explain. Rebecca can blend in quickly with her cover. Elisabeth, your cover is that you quit

Omaha for StoneHead. Jackson, I'm sure you'll pick up where your practicum left off. Your cover is you wanted out of Michigan and took this temporary opening hoping it will lead to a full-time position. Sorento went to school with the Stone County Schools Superintendent. They graduated from New Mexico together.

Sauldez went into teaching and then administration. He landed in Wyoming a while ago. The guys have kept in touch over the years. Sorento's paved the way for your employment. Elisabeth, you're teaching computers at StoneHead Middle School. Jackson, you're doing grade twelve History at StoneHead High.

You'll have time to brush up. Your time at each school will be about what you did for your practicum. Sauldez has created a curriculum development team with the two teachers you're replacing. Their project will last your cover. He's created a paper trail showing the positions advertised, applicants interviewed and you two being selected. There will be no backlash. You came directly from your previous teaching/practicum experience to StoneHead."

"That leaves Jason and me. We'll come as agents doing a low key by the book community evaluation. Everyone in the community knows Bakus. His family has been in the area for decades. So it will be a natural for us to be there.

"Questions?" Receiving none, she moved on with, "Okay, let's get to the gym."

Rowley's gym was state of the art, with a separate weight room which would be the envy of any university coach. Moments after they arrived, Hassanali walked through the door in sweats with the Secret Service logo on the chest/back and down one leg.

"Good morning all, I'm Noor Hassanali, agent in charge of your physical upgrading," he said as he shook hands all around. "I understand we have a variety of physical readiness levels based on your previous assignments so we'll take it easy at first so there are no injuries, and everyone comes up to speed at the conclusion. If what we start with seems elementary, I trust you'll be patient while your teammates catch up. Everyone is capable of attaining the required level, which isn't much different than your basic training. The only difference will be running, and that need is based on your assignment.

We'll be doing a lot of flat running, not for time but for endurance. Once you attain that level, we'll head up into the hills for bush running. The rest of it will be free weights, relying on light poundage with twenty to thirty reps per set. We'll be developing your fast twitch muscles in contrast to your slow twitch. Again, this is the need based on your assignment.

There is no weight goal. You'll each start with a weight with which you can do three sets of fast reps. You'll massage the worked muscle between sets. After three sets, give yourself two minutes and move on to the next muscle group.

Our sessions will last two hours every morning starting at 0800 hrs. We'll start with stretching then run the basketball gym for forty-five, then hit the weights for forty-five. That gives me a thirty-minute window if I want to extend the bush runs. Questions?"

There were none, just anxious and hyped eyes watching his every move. Jackson and Pennington bouncing on the soles of their feet.

"Good. Here is the weight circuit," he said, as he handed out several stapled pages. "Give it a read, then hit the court for your forty-five, and then join me at the first weight station over there."

Everyone stuffed their paperwork into leather folders and filed out of the weight room and started running around the court, each concentrating on her/his personal development. Concluding that, they joined Hassanali back in the weight room, properly warmed up.

The two hours passed quickly with everyone working up a good sweat. They did dumbbell flies, straight -arm pullovers, one-arm dumbbell rows, barbell curls and dumbbell kickbacks for triceps. Between each set they did as many crunches with their legs in the air as they could.

Everyone was working at their maximum when Hassanali yelled time. "Okay, agents, that's it for today. Take a long hot shower and a couple of Advil. See you tomorrow at 0800." With that he walked out of the weight room. The team headed for the showers, chatting among themselves. Jessica noted there was no whining or complaining. Good start, she thought.

The guys headed to their change room while the women angled off to the right to theirs. Each had a change of clothes, almost identical to what they were wearing. The women striped and headed to the showers. Jessica couldn't help but note Rebecca's physique. She had kept her competitive shape in spite of her grueling Service schedule. She had an upper body similar to Winthrop's, wide shoulders and defined biceps and triceps.

Elisabeth wasn't a complete contrast, but close. She just hadn't kept in shape. Jessica could tell Elisabeth's arms and legs had the potential for development. She had a flat but soft stomach. Noor would take care of that, Jessica assured herself. The women showered with little chat, dried, and dressed in relative silence.

Jessica wasn't sure whether they were tired, intimidated by her presence or just shy. She figured it was a combination of the first two as neither agent impressed her as lacking in chat skills.

They met Jason and Jackson as they were coming out of their changing room, and they all headed to the cafeteria for a break. After coffee and muffins, they moved to their assigned classroom. Jessica locked the door after them and sat at a round table with her team.

"Okay, let's get to work. First off, other than personal information, our team has to be an open book. If during these next few days and weeks you find you can't keep up or have a problem with any aspect of the operation, let me know and we'll discuss. But we can't keep secrets from each other. Agreed?"

Heads nodding all around. "Good. The reasons for choosing each of you. The team needs to know my objectives. I'll keep it brief. Elisabeth, your hacking abilities are infamous. MI6 was foolish not taking full advantage of your skills. Add to that your time in commercial crime in Nebraska and your teaching. You'll see in a minute where this is going. Sorento has authorized you to request any and all equipment for monitoring. Deal directly with Procurement. He's cleared the way. You have accommodations in StoneHead. A furnished house has been rented for you. You can have Procurement send everything there or wherever you choose.

"Jason, your L.A. Street creds, your dialect gift, your undercover with the guns division and your time in Africa are a mix that will produce results here.

"Rebecca, we needed an agent with equine experience, and you popped up front and center with your kick-ass attitude, your leadership in Arizona, your perseverance, and your ability to find the proverbial needle were the attraction.

"It's a combination of attributes you all have. Put them together and the mix is unbeatable. Jackson, your time in Idaho is becoming more and more the assignment's catalyst. Everyone, Jackson is ex-Delta with a B.A. in History as he mentioned previously. He came here from Idaho where he reconned a mountain top settlement of Christians for a Better America which had stockpiled a shit load of explosives. This group hero worships Timothy McVeigh, our famed home-grown terrorist whose death was at the hands of the state.

The Seattle office has the intel on these guys from their interrogation. They bragged about their plans. There are numerous cells around the country with the same objective, all stockpiling the necessary explosives. We have no idea their ETA at The Ranch, but we're positive that is their goal. Sorento is concerned this group has Wyoming members and he's placed this as a high priority. So we're three pronged; shed the area of any McVeigh wanna-bees and get intel on where other members are country-wide, determine if there are any Al Qaeda sleepers and close all approaches to the Wyoming Ranch.

"Elisabeth and Jackson, you guys have to come off sympathetic to the Christian right's cause. You know how to do it. Rebecca, you will be neutral, but all ears. The red necks are going to gravitate to you. That you can exploit.

"Let's be straight here. We are obviously a country in the midst of a cultural change but folks in these Western hamlets are going to be a mixed bag. That's one reason Jason and I are going in a-la-natural, since one look at us and they wouldn't believe any cover we could imagine. Questions?

"Okay. Jason, I gotta ask you. What the hell happened when you got to Rowley?"

"A major fuck-up Jessica. I just forgot. I received my transfer while in the middle of the desert and hustled back to Morocco and grabbed the first plane out. I should have thought it through, but I had no apartment, no clothes. I hadn't been in a town for months and hadn't given any thought to my appearance. I hope I didn't create any problem for you or the team."

"Are you kidding? Never. You handled yourself very professionally laying prone on the pavement with the MP's training their M16s at you. I'm not being sarcastic. You handled it well.

"Rebecca, what's this I heard about you makin' it from Phoenix to Rowley in twenty-four hours?" Jessica said with a smile.

"Well, I was kinda in the same boat as everyone else. I was excited about getting a new assignment. I packed and was out of Flag' without making a flight reservation. Found out I wouldn't make your deadline by flying-would take me two days. So I rented a truck and drove. Some very helpful state troopers assisted me along the way by greasing the speed limit."

Everyone laughed. "That's the kind of attitude I was talking about that will propel our team to success. You all have that personal kick-ass philosophy that meshes with mine. And Rebecca, your ability to get that co-operation points to your assignment. I've told many female agents and cops that a woman can use her gender as a tool. No, not like that!" she laughed. "But to disarm a male antagonist, just before you destroy him. I'll mention more about that in defensive tactics. Sorry guys, I've never heard of men using the technique with the exception of feigning compliance before you attack.

"We're good here. You guys can exchange information with each other so you're comfortable. It's almost noon, so let's do lunch and meet in the defensive tactics room just down from the gym at 1:30."

Lunch was light for everyone. Salads and pita bread sandwiches. They sat at a round table off in the corner where they were assured privacy, no one wanting to be overheard.

Chapter Thirty-Two

Jenewein managed another couple of hours sleep, albeit restless given his nocturnal visitor. He dressed in sweats, grabbed a quick breakfast of leftovers, stuck the semi in his waistband then a semi-automatic Russian rifle with a 30-round clip over his shoulder and headed out the back door just as the sun peeked over the foothills.

He picked up the trail just as his visitor hit the bush earlier. The swath through the dense brush was easy to follow as he maneuvered through the bent Aspens with the SKS at shoulder ready, safety off ready to strike the intruder.

He followed the recently made trail, the pungent odor becoming stronger as he passed deeper into the bush. An hour into the pursuit he found the trail dead-ended by a creek bed, almost as though Behemoth was covering his trail. He followed the creek up and down stream for 30 minutes each way, finally having to withdraw to make it to Denver and then to Cow Springs and back to Denver that day. He arrived back at the retreat, grabbed food, filled his thermos with coffee, secured the buildings and was airborne by 0900 heading southeast.

Rowley's defensive tactics training room was similar to TPS where Jessica and Karen had worked out but with the addition of red training M16 rifles and H&K's MP5 SD. Jessica had everyone gather around in the middle of the wall-to-wall floor mats.

"Firearms, physical conditioning and defensive tactics are the three pillars on which our operation stands. If one is weak, it threatens the operation as a whole. We may get west and find no evidence of the domestic terrorists, secure the Wyoming Ranch and be done. Based on Seattle's intel, I doubt that's going to happen. So many of our colleagues have become complacent jeopardizing themselves and any operation in which they're involved by allowing one or more of these pillars to deteriorate. That's not going to be us.

"You will practice the Color Code of Awareness every minute, every second of every day. You will be in Yellow from the time you get out of the sack until your head hits the pillow again. When you're out and about with your covers, you'll be in Orange, without exception. You'll practice it here at Rowley until you live and breathe the system. Any questions on that?"

There were none and Jessica's gut was telling her that the team choices were right on the money.

They listened.

"Good. I want to see you using 360s everywhere. You recall the concept from tactical shooting, so all we're doing is extrapolating. Don't let me catch you by surprise entering a room or exiting the restroom. Ever. I need to know you have the system down pat and will have my back and that of every team member.

"No disrespect to the Service, but their training is liability motivated. For the Presidential Detail they've pretty much thrown out that rule book but many detail members have not adjusted their skills or their mindset. For our purposes it is kill or be killed. I believe Jackson and Spencer have it and our training here will hone both the set and skills. So, to the skills.

"I'm going to presume you're all competent at takedowns so we're going to concentrate on attacks with handguns, shotguns, rifles, automatic rifles and knives. We'll start with going through the movements so I can be sure your body has the motor skills. Then we'll move into using the Red Man. Elisabeth, you studied with Ricardo Montabo, correct?"

"Ya, I did. In Florida."

"What's your opinion of Chilean Jujitsu's ground fighting for our purposes?"

"The take-down is very smooth and efficient but it makes the assumption your attacker isn't going to pull a knife. When you lay your head against your attacker's chest and prepare to drop him with your hip movement, you're very open to being stabbed because his arms are free. As we all know, it only takes a second to slip a knife free and into your side. As far as being pinned on the ground is concerned, the skills are excellent for moving your assailant off regardless of a weight disadvantage. However, I prefer using my knife immediately and ending the issue."

"Okay, I agree. I trained with Ricardo in Berkeley and have the same evaluation. You did your martial arts in combative in New Orleans, right?"

"Yes, when I was stationed there. Originally because of boredom and a free time activity, but the more I learned and advanced the more I was convinced combat martial arts was the only system for law enforcers, regardless of department regulations."

"Good. Speaking of knives, do each of you carry a belt clip knife?"

Each nodded.

"I carry a Spyderco Police in the stainless. I find it a good balance and weight. What about you guys?"

"I carry an H&K Nitrous," said Jackson.

"Mine is Osborne's Opportunist," added Spencer. "I carried a boot knife in the desert as well."

"An Apparition," said Rebecca. "And I too have a boot knife in my cowboy boots. Actually Smith and Wesson's HRTs in each boot."

"Smith and Wesson's Tactical is my baby," said Elisabeth. "I've carried that since college. MI6 told me I had to lock it up as knives were prohibited by British law. I put it in my belt the moment I passed through Reagan security. Thanks for Buster by the way Jessica."

"You're welcome. So, we're all on the same page with knives. We'll go over both defensive and offensive tactics of an approaching knife attacker after we're all comfortable with defending against a knife at your throat, back and neck. Okay, lets' get started. Jason, grab five handguns from the cabinet and let's pair up. I'll show you the technique I prefer and want you to learn. Again, we're going to be a tight team and need to know of what each of us is capable."

They spent the remaining afternoon and early evening hours working in pairs on the various defensive tactics Jessica demonstrated. Everyone had some understanding of the movements from their basic training. Jackson had them all. Plus several of his own.

Delta didn't deal with liability issues.

Each day was identical to the previous. Run at 8-the last week was bush, up, and down hills, through the brush at full speed. Then weight training till 10:00. Break. The Service's Hogan's Alley till Noon. Lunch. Defensive tactics 1 to 3. Break. Strategy meeting from 3:30 till 6. Dinner. No booze. Bed by 9.

The team found the routine stimulating and exciting, particularly as their briefings began to solidify their mission. Rebecca had contacted her former Montana Sheriff's Department partner, arranged to pick up the truck at Missoula Airport and Sorento had confirmed the signing of the Secrecy Act papers. On the final day at Rowley, Jessica spent the morning going over the last-minute details of their mission and movement to Wyoming.

"Welcome to our last day at Rowley and the first day of the rest of your life." Everyone laughed at her attempted humor. "Everyone has their encrypted Blackberry with your individual codes. We're bound to see each other out and about in StoneHead so let's work on our lack of recognition. As always, be vigilant and use the Color Code 24/7.

"You know your jobs. I'm confident. You're physically ready. But I want to reiterate the magnitude of our mission, aside from setting up the Wyoming Ranch. McVeigh killed 168 people when the idealistic degenerate bombed the Alfred Murray Federal Building in Oklahoma in '96.

"Also remember Eric Rudolph, the Olympic Park bomber who killed two and injured 100 over a period of three years. He targeted abortion clinics and gay nightclubs and killed one of ours. And finally, Kamran Akhtar who ignored his deportation order and proceeded with his plans to destroy the Mansfield Dam in Texas, then moved on to Atlanta, Georgia's transit system and New York's FBI building.

"Our home-grown religious fanatics create their western brand of Fatwa-religious order. Omar Rahman was convicted of encouraging acts of violence against America. He directed his followers, 'to destroy Americans, ruin their economy, sink their ships and bring down their planes.'

"And let's not forget our New Mexico born Anwar al-Awlaki 40-year-old who was the inspiration for the 2009 Christmas Day bomber over Detroit, the May 2010 Times Square bomber and our very own Major Nidal Hasan, who killed 13 at Fort Hood. These factions are becoming successful at destroying our country from within, like a festered wound untreated consumes the human flesh from the inside out, destroying all the supporting vessels.

"We need to locate these cells and destroy them. Remember, we're not the FBI. We're the President's Protection Detail and as such we have powers far beyond that of any other American law enforcement agency which we will use, with discretion, to eliminate any threat against the President.

"Rebecca, you're out of here for Missoula. Do you have a residence in StoneHead?"

"Yup! Derrick got me a cabin just outside of StoneHead on Dry Creek. Never been there but I Googled, and it looks like I can get into town quickly. So I'm good to go. I'll give myself a day to settle in, go to the grocery store and introduce myself etc. and then meet my client. You want us to check in via the unit every couple of days, right?"

"Yes. Jason and I will record our communications back and forth and Elisabeth, you can give us whatever you get from your monitoring. You and Jackson are so gregarious you'll be up on the party list the first few days and be mingling and partying the first Friday." Everyone laughed but Jessica knew she was right. She had a perfect team.

"One last thing, you guys need to make sure Rowley administration has all the info for storing your personal affects. I'm the only one with a wardrobe. Sorento has authorized funds for a shopping spree for each of you. No makeover but buy whatever you need for your covers and a prolonged stay.

Use your personal credit card the government issue would be a tell.

Even though he's authorized the spending, he'll be scrutinizing the statement, so keep away from silk boxers or thongs," she said with a smile. Everyone considered her humor represented the team's cohesiveness. But the guys wondered if she really thought they wore silk thongs.

"Pick up your travel packs after we're done here. You're scheduled to leave separately. You're under cover when you leave this room. Any questions? Okay, let's do it. We'll meet up in StoneHead in a couple of days."

With that, they rose in concert, high fives all around and walked out of the room and headed out.

Karen did two four-day rotations before getting a few days off after her final leg ended in Toronto. Even those with a passion for flying would groan at the grinding pace: Toronto, Washington, Miami, Los Angeles, Vancouver, and Toronto. Then do it all over again. She used hotel laundry services extensively but longed to wear something new after living out of a suitcase. It usually took her only a couple of days down time before she was ready to go again...being idle too long worked havoc on her psyche.

This last go round was pretty uneventful. She dealt with two Cuban immigrants who spoke no English, no French and were dissatisfied with their Coach seats on the Miami to L.A. flight. The men were creating a disturbance near the rear of the plane, next to the flight attendants' jump seats. At the sound of raised voices, Karen eased around the curtain. She saw both men standing, waving their arms aggressively, indicating they were cramped and pointing forward in the direction of first class, presumably indicating their desire to move. The attendant was having zero success in communicating. Without a language Karen felt hobbled but quickly came up with a plan.

She eased around the curtain, moved forward catching the attendant's attention and slipped by her to stand in front of the men. She nodded acknowledgement then flipped open her Ellen Tracy coral light weight belted wool coat, revealing her Smith and Buffalo. She accompanied this maneuver with a stare that cut the two men to the quick. Verbal skills my ass, thought Karen. Mr. Smith and Mr. Buffalo spoke volumes. The two sat down with the most dumbfounded expression Karen had ever seen. It was obvious their intention was to intimidate the attendant to a seat change. Their faces indicated they hadn't counted on what they'd just experienced.

Karen nodded again and returned to the galley amid smiles from the attendants. She adjusted her jacket, retying the belt with just enough tautness to keep it closed but sufficiently loose for her to whip open with one motion. She felt good in the jacket with matching silk jersey tee and Linda brand stretch denim pants.

Winthrop staggered into her condo bushed. Checking her messages the first was a blocked call. The second was from Tom Hortonn. What! She hadn't seen the guy in eons until the academy and now he calls?

Mumm, she thought, wonder what he wants? She rolled her luggage into the bedroom, stripped, jumped in the shower, and dressed in her usual sweats from the U of Ottawa. Back to the living room with her view of the golf course through which she and Jessica had jogged, she chose a tall, long stem wine glass, topped it up with Cuvee St-Denis chardonnay, sipped, then went to the kitchen and came back with a section of brie and oyster crackers.

As Karen savored the view, wine, and snack she pondered her non-existent love life which had been non-existent for so long she wasn't sure how to approach the call. She felt silly considering he may have called professionally. Up out of the couch, over to the answering machine and hit the play button before she chickened out.

"Hi Karen, Tom Hortonn. I know you're out of town, but I wanted to leave a message you could consider while you're away. It was excellent seeing you at the academy and I was wondering if you'd like to grab dinner when you get back. It would be fun to catch up. I thought maybe The Calgary Steak House. I heard Soul Train is the manager."

Well, there it is, she thought. What now? She liked Tom but they had always been just friends, studying together, pizza and beer after class and such. She'd never thought of him in a romantic way. But hell, her love life sucked, so why not. At least she knew he wouldn't stand her up or be an asshole like the last guy.

She picked up the phone and called the cell number he'd left. "Hortonn," he answered in his very cop commanding voice.

"Hi Tom, Karen Winthrop."

"Hi Karen, great to hear from you, you got my message?"

"I did. I just got in a little while ago from an eight-day rotation and am beat. But your invitation sounds great. Tonight would be terrible as I'd probably drop my face in the steak. You available tomorrow night?"

"I am. How about six? May I pick you up?"

"I'd be delighted. Six o'clock it is. Save you parking, I'll meet you at the front door. Is that okay? You know where I live? "

"I do. See you then. And Karen, I'm looking forward to catching up."

"Me too Tom." And they clicked off.

After Tom hung up, he did the one arm pull down and yelled, Yes! Then called The Calgary for reservations and to see if Soul Train was working tomorrow night. Reservations for two at 6:30 and The Man was on. He left word with the hostess to let Craig know they would be there.

Jason and Jessica met up in the administration building. "We've a two o'clock flight on Frontier from Reagan to Denver, overnight there. We have two rooms booked at the Hyatt not far from the airport.

Then a connecting flight at nine in the morning. Nothing but economy available, so we're knees in the face for four hours. The Service will have an SUV for us from our Meeteetse office. And no, I have no idea what the Service is doing in Meeteetse. It's an hour and a half from Cody. Then it's only an hour to StoneHead," said Jessica.

"Sounds good to me. I'll grab my meager belongings, cab to the mall, and meet you at the Frontier counter at, what, one?"

"Okay. Let's go through security with Buster first, and then get lunch while we wait for the flight. That okay?"

"Yeah. See you then." And he headed out of the administration building for the townhouse.

Chapter Thirty-Three

Jackson and Jason arrived at the townhouse simultaneously. As they entered the unit, Jason said, "So, what do you think of our assignment? Certainly different for both of us I would think."

"Yeah, it is. I'm looking forward to working with a team that's solid in its objective rather than with other agents making decisions based on what's in it for them."

"I hear you. It's really going to be interesting to work off your Idaho experience. I find that quite exciting having worked solo for so many years. I've missed bouncing ideas and procedures off colleagues, said Jason.

The guys packed in silence and headed to the main gate together, checked out through the MP's, retrieved their Sigs, checked the magazine and the chamber, holstered, and headed for the gate where two Alexandria Yellow cabs sat waiting their arrival.

The men shook hands, clapped each other on the back and headed to a cab, Jason for Dulles Town Center for his shopping spree, Jackson to the Beltway Mall in College Park, Maryland, about four miles from Rowley.

They knew what they wanted and went store to store purchasing runners, socks, sweatpants and tops, jeans, long sleeve shirts, underwear, dress pants and shirts and shoes. Jackson went a little extra on the dressy stuff for school but figured if StoneHead was anything like his Michigan teaching high school, jeans and a casual shirt and boots would be acceptable. Jason purchased two new pieces of luggage while Jackson stopped by a thrift shop across the street from Beltway and picked up two duffle bags. He figured they would be more in keeping with a destitute new teacher. Each were done in two hours and headed to Reagan.

Jackson was scheduled to fly direct to Seattle where he would pick up his truck. He'd cleared it with Jessica several days ago, thinking the truck would fit his cover perfectly. He'd called Carver at the Seattle office who had obtained a Marquette, Michigan registration and license plates and installed them on Jackson's truck himself. Carver previously had Jackson's belongings packed and shipped to Maryland for storage. The truck was all that was remaining of Jackson's time in Seattle. His plan was to drive from Seattle taking Highway 90 all the way to Laurel, Montana and come into StoneHead from the north on Highway 72/120 to create the illusion he'd traveled west from Michigan.

Jessica met up with Elisabeth and Rebecca at their town-house. The agents went about their packing chore with little conversation, each concentrating on the task at hand, getting to their assignment and cover.

They were packed and at the guardhouse within forty-five, checked out, received their Sigs and were off in the Alexandria caravan. Elisabeth went directly to Reagan where she was scheduled for a four-hour Northwest Airlines flight to Des Moines, Iowa where she'd rent a vehicle for the two-hour drive to Omaha.

Sorento had a used vehicle in Omaha with a registration showing she'd owned it for ten years. She'd overnight in Omaha, and then headed west on Highway 80 into Wyoming, and then north on Highway 25 and eventually west on a series of state highways to StoneHead. She'd scrutinized the area maps at Rowley and knew her residence address. She'd been over and over her cover until she felt she was leaving Omaha High school for StoneHead. Sorento had greased the Omaha school district bureaucratic wheels, so their records indicate her continuous employment since obtaining her Masters. She knew her computer knowledge was superior and felt confident she'd be successful with her cover. She would shop somewhere in Cheyenne before heading to StoneHead.

Rebecca knew she didn't have much to purchase and felt guilty she wasn't going to run up a sizable bill for Sorento. She was flying into Missoula today, would meet Derrick at the airport with the truck and cover information. She'd stop in Bozeman, Montana as a break from her five-hour drive to StoneHead and shop at one of her favorite western wear stores, The Corral. She'd be able to get just about everything needed, maybe even a new pair of Tony Lama boots, considering her current pair had a rip across the instep. Good soles though, she'd just had them redone in Flagstaff.

Jessica watched the two agents head out then went back to grab The Bug and get home to pack. She had run this process through her mind numerous times and knew exactly what was going with her. Armani would stay home. She'd take casual boots, jeans, sweatshirts, blouses, and a heavy jacket. She was packed and in an Alexandria cab on her way to Reagan within ninety minutes from leaving Rebecca and Elisabeth.

She'd stopped by her neighbor to let her know of her extended absence and left Sorento's number in case of an emergency. No hamster. No cat. No fish. Geez, she thought, the only heartbeat in this place is her own. She'd fix that when she got back.

Fukishura arrived at Buster's office as Jason strolled up, his dreadlocks flapping with his quick movements.

"Hey Jessica, been waiting long?"

"Nope just got here. Let's get through security and eat. I'm starved."

"Lead the way. I'm ready for burgers and fries."

They headed to the security office and found Buster in his office busy with another potential problem with an aircraft which just landed from Italy. "Hi Buster! We're heading to Denver. You have a couple of minutes to process us?" asked Jessica.

"Hey, Hi Jessica. All done at Rowley? And I see that Agent Spencer cleans up well" he offered with a smile. "Welcome back to Reagan. I'm starved. You guys have time for something to eat before your flight?"

"Thanks for the compliment, Buster. I was pretty bad when I arrived, I admit. And yes, we have time. We're heading to Sam's Brew House in the post security area."

"Sounds good to me. Leave your luggage with the duty guard and he'll see it gets to Denver with you. I'll just tell my staff my whereabouts and we can go through security."

Buster rose from his desk, shook Jessica's and Jason's hand in welcome, held the door open for them, walked into the main office and told the security officer his destination and they headed out into the main corridor. He passed them through security quickly, then went on his handheld and advised Frontier of their carry status. Sam's was just on the other side of security, and they were able to find a seat in a corner facing into the corridor.

"Hi Buster, what can I get you guys?" said the twenty something brunette.

"Three coffees and some menus, Bonnie. Thanks."

After the caffeine arrived, Jessica said, "Buster, how are things going, generally speaking, with passengers and security?"

"Depends on where and when. If we look at the country as a whole, there are leaks a plenty. Take Phoenix Airport for an example. They call it Sky Harbor Airport. An ABC investigator did a piece on them recently where she found a 4.5-hour time frame each night when TSA-Transportation Security Administration guards left their posts with security guards taking over.

The security guards were allowing anything or anybody into the secure side of the airport. She found, with hidden cameras, there were no metal detector or X-Ray machine. Guards were observed admitting employees with backpacks un-searched. Suitcases passed through unchecked, and pedestrians strolled through checkpoints unchallenged. Information from Phoenix law enforcement indicated one guard admitted he was asleep for twenty minutes while on duty.

"And this isn't just us. Your agent Peltowski? When she came through here for Rowley, I thought I recognized her name. She was the author of an internal MI6 report on Heathrow's security. This was several years back. She documented security guards socializing while passengers walked right by, checked their luggage, and boarded international flights. She had one of her Brit friends do exactly that and photographed the incident. I thought for sure it would be her demise with MI6 and she'd be persona non grata."

Jessica couldn't help smiling to herself. Although MI5 and MI6 were two different agencies and co-operation was often minimal, similar to the FBI and CIA, or CISS and the RCMP, but in this case she could see them sharing, MI5 being responsible for internal security, and ostracizing Elisabeth.

That was the reason for Elisabeth's being frozen out of MI6, not her gender and not her skills. Son-of-a-bitch. Well, nothing Elisabeth could do about it other than make sure she never got posted to England again. Not much chance of that. A screw-up on the Protection Detail would probably get her posted to Haskell, Vermont (small town on the Quebec border).

She made a mental note to contact the Seattle Agent in Charge to see if they had any intel on the Phoenix airport in relation to *Christians for a Better America.* How easy would it be to load explosives at night at this airport? Ditto Phoenix. Scary she thought.

"I never heard a thing about it Buster, must have been kept in house with MI6. I wanted to ask Karen about the Canadian border and if they had any specific problems, but we got to shopping and I forgot."

Buster gave a huge guffaw with that comment, and everyone joined in. Buster had three teenage daughters.

"Jason, Karen Winthrop is an Air Marshal with the RCMP. We met on my flight to visit my folks in Toronto last week. She is one tough cop I tell you. I hope you get to meet her. Actually if I could figure out a way to get her to join us, I'd do it in a heartbeat."

Seattle's Secret Service Agent in charge, Carver, was fastidious in the interrogation of the Christians for a Better America leadership arrested in Idaho. The FBI SWAT-Special Weapons and Tactics team had flown their captives to Lewiston where the chopper was refueled for the remainder of the flight to the Bureau's secure site at an unknown airfield northeast of Twisp, Washington, between Little Buck Mountain and Blue Buck Mountain where the FBI maintained a renovated farmhouse and outbuildings.

Carver was flown from South Boeing Field in Seattle to the secret location.

The team was met by other agents who took charge of the prisoners and their interrogation. At first glance, a hiker or ranch hand would assume the facility was nothing but what it appeared; a small hobby ranch, operated by a retired couple from Seattle. Chance visitors would have no idea that the couple were counter terrorism FBI agents who supervised the facility.

The CIA conducted interrogations at Guantanamo Bay, using waterboarding, a process of pouring water over a suspect's face not allowing them to breath, forced sleep deprivation and similar techniques which were the key to obtaining information.

However, the FBI had years of successful interviews and knew what worked. They didn't have to threaten to kill captive's family, rape their mothers and similar atrocious acts. Gaining trust, explaining options, and creating a positive environment produced results.

Or so they claimed.

The social workers who questioned the women from the compound found several who were disenchanted with the commune relationship, wanted out and saw an opportunity to tell all to the FBI in exchange for the witness protection program for their children and themselves.

These women were flown to the Twisp location for interrogation. It was there and with these participants that the FBI discovered the compound was really nothing more than an Idaho based polygamous community but had done nothing illegal. The women told agents that there was nothing at the compound that was illegally acquired and therefore they couldn't be detained.

The women further sited the British Columbian Bountiful polygamous group under the leadership of Winston Blackmore and James Oler where charges against the men were determined to be in violation of their religious freedom, Bountiful being a faction of the Fundamentalist Church of Jesus Christ of Latter-day Saints based in Utah.

U.S. federal attorneys present couldn't connect the women or children with the explosives but couldn't determine the validity of their statements. Some of the interrogators questioned the compatibility the women who professed to be living their chosen life at the compound, wondering if it was rehearsed.

Chapter Thirty-Four

The server left with their order and the three continued to chat about general law enforcer issues, everyone staying away from any hint as to where Jessica and Jason were headed. Buster could find out their destination if his curiosity got the better of him, but his years of experience told him otherwise. He was always curious though.

They'd enjoyed their meal and had just finished when they heard their boarding call. Jessica placed four twenties on the table telling Buster it was her treat and no arguments. Jason and she bid Buster a farewell then headed to the boarding tube for Denver. They introduced themselves to the attendants, stored their carry-on in the overhead and settled into their seats. They hoped their flight would be uneventful and were looking forward to a good night's sleep at the Hyatt. Their Rowley experience had been grueling, and they both needed down time before they started all over again in StoneHead.

Jackson, Elisabeth, and Rebecca arrived separately but almost simultaneously at Reagan, each spotting the other heading for security. Jackson held back and grabbed a seat at the Starbucks, while Rebecca did the same at a Cinnabon, allowing Elisabeth to go through Buster first.

Buster wasn't fazed by the stream of agents heading through his airport making for different destinations. He greeted each with enthusiasm, processed and walked them through security; bid them all the best and returned to his office to process the next. Jackson was the last through.

Jackson arrived in the late afternoon to the hustle of one of the west coast's busiest airports. He grabbed the first cab in the cue and headed for the federal building on Second in Seattle. The weather was unusually mild and sunny as he made his way through the government building's foyer, showing his ID to security and heading to the underground secure parking area.

Down the elevator and out on the lowest level. Few vehicles. He spotted his beauty immediately, parked in a corner under a bright overhead light. He removed his spare key from his wallet, threw his bags behind the seat, not wanting to chance rain or snow ruining his new threads. He did a few knee bends, jumping jacks and push-ups, getting the flight kinks out, then slid behind the wheel.

God, he loved this truck, he thought, as a big grin came across his face. He ran his hands around the steering wheel, over the dash and the seats. He extracted Andre Bocelli from the console. Into the disc player and cranked it. He sighed as Bocelli's voice sent the familiar tingles up his spine. Turned the ignition key. Hit the accelerator and let the engine's rumble echo and bounce around the garage's acoustics.

As Bocelli hit a high note, Jackson put the truck in reverse, backed out and headed up and out onto Second. He was anxious to get across the floating bridge, through Mercer Island and up into Snoqualmie Pass where he'd hit the afterburners.

Elisabeth landed in Des Moines without incident. She'd had her bags flagged at Reagan, so they'd bypass the passenger luggage area in Des Moines. They were waiting for her at the security office. She presented her ID to the duty guard, grabbed her bags, got a rental and was on the road to Omaha within an hour. She had to admit she loved the perks the badge offered. She breezed along Highway 80 into Omaha and headed for the Hilton Garden Hotel on Dodge.

Five minutes around the curves of Abbott Drive and the seven-story haven loomed in the foreground. Parked the rental. Overnight slung over her left shoulder, her jacket open, she headed for registration. Her Nebraska College of Teachers' identification got her a suite for $100.00 a night. Sweet! She smiled as she headed for the elevator and the seventh floor. She found her suite, used the pass card, and entered.

Peltowski closed and locked the door immediately and then walked around assuring herself of the room's security. Satisfied, she did a quick clean-up and headed back down to the lobby to the Nebraska Steak House. The restaurant was almost empty, spotted a corner table and had the hostess escort her.

She settled in, ordered a chardonnay, fillet, baked russet, and grilled vegetables. After her wine arrived, she relaxed and watched the other diners, wondering what inner secrets each had that were hidden by facades. This was always an activity on which she could never flip the off switch. Tomorrow she'd collect the computer system held for her at the Omaha Service office on Capitol, just a few blocks from the Hilton. But for now she would enjoy the time alone, a nice meal and a good night's sleep...if she could shut her mind off configuring the high-tech security systems she would install.

Jackson basked in the joy of the truck's performance, complimenting himself on the wise decision to take it with him to StoneHead. The miles flew by with a fuel stop in Moses Lake, Washington and one in Green Acres. He arrived in Coeur d'Alene just after the dinner hour and booked himself into the Shiloh Inn for the night. He freshened in his room then headed out for a relaxing evening before having to deal with tomorrow's drama. Shiloh's night manager suggested the Hot Rod as something different for dinner. With a name like that, Jackson knew he had to give it a try.

He found it easy enough with the manager's directions-town not really that big. The decor did the name justice. The exterior reminded him of fifties drive-ins. The interior was wall to wall cars and truck photos. He settled into the booth furthest from the front door. A server appeared immediately with a menu and asked if he'd like a drink. He ordered a coke. A quick menu glance and he found what he wanted. The Blue Lincoln Burger: ¼ pound patty-coated in a black peppercorn crust and smothered with Lincoln Shire bleu cheese. He motioned the server over and gave his order asking her if she had Hot Rod Wings to go with his coke. She had. She did.

He sat back with one leg on the bench, eating with his left hand, instinctively leaving his right hand on the table. He was engrossed in wide screen racing events when his burger and fries arrived. He ordered coffee and dug in. Man, he thought, this is some burger. Good combination the blue cheese and peppercorns. He was ravenous and the meal disappeared quickly.

He sipped his coffee watching more races. His server came with the check, and he asked her what was happening in town that night. She said that Coeur d'Alene was a hockey town with a game that night at the Skate Plaza between the local women's team and the University of Idaho. It had been a long time since he'd been on skates and even longer since he'd seen a woman's game. He recalled with fondness the games at Northwestern where the women played with skill and not force. He had been glued to the television during the Olympics watching the Canadian Women's Hockey team dominate the games with the American women taking the Silver.

This would be good he thought. He had time to burn and couldn't think of spending the evening with television, so he paid his bill, left a fifteen percent tip, and headed over to the rink, arriving at the end of the first period.

Rebecca was the last to leave Reagan after Buster's processing. Her Delta flight was uneventful albeit the annoying male stares. She realized, as she walked the Missoula airport concourse, that she was getting tired of it and at the same time acknowledging she brought the larger percentage on herself. But fuck, she thought, why must I wear clothes to downplay my looks? Her mom tried to get her into skirts and blouses and as early as she could remember, and she'd change the first time her mom's back was turned. By the time Rebecca entered kindergarten, her mom had given up and Rebecca was the only girl in class with the boots and jeans. She smiled to herself as she continued her walk, remembering her teachers trying to get her to remove the hat.

When she was in her early twenties she found it flattering, but since she hit thirty and had been competing with men for so long, she found it both boring and annoying to have to deal with what she felt were intrusive looks. Get a life, she thought. She really wanted to flip them off. My God, she thought, those guys over in the corner wiring the lights, actually stopped work to glare. Morons! Screw it, not my problem. Although she did wonder now and then if her anger was what she was getting out her system when she arrested bad guys. She'd never had a use of force charge against her, but she often wondered if it was just a matter of time.

She spotted Derrick as she rounded the corner from the Delta desk. He was leaning against the restaurant's entry dangling a set of keys as he spotted her. Derrick was one of the good guys, married to a classmate from the U of Montana with three kids. He'd moved into management with the sheriff's office and was one of the team a woman could feel comfortable working with knowing there would never be a gender problem or a come on.

They'd worked many cases during her time with Flathead law enforcement, many dealing with drug smuggling from Alberta and Saskatchewan. They'd made a good team with solid arrests, Derrick having to pull her off more than one foul mouth asshole.

She grinned as they spotted each other. She strolled up and gave him a high five. "You're lookin' great Derrick. Nice to see you and thanks for coming. I hope we haven't put you out too much. Looks like the Airport Restaurant is nice. Can I buy you a burger?"

"Nice to see you too Rebecca. I see you still draw the male crowd. I watched them as you left the arrival area. I often wonder how you get any work done having to deal with that all the time."

"Not a problem Derrick, let's get something to eat. How are Sue and the kids?"

They headed into the restaurant and grabbed a corner seat sitting side-by-side so they could both observe the doorway. Habit they both accepted. Derrick no longer wore a uniform, so his firearm was in a hip holster on his right side. He adjusted himself so his right leg extended somewhat outside the booth. Rebecca sat on his left with her jean jacket open. She had a tactical advantage over Derrick. Seated, she had quicker access to her Sig than he did his Berretta.

"Sue and the kids are doing great. Sue's back teaching elementary and the kids are active in just about everything available. I often wonder if they're too active, but they choose themselves, so we let it be."

"Great to hear it. So, tell me about my job in StoneHead. Who's my client?"

"His name is Tom Radke. He has a two-year-old colt he wants you to saddle ready. He has a round pen, so you don't need anything but your skills. You're working for me, and I have a pick-up outside for you with my stable name on it. Should add a little to your cover. If there is anything I can do either professionally or personally without breaking protocol or your cover, call me on my cell. Will that work for you?"

"It will. And thanks Derrick. From me personally, my boss and the Service. You've gone above and beyond, and we appreciate the support."

"My pleasure. I knew the minute the Service snagged you away from Flathead, you'd be a success and I'm getting a kick out of helping."

"How about we order and go over any details?"

"I'm good with that," said Derrick. He raised his hand and got the attention of a server. She came over and he said, "Pattie Melt and fries for me."

"Make that two," said Rebecca. "And two coffees please."

The server left and came back quickly with two coffees and left a stainless thermos.

Rebecca and Derrick exchanged a few additional details then chatted about their time together in Flathead. "Do you remember one of the first cases we were on together," asked Derrick. "The one, what was that guy's name, fancied himself a mountain man. Can't remember but you'd just joined the department and our RCMP intel indicated Mountain Ben was coming into Glacier with a pack train of Methamphetamine through the Trail Creek valley from Alberta's Waterton Lakes National Park. We cut his trail early one morning, and you tracked him for what, about five miles when he stopped for a leak. You remember that?"

Rebecca laughed, "I do. I was so rushed with getting my first doper, I almost screwed us if it hadn't been for you telling the guy we were newlyweds. I was going to take him down immediately, but you wanted to get between him and his horse to prevent a getaway.

I'll always appreciate your giving me the nod that day. Man that guy almost shit himself when I pulled my jacket back to show him my shield and Glock. When he bolted, I felt like a million bucks running him down then cuffing the bastard. Great fun wasn't it?"

Derrick was smiling at the memory. "The guy was so sure he only had me to take out. The look on his face when you dropped him and stuck your Glock in his ear was a career memory for sure. You know Rebecca that arrest made your bones with the department and probably was instrumental in the feds looking at you down the road a few years later with a few more arrests like that. You miss that action?"

"I do. I was hoping to get back into it on my last assignment, but I guess that old adage that you can't go home again applies to careers too. But I think I just might have another shot, no pun intended, at action with this new assignment."

With what seemed like no time at all their food arrived. They concentrated on their meal, stopping between bites to comment about a cover question or related query.

They'd been colleagues and friends for a number of years, had kept in touch, so it wasn't a surprise or disappointment when Rebecca said she had to be moving. Rebecca pocketed the truck and cabin keys Derrick had slid across the table, picked up the check.

"Dinner's on me," she said.

"Thanks Rebecca. It was great seeing you again. I know we won't have an opportunity to get together in the next little while so take care of yourself and be safe."

"I will Derrick and thanks for having my back on this, my best to Sue and the kids when you get home. How are you getting home, by the way?"

"One of the Lake County deputies is meeting me here. I just have to call him. He'll take me to Ronan and Sue is meeting me there."

"Sounds good, I promise to take good care of your truck," Rebecca said, as she dropped three twenties on the table and headed for the door, her carry-on slung over her left shoulder.

They headed out the main terminal door and Derrick casually pointed out the truck parked close to the main entrance. It was a late model silver Ford ¾ ton 4 X 4 pick-up extended cab. Geez, pretty fancy. She hoped Sorento was paying for this, but she kept her thoughts to herself. They high fived each other and

Derrick returned to the concourse to be swept up by the hustle of bodies. Rebecca strolled over to the truck, chirped her way through the driver's side, opened her duffle and extracted a couple of CD's, put the duffle in the back seat and climbed in. Missoula Airport was right on Highway 90, so Rebecca was out of the parking lot and heading to Bozeman within minutes. Once on the freeway, she slipped in Toby Keith and cranked. She was in her zone; heading to what she knew would be a career highlight.

Denver's Mile High Airport loomed in the distance as Jessica and Jason stretched, yawned. They were sure the flight had taken eight hours instead of four. They both wanted to sleep during the flight but knew that their inner Yellow wouldn't allow it until they were in the Hyatt. They waited till all passengers disembarked, grabbed their over-nights, and headed for the exit. The captain was thanking the passengers for flying Frontier. As the agents approached, the captain said, "Agents Spencer and Fukishura, my sincere appreciation for flying with us. This is the first flight any of us can remember where we felt 100% safe. Thank you."

Both Jessica and Jason could feel the flush of embarrassment rush to their cheeks but managed to recover enough to say, "Our pleasure captain. Thank you for a safe and enjoyable flight," said Jessica.

They shook hands and departed with waves backwards as they entered the concourse. "Can you believe that guy?" asked

Jason. "I can't recall any time I've ever been thanked for doing my job. How about you?"

"I agree. We don't get that too often. I got a thank you from an Air Canada pilot recently and that was nice."

They walked through the long corridor and exited to the hotel shuttle area and boarded the first one to the Hyatt.

Chapter Thirty-Five

"Young sheepdogs yearn for a righteous battle."

Lt. Col. Dave Grossman

A few minutes post dinner, Jackson was in the rink's parking lot, truck locked and headed to the game. The second period was just starting as he settled into one of the few remaining seats. The University of Idaho was up 3-2 with Coeur d'Alene having a woman advantage on a U of I two-minute penalty. He was pleasantly surprised at the almost sold-out crowd. Usually women's sports drew small crowds making it difficult for universities to obtain a fair share of athletic funding. He wondered if this imbalance had righted itself with the success of the American Women's Hockey team at the Olympics.

The game ended with the U taking the victory with team members congratulating each other in a celebration line after the final whistle. The crowd was happy as they filed out of the stands and into the parking lot.

He let himself be one of the last to leave so he wouldn't get caught in the traffic jam. As he left the arena and spotted his lone truck, his heart sank with the site of a police car parked behind it. "Shit", he said out loud. "What the fuck now?"

Jackson walked up to the truck ignoring the deputy leaning on the cruiser, unlocked the truck and started to get in. "Hold on there partner, I need a word," said the deputy.

Jackson turned to his left facing the cop, "What can I do for you deputy?"

"How about a driver's license and registration for starters?"

"Why? I just drove into town a few hours ago and have been sitting in the arena for the last two?"

"Probably just because I said so partner."

Jackson opened the door, crawled over the seat, and got the registration out of the glove box, retreated back to the driver's side, and handed it to the deputy.

"Okay, now your driver's license."

Jackson reached into his back pocket to get his wallet making sure his jacket stayed closed, pulled the wallet out and slid the Michigan license out and handed it over.

"Well partner, you see we got a real problem here. This truck was run not too long ago in Lewiston by a Nez Perce deputy. It had the same VIN number but a different license plate. You couldn't have been back to Michigan to establish residency. So I got to thinkin', maybe the Nez Perce guys had something when they suspected you might be involved in the drug business down south and also maybe the death of the chief of police there. Any thoughts?"

"You have it wrong deputy. The license and registration are legal and accurate. You have no reason to hold or interrogate me."

"Oh, but I do partner. This here is Kootenai County and I'm kinda the law hereabouts. So if I say we're going back to the station and chat a bit, that's exactly what we're going to do. Now you can come nice and peaceful like, or I can cuff you. Your choice."

"I don't think so deputy, what's your name? Deputy Dog? No, Smith." He glanced at the name tag. You're being an asshole Deputy Smith. I'm going to leave without an incident and you're going to back off this absurdity and have yourself a nice evening." Jackson turned to enter the truck.

Jackson's refusal to co-operate set the deputy off and he went from zero to deadly force as he drew his service pistol and stuck it in Jackson's right ear. Jackson was facing the truck's open door and turned slightly to see the pistol.

"I think you should reconsider my offer partner. I don't want to wake up the coroner just after he's gotten himself all settled for the night."

Jackson couldn't believe this guy's stupidity. He had no justification for his intimidation other than that he could do it. Without hesitating Jackson pivoted on his right toe and stepped with his left pulling his body out of the line of fire (action faster than reaction) grabbing the deputy's handgun with his right hand and then hit the elbow with his left palm locking the deputy's arm. He forced the deputy to the ground then dropped his own body straight down, putting his entire weight on his left knee into the deputy's rib cage and took the gun. While the deputy was on the ground, Jackson removed the deputy's pepper spray canister and collapsible baton tossing them into the nearby bush. He released the deputy's arm, removed the pistol's magazine, and chambered round and tossed them into the bush to join the equipment.

"You just made a major fuck up there partner. You don't have a hope in hell of gettin' away."

"Oh, but I do deputy," Jackson said as he pulled his ID from inside his jacket pocket revealing his holstered SIG. Jackson bent down and showed the deputy the ID and badge.

"If you hadn't insisted on being such a prick, this would never have happened. This vehicle complies with all legal standards. You just wanted to get in a pissing contest and chose the wrong guy. Your ego fucked you. If you don't want a swarm of federal cops down here immediately jamming your head up your ass, you better forget you ever saw me and pretend that your stupidity was a nightmare."

Jackson removed the police car keys from the deputy and tossed then and the pistol in the opposite direction and got into the truck. He drove immediately back to the motel, grabbed his bag and was on the highway within fifteen minutes. He wasn't going to give the moron any opportunity to regroup. He'd drive for several hours and sleep in the truck if necessary, giving some space and time to the incident, letting the deputy cool off.

In hindsight, he knew it was a stupid thing to do. He could have easily shown his ID immediately but pricks like that guy just pissed him off. They abuse the power society gives them. He probably does the same thing to locals who accept it.

He drove for about an hour and realized he wasn't sleepy and was in a groove, so he decided to keep at it. Six hours later he was in Laurel, Montana and pulled off the highway onto a forestry access road, then backed into a clearing, shut the truck off, slid his Sig out and laid it across his chest as he spread across the truck's bench seat. He was asleep instantly.

"Sheepdogs are often female."

Fukishura

Elisabeth was up early and decided she'd maintain the physical fitness she'd gained at Rowley...primarily for her professional survival but also for her personal piece of mind. She had missed physical fitness in London. She threw on sweats and runners and headed down to the hotel's gym where she used the Stairmaster for twenty, then the universal gym for thirty and finished off with the treadmill for a final twenty. She felt alive and excited with endorphins cascading through her blood stream as she headed back to her room in the first elevator available.

She entered the elevator and went immediately to the opposite corner, reached, and buttoned her floor, closed the door then leaned against the back wall with her right leg pulled behind her braced against the elevator wall. At the next floor, the door opened bringing with it a man, in too much of a rush for her instincts.

Presumably a guest, but no guarantees. Five ten or so, fifties with medium length curly grey hair, boozers complexion, 190 maybe. Stocky build. Wearing a dark blue running suit with white leg strips. What brought him to her immediate attention other than his mere presence was his lack of surprise at seeing her at the early hour. A smirk grew on his unshaven face.

Flash to Orange.

He entered, turned, and pushed the button for the top floor then walked to stand beside Elisabeth. "Good morning, great day to be up early. I'm Stan Pinette from Iowa and you are?"

"Someone you don't want to know Stan."

"Oh, now don't be that way. I was just going to ask you to have coffee with me. Good lookin' woman like you shouldn't be alone first thing in the morning. What's your name?"

"Stan, you don't want to be doing this with someone like me."

"Ooooh, what are you some kinda undercover cop, female ninja? Don't think so sweetie. Not someone your size. Come on now, just tell me your name so we can be best friends right off the bat," Stan breathed as he leaned close to Elisabeth's left ear.

He let his right-hand slide down Elisabeth's left leg and snaked it around behind her and cupped her left butt cheek. He was enjoying himself more so because this woman wasn't scared, which could only mean he lucked out this time and found a woman who really wanted the attention. This would be easy he thought as the bulge grew in his sweatpants. His boldness grew with the increase size of his erection as he slid his hand down Elisabeth's butt crack on his way to her crotch, through what he liked to think, the back door.

Elisabeth smiled to herself knowing her reaction was prompting his advances. Just as his hand slipped from her butt she stepped forward with her right foot putting her body at a forty-five to Stan. Immediately, she spun on her left foot twisting her upper body and delivered a whipping back fist forearm smash to Stan's face snapping his head against the elevator wall and forward again. Blood immediately began pouring out his broken nose.

"What the fuck. You broke my nose you bitch," he said as he sprinted forward to hit the stop button. As Stan moved, Elisabeth pivoted again on her left foot, twisted her upper body and hips, and drove her right knee into his chest whipping his upper body back against the wall. She followed that with two knee smashes to his groin forcing Stan to double over screaming. His head was down, hands cupping his groin. Elisabeth placed two hands on the back of his head holding it in place while she drove her right knee up into his face breaking his jaw. Out. She stepped back to let his body drop to the now blood-stained carpet.

Elisabeth reached over and punched the button for the exercise floor where she could exit and take another elevator to her room. She used her elbow to remove her prints from the control panel then noticed the lack of blood on her sweats as the door opened to an empty corridor. She exited, walked the few short steps to the next elevator and entered, her heartbeat never rising above 60. She smiled to herself as she hit the button for her room.

Don't get many dates that way, but it sure was gratifying, too bad more women couldn't experience the rush she thought.

Back in her room, she showered and dressed in jeans, yellow blouse, and hiking boots. Light make-up, brush through her short hair and out the door. She wore a lightweight jacket to cover her SIG. She was out of the room and back down in the steakhouse for breakfast before most of the other guests were stirring.

As she exited the elevator she was met by the cacophony of paramedics and cops hovering around one of the elevators. She could just make out the paramedics talking as they brought their patient to consciousness. The cops were standing back waiting their turn to question the person.

She entered the restaurant and waited for the hostess to seat her. As they were walking to a booth, the server said, "Never seen that happen here before."

"What's that?" asked Elisabeth.

"A guest was waiting for the elevator apparently and when it opened there was a guy lying in a pool of blood. People didn't know if he was dead or unconscious. No one wanted to touch him, you know, because of aids and all that. The paramedics arrived within minutes and that's what's happening now.

Weird."

Elisabeth didn't respond to the server's comments but took her seat, accepted the menu, all the time watching the lobby scene.

Fruit, bagel with cream cheese and coffee. Had to keep with the Rowley diet if she was going to keep the weight off.

By the time she'd finished her meal the lobby was back to normal with a yellow tape across the now closed elevator. She checked out, loaded the rental, and headed up the street to the Service office. Ten minutes total. She flashed her ID at the guard station just inside the federal building and was directed to the fourth floor where was asked to take a seat while her contact was located. She left her luggage at the guard station.

Momentarily a forty something man approached her, hand extended. "Hi agent Peltowski, I'm Jerry Braun, agent in charge. Welcome to Omaha. If you'll follow me to the office area, I'll get you set up."

Elisabeth shook hands with him, commented on the community's friendliness and followed him behind a card keyed door. They walked down a long hall to an end office. Braun opened the door and allowed her to enter, followed her in then closed the door locking it. He moved behind a green, plain, metal government issued desk, sat, spun the chair around and scooted a short distance to the back wall to a safe.

A few twists of the dial the door opened, and Braun produced a large brown envelope and extended it across to Elisabeth. Her name was all that was on the front, plus, "Top Secret. For Peltowski's eyes only."

Braun said, "You can take that into the room next door and secure yourself. The entire office is swept for bugs daily."

Elisabeth thanked him and headed for the secure room's door, opened, checked that it was empty then closed and locked the door.

Package opened. Two sets of keys, one for a vehicle and one for a building door. She pocketed both. The paperwork was simple and brief. Her address in StoneHead was 218 Broken Arrow Trail. There was a photo. It was a 1400 sq. ft. rancher, three bedrooms and two baths. It was a year old with a double car garage. The vaulted ceiling in the huge kitchen was the only exception to an otherwise plain Jane house.

Just what an underpaid teacher could afford. Furnished. The cover team did a good job. Sure looked like it was out in the middle of nowhere. She made a mental note of the phone number, her mailbox number and pocketed the mail key. The vehicle was a five-year-old GM with Nebraska plates and registration. The note stated the registration was in the glove box.

There were copies of her university transcript, a letter of recommendation from her former employer showing she'd terminated recently with a successful teaching history and impressive recommendation. Elisabeth smiled, amazed at the work that went into a cover operation. The Service's paper jockeys were incredible. How they did it was beyond her. But without them, this operation wouldn't be happening.

She double checked all the material making sure she had it memorized, checked her pockets for the keys and returned to the attached office. Braun said, "The shredder is in the corner. I've been directed to have you shred the contents and envelop yourself."

Elisabeth complied, shredding each paper separately. She knew the contents were classified and would be shredded again at the day's end, locked in a secure vault until a contract security firm would arrive to shred it a third time, then remove it to be incinerated.

Braun walked over to the window that overlooked a parking lot and pointed out her ride. "Your requested equipment was just placed in the car which an agent is guarding until you take possession. He has your description so there is no need to make contact."

She noted the car's color and location, gave her Hertz rental contract and keys to Braun, and thanked him for his help.

Chapter Thirty-Six

"Do not speak- unless it improves on silence."

Buddhism

The Christians for a Better America leadership, William Shepherd, and Ken Marrington were hooded and airlifted from the eastern Washington interrogation site to the FBI's Seattle Third Street building, landing on the roof. They were processed then housed in windowless top floor cells. The suspects were kept in separate enclosures; each unit lighted with harsh 500 watts overhead 24/7.

Marrington lay on the bunk wondering what the hell happened. They were sure their mountain position hadn't been compromised. They'd had no fly overs, consequently the government's satellite system couldn't have picked up any intelligence from the buildings and they couldn't know how many were grouped there.

He was unaware of the government's satellite system that can read a license plate number from space. There had to have been a leak somewhere within their cell, but whom the hell was it? He had no time frame concept. He could have been held for days or weeks. He remembered vaguely meeting a masked male outside the barn but no details.

He didn't know their attackers. The helicopters were unmarked. The heavily armed assailants were masked with balaclavas and no uniform markings. He couldn't even tell if they were male or female. But he figured some had to be women, assuming they were law enforcement of some kind, women who didn't know their place in God's design.

None of his and Shepherd's children would ever have such a desire. Well they'd all find out soon enough where America should stand on the separation of gender. He laughed out loud, knowing of course that he was being recorded visually and verbally, thinking about the misdirection he'd given his interrogators.

He knew Shepherd and the women designated to be "ready to co-operate" had given the FBI the same information as they'd rehearsed a thousand times. They convinced their captors that nothing ominous was occurring at the Idaho compound, that the men, women, and children were simply members of a shared faith following the direction of their elders. They offered no explanation for the massive storage of chemicals; for they knew they couldn't be compelled to do so.

The truth of course was that *Christians for a Better America* was designed in typical terrorist fashion with the country divided into cells, locally led, with none in a single cell having any knowledge of the other cells. The group had a leadership school where students, all in their early twenties, studied fundamentalist conservative philosophy and learned to spread their conservative beliefs among the general public.

Colorado Fundamental University appeared innocuous at first glance. Students who displayed aggressive right wing social and religious personalities, fanatics if you will, transferred to a remote Denver campus where they were guided into a subversive society. They learned bomb design and became convinced that liberal political leadership was driving America to financial and moral destruction. Their objective was to destroy anonymously, pointing fingers at mid-eastern terrorists and creating a national fear from which only a conservative federal government could lead the country.

The targets were all the stops during the upcoming senate and congressional campaigns the president would attend on behalf of the Democratic candidates. And the bombs were being delivered by divinity college graduates in stylish SUVs. There were many faithful devotees willing to give the ultimate for the Lord and to get America back on track, back on a God-fearing Road, following His directions.

William Shepherd had faired physically better than Marrington. When the raid began he was asleep with two of his disciples. The attack helicopters shook the main complex as they hovered in the compound's clearing to disgorge its HRT members. It took his brain nano seconds to know he was in trouble, but by then the reinforced front door had been breached with explosives and every room was flooded with masked assailants. His bedroom door flew open, and two assault rifles were in his face before he could get out of bed.

He and his girls were pulled from the king size bed, forced to the floor where additional attackers put knees to his back and forcibly handcuffed his hands behind. He was hooded then lifted and carried to the Apache Helicopter with its rotors at fast idle and chained to a seat with a guard by his side.

He'd heard later that Marrington was found unconscious by one of the outbuilding from a source unknown at the time. He too was cuffed and brought to a second helicopter. Within fifteen minutes the two choppers rose as one and headed west. He had no idea what transpired next at their compound. He was kept confined for an indeterminable time, and then questioned relentlessly.

His interrogators didn't tell him that after he was airlifted off the mountain, other helicopters arrived and took all the women and children to a prearranged secure housing complex at the Ft. Lewis Military base south of Tacoma, Washington where they were met by a bevy of social workers and female FBI agents who interrogated them as well, albeit, in a less physical manner.

Shepherd knew few people understood their motivation, least of all his captors. So many had forgotten history's lesson put forth by America's founding fathers; Patrick Henry said in Virginia's Ratifying Convention in 1778, "Guard with jealous attention the public liberty. Suspect everyone who approaches that jewel. Unfortunately, nothing will preserve it but downright force. Whenever you give up that force, you are inevitably ruined."

Shepherd knew that with Bakus' overwhelming victory and the Democratics controlling the House and the Senate, public liberty would be consumed by exorbitant taxes, firearms control, and negotiations with America's enemies abroad. His solution was the only answer. Americans had to know the reality of the Democrats' evil path and the direction it was taking the country. With Bakus and a large number of democrat legislators out of the way, conservative Republicans would rise to the challenge bringing America back to the Lord's intended political right.

Already a number of Republican legislators, both state and federal, were seeing the value of the conservative Christian message, that the combination of intellectualism and force was the only way to return the country to the successful leadership of the early '80's and the likes of Ronald Reagan.

He knew these politicians acknowledged the success of the Republican presidency in using a big stick in dealing with foreign governments. The Tehran hostage disaster still made his blood boil, knowing that a conservative president with conviction would never have allowed Americans to be humiliated and tortured by those rag head Islamic fanatics.

Christians for a Better America received confirmation of their direction constantly, albeit not the ultimate objectives, by conservative think tanks across America. One in particular stated in a national press interview that, "The push to recruit young intellectuals is an investment in future allies."

Shepherd interpreted such comments as being words from God. Even a number of university deans were supportive as noted by one California educator, "Education in the last few decades has ignored religion and the *CFBA* is creating resurgence in traditional intellectualism and the recovery of our historic roots."

Shepherd smiled to himself as he settled back on his spartan bunk, knowing his and Marrington's physical presence wasn't necessary to reach their objective.

Shepherd felt smug and confident that he and Marrington had succeeded in blocking the government and directing them to defend their position against *CFBA's* religious freedom. Oh, the Lord gave him tremendous ingenuity and conniving skills he acknowledged.

Jessica and Jason were the last aboard the hotel shuttle. The Hyatt was the first on the driver's route and they were there in less than five minutes. They struggled with getting their bags out of the center luggage area and barely had two feet on the tarmac when the bus pulled away. Jason yelled, "You have a nice day too fella!"

They made their way into the hotel's lobby and the registration desk. The clerk addressed Jason first. He nodded to Jessica who said, "We have reservations for two rooms for tonight under Fukishura?"

"Yes, ma'am," responded the clerk as she keyed her computer, coming up with the required data. She slid two registration forms forward with two pens. The agents completed them as vaguely as possible and slid them back across the counter. Jessica offered her personal credit card to the clerk who swiped it and returned it to Jessica.

Five minutes got them to the top floor. Rooms side-by-side.

As they were heading for the elevator Jason said, "I don't know about you Jessica, but I'm beat. Any problem with us each doing room service then having breakfast together tomorrow?"

"I was thinking the same thing. I'm game."

"Okay then. What time tomorrow?"

"How about seven?"

"Good for me. By the way, no discount?"

"I sometimes do. Depends on the situation. We'd have to show our ID's then she'd get emotional, run for the manager, and create a lot of kafuffle. For two bucks? I think Sorento will forgive me."

They exited on the sixth floor and found their rooms quickly, each keying their door while the other watched the hallway. Instinct. They entered their separate rooms and said they'd see each other at the Gallery Cafe in the lobby at 7 am.

Jason locked the door behind him, made a security check, then threw his luggage on the rack. No mini bar. Shit, he thought. He found a menu, chose a large Greek pizza, dialed room service, and added two Buds. Twenty minutes they said. He peeled off his clothes, taking the SIG with him into the bathroom. Laid it on the toilet. He lavished under the warmth for ten minutes, toweled and donned the complimentary robe.

The knock came just as he exited the bathroom. His SIG was in the robe's left pocket as he viewed the peep. Room service. He opened the door, stepped back allowing the busboy access. His left hand never left his pocket. He scribbled his name on the bill and showed the fellow out. Lock. He placed the SIG on the bed beside him and dove into the pizza and Bud. Oh, the beer was so smooth. He downed half the pizza and the first beer before he grabbed the remote and started surfing.

Jessica showered, passed on dinner, turned on the television, climbed under the covers and fell asleep, waking seven hours later with her phone alarm.

Rebecca covered the miles to Bozeman quickly and with excitement and anticipation, alternating her listening pleasure between Toby Keith, Beyonce, and Michael Bublé. At her last fuel stop before hitting Bozeman, she asked the gas station attendant if he knew of any good places to overnight in Bozeman. She was sure by the expression on the teenager's face that he wanted to say, "With me." Instead, he told her of his aunt and uncle's B&B called Fox Hollow.

The way he described it, she figured it was as good as any place and certainly out of the way and the limelight. She was using her personal credit card with her real name for the first time in months and it took her a little while to realize that clerks could obtain her personal information.

On the final leg of the trip to Bozeman, she changed her mind about the B&B. She figured it would be too difficult to conceal her SIG, she couldn't very well come to breakfast wearing a jacket without drawing attention to herself. She blew into Bozeman, stopped at Bubba's Burgers, chicken burger, fries, and a chocolate shake. She woofed it and stopped at the first decent looking overnighter, Big Country Motel.

She was beat. No chit-chat with the front desk clerk. Gave her personal credit card and off to the requested ground floor room. No high-tech key card here, just brass. Better than the easily copied magnetic strip she thought. She opened the door, checked behind her once more, into the room, shut and locked the door. Check the security. The bathroom window was pretty flimsy and easily breached. She left the room, down the walkway and around back to a small grove of aspens. Used her Apparition and cut a four-foot sapling, trimmed the branches, and headed back to the room. She jammed the natural dowel into the window slide to prevent it being opened. Next, she moved the desk chair to the door, tilted it backwards and jammed the back up under the doorknob, wiggling it into place. Sig across her chest, she drifted off.

Chapter Thirty-Seven

Jackson woke with a start as the sun bounced off the truck's side mirror hitting his eyes, jarring him to consciousness. He sat up slowly, his Sig in hand, craned his neck to check out the passenger window, then swiveled, checked out the driver's window and slid out, belly first, dropped to the ground and slid under the truck. He laid motionless, listening for any human sounds, grass or pebbles disturbed, twigs breaking or the shallow breathing of an attacker in waiting.

Nothing.

He crabbed to the rear, just under the differential. Waited again. A fast crawl, out and into the bushes to do surveillance again. Satisfied he was alone; he relieved himself with his back to a large aspen, then quickly returned to the truck, did thirty push-ups, one hundred crunches and fifty jacks then motored back to the Interstate.

He found Mickey D on Fourth Street was just opening for the day. Everything fresh. He loved the Chipotle BBQ Snack Wraps. Ordered two, plus an Angus Burger, loaded, and a large coffee. He sat in a corner booth, watching the main door and parking lot. He didn't expect deputy dog to arrive since this wasn't his jurisdiction, but he could have radioed ahead. Not too likely either given he'd be out of a job, but instinct ran Jackson's behavior. He was surprised he was relaxed and enjoying the morning quiet with a fast-food dining icon.

Thirty minutes later he was feeling pretty good. Hit the restroom then headed out. He found Interstate three-ten, took that south; hooked up with seventy-two to the Wyoming border where it became their one-twenty. If any locals spotted him coming into StoneHead, his direction would be a logical choice from Michigan. He had no idea if Elisabeth had arrived or her residence location. He stopped to refuel and freshened, then headed for the school district office on Cody Ave.

Superintendent Sauldez didn't keep him waiting. He greeted him cordially and led him down a narrow hallway to his office. Shut the door. Lock.

"Great to meet you Jackson, Sorento has everything ready, and I've done my part. There won't be any question about us hiring outside the district since we advertised, and no one wanted a temporary job. Your paperwork is in order. You're coming here from Marquette Senior High where you taught World History.

Considering your background I think the students are getting the best of this deal. Here is the text they've been using and a synopsis by the teacher of what she's covered to date. They'll be prepping for their state exams during your time here and I've included copies of several previous state exams for your perusal. You have a couple of days to prep and maybe you'll want to drop by the school and meet Brenda Scarsdelli, the teacher you're replacing."

"Sounds good Mr. Sauldez. Thank you for all your support. We couldn't have pulled this off without your relationship with our boss."

"My pleasure agent. If there is anything, anytime, anywhere, with which I can assist, please don't hesitate to ask."

"I will keep that in mind sir. Thanks again. I'd better find my accommodation and get settled in. I'll see Ms. Scarsdelli after lunch."

His paperwork noted his digs were on Nez Perce Creek. A two bedroom, 1 ½ bathroom house which would give him privacy but not seclusion; the latter would tend to alienate him from his new colleagues. Five minutes from the district office. He drove right past the high school on his way to Nez Perce Creek. As he approached his new residence, he was taken aback with what he saw.

He parked in front, grabbed his bags, and headed up the walk. As he made his way to the front door, he 360'd, giving himself a good idea of his surroundings.

An open field across the street that ran for about ½ mile in each direction without any structures. The house was a refurbished ranch house with a well treed lot/acreage. He walked around back and noted a garage set back to the right and what looked like a heritage barn further back on the property. He had no idea of the lot or acreage size, but there weren't any other houses within sight.

He keyed the back door. Bags down. Locked the door. He spent a good thirty minutes reconning the house. No basement. Crawlspace. Nothing there but a water holding tank. No spiders. Exterior doors were quality heavy wood with three-inch dead-bolts. He'd add another to the bottom of each. The windows were double paned and opened out with a quality lever latch.

The living room's vaulted ceiling was pine paneled with a glass front wood stove. Auxiliary heat was individual room baseboard electric. The furniture was a classic western well-worn couch with two matching occasional chairs, Navajo pattern. Sorento would love this, he thought. The kitchen had knotty pine cabinets with a breakfast bar and two stools. The dining room looked out over an expansive yard and a view of pastures beyond the weathered barn. Each bedroom was decorated with a double bed, a highboy and dresser.

He chose the room furthest from the living room and dropped his bags on the bed. The ½ bath was off the kitchen which made it convenient coming in through the back door. The main bath was off the hallway leading to the bedrooms and was standard fair with a tub/shower combo with curtain, toilet, and sink. There was a pine medicine cabinet over the sink and another on the wall behind the toilet. Very comfortable he thought. He'd add his own alarm and intruder system in the next few days.

Pennington walked out the back door. Locked it. Meandered to the detached garage and opened the side door to find nothing but an empty work bench with a long florescent light system hanging overhead and several beer neon signs on the walls. Jackson walked back outside and noticed the lack of a garage lock. He'd rectify that too. He headed back to the truck and drove to StoneHead Secondary to meet Ms. Brenda and see what she thought of her temporary curriculum writing assignment.

Jason woke before his wake-up call, hit the bathroom, did a hundred and fifty crunches, fifty push-ups, slipped on his sweats, runners, fanny pack with the Sig, his ID and was out the door by 5:30 putting in a forty-five-minute run around town in the dark. On his return to the hotel, he hit their exercise room for another thirty-minute work-out on a universal gym.

Back in his room he showered and dressed in jeans, solid red long sleeve button down and hikers. He was enjoying a coffee in the Gallery when Jessica arrived. Their server sprinted up just as Jessica sat down. The detail lead ordered black coffee as the server gave them menus. A quick perusal and they had made a choice. Jason was having their el burrito-scrambled eggs, pepper jack cheese, tomato basil tortilla and salsa. Jessica was having the gardener's frittata-basil pesto, tomato & asiago cheese, and roasted pepper sauce. They were early so their food arrived quickly.

The duo small talked about Denver. Neither had been there before. Jessica asked about Jason's family. A mother in Los Angeles still enjoying the family home.

They finished their breakfast, paid the bill, headed back to their rooms to hit the bathroom, brush teeth etc. and were at the Hyatt's shuttle with plenty of time for their flight. Sky West Airlines had curbside check-in, so they received their assigned seats and were headed to security within ten minutes. They knocked, then entered the airport's security office and were greeted by a female security agent. Jessica introduced herself, presented her credentials and introduced Jason who did likewise. Very quick and efficient. The security agent took their bags, walked them past the security check points, and introduced them to the flight attendant taking tickets. They were whisked into the back of the coach section taking their seats right next to the flight attendant jump seats.

Jessica had called the StoneHead Ranch the previous night to advise Lela and Kate their estimated ETA. The flight was short, and they had a vehicle waiting at the local airport with keys left at the security office. They relaxed as the plane taxied and was airborne with no waiting in a take-off queue. Ninety minutes went quickly. Coffee, a Danish, a trip to the restroom and they were there. Passengers paid them little if any attention, a credit to their years of experience blending in.

The senior flight attendant took them personally to retrieve their bags and the keys to their vehicle at security without any questions, although Jason and Jessica knew she was just bursting to know what they were doing there.

Thank god she said to herself, the SUV wasn't black. She figured the only reason they got metallic green was the blacks were all taken. She checked the registration and found the Service actually had leased it for an indeterminable time. They threw their bags into the large cargo area and headed to StoneHead, Jessica driving.

Elisabeth drove six hours to Cheyenne without incident. The hacker chose a Hampton Inn with secure underground parking for the night. The rooms were comfortable with complimentary blow-dryers and an in-house restaurant.

The agent checked in using her personal credit card and chatted with the clerk, telling her she was relocating to a new job in Wyoming. Never too soon to start spreading deception, she figured.

Peltowski used a key card, accessed the underground parkade, checked to ensure there was twenty-four-hour vehicle surveillance, and brought just her overnight bag to her room, ensured the surveillance equipment would be safe in the trunk. Room service was offering ribs, slaw, and fries. She grabbed the phone immediately and ordered, changed into sweats, removed what little make-up remained, threw some water on her face and was ready when the food arrived twenty later.

Chapter Thirty-Eight

Jason and Jessica were motoring from the airport to StoneHead and the Western Ranch when Jessica's encrypted Blackberry went off. She pulled it from her waistband and handed it to Jason to check the message. The message read, "Welcome to the ranch on a beautiful sunny day Jessica and Jason. Dinner is ready. See you soon, Kate and Lela."

Jason asked, "Do you know these women?"

"You bet. They are the best. They run Bakus' ranch with their husbands' help. They all have top security clearance from the Service. I think you'll like them. Lela is Kate's daughter who taught at American military bases for years before she met Dean, then taught in Washington until she and Dean retired to StoneHead. Retirement wasn't for them so now they manage the Ranch along with Lela's mom and dad, Kate, and Andy. I don't know if you've ever seen anything like this place or not. I often compare it to British Columbia's Douglas Lake Ranch near Merritt which runs about twenty thousand head of cattle on about thirty thousand acres of public grazing land.

"StoneHead has about three thousand deeded acres with access to another ten thousand of BLM-Bureau of Land Management land for grazing. Bakus' herd was considerably larger before politics. I don't know if you're aware, not everyone is. Bakus is a structural engineer with a law degree who got in on the ground floor with wind and solar alternative energy.

"When he accepted the Democratic Party's nomination, he had to divest himself of all his interest but was able to keep the ranch as long as it was scaled back. Kate and Lela run about eight hundred head with hand-picked ranch hands that have either been with Bakus forever or with Kate and Lela for at least five years. All have the highest security clearances as well, making it very easy to set up our security system.

"The structures are very impressive but are going to be a challenge for our installation team. The ranch house is turn of the century with eleven bedrooms and six baths on three floors over eight thousand square feet. There are a number of other smaller ranch houses for the managers, ranch hands and guards, before scaling back, Bakus had separate managers for the crops, machinery, cattle, and cowboys. Then there are the bunkhouses for the single hands; two for female employees and two for the men. And yes, there were quite a number of female wranglers and still are for that matter.

"Often the female sheepdog is superior to the male sheepdog."

Fukishura

Winthrop spent the day running errands, doing laundry, and cleaning her condo. She was ready at 5:30 in an Italian white/brown striped buckle caban, brown halter top and wide leg cuffed off-white pants. The evening was going to be warm enough-no need for an additional jacket. It was on evenings such as this-dates-that she felt naked without her Smith, but the force was adamant about off-duty carry. She compensated by carrying her Bench Made belted knife in her waistband.

She was ready for the evening and spent the remaining few minutes commiserating its ramifications. What was Tom up to? Did he really want to catch up or did he want something more? This will be a very interesting evening," she told herself as she headed out of her condo after setting the intruder alarm.

The U of Ottawa grad had just stepped out the condo's main door when a brilliant candy apple red '69 Pontiac GTO Judge rumbled to the curb. Out stepped a smiling Hortonn wearing a white and blue pin stripped long sleeve button down oxford, two button camel hair sport coat, pleated tan slacks and cordovan tassel loafers.

Very impressive thought Karen as he swung around the GTO, gave a cheek kiss to Karen, took her gently by the arm and guided her to the passenger door. She swore Tom actually skipped around the rear of the GTO and into the driver's seat. Bigger smile now. "You look fabulous Karen. Very nice outfit. Gucci? You do his design justice and acclaim."

"My, my, you do know how to turn a girl's head Mr. Hortonn with the flashy '69 GTO and GQ attire. Thank you for the compliment. You look pretty fab yourself."

The Calgary was a five-minute drive so no time to chat as Tom maneuvered the commuter traffic. The Judge growled to the curb at the Calgary. Two valets immediately. The GTO's buckets were so low, she was thankful she was wearing pants. The teen helped her up and out and Tom was there to take her arm into the restaurant. As their eyes adjusted to the interior's ambiance, they saw Soul Train leaning against a mirrored wall watching them. He pushed himself off the wall and walked slowly forward with his hand out in greeting. "Karen, great to see you again, and Tom, what has it been, twelve years?"

"Hi Craig, something like that. Karen told me about the great time she had here recently. How long have you been the GM with Calgary?"

"About five years. I came from their Whistler operation. It was a great opportunity. Jamie and I love Ottawa. Never thought I'd return but I found I'd actually missed it and then I was transferred here the same year the last of our two children graduated from high school.

"I have a table for two off by itself. The evening is yours. No second seating" He laughed at his reference to restaurants working to have two and sometimes three rotations per table in an evening and staff working the service to coincide with that policy.

Craig lead the way past the impressive bar to a corner table with white linen, two tall dark red candles in brass holders with a low white daisy arrangement nestled between the holders. Craig held a seat out for Karen, then for Tom, handed them the wine list and said he'd return shortly. Karen was wondering if he was going to complement their meal as he had the last time but figured he'd upstage Tom by doing so.

She was right.

"This is really nice Karen. It's been quite a while since we've been out together, and I don't recall us ever being able to afford The Calgary. Anything for which your taste buds are clamoring?

"Fillet and roasted vegetables would be fabulous. How about you?"

"Let's make that two. How about a Caesar salad too?"

"Okay by me." She was hoping the evening would progress to mouth-to-mouth garlic, then was surprised by her thoughts.

Tom was glancing at the wine list, "How about a Pelee Vineyard 2007 Cab/Sav? It received good reviews in the Ontario Wine Review."

"Why Mr. Hortonn, are we showing off our sophistication?" Karen laughed.

"I gotta have something. I can't impress you with my employment accolades."

"The wine sounds inviting. So, yes, the Pelee would be great. And Tom, you impressed me many years ago and I don't think you could move that needle further up the scale."

Tom was so taken aback by the comment; he felt his face flush with embarrassment. He swallowed a couple of times and was figuring out what to say when their server arrived.

Saved, thought Tom.

"Mr. Stevenson said you folks are very VIP so I'm doubly honored to be your server. I'm Janis. What can I get you folks to drink?"

"Karen, would you like a cocktail?"

"Yes, please. Tell Mr. Stevenson, I'll have his Blue Goose special. Tom?"

"I'll have a double Chavis straight."

After the server left, Tom said, "That was so hilarious Karen. Craig is going to be blown away."

"Spur of the moment. Let's see what I get."

They were commenting on The Calgary's decor and how happy they were for Craig to be so successful in a very competitive business when Janis returned with their drinks. "Sir, a double Chivas, no ice, and ma'am, an Orgasm on the Beach. I know there's a story behind that because Mr. Stevenson just about fell off his stool laughing and insisted on making it himself.

Enjoy. I'll be back shortly for your order."

"Actually, Janis, we know what we want."

"Okay."

They gave her their request, Tom asking for his fillet medium well and Karen medium. Janis left smiling trying to figure out the relationship between this couple and her boss.

Tom took a couple of large swigs and immediately felt better, the nervous pit at the bottom of his stomach starting to quiet itself. He was looking at Karen enjoying her Orgasm as she glanced around the room getting her bearings. She caught him looking at her.

"What?"

"Nothing, I'm just thinking how beautiful you look tonight and that my returned call produced this enjoyable, fortuitous experience."

It was Karen's turn to be embarrassed and she wasn't hiding it. "Thank you Tom. I must say your message created considerable consternation given we spent all those years hangin' without a hint of interest beyond friends."

"I figured that but couldn't think of any way around it. I appreciate your accepting the invitation. It's been quite a few years since Ottawa and after seeing you at the academy and hearing all of what you've accomplished, it brought my morbid and unsuccessful dating experiences to light. Finding a woman with beauty and brains without a desire to crush a guy is pretty difficult. I realized after seeing you that I had to give it a try, to see if you might be interested in seeing me socially."

"Interesting you should feel that Tom because I'd given up on dating. The last guy I went out with met me at a hole in the wall. Wasn't only a bore but five minutes there and he wanted to know if I'd come back to his apartment. This is what's out there. Or so I thought until your message." She raised her glass, not realizing the symbolism or her drink's name.

"Why thank you ma'am," said Tom. "I hope I live up to such praise."

"You already have Mr. Hortonn."

Tom quickly changed the subject, feeling the return of the face flush. "Tell me how you know about GTOs."

Karen laughed at his embarrassment. "Some of my layovers are long and I try and find something to do in each city. I was drawn to muscle car displays at malls. I remember one in particular in New Orleans held in the Louisiana Super dome. I admired the Pontiac GTO and fell in love with a burgundy one on display. It had thousands of dollars in restoration and modifications.

"When you drove up to my condo, yours sounded identical to the New Orleans one. Which I must add, I saw demonstrated on a quarter mile track behind the stadium. The female driver clocked nine seconds at 135 mph. The sound sent chills up my spine. I loved that car but at the time I figured it wouldn't fit my lifestyle. I'd end up paying to have it parked 365."

"Wow, I'm really impressed," Tom said raising his glass just as their wine arrived.

The sommelier arrived and presented the 2007 cabernet sauvignon. Tom nodded his approval. Calgary's wine expert removed the wrapping in one motion, swung her corkscrew from her waistband with such precision Karen was taken aback. The cork slid out with ease and Tom was offered a taste. He approved and nodded. The sommelier poured Karen's glass then filled Tom's, nodded, and backed away.

Tom raised his glass, "To a beautiful evening with a beautiful woman. I hope this is the beginning of many more enjoyable times together."

Karen raised her glass, caught Tom's eyes, held his stare, and smiled taking a sip while she held his gaze.

"Where did you get the Pontiac, if I may be so bold as to ask?"

"I needed new wheels and wanted something different. Not that I want to stand out, I just didn't want the same ol, same ol, that every other guy has. I was browsing through a Buy and Sell in Timmie's, referring to the national donut icon, Tim Horton's, and saw the ad. Called the guy. Fell in love with the first key turn, made him an offer. The guy let me take it to the bank and we sealed the deal in RBC's parking lot.

"I know it probably sounds juvenile, but I love driving it. I love the vibrations the engine's rumble sends through the vehicle and into my body. I love the elaborate sound system and the cornering. I often wonder why I don't have a slew of tickets from squealing corners. It will do 160 mph in eight point six seconds in the ¼ mile. It has a rebuilt 400 cubic engine with added body suspension to prevent side rolls, oversize tires as you saw and a K&N air filter system.

Tom had just finished his discourse when their meal arrived before Karen could respond. Janis placed their respective plates then stepped aside, waiting for their approval. Karen took a bite of her roasted red peppers. Karen heard herself, "Mumm," produced a side glance and nod to Janice, who smiled, nodded in return, and walked away, leaving her guest to enjoy.

Their meal was exquisite, in keeping with The Calgary's reputation. The meat required little cutting and melted in their mouths. The red, green, and yellow peppers, red potatoes, parsnips, rutabaga, turnips, and red onions were tossed with olive oil, salt, pepper, and a hint of heat from Mexican jalapeños. The Caesar was strong with garlic and anchovy but not overpoweringly so.

Their meal was so captivating neither spoke. Communication was an occasional smile and staring at each other trying to prevent the other noticing. Each commented briefly on the delectability of the meal and wine but otherwise neither spoke until knives and forks were placed on empty plates.

"Unbelievable meal. I can see why The Calgary is almost impossible to get into on short notice. I read in MacLean's recently that Toronto's hotshot politicians are regulars. No wonder Craig is so successful."

Karen signed audibly, took a sip of wine, and said, "I agree. That was so delicious."

She wasn't able to complete her thought as Craig appeared in her peripheral with a bottle of Inniskillin Vidal Ice-wine and three dessert wine glasses held between his right-hand fingers. "May I join you two for a couple of minutes and find out what you've been up to recently?"

"Of course you can. Please pull up a seat. Tom and I were just praising the fabulous meal. We can both see why The Calgary is so popular. The combination of fillet, roasted veggies and salad were to die for."

"Thanks. Glad you enjoyed and I hope you'll be back." Craig sat down, placed a glass in front of each and poured a generous portion of Vidal.

"So, tell me, what have you guys been up to for the past twelve years?"

They spent the next hour or so bringing each up to date, enjoying each other's company and laughing when one or the other recalled a particular eventful antic at the Blue Goose or the U itself.

Before they knew it the clock was pushing ten. Tom apologized that he had an eight am meeting and begged his leave. Craig shook their hands and they all promised to keep closer in touch now that they were all in the same town. Craig headed off and Janis appeared from a side anti-way with the check.

Tom perused it and found that the dessert wine was conveniently absent. He peeled off ten twenties and placed them inside the check folder, rose and helped Karen from her chair. As they headed for the foyer, Tom noticed a number of turned heads of several men and smiled to himself. If they only knew her identity... women with guns, they'd run for the back door, he thought.

As they exited The Calgary, a valet ran up requesting their ticket. Tom asked the teen the GTO's location, saying they'd like to catch some air and would walk over to it. The teen handed Tom his keys with Tom responding with a twenty.

Tom took Karen's right hand as they meandered down the block and around the corner to the rear parking area, each maintaining Yellow...with a struggle, finding they were concentrating on each other instead of their personal safety.

As they approached the GTO a dark figure, cloaked in a hoodie, approached them from between two parked vehicles, one hand extended holding a single bladed knife. The thief didn't say anything, just flipped the knife in the air a couple of times and motioned with his other hand in a "give me" motion.

Tom and Karen instinctively separated themselves, Tom moving slightly to his right and Karen stepping left at a 45-degree angle.

"Just stop there lady and give me your fuckin' purse. And you asshole, throw your wallet here and no one will get hurt."

"Sorry my man. I don't carry a purse. What can I give you instead?"

"Don't fuck with me lady. Every woman carries a fuckin' purse for christ sakes. Just give it here and I won't have to cut you."

"Tom, would you like to communicate with this young man, or may I have the pleasure?"

"By all means my lady, the pleasure is all yours."

Karen had never taken her eyes off the thief whose attention had been on Tom. As Tom had just mouth "yours", Karen stepped forward with her left foot while swinging her right leg forward and delivering a bone crunching kick to the thief's right knee. As Thief started to crumble, Karen grabbed the wrist holding the knife with her right hand, pulled sharply to her right straightening Thief's' arm, then delivered an open hand blow straight down against his elbow. She heard the familiar snap. Thief's scream could be heard some distance as several diners came running with the parking lot attendants.

"RCMP folks. You, with the blue jacket, call 911?"

"Very well executed Corporal, thank you for your expertise," said Tom as they both leaned on the Judge hearing sirens approaching. Thief was alternating between holding his arm and knee, crying out in pain. Karen hadn't removed the knife which remained on the pavement by Thief's feet.

TPS was on the scene in less than two minutes with three cars screaming into the parking lot. As the officers exited their vehicles and ran to the scene with drawn pistols, Karen and Tom raised their arms holding their respective ID's. Tom was the first to speak.

"Sergeant, I'm Tom Hortonn with Toronto Transit Police and this is Karen Winthrop with the Horsemen."

The lead officer holstered his weapon as the other two took up positions at angles covering Karen, Tom, and Thief with their weapons. The ID's were offered and inspected by the TSP who returned them and nodded to the other officers who then came around the Judge to inspect Thief.

"What the hell happened here Sergeant?"

Tom explained the event to the incredulous officers. The lead officer wearing black Kevlar gloves, bent down and retrieved the knife, placing it in an evidence bag. Thief was howling in pain asking for a hospital. Lead smiled at him. "You've got to be the dumbest fuck I've ever met. You chose two police officers to rob."

Lead said to his colleagues, "Get him an ambulance. One of you ride with him and come back for your cruiser later." Speaking to Karen and Tom, he said, "This has been one crazy time. We've had a rash of petty thefts, mostly purses, wallets and iPods recently and to top it off one of the petty thieves was executed just around the corner in an alley. Had his head split in two with a .50 caliber. Man what a mess. That's what we thought we were coming to again just now."

Tom asked, "Any leads on the killer or killers?"

"Not a one. No reason for the guy to be offed like that. Stole purses from women, and men for that matter, up and down the main drag. Would throw the empty purses in alley dumpsters. Was probably what he was doing when he was killed."

"Anyway, can you guys come back to the office and do the paperwork?"

Karen said, "Any chance we can do it in the morning officer? We're both pretty beat?"

"Sure. Any time tomorrow will do. You know the way? Just let me write down your respective job locations etc. and you can be on your way."

"Yes, we do. And thanks officer," said Karen as the duo provided the required information.

Tom opened the door for her and rounded the GTO, trying to keep a straight face while passing the three TSP guys. He gunned the Pontiac, backed out and rumbled out of the lot heading to Karen's condo. As soon as they were out of the parking lot, he started to laugh, and Karen joined in.

"What's so funny?"

"You are. That was so expertly executed I wished I had it on tape for training purposes. And us being too tired, what was that all about?"

"I just thought we might have other things to do with the remainder of the evening."

Tom was so taken aback he almost rode over the curb leading to Karen's condo parking lot. Karen laughed as he regained his composure and found the guest parking spot. He casually exited. Around to Karen's side and opened her door and assisted her out.

She led the way to the condo's rear entrance, entered her security code and pushed the door open, closed and locked it after Tom crossed the threshold. She took his hand as they walked to the elevator. Neither spoke as she pushed the up button. The door opened immediately. Empty. As the doors closed, Tom turned to Karen and let his hand grace her cheek and jaw line, bent down slightly and gently kissed her. Karen closed her eyes and returned the kiss...which was broken by the floor ding and the doors opening. Instinctively they both turned and separated as the doors slid open. Nobody. They walked the short distance to Karen's flat, entered, closed/locked the door. No lights on.

She took him into the living room where Toronto's nightline was resplendent in soft neon with ribbons of taillights heading to the burbs. Karen turned him and pushed at his chest till he collapsed on the couch then gestured with her index finger-one minute-and went to the kitchen. Moments later she returned with two long stems and a cold bottle of Cuvee St-Denis' Chardonnay, placed both glasses on the glass oak trimmed coffee table and half-filled each.

Holding both glasses, she turned slowly and sat to his left, angling ever so slightly and placed her right leg over his and offering one long stem. As Tom accepted the wine, Karen clinked his glass and leaned back, feeling her body sink into the couch's elaborate comfort. Neither spoke, allowing the evening's pleasure to combine with the leather's embrace and the bay window's lure.

Karen's eyes were closed when she said, "I wasn't sure of my reaction to your message and invitation until you drove up. Your smile and gentle manner shouted that this male was very different from the species norm. I'm very happy you called Tom."

"I'm very glad you accepted my invitation. When we met at the academy I realized immediately why I'd pretty much given up on dating."

"What do you mean?"

"I don't mean to sound like a snob, but I just got tired of dating shallow, un-energized, unmotivated women. Like I said earlier this evening, most have but one thing going for them, and they think their looks are all they need. I knew when we were at the U that you'd accomplish your goals, but I was too immature at the time to consider dating someone of your caliber. To be honest, I was intimidated."

"Thank you Tom. But I hope you are not intimidated now." Karen said as she raised her glass, her turn for embarrassment.

Tom laughed, "There are very few attractive, smart women and I'm blessed to have the chance tonight to enjoy your company."

Karen leaned forward and placed her empty glass on the coffee table, reached over and took Toms and placed it beside hers. She swung her leg off his, wrapped her right arm around his neck and gently kissed his ear. She could feel him melt. She reached up and turned his head toward her and kissed him. Gently at first until their tongues met, then more passionately.

Tom felt her body heat as he pulled her tight against him. Karen moved her left hand down his chest and onto his thigh. She broke their embrace, leaned back, and unbuttoned her blouse, revealing a light pink lace push up. She squirmed out of the blouse, bra then helped Tom out of his shirt and pants.

Afterwards, neither spoke until the apartment's coolness caused them both to shiver. Karen got up, took Tom's hand, and guided him into her bedroom, pulled back the sheets, crawled under with Tom beside her.

Chapter Thirty-Nine

Elisabeth woke precisely at 6 am, glanced at her surroundings, taking a few moments to orientate. She dawned her sweats, opened the drapes, hit the bathroom, made coffee, and turned to Fox & Friends. Nothing earth shattering. Finished her coffee and turned to fifteen minutes of yoga, put on her runners, her fanny pack with the Sig and put in thirty minutes around the hotel's neighborhood.

Showered, dressed in what was left of her meager belongings, repacked, and checked out, asking the pleasant front desk clerk for a clothing store recommendation. Christopher & Banks was suggested, and she gave her directions on Dell Range Blvd. Elisabeth figured she'd get a few things to last her for a couple of weeks then shop again in StoneHead.

She found the store quickly and spent the next few hours getting essentials-underwear, bras etc. several blouses, skirts, slacks, jeans and two lightweight jackets, one casual and one a little dressier for school. The clothes were within a teacher's budget even though the bill seemed outlandish. She struggled with getting the packages into her car then headed north out of Cheyenne, put it on cruise and waited for an opportunity to pull into a rest stop.

Traveling Highway 14 along the Pawnee River, about twenty miles west of StoneHead, Jessica and Jason hit the eastern most point of Bakus' property; the land marked by a massive hay field on their right. As the road elevated slightly they could see the field extended to the north for as far as the eye could see. Jessica slowed to show Jason. "This is the edge of the President's property. I don't recall the hay field's acreage but as you can see, it runs to the north to the horizon. The barns to store the crop are equally massive. A lot of his neighbors use round bales, which range from fifty to twelve hundred pounds, but Bakus feels these create too much waste. The cows congregate around the massive quantity of hay, shit and piss and destroy a great deal. Then there are the elk who love a free meal. With traditional square bales, the wranglers put out enough for each cow, spread it in a long trail and when it's gone in a few hours, it's gone. Each cow eats from the strip and can't contaminate the feed." Leaving her discourse, she said, "The main gate is still some distance west but comes up fast on your right."

Jessica kept the large SUV to about forty allowing Jason a tourist's view of his boss' property. After some time, Jason expelled a huge breath and said, "Man, this place is massive."

"About three thousand deeded acres and about ten thousand of BLM land. The Bakus ranch reminds me of the King ranch in Texas, the Douglas Lake ranch, as I mention, in British Columbia or the Gang Ranch also in B.C. Massive operations. Douglas Lake currently grazes twenty thousand head. It's mind boggling."

She slowed as they approached a road opening on their right. She made a sharp turn and came upon a standard metal gate. Jason got out and opened it. Jessica drove through, stopped while Jason closed and latched the gate and got back in the SUV. They drove on for several more miles over the rolling hills until they came upon a massive fourteen-foot wrought iron gate with StoneHead Ranch emblazoned across both gate panels. To the left and right extended a fourteen-foot chain link fence topped with razor wire extending beyond sight east and west. Jessica drove ahead to an intercom and a CCTV's-closed circuit television nested in the chain link fence's barbed wire. She could see two guards with M-16s on the other side of the gate watching her every move. Rolled down her window and pushed the button.

"StoneHead Ranch, may I help you?"

The greeting was somewhat unorthodox in that the guards were not communicating with the agents.

"Hey, Kate, Jessica and Jason here?"

"Hi Jessica, how is my favorite agent today? Jason, nice to have you at the Ranch. What's today's word of the day?"

"Today's word is Athabasca."

Within seconds, the massive gates slid away and after about ten seconds, there was sufficient space to drive forward. She stopped just inside the gate and watched it close behind her. Two guards were watching the process, one to each side of the SUV.

The first guard came forward and asked her for ID. Jason handed his over to Jessica who gave both chip embedded plastics to the guard who stepped backward to the guard house while the second soldier watched them both with his M-16 at the ready. The first guard returned. Jessica and Jason had just accepted their ID's when a third guard and a Cocker spaniel appeared and walked around the SUV several times then left. Next, the second guard appeared with a mirror on a long pole and inspected the undercarriage.

The first guard asked Jessica to move the vehicle just slightly forward to the stop line and cut the engine. She did, allowing the undercarriage to be scanned and viewed by a guard in the guard house operating a high-tech device designed to detect, which Jessica had no idea.

This was all new to Jessica. Her last time here was just after the election and obviously considerable security upgrading had occurred in her absence. She noticed the first guard speaking into his shoulder mike and about five minutes later an armored jeep with four guards appeared on the other side of the second gate, did a U turn and waited for the SUV to clear inspection.

The second gate opened, and they were motioned through. One of the jeep guards motioned for her to drive forward. She did. Jason and Jessica proceed up the long narrow driveway to the main ranch house followed by the Jeep.

Good process she thought as she said, "Takes your breath away doesn't it?"

"Geez does it ever. I've never seen anything like it. I'm talking about the ranch, not the security. I'm glad for his sake that he didn't have to give this up entirely to take office."

Just then they came upon the main ranch house. The jeep pulled away and headed down a lane toward outbuildings. Jessica stopped just as the driveway opened to an expansive parking area. They gazed upon a three-story log house that an urbanite would call a mansion. But this was different. It wasn't pretentious.

It emitted warmth most houses of this size could never accomplish. The house was asymmetrically designed with the main door set more to one side, closer to the six-car garage to the right. The parking area was bordered by three-foot-deep flower gardens with the lawn stretching beyond to the paddock fencing. The curious studs, mares and foals were lined up around their respective areas watching their approach. As Jessica moved the vehicle slowly forward into the area in front of the main door, three black and white border collies appeared from around the garage and approached the SUV with swinging tails and loud barks of welcome.

Just as the vehicle stopped, Kate, Lela, Dean and Andy walked out, the men sporting western style holsters carrying what looked like Ruger .44 Magnums with six-inch barrels. Jessica and Jason got out as the Ranch crew approached. Kate made the introductions with Jason's eyes concentrating on the Rugers. Not able to contain himself, he said, "Guys, just curious, why the handguns?"

Andy replied first, "Everyone is armed here Jason. We carry rifles in our vehicles, on our horses, in the tractors and we have our favorite right here. 250 grains will put a major hole in anybody."

"We've been doing it for decades here Jason," said Dean. "Between bears, wolves and other predators it's just common sense, besides, this is Wyoming. When Mr. Bakus, excuse me, when the President got into politics the need expanded to include two legged predators. The Service was somewhat nervous at first, but the President assured them we were an asset rather than a liability. Jessica, remember Mr. Sorento put us through training so we'd know the routine if the shit hits the fan. You recall those sessions?"

"I sure do, and we sincerely appreciate the support. Not to my knowledge has a president ever had his own civilian protection detail and never like you guys."

"Oh, by the way Jason, Kate and Lela are armed as well. What do you have on you Kate?"

Kate patted her mid-section and pointed to Lela and said, ".25 Seacamp in a waistband holster. Let's get your bags and set you up so we can uncork some wine."

Dean, Andy, and Jason grabbed the bags and headed up the stone entryway depositing the bags in the foyer. Jessica said, "We'll do the bags later, lead us to the vino. It's been a long two days."

"Sounds good," said Lela, as she led the way down the long foyer lined with various western artwork, two antique saddles and various turn of the century tack. The foyer opened into a huge kitchen, resplendent in state-of-the-art commercial appliances and various pots and pans hanging above a preparation island.

At the far end was an equally expansive dining area that was considered part of the kitchen. The dark wormed pine table which sat eighteen was decorated with several large brass candleholders on a long eighteen-inch-wide quilted runner. There were two matching sideboards, a credenza and two China cabinets all polished to a brilliant glow. One wall was devoted to a bay window overlooking paddocks while an adjoining wall held a stone fireplace with a fourteen-foot hearth, mantel, and a fire pit large enough to roast a side of beef.

Creating an oval in front of the fire were two burgundy leather couches and several matching oversize chairs. The fire was pumping soul absorbing warmth which drew Jessica like a moth to flame.

She plopped herself heavily in the corner of the couch closest to the fire and reached over to the oblong ten-foot coffee table, accepted a glass of a 2006 Cowboy Reserve Red from Dean who said, "This is a Wyoming wine from Table Mountain Vineyards in Huntley, Wyoming. We quite enjoy the light body that seems to compliment a meal rather than overpower it. Salute," raising his glass and taking a seat beside Lela, shifting slightly to make room for his thigh holster.

Everyone chatted the language of newly arrived travelers for about 1 ½ glasses then Kate said, "Jessica, why don't you show Jason around while I finish with dinner and the boys wrap up their chores?"

"Sounds good to me. May we take the bottle?" laughed Jessica. "Where do you have us bunking down Kate?"

"Sure. Glad you're enjoying it. How about the last two bedrooms in the first-floor west wing?" Kate said as she made her way back into the kitchen.

Jessica and Jason got up and meandered into the living room with expansive windows designed to follow the vaulted knotty pine ceiling's straight lines right to the twenty-foot peak. Across one wall was another stone fireplace, this one adorned with a mounted horned antelope. The seating arrangement was created to appreciate the rolling hills view and the fireplace.

Jessica explained that the exterior lighting resulted in a twenty-four-hour view beyond the wrap around covered porch and railing system. The floors were tongue and groove knotty pine allowed to age without a sealer or lacquer creating a dull but alluring charm. Jessica often wondered how many cowboys walked these floors wearing boots and spurs before Kate shooed them out.

Jason suggested they get their bags into their respective rooms and wash up. Jessica shared the remainder of the wine, toasted their arrival then headed down the stairs, wine bottle swaying in her descent just as Kate came to the living room and yelled that they had ten minutes to dinner.

Everyone was seated when they'd made their way down the circular staircase. Seating was around the table-end closest to the kitchen. Kate and Lela presented the meal family style, and everyone was helping themselves as Jessica asked, "Kate, this corned beef is incredibly tender. You mind if I ask how you get it to fall away like this."

"Not at all Jessica. Nothing secret about it. My grandma came from Dublin and taught me to simmer it all day in the brine and spices. Glad you like it. Everyone dig in, there's plenty."

"Kate and Lela, do you guys cook for everyone like this?" asked Jason.

"Lela laughed, "No, this is just a special time having Jessica back. We'll cook for you guys for a day or so. Marc Stucki is the President's chef and since the President is out of the country, he offered to assist your team. He'll be here tomorrow. He'll take over and we all can get some royal treatment before all the big wigs arrive."

Everyone had their plates full and was enjoying the corn beef and cabbage. Jessica said, "Are you guys available tomorrow morning for us to bounce security ideas off you for a few hours? We have a solid plan and proposal firmly in place and want to clarify a few details before we contact Washington and get the contractors here."

Full mouths produced nods all around. "Great. How about 8 am? Everyone nod again if you're game."

People were trying to keep from laughing as they agreed to tomorrow's agenda with nods all around.

After dinner, everyone chipped in and bussed their dishes then headed for the living room where Andy had brandy poured. The rest of the evening passed with folks sinking lower and lower in the burgundy folds, absorbed in the fire's warmth as they discussed everything but politics. When eyes flittered, Kate got up and said it was time to bring this day to a close. The rest rose as one, saying their goodnights and headed off.

Jessica closed the bedroom door, dragged over a high back chair, and propped it under the doorknob, acknowledging her actions superfluous given the property security but unable to break the habit...threw her bags in the corner, grabbed her toiletries, brushed her teeth, stripped, crawled under the flannel sheets, and conked.

Jason had refilled his brandy and stepped out of his bedroom through French doors to the backyard and meandered around absorbed in StoneHead's beauty. He found a swimming pool that was twelve feet deep end to end, a hot tub right next to it and what must be a sauna tucked into a corner of Ashleaf Spirea, a white flowering shrub he remembered from his university days.

He walked beyond the pool and could see several large barns, the whinnying brought to him by a cool breeze. Other horses were in large paddocks that wrapped around the property. He could make out wranglers completing their evening chores, closing the barn doors, and heading off to their respective bunks in quads-all terrain vehicles.

He finished his brandy, retraced his steps, closed, and locked the French doors, propped his bags against it, grabbed his shaving kit, brushed, threw his clothes on the floor beside the bed, grabbed a novel he'd picked up at the Denver airport and read about a horse trainer in Florida who got herself entangled in crime investigation.

Chapter Forty

Rebecca woke with a start as the sunlight crept around blinds and caught her right eye. She jumped as though a bolt of lightning had hit the motel. Her right hand slapped and grabbed the Sig as she rolled off the bed, braced her forearms across the covers with eyes lasered at the door waiting for it to burst open.

What the fuck did I hear she thought? Nothing? Man, am I fucked up or what? Couldn't remember any dream, just the head pain. She thought. Fuck, that's it.

No dinner. No wonder she was freaking out. Low blood sugar. She made coffee from the room's machine, found a granola bar at the bottom of her bag, wolfed it, drank the coffee, and felt a hundred percent.

Sig in a fanny pack, knife in her waistband and headed out for the wilds of Bozeman for a forty-five.

She ran through the town's residential area admiring the early morning activity of Middle America. Guys were out grabbing the paper catching sight of her sprinting down their street giving them a twinge of excitement as though Desperate Housewives' Edie was moving in.

Back in her room, she showered and dressed in her usual, slipped on her shoulder holster, inserted the Sig, and loaded back into the pick-up and headed to the Corral on Main Street. She drove by a corner restaurant, Deb's, which looked friendly and as good as any she figured. She rounded the block, found a parking spot on the street, and headed in, her stomach growling. Sat at the back. Server there immediately with the coffee but no menu. "Good morning doll, how are you?"

"Just fine," said Rebecca, "How about you?"

"I'm feeling super doll. Thanks for askin'. What can I getcha?"

"How about a couple of eggs, over easy, bacon and some pancakes?"

"You got it doll, won't take but a minute. Here's this morning's paper. You enjoy the paper and coffee; I'll keep an eye on the door for you."

As she left, Rebecca took a few to try and figure that out. She was used to small town hospitality, hence the 'doll' but the door comment. That puzzled her. She was very capable of multitasking in yellow, reading the paper while watching the door.

She was into the second section when her meal arrived. One glance and she smiled. Good ole country restaurants; great food and lots of it. Her plate was a platter with three eggs, four pancakes and four pieces of hand cut bacon. Deb filled her coffee and was about to leave when Rebecca asked her, "Deb, mind if I ask why you commented about the door?"

"Not at all doll, I took you for law enforcement the minute you walked in. You're carrying under your left arm pit." Her face broke into a mile smile, "My hubby's a deputy sheriff. Ya get to know these things. Enjoy. I'll be back to refill your coffee in a bit."

Rebecca smiled at the comfort. She dug into her meal as though she hadn't eaten in forever, relaxing visibly with a sigh, remembering the constant tension in Arizona.

She polished off everything but the pattern as her mom used to say and was finishing her coffee when it dawned on her. I had dinner last night! At Mickey D's. Geez, good thing I have a high metabolism, or I'd be in big trouble. She got up, left a ten-dollar tip, and paid her bill at the counter, thanking Deb for a great breakfast. As Rebecca was almost to the door, Deb said quietly, "You be safe doll."

"I will Deb and thanks, more than you know."

Rebecca climbed into the pick-up and continued her short leg to the Corral.

The store had just opened as she parked in the small parking lot and entered. She chose a couple pair of Wrangler jeans, several shirts of various colors and styles and a pair of Justin Bay Apache brown cowboy boots. Done in an hour, paid with her personal credit card, put the packages in the back seat and drove back the way she'd come.

She was comfortable with her cover and felt confident she'd find the information Jessica required. Toby Keith and she were off for StoneHead.

Two hours into her seven-hour trip, Elisabeth pulled into a truck stop and slid behind a dumpster. She removed the price tags, threw the boxes into the dumpster, and packed her new clothes in her luggage. She filled the tank, grabbed a coffee and was back on the road in thirty.

The trip was monotonous with flat, barren, arid terrain. She stopped for fuel, the restroom and food but otherwise kept a steady pace at 80-speed limit was 75-and made it in five hours. Plenty of daylight left when she found her new residence on Broken Arrow Trail.

She parked in the breezeway, got out and walked the house's perimeter noting the lack of tracks in the sandy soil. She did a house walk-through with her hand on the Sig. Satisfied the house was empty, she returned to her vehicle and unloaded the equipment through a side door then returned for her luggage. Locked the car. Locked the house doors then settled in to set up her equipment in the spare bedroom.

The agent quickly fell into a smooth rhythm arranging the equipment to maximize space and programming efficiency. Within thirty minutes she was operational on encrypted high speed transmitted via a small portable satellite dish attached to the outside back wall of the house. She sent a message to Jessica advising of her arrival, that she would see Sauldez in the morning and start her job in two days.

She was recording all flagged email activity in the immediate vicinity and those isolated through the NSC-National Security Agency satellite. She programmed for everything relating to the *Christians for a Better America*, religion, explosives and their components, and a variety of related topics to isolate all communications to and from *CFBA* bases.

She created a second tracking system for any Middle Eastern visitors by isolating a variety of middle eastern languages, religious terms/phrases and air traffic control chatter and related traffic.

Finally she created a third tracking system which isolated all the same information transmitted from the Arizona and New Mexico area. Her tracking software allowed her to pinpoint Internet Protocol (IP) addresses to within a few meters of any questionable activities.

Satisfied the system was functioning properly, she set up her personal security system on the equipment itself, the window, bedroom door then the front and back doors and finally an infrared beam across the hallway leading to the end bedroom. If any of the contacts were compromised a signal was sent automatically to her and Jessica's encrypted Blackberry.

Jackson found the high school on tenth, parked in the staff lot, adjusted his undershirt holster with his pistol.

Schools are schools anywhere in the country and he found the office quickly, asked the secretary for Ms. Brenda and was directed to the staff room down the hall.

Ms. Brenda was enjoying an afternoon coffee with colleagues. Jackson introduced himself to Brenda and the others and after a few minutes of chit chat-where he was from, what he teaches etcetera, he and Brenda moved over to a corner couch where they went over what Brenda wanted done in her classes.

The afternoon went well. Brenda shared her surprise at the superintendent's choosing her to develop an overall district approach to professional development but was quick with her appreciation of the opportunity to explore the needed policies and procedures.

Jackson felt ready for the morning and several hundred teenagers. He was excited about being in the classroom again. He knew he could enjoy his short time while drawing out information from the kids.

He knew that teens, once you gain their trust, were incredibly communicative and anxious to impress adults with their local and worldly knowledge. Jackson felt confident he'd acquire whatever *CFBA* intel was available; if not specific to their cause, then about who they were and some necessary background, particularly the who's who in the hierarchy.

Pennington left school about an hour after the last class was dismissed and headed to the Maveric Grocery Store on seventeenth. He introduced himself to several clerks, purposely ran into the assistant manager and made sure his face and teaching position would be remembered. He impressed the employees with his desire to make StoneHead his home. He loaded up on groceries, several bottles of local wine, thanked the staff at the check-out stand and accepted the teenager's offer for help with the bags. Turns out the box boy was an honor student whom he would see first period in the morning.

Next stop was the hardware store for several quality deadbolts and a few basic household tools. He chatted with the staff, telling them where he lived and they in turn giving him the scoop on the property's history. He gassed up at Ron's Exxon and headed to his new home.

He put the truck in the garage, groceries away, poured a coke and spent time installing the deadbolts on the garage-the truck door was barred inside, the front and back house doors and his bedroom. Then he placed the personal wireless security system he'd picked up from Rowley throughout the house-back, front and bedroom door contacts, infrared motion detectors in the living and dining room, kitchen, main hallway, and his bedroom.

The control system was in his bedroom with a battery back-up and activated by a key fob, which was obscure on his keychain. His encrypted Blackberry would be notified of a breach.

He found a barbeque on the back porch with a full propane tank, put on a steak and a foil container of chopped vegetables then sat back in a porch chair and enjoyed the view.

Karen woke with a slow, sloth-like comfort she'd forgotten was possible. Rested, relaxed, and curled up with her head on Tom's chest and her right arm across his stomach. Tom was out for the count.

Winthrop nuzzled his ear and ran her hand across his chest bringing the desired result as he moaned slightly, opened his eyes, and smiled.

"Good morning," were his first words followed by, we need to do this more often."

Karen replied, "We need to make up for lost time. What are you doing tonight?"

Tom laughed, "Anything you'd like, just so long as we end up in yours or my bed."

"Perfect. Now, we'd better get you going, or you'll be late for your meeting. How about I get coffee and some breakfast going and you can shower. You okay in those clothes for the day, or do you have to go home?"

"I'm okay. What did I spend, three hours in them?" he laughed.

Tom got out first and Karen rose on one elbow and watched him walk toward the ensuite admiring the firmness of his butt and thighs.

Better get going girl, she thought, or you'll get him back in bed for more. She threw on her sweats and headed into the kitchen. Coffee going, orange juice from the fridge, sausages from the farmer market down the street, toast and honey and she was good to go.

She had it ready when Tom came in looking very appetizing but already in a business mind set. Damn, she thought, just one more before he left. She should have got in the shower with him. Next time, she promised herself.

Tom came over with a huge grin, put his arms around her waist, kissed her, backed away and kissed her nose, then her forehead. He laid his jacket on the high back stool adjusted his holster and said, "You've been busy, smells divine."

"Juice first, then sausages, toast and coffee. Will that do you for a while? Want to keep your strength up for tonight."

Tom laughed, "You're off for three more? Do I have that right?"

"Yup, next flight is counterclockwise. Gotta keep my brain from winding too tight."

"You hear from Jessica?"

"Why do you want to know about Jessica? Do I have competition?"

"No," he laughed. "You have competition from no one. I've waited a long time to find you. I was asking professionally. First time I'd met a Secret Service Agent let alone one who's with the Presidential Detail.

I've partnered with London and New York Transit personnel seeking better ways to protect travelers and there's always the red tape, the protocol, the egos. But listening to you and Jessica communicate, I'm hoping to learn some techniques to duplicate that with New York. Besides, from the way you guys talked and your training session incident you'd be a great team."

Karen laughed and turned a little red. She hadn't heard much past the first sentence. She was feeling the same about Tom. "Nope, haven't heard from her. Didn't really expect to since she'd mentioned her assignment was classified." Karen didn't mention that she had the encrypted Blackberry or the excitement she felt about the possibility of working with CISS and the Service.

They finished their breakfast; Tom brushed his teeth with her toothpaste and his fingers then gargled. One more embrace at the door and he said, "I'd better go, or my heart is going to bust." He walked to the elevator and was gone. Karen closed and locked the door and headed for the shower to get on with her busy day.

She'd call him on his cell later in the day and to make plans for that evening. The marshal thought of stopping by the market and doing a Mexican dish with a few Coronas. She smiled as she stepped out of the sweats and into the shower. As the hot water hit her breasts a shiver rippled through her body thinking of Tom.

Tonight she thought.

Jenewein was able to skirt the Air Force's SAC, Strategic Air Command's tracking system by following Colorado's canyons, often flying dangerously low over ranch land. He landed and refueled and was airborne for Cow Springs before noon.

He approached the Arizona flatlands skimming sagebrush and rattlesnakes and landed next to a topographic abnormality, a small two-hundred-foot sand mound, the sight of which he obliterated with his propeller driven dust.

He stayed in the Otter while the prop slowed, and the dust settled then exited and walked the short distance to the sand mound shade where he greeted four camouflage attired men, who by all appearances were locals. He spoke briefly to each in Arabic, acknowledging their dedication to Allah, and then guided them to the Otter.

Abida Chahine, Qalat Ghazi, Zaranj Beydoun and Meymaneh Rahmani waved good-bye to their guide who was heading south with the rider less horses to wait his brothers' return. The instructors had been training at the Christian center for several years, spending their down time, from which they were returning, by destroying small targets, usually businesses or community centers, always choosing a different community and different target to prevent authorities an opportunity to develop a pattern.

Jenewein recalled the time he was assisting the newly inducted explosive experts assemble bombs in a hidden cabin in the rock crevasses, when they spotted what turned out to be the FBI approaching. He laughed at the memory, seeing the huge dust storm behind each vehicle, knowing all those following the lead Jeep were blinded by the flying sand. It was so easy to outwit the city boys.

He recalled being able to pack everything valuable on the horses and head into the hills, leaving little trace of their presence. He could never figure out why the government wouldn't hire the locals to track. Now that would have given him a challenge but of course he was thankful the feds remained ignorant. It made his job much easier and so much more fun.

While Jenewein prepared for take-off he offered several thermoses of sweet tea, a favorite in Arabic communities, which he'd prepared at the research facility. The passengers chatted while the plane taxied the short distance to lift-off.

They arrived after dark at the deserted airport, deplaned next to Jenewein's Chrysler Caravan and headed for the Christian facility where they'd begin their next round of instruction in the morning.

The center had its geneses in the Tea Party political movement. Thousands spoke their dissatisfaction with Washington and state politics sending scores of Republicans to Congress tipping the balance of power in the GOPs favor.

Much was expected of the newly elected legislators, but it became clear to many that Washington business was going to be the same old, same old with the national debt continuing to soar, China making greater inroads into American politics by loaning the country close to a trillion dollars and influencing policies.

Many political organizers dropped out in disgust, to put the bitter experience behind them and move on with their lives, albeit with trepidation. Others spoke quietly among themselves and chose to make a difference, in a permanent way.

They were unable to see beyond their disdain for the way politics and politicians refused to change and it was this zeal that propelled them to develop the center and recruit young zealots who shared their convictions and were willing to risk all to achieve their joint end. It was this fervor that drove them to contact Jenewein.

The group's political hatred deepened over the years with some having to be removed from the operation due to their inability to see the bigger picture and the end goal of eliminating the majority of Washington legislators in one fell swoop. Those who were eliminated wanted immediate results, having grown tired of what they considered CFBA conservative diatribe, all talk, and no show.

For the group to have given in to their minority demands would have provided small gains but destroyed not only the long-term goal but imploded the organization. The naysayer were ejected and silenced.

CFBA was primarily older, white educated males, many with ivy league schooling who enjoyed pointing to the American Constitution and those who drafted the historical document and how the writers would be appalled at America's degeneration.

Chapter Forty-One

"Sneak across the ocean in broad daylight"!

Thirty-Six Strategies of War

Rebecca had no difficulty finding the cabin on Dry Creek. She'd Googled from the hotel lobby and found their directions incredibly accurate. Numbers on a post box.

She pulled into the long driveway slowly as it rose slightly. She took in the terrain and got her bearings. The driveway was lined with huge cottonwood trees with a density that blocked out most of the sunlight as she made her way. The creek ran on the other side of the highway and the cabin was nestled across the road and at the base of rock outcroppings about two hundred feet above the roof. No lawn or flowers.

Simpson would rectify the latter when she got to town. She drove into the car port, got out and did a three sixty around the property. Pretty simple structure she figured, probably about eight hundred square feet, property sloping down the driveway to the road and creek. She opened the front door and did a walkabout.

Smelled nice as though someone had just cleaned. Back to the truck and her gear. Lock the truck and into the cabin; one bedroom, dining room/living room and kitchen all one. Should be cozy she mussed. Stone fireplace; probably taken from Dry Creek years ago. Well maintained.

She put her gear away, then called her client, Tom Radke, on her cell, the number and location untraceable, and arranged to meet him the next morning.

She got back in the truck and drove to town for supplies. Dry Creek Road dropped gradually into the community. East and west of the road were more cottonwoods, some groves creating a dark and foreboding aura, dense to the skyline, while further into town, the landscape opened to massive hay fields dotted periodically by small cottonwood groves which would indicate a water source.

She stopped at the White Grizzly on seventeenth, one of the main roads. She gassed up first, chatting with an older guy doing the pumping. Kinda out of the ordinary...having someone pump your gas, so she was somewhat suspicious as to the why. She knew the attendant was prolonging the task, so she encouraged him by asking him to check the oil and washer fluid.

"You in town doing some trainin'?"

"I am. You know Tom Radke? I'm going to start one of his colts tomorrow."

"I sure do. Tom and I go way back. He and his folks and those like them are becoming a rare breed around these parts lately."

Rebecca sensed an opening with this guy. Her years of training and interrogation tweaked her senses. All the years growing up in Montana, she never experienced racism but then there were few non-whites ranching an oddity she never understood.

Never in her years with the sheriff's office or with the Service did she encounter behavior motivated by ethnicity.

In nano seconds her mind raced back to her first university criminology class in which she learned of similar attitudes that manifested themselves in the race shootings in the early '60's in the south. She needed to draw this guy out.

"Things changing here probably just like back in Flathead. Don't know what it really is. Folks movin' out, retirin', kids not taken over the ranches and farms. But not like it is in the prairies with the large companies takin' over whole sections and operating them like factories. You get some of that here?"

"Yeah, we do, same thing. We had hippies move in here during the '70's but they left quickly when they found out the government weren't gonna give them a handout sittin' around doin' nothin'.

So we had a lot of empty ranch houses. With no real work available they were left vacant. Some got sold for back taxes cause folks couldn't sell them or the owners died with nobody to take them over."

"I know what you mean. You remember that group in Idaho livin' on the mountain top? Guy's name was Weaver. His kid and wife were shot by the FBI and ATF? You wonder what brings folks like that to the boonies. Certainly not to try and hide cause everyone knows them. We haven't had anything like that around the Flathead. The most excitement we have is folks gettin' lost in Glacier Park. You get anything like those folks in Idaho?" He'd finished pumping gas, washed the windows, checked the oil and washer fluids and was working on the tire pressure.

Rebecca backed off a little to make sure she didn't push it.

He avoided the question and said, "That Weaver fella, I can understand how folks would come to our area tryin' to get away from regulations and stuff. I can understand folks gettin' frustrated with the President saying he's gonna make changes to the national food stamp program to help folks hit hard by the recession.

What we need is to get a good Republican back in office as Bakus is gonna spend us to poverty. President Bakus, you know he's from around here? Some folks are sayin' that the President is the devil himself in charge of the country. Folks here abouts liked Mr. Bakus until he went all political and favorin' givin' the country away. Family has been around here since forever and him runnin' that ranch out towards Yellowstone. Anyway, your rig is all set there Miss. And thanks for listenin' to an old fart ramble on."

"Thanks for all your work and I enjoyed chattin' with you. I'm Rebecca. What's your name?"

"Mike. Hope you'll make The Grizzly your shoppin' spot while you're workin' with Tom."

"I will Mike. I'll just move my truck over there and do some grocery shopping."

She moved the pickup and smiled to herself. It was so easy and to think she gets paid for this. Went into the store and loaded up on groceries and a few bottles of Flathead Winery's Gewurztraminer. It was a nice dry white wine she'd grown fond of in Montana.

She chatted with Grace at the checkout, so she'd remember her, paid her bill and accepted Mike's offer to carry out her groceries. She offered him a tip, but he refused saying it was his pleasure, repeating himself with hoping she'd make The Grizzly her one stop shopping store. She said she would and got into the truck and headed back to the cabin. Rebecca was sure Mike was whistling *My Town* by Montgomery Gentry.

Parked in the carport, hauled the bags into the kitchen then went into the bedroom, locked the door, and sent an encrypted message to Jessica detailing her conversation with Mike. That done she returned to the kitchen, put the groceries away then poured a generous mug of Flathead and went about setting up the security system she'd been assigned at Rowley. When completed, the cabin was secure with a portable satellite dish on the cabin's backside that would send a signal to her Blackberry if breached.

She made mac and cheese, ate it on the front porch with her SIG on her lap looking down to the distant country road wondering what tomorrow's training session would bring in the way of information for Jessica and Jason. When the sun set, she put her dishes in the sink, checked the security system, and climbed under the fresh sheets, saying a silent thanks for the Service's location specialists.

Jason woke as he often did, naked with a violent jerk, grabbed the Sig before his brain kicked into his surroundings. Survival years. He sighed, threw the covers off and walked over to the window, pistol hanging from his right hand. Gorgeous day with an early morning mist hugging the paddocks and pastures and the sun just peeking over the corner of the barn.

He stretched, ran his hands over his face and hair, ran his fingers through his dreadlocks. Maybe time to get them trimmed a little, he thought. Doubt there'd be anyone in StoneHead who could do a decent job.

He laid on the hardwood floor and did fifteen of yoga, rummaged through his gear for runners, socks, sweats and fanny pack. Stuck the Sig into the pack, checked the zipper's quickness then headed down the long hallway to the front door.

He was surprised to see someone in the kitchen. Guy in his early twenties, about five ten, good looking, oval face with short dark hair wearing chef whites.

Jason purposely made noise as he rounded the dining room table so the person would hear his approach. As Jason entered the kitchen, the guy turned around and said, "Hi, good morning. I'm Marc, President Bakus' chef."

"Hi Marc, I'm Jason," he said as he stretched out his hand to shake.

Marc took it and gave a firm hold.

"When did you get here man, it isn't dawn yet?"

"I got here about two hours ago. Kinda took the night crew by surprise. I'd forgotten the ranch would have security even when the President wasn't in residence. You staff here?"

"We work for the same guy. I'm with his protection detail. Jessica is my boss and she'll be dropping in pretty soon. She's next door to me."

"Well, nice to meet you Jason. I'd better get on with breakfast. Figuring this is my debut, I want it to be perfect. Hope you like Eggs Benedict."

"Love them."

Just then, Jessica came around the corner, "Hey, you weren't going running without me were you?"

"Didn't know what the protocol was for running with the boss," Jason said lightly.

"Don't be silly. Hey, I'm Jessica, the other part of team J and J."

"I'm Marc Stucki, the new chef. Nice to meet you ma'am."

"My pleasure Marc, and please, it's Jessica."

"Okay, Jessica. If you guys want to do your run, I'll have fresh orange juice and coffee ready for you when you get back."

Sounds good to us, J and J echoed, as they headed to the front door.

They were just about to approach the door when a male voice called from down a short hall to their right, "Good morning agents. Do you have a moment?"

They walked the short hall and into a large room filled with monitors. "Bruce Bowe, security detail. Sorry we didn't meet yesterday. We were tied up with electronic maintenance. I saw you guys were up, so I thought I'd introduce myself. Kate told me you would have a meeting this morning to go over the existing security."

"Hi Bruce, nice to meet you," said Jessica.

"Jason, I neglected to mention this last night. Must have been too tired. Bruce heads up the twenty-four seven electronic security. We'll be building on his system."

"Hey, no problem. Good to meet you Bruce, Jason Spencer, " Jason said as he stuck his hand out to shake.

Bruce took it, smiling. Hope I wasn't too forward catching you with the monitor. All the halls are covered of course, and I didn't want to miss you again. You guys going for a run I assume.

The front door will lock automatically behind you and if it were to miss, an alarm will sound in here. Have a good one."

"We will Bruce. Thanks. Marc said he'd have juice and coffee ready when we get back. I know you can't leave here without a replacement, so we'll bring some back to you," said Jessica.

"Sounds good. Thanks."

With that Jessica and Jason walked back to the front door, exited, and ran down the steps and headed out the long driveway they'd entered just a few hours previously. They were serious runners, not chatters, and they ran with a steady pace until they reached the main gate. Twenty minutes. They turned and ran back, both enjoying the brisk clear air hitting their lungs, pushing the red blood cells through their bodies. They could feel the adrenaline soar through their muscles and envelop their souls.

The runners' high.

As they approached the parking area, they slowed to catch their wind and walked up to the main door. Jessica had been here before of course and as her right foot hit the landing in front of the door, she pointed her left-hand wand like, and the door opened.

"Estrogen," she said with a straight face.

Jason was speechless and just smiled as they removed their runners and entered the foyer. Bruce yelled from the surveillance room, "Pretty cool hey guys?"

"You got me on that one you two," laughed Jason. "We'll be back shortly with coffee and juice."

They showered and were in the kitchen in thirty just in time for Marc's promised coffee and juice. He'd just poured when Bruce rounded the corner looking like he was joining them. "Your relief arrive Bruce? asked Jessica.

"Not yet but I'm covered with portability monitoring. This is new since you were here before Jessica. The computer is programmed with face recognition, fingerprint and iris scanning software, so it monitors staff activity but won't buzz me unless an unknown makes a hit on the close circuit televisions. The system covers every camera from the main gate to those on the barns, paddocks, and the outer fence. You guys knew the fence was electrified, didn't you? That's new too."

"Shit, no we didn't," exclaimed Jessica. "Ouch, that would set my hair on end."

"More than that. It would be the end of your career. There's a sign at the main gate and spaced the entire perimeter every ten feet. Touch the fence and the person is coyote breakfast. Speaking of breakfast, Kate and the crew are on their way."

"Great timing," said Marc. "You guys have a seat and I'll bring it in."

Everyone was just sitting down as the rest arrived, kicked off their boots at the door and made their way to the kitchen table. "Good morning you guys. How did everyone sleep?" asked Lela.

"Great," said Jason.

"Me too", added Jessica. "How did you guys get in the house? There are no keys and Bruce is here."

"Whoa, sorry Jessica. That's new too. I'll bring you up to date after breakfast. These guys have a code that allows them to enter the back door only. The computer recognizes them and responds to today's seven-digit code, plus of course they have to scan their fingers and eyes. If they had anyone with them, the computer would have sent an alarm before they got anywhere near the ranch house. The software picked them up as they left their house, which is also under constant exterior surveillance, so no one can approach it without the computer alarming us. Anyway, more of that later. Here comes Marc."

"Good morning everyone. I'm Marc Stucki," he said as he set a platter of food on the table. "My appreciation to Kate and Lela. This morning you're having my Italian Eggs Benedict. There's fresh orange juice in the jugs, coffee in the thermoses there. Toast and jam are in the covered server in the center. If you'd like anything else, just let me know. These Bennies have rosemary, basil, arugula, ham, grape tomatoes, onion and garlic, sherry vinegar and of course eggs. Enjoy."

Marc walked back into the kitchen to bring out additional platters. While he was gone Kate said, "It was the President's decision for Marc to be an intricate part of our team, so he'll be joining us each meal.

Marc came back with two platters filled with his Beanies, set them on the table, removed his chef hat and sat down. "How's your breakfast everyone?"

"Devine Marc. You have quite a talent. And I apologize, but you are too young to have this expertise, "commented Jason.

"Thank you," replied Marc. "I appreciate the confidence. Actually I've been doing this a long time. I started as a dishwasher at the Tack Room restaurant in town while in high school. After graduation I asked for the kitchen and started prepping.

The chef at the time took me under her wing so to speak and sponsored me for my apprenticeship after I obtained my Associate of Arts Degree. Anyway, here I am and very happy to join you guys."

"Here, Here," said Dean as he raised his glass of orange juice.

Everyone joined in the toast with Marc blushing and trying not to show it by serving himself.

Twenty minutes and everyone was done and bussed their dishes to the kitchen. Marc said, "That's not necessary you guys, that's my job."

"No it isn't," said Kate. "Your job is to do your magic, we can bus our dishes and put them in the machine.

Chapter Forty-Two

"Teaching is not an either-or-issue. It is about
what works with particular students."

Dr. Barrie Bennett

E lisabeth had been so exhausted after setting up her security
and monitoring systems, she dumped her clothes on the floor
and crawled under the sheets. Mm, she thought, flannel. It was the
last thought before blissful sleep.

She woke slowly with her 6 am inner clock and slid from the
covers, shivering in the house's morning coolness. She rummaged
through her luggage and shrugged into sweats, wandered into the
hallway, and found the thermostat. Seventy and she heard the oil
furnace kick in. Within moments she felt the warmth blasting
through dozens of floor vents. She peeked into the cabinets hoping
there might be coffee.

Nope.

It took her a few minutes to put the day's schedule in
perspective. Once done, she headed for the shower accepted that
with no food and an appointment first thing at the Middle, she'd
have to skip exercise. She did a few stretches and isometrics
waiting for the shower to heat, stripped, and stepped into the stall.

She dried, dressed in one of her teacher outfits being careful
to pull her blouse out to cover her mid-section holster and the HK
pistol with which the team was outfitted at Rowley. She locked
her Sig in a secure lockbox, also provided by Rowley, that she'd

bolted to the bedroom closet floor the night before with tools she'd found in a kitchen drawer. She returned to the bathroom to dry and set her hair and was out the door by seven.

She headed to "Chris' Cafe and Bakery" on Sheridan which she'd passed on the way in. She was famished and the whiff coming from waffles as she parked and approached the diner was a magnet to an empty stomach. She entered, making sure she was wearing her teacher persona. She'd be dead in the water if anyone picked up on her true identity. Thank goodness, she mused, she was a teacher, otherwise she'd be winging it with questionable success.

The cafe was just starting to fill up, giving her a good sign that she'd picked a local hot spot. She waited until a server came and took her to the middle, gave her a menu and poured coffee. Black. A quick glance at the menu and she knew what she wanted; A two cheese omelet and wheat toast. The server had just seated a couple when she caught Elisabeth's eye and came over. "That was quick. What can I get you?"

Elisabeth gave her order and the server asked, "You new in town?"

"Yes, just starting at the middle school tomorrow. It's a subbing job but I'm hoping it will work into something permanent. I love your town."

"Well welcome." I'm Deb. I've two girls at the Middle, one in sixth and one in eighth. I'll tell them we met. It'll help your first day for the girls to spread the word. What are you teaching?"

"Computer Science. Actually it's keyboarding or touch typing but I'm hoping to liven it up a little with some games they'll enjoy but still learn the keyboard. One eighth grade class is entry level computer analysis and that's a fun course. But kids need the keyboard mastered or else they can't keep up."

"Sounds exciting. Like I said, I'll let my girls know. I'll be back with more coffee and your order won't take long. You timed it just right. In another hour this place is a zoo. Good zoo but crazy."

Deb headed to the order wheel, slipped Peltowski's under the spring, and returned to seat another customer.

Elisabeth spent her waiting time getting a feel for the town and its residents. She'd learned to feel, to interpret vibes, which had helped her in numerous situations, save her London experience.

She was covertly observing two construction workers two tables away when Deb arrived with her meal. She caught the guys' astonished look as Deb set the spread down. Deb caught their look and said, "Don't pay those boys any mind. They're just used to seeing women with your build eating a bagel for breakfast."

"Thanks Deb. It smells heavenly. I haven't eaten since yesterday morning some time."

The mom filled her coffee and headed back to double as hostess.

Elisabeth bent over and drew in the aroma and took a bite of omelet. Just as she'd predicted. Delicious.

Deb came back with another coffee refill fifteen into her meal and dropped the local paper. Elisabeth smiled through a mouthful and nodded her appreciation. She spent the next hour savoring her meal and reading the health section and the latest news in breast cancer survival. She moved on to a piece about a resident who donated a half a million dollars toward a hospice house. Other stories that caught her eye were about an assisted living management company being charged by the SEC-Security Exchange Commission for fraud. This is one impressive community of eight thousand she thought, generous with their money and time and uncompromising in their justice.

This will be interesting to see how folks view the *Christians for a Better America*, if in fact they're here. Her intuition told her they were. It would be unusual for a group to be just over the mountain in Idaho and not be here and elsewhere in Wyoming. She knew from Rowley briefings that the group was huge with the national training center in Colorado; just a stone's throw, so to speak, from here.

She finished her breakfast, left a twenty percent tip, thanked Deb for a tremendous meal and paid the cashier. By now the place was abuzz and two additional servers had joined Deb. Deb hollered after her, "Make my girls behave!"

Elisabeth waved over her shoulder and said she would and headed out to her vehicle, assured she'd made the right impression and that every one of the eight thousand residents would know in an hour that there was a new teacher at the Middle.

She located the school on Cougar easily, parked in the staff lot and headed to the office. She found that the teacher was absent that day and that a temporary sub was in just for the day. The principal expected Elisabeth in tomorrow for the long term. But there wasn't an opportunity to see the lesson plans since the sub had them and she had noon hour hall duty. The secretary asked, "How are you at winging it for a few hours on your first day?"

"Sure. Not to worry. I can handle it. See you about seven thirty tomorrow. And thanks for the support. Almost forgot. I need to stock up on groceries. Any store you'd particularly recommend?"

"Sure. There are several good ones and a couple of the chains but for good products and friendly service, I go to the White Grizzly. You can't miss it just down the road a bit."

"Thanks, I'll give it a try."

Seeing the principal wasn't protocol. With so many substitutes coming and going in any school on any given day, chatting with every sub wasn't practical. Besides, every teacher handled the sub's preparation and lesson plans, making a principal superfluous.

That was a wasted trip she thought as she made her way back out to the parking lot, but not really considering the time spent was an investment given the school clerical staff's support was crucial and she figured she made a few points with them today.

The grocery store was easy to locate. The Sub had cash left from an ATM visit in Cheyenne, so a credit card wasn't necessary, less personal information the better.

Walking into the store a woman greeted her, "Welcome to the White Grizzly. If there's anything you don't see, ask me or ask Mike over there."

"Thank you very much. I'll do that."

She grabbed a cart and started up the first aisle picking up fruit and vegetables then headed along the short dairy section for butter, eggs, orange juice and cottage cheese. The new resident turned down the cracker and pasta aisle and almost bumped into an older fellow stocking shelves. "Woops, excuse me. Sorry about that."

"No apology necessary. I don't need to be takin' up so much space. You findin' everythin' you need?"

"So far Mike", having read his name tag.

"You must be the new teacher we've been hearin' about."

"Wow, news sure moves fast. I just left Deb at the cafe a while ago."

"Oh, we heard about it about an hour ago. All the guys stoppin' for coffee figured you for the new sub in for the computer lady who's gonna try and figure out why teachers need all those professional days and nothin' ever changes."

"Don't know anything about that Mike but, yes, I'm the sub in for the computer classes at the Middle. I'm Elisabeth by the way." She stuck out her hand to shake and Mike accepted.

"Mike," he said and shook her hand. "I gotta get back to work. You let me or Grace know, that's the gal you saw comin' in, if you need anythin'."

"I will, thanks Mike."

She continued her shopping then made her way to the cashier. Grace was as hospitable as Mike and Peltowski could see why they obviously did a good business. After the groceries were packed,

Grace called to Mike over the PA system, "Hey Mike, Elisabeth needs a hand with her groceries."

Mike was there in seconds, loaded the bags in a cart and headed out the door with the hacker rushing to keep up. Elisabeth pointed out her vehicle, opened the trunk and Mike loaded the bags. She offered to tip him, but he refused, saying it was regular Grizzly service. He even tipped his feed hat as he walked back to the store.

Small towns Elisabeth mused. They're the best. She drove back to the house and parked under cover, fobbed the system, and unlocked the door. After the groceries were put the groceries away and a tuna sandwich with pickles, popped a coke, downed, the afternoon was spent with lesson plans.

The computer teacher thought of an approach during the drive from Cheyenne and came up with a plan. Students' computers would be programmed to automatically segue to one of their favorite games once they'd completed the assignment. The task would be timed, therefore key pecking wouldn't work. Too slow.

The agent would also tweaked the games she knew they'd like so they'd be forced to use their Math and English skills as well as basic software knowledge to move from one skill level to another. By late afternoon the lesson plan and the program were designed. She grabbed a coffee and entered the second bedroom to check her monitoring system.

Peltowski just keyed the recorder to view when an email popped up as it was being transmitted. The sender was JohnBoy@yahoo.com and was being sent to a similar ambiguous address, the location of which would obtained with a few keystrokes. The message read, "Need to talk about new material just arrived today. Meet you at regular tomorrow 9 am." The sender was Harold Richards with a home address on Rumsey Ave.

She changed screens and keyed the satellite system and the Service's server, keyed in her passwords and codes and came to the main frame. Harold Richards was a forty-five-year-old white male who listed his occupation as welder with a business address the same as his residence. Mumm, she thought.

Screens switched and his home address was revealed. The property had no outbuildings that would accommodate a shop. Back to the satellite and the main frame. Richards had been deacon of his home church prior to moving to StoneHead two years ago. Coincidence it coincided with Bakus' inauguration. Married, no kids. Wife a homemaker.

The recipient was almost a carbon copy of the sender. Joe Sarkowski was also in town but with an occupation as an insurance broker. An office on Stampede Ave. They lived a few blocks from each other. Rather strange they'd email and not use the phone.

The next two hours were spent reviewing the system's monitoring and storage results. Satisfied she had lucked out in hitting the system; she logged off then sent an encrypted message to Jessica giving her the details of her first monitoring success.

Elisabeth wasn't a believer in coincidences. Mike commented about another newcomer, which of course was either herself or Rebecca. Could Mike be more than a retired guy keeping busy stocking shelves and getting off taking groceries out for women. Too late tonight to deal with it.

Back to the kitchen, the programmer topped the coffee mug and sat in the darkened living room, gazing out the window at night's approach. Her H&K lying next to her on the couch was incongruous with the peacefulness the awakening stars emitted.

Chapter Forty-Three

After the steak and vegetables, Jackson washed the dishes then returned to the deck. He felt himself blending with the corner darkness becoming part of total blackness' unpredictability, energy, and wildness. Stars were the backlight of extended openness and coyote chatter...the entertainment. As the banter grew closer he joined in becoming one with the pack. He saw them in the distance, under a full moon's spotlight, cross the field, stop periodically to woof down a mouse or other unlucky critter. With each of his yip, yip squeals, they'd stop and move closer to him, confused as to the identity of an outlaw canine taunting their society.

Jackson would stop and they'd renew their feeding, circling the huge field, jumping straight in the air then coming down forcefully with their front feet and snapping jaws coming up with a morsel. What he didn't immediately notice was their tight circle was advancing on his location moving five or ten feet closer with each configuration.

He smiled at their cunningness, yip, yip several more times, agreeing to play the deadly game. For if he was in fact another of their kind, they'd decide immediately if they'd invite in or kill. The former would be automatic if their playmate were female. The latter the result if male.

The game continued as they approached. When they were within twenty feet, he changed his sounds to the squeal of an injured rabbit, a skill he'd found invaluable in the hills of Afghanistan. Their reaction was as predicted; immediate stop, regroup and quickly advance on Jackson's location intent on taking advantage of the situation. The six were at the porch railing when his scent hit them like a door slammed on their muzzle. All six stopped abruptly, did a one-eighty, and sprinted across the field yelping madly as though they'd been shot and would never survive.

Jackson rose from his shadows and grinned at the game played countless times while waiting for Taliban convoys he's been assigned to destroy. Waiting for days in the one-hundred-and-twenty-degree furnace and huddled in the twenty degree nights with the Middle Eastern coyotes and stars his only entertainment and sanity.

Back inside. Doors locked. System on. Clothes dumped on the floor. Jackson acknowledged happiness and relaxation he'd forgotten was possible. The H&K lay across his chest, his mind drifted off with positive thoughts of tomorrow's task.

Breakfast done, Jessica, Jason, Kate, Lela, and Bruce excused themselves, grabbed a coffee refill and headed to one of the small conference rooms which Bruce had previously swept for bugs. The room's walls, ceiling and door were lined with lead, preventing the retrieval of outgoing or incoming radio waves. Door locked, they sat at the oval table and started in on their security programming.

Jessica began, "Okay, thanks for taking time this morning to brief us on the property needs. Bruce, other than what you covered earlier, is there anything else that's been added since I was here last?"

"No, that's it Jessica. The perimeter fencing is electrified as I mentioned previously, preventing anyone scaling and trying to get over the razor wire. The identity software is on all the closed-circuit television feed including the front gate. It's not one hundred percent, of course, nothing is.

If the system doesn't recognize the face, it will advise the monitoring operator who will challenge or reject the person at the gate. If recognized, and the person is expected, the guard opens the first gate, and the vehicle enters. The guards then inspect the vehicle-interior, exterior including the undercarriage and the occupants and their identification. Each visitor undergoes a full body scan and complete body pat-down. If the dog doesn't detect explosives and the visitor is accepted, the guard radios ahead and we send four guards to escort the vehicle to the main ranch house. If the system recognizes the face but the person is not expected, or not a staff member, they are either rejected or detained at the main gate. The latter would occur if the guards had an Interpol, FBI, CSIS, or CIA flag on the person.

"ID's are similar in technology to the new passports that contain a chip. The ID is scanned by the guards. Any irregularity of course is reported immediately, and the vehicle and occupants detained. At gunpoint I might add. You can't get in here with just a driver's license. You guys experienced all of this when you arrived.

"What we're most concerned with is explosives at the main gate or anywhere on the perimeter. I believe we need to add another fence identical to the first, the entire perimeter about twenty yards wide starting and ending at the present guard station patrolled with dogs and two person teams with sporadic scheduling and electronic check in points. The guards would be monitored every step of the way by our existing system. We also need to add explosive detecting equipment inside the corridor that will cover the entire perimeter.

"The cameras swing in opposite directions so the entire perimeter is covered one hundred percent, leaving it unlikely explosives could be set next to the fence. But our security system is layered, leaving the next level to the dogs and guards in the fenced corridor.

These guards will be on foot and ATVs, never being out of sight of each other. The next level needs to be a seismic intrusion detection system between the last fence and the buildings. Geophone sensors placed in the earth and the software integrated into our existing system which discriminates between actual intruders and natural disturbances.

"The final layer is the interior security and guards, including Dean, Andy et al."

"That's very comprehensive Bruce. I can't think of anything you've left out. How about you guys?"

"No, I think he's got it covered," said Lela.

"One thing I forgot to mention," noted Bruce.

"We get all our supplies delivered. They're unloaded inside the second perimeter at the guard house then the delivery truck exits, the gate is closed. The dogs check for explosives and the guards scan for electronics. Then the second gate is opened, and our van enters, loads the supplies, and comes back to the house followed by the armed jeep personnel. They stand guard while the supplies are checked again for bugs, unloaded and the supplies opened and stored.

"A problem I have is incoming rockets. I discussed this with Sorento and he's confident the air force's no fly zone and radar coverage will prevent such an attack. The air force's anti-ballistic missile system covers this entire area. If a shoulder launched missile were deployed anywhere within the immediate vicinity, the air force's system would have it destroyed immediately. Also, the army will have continuous recon patrols surrounding the ranch.

"Okay, I'll get this off to Washington and Sorento will have the security team here immediately and install the additional layers. Now, for the next agenda item, we have an exterior security problem."

Jessica explained Jackson's participation in the take-down of the *Christians for a Better America* a short distance northwest of StoneHead, the FBI's interrogation of the two main leaders and the presumed plot to attack The Ranch. She went on to explain the data Rebecca and Elisabeth sent outlining their preliminary observations.

"I'm going to have the Service's surveillance team take over the control of the two suspects in StoneHead Elisabeth discovered as well as Mike at the White Grizzly. I agree with her that the email was not coincidental. I'll keep you posted and if you hear anything weird in town, let us know. Let's make sure we have sufficient housing for the additional guards and installation crew. They might have to double up in the bunk houses for now, but the military cook should be able to accommodate the additional staff."

Everyone headed out to get on with their day and carry out the upgrading. Jessica and Jason went with Bruce to peruse the added security requirements Bruce had described. They came back for lunch and spent the remainder of the day on quads measuring, photographing, and developing the preliminary installation plans.

"Direct Instruction-Stand and Deliver
teaching, thwarts creativity."

Dr. Barrie Bennett

Jackson was up and out on a run before the sun brushed the nearby hills with its early morning blindness. Back at the house he showered, gathered his gear, and headed into town for breakfast. He stopped at *Cassy's Breakfast Nook* on Yellowstone Ave. slipping in between two other older trucks.

The building was designed as a general store taking up half the length and the *Breakfast Nook* the remaining space. He entered and was immediately taken aback to Buffalo Bill days with all the trappings of the eighteen hundreds. Saddles, brass spittoons, a miniature carriage, and untold number of metal signs advertising; everything from Brylcream to itching powder welcoming diners.

Typical of small towns, he was met at the door by Cassy, a woman in her mid-forties, who welcomed him and offered a seat by the window. Not his choice but a teacher wouldn't be particular.

Last night's steak and trimmings seemed forever ago as his stomach growled in anticipation of waffles and bacon. Cassy took his order, filled his coffee mug, and headed to greet another customer.

He was early and his order was ready quickly. He ate, people watching from the large plate glass window, wondering what today's teen adventure would bring. He'd made a tentative lesson plan that laid out Monday, Wednesday, and Friday for co-operative learning experiences. The school ran on a yearlong program with each major class meeting three times weekly for the entire year. He needed to develop student dialog to discover any radical religious intolerance pockets during the short undercover timeline.

He finished his meal, left a moderate tip in keeping with a teacher's income, paid his bill, thanked Cassy, and headed to school. Parked in the staff lot, in the back door and up to the History classroom section.

He didn't pause at the staff room for socializing, wanting instead to get a jump on the day. He busied himself putting the final touches on his lesson plans and rearranging the desks so there were five rows of four on each side of the classroom facing each other.

When the bell rang, he opened his door and stood to the side as students wandered in disheveled and caffeine deprived. He greeted each student and within minutes his class was complete. Close the door; walk to the center-he'd moved the teacher desk to the far corner out of the way. The kids were still confused about the seating arrangement, several of them with deer in headlights expressions.

"Good morning, I'm Jackson Pennington, your sub for the remainder of the year while Ms. Brenda works on the professional development team. She said you were pretty sharp and probably wouldn't need a great deal of time prepping for the state exams and that we could work on something different...if you're game.

In trying something new, there is no jeopardy to your grade if this process doesn't work for you but if it does, those of you going on to college or university will find the skills/knowledge invaluable. Those of you going into the work force will have an advantage over other applicants. Here's how it works. You've been studying World History all year; conflicts, cause, and effects of past events on the present. But it's often difficult for students to grasp the ramifications of hundreds of years of tradition and religious involvement and the violence that the combinations bring to current citizens.

I suggest we start with the Israel/Gaza/Palestinian conflict. We'll work on the research Monday and Wednesday and do the presentations on Friday. Here's how it will work. There will be six heterogeneous groups of four. So to get those, let's start here to my left and count off one to four."

Students were still puzzled but amiable and obviously a little titillated by a change of pace. They numbered off. Then he asked everyone to stand and arrange the desks in six groups of four in a circle. He then asked for all the ones to raise their hands, which they did. "Okay, now you guys take a seat at one of the six arrangements."

When done, he had six groups of four students whose academic abilities spanned the grade curve. "Good arrangement. Thank you for being so quick. Now you need to decide among yourselves who will be the presenter, recorder, evaluator, and cheerleader.

The first two are self-explanatory. The evaluator checks your process and decides as to how effective you were. The cheerleader's job is to keep every action positive, in effect, cheerleading. Let me know if you have problems with this. Mondays we have the library computer room to ourselves leaving Wednesdays to put the presentation together here and Friday for the presentation itself. You can take any position on the subject you like. What we're looking for is an exploration of the cause and effect and conflict on each country and the world ramifications, and possibly a conflict resolution. Ask any questions you like as we proceed through this and remember, to use a cliché, there are no dumb questions. Your librarian has been kind enough to give us today, Thursday, and tomorrow in the computer room so you can get a jump start. Everyone ready?"

Jackson headed for the door, opened it and the students exited in mass, all talking at once. He caught a hint of the general conversations as they passed him with questioning glances, "Who is this guy?"

Jackson followed the students as they headed to the library in another building. He was smiling, remembering the joy of this segment of his practicum. The students gathered around the computers, booted, and began their research.

He was taken aback by their enthusiasm; he figured he'd need more of a sell than this. But he realized he was coming into the tail end of a year's study and maybe a change was welcome. The period went well, a number of questions regarding the assignment, but most were about his background and what brought him to their small town. The rest of the day went equally well with the grade ten classes choosing to work on cause and effect of American History.

"Always change a losing game."

David B. Posen

chey and Brian Sawyer were high school classmates in Lethbridge, Alberta where they followed the curricular programs for success. Del took high school pre-apprentice plumbing courses then entered an apprenticeship program, obtaining his journeyman papers by the time he was twenty-one. He was making thirty dollars an hour in the Alberta oil fields, had a new Ford Mustang, was leasing an upscale condo, had an active social life and thought he was well on his way to financial and personal success.

Brian didn't know what he wanted to do after high school but was convinced he had to decide in grade ten so he could take the necessary classes in eleven and twelve. Counselors gave him a battery of tests to determine his interests and aptitude.

He was shocked to find he had a flare for welding. The school didn't have a pre-apprentice program, so he took the regular high school graduation program and enrolled in the apprenticeship program at his local college, attending evenings.

When he graduated, he had completed two of his four-year apprenticeship program. He too obtained an employment/apprenticeship program with an oil firm and excelled, completing the required hours in fourteen months.

He stayed with the company and thought he was on his way until the first extended spring thaw put him out of work for four months, the length of time Mother Nature took to dry out the terrain. He hadn't saved a dime, thinking he'd always have a continuous money flow.

It was during the sixth week of unemployment that he ran into a fellow partygoer who was passing around dope. Brian thought the guy was another victim of the economic downturn, but the supplier wasn't unemployed; he grew pot for a living and said he netted twenty-four thousand from his six-week crop.

This revelation weighed on Brian for several weeks as the prospect of his return to work became more and more distant; his unemployment didn't come close to maintaining his lifestyle.

By chance he ran into Stan again at another weekend beer party at a neighbors and Brian brought up the topic of entrepreneurship. It just so happened that the guy was branching out and needed someone to run his new operation.

Applying for a drug dealer position wasn't exactly what Brian had in mind when he took the aptitude tests in high school, and he couldn't prepare a resume to present to Stan. He told Brian that his operation was at arm's length and if Brian ever got busted, he was on his own, there would be no trail leading to Stan.

At first Brian was apprehensive to leave what he'd previously thought was a steady job, but the financial possibilities of pot growing were mind blowing. Stan told him he would cultivate acreage southeast of Lethbridge, Alberta to fill orders in the U.S. Between harvests Brian was to produce large steel boxes which would be installed on Canadian Pacific rail cars disguised as toolboxes. The marijuana would be packaged and transported to eastern Idaho to Stan's contacts at a Native American reservation in Idaho where it would be distributed to local dealers.

Turns out Brian's trade was applicable after all.

Brian took the deal, leaving Lethbridge without a fanfare. He just left. Months later friends had no idea where or when he'd gone. Pretty soon he was forgotten as folks moved on with other relationships. He'd hauled a twenty-six-foot trailer with his pick-up and installed it in a remote area southwest of town where isolation was maximized, the growing season the most favorable and transportation to the CP rail cars the quickest.

Stan had purchased an isolated farm left to seed years ago by a family death. Its remoteness kept the property on the market for several years with the price dropping repeatedly until Stan purchased it through a dummy Ontario firm as an investment. The transaction was done completely over the internet and via snail mail with no realtor or buyer ever being on the property. Brian's trailer was miles from the farm providing him a security buffer.

He hauled a small backhoe behind his trailer that was rented in Edmonton for a week telling the rental company he was digging a foundation for a home. The reality was a room ten feet below ground with a twelve-foot ceiling entirely encased in cement. He had the backhoe returned within a few days and spent weeks getting the foundation poured using just a gas operated cement mixer.

He found patience was his most valuable virtue as it took weeks to develop, frame, pour, and wait for the cure, then start the entire process again. When completed it had a 3,000 square foot room with a high-tech hydroponics fertilization system that circulated the nutrients. There were rows of plants with overhead lighting 24/7. Electricity was provided by a diesel generator buried ten feet below ground next to the main grow room with its exhaust coupled with the moisture exhaust from the grow room. He had buried three 500-gallon diesel fuel tanks that fed the generator in series with one filling tube up to the surface.

Brian's pick-up was equipped with one five-hundred-gallon tank in the bed which he built himself. Each hygiene visit to the big city brought back a full tank which he transferred to the underground storage units. The exhaust system was filtered through an elaborate scrubbing arrangement similar to that used in pulp mills to eliminate odor from the manufacturing process...the smell of which is often equated to rotten eggs.

The landscape was returned to its original terrain with grass, rocks and scrub bushes transplanted from further in the bush. Entry was gained through a trapdoor accessed through an adjoining cave. Any aerial surveillance would find no heat emitted from the operation, no vapor trail or odor to identify the presence of humans let alone a multi-million-dollar drug operation.

Producing the first crop was incredibly easy and almost maintenance free once the plants were in pots. While nature took its course, Brian produced the boxes which would be attached to the rail car's undercarriage while the cars were on a side-rail waiting for on-coming trains to clear the track.

One box held a huge quantity of product, and he could install and load ten boxes at a time. Once installed and he was out of site of the rail cars, he would text Stan the box car ID numbers and return to his operation.

The business was cell organized. Stan was growing all over southern Alberta and British Columbia with one grower not knowing the identity of another. Brian took three weeks during the winter when the operation could be self-sustaining in Cancun. His marijuana brought a premium price due to its strength compared to its Washington and Idaho competitors.

One ounce (28 grams) of premium marijuana was sold in major Canadian cities for $400.00 but exported to a much larger and discriminating U.S. market, the price skyrocketed.

Brian seldom saw Stan. His financial share was always left in the Greyhound bus station locker in an athletic bag. Brian would take his share and hide it in a weatherproof cache he'd created near his trailer in another cave. He'd learned from Stan that the quickest road to arrest was a paper trail and he figured few if any hikers would stumble upon his stash. He'd smuggled thousands into Costa Rica over the years flying his own plane from Washington to Limon.

Every two weeks he'd trip to Calgary and treat himself to a motel night with a proper shower, shave, and a once-a-month haircut. He'd learned from Stan that neglecting personal hygiene brought unwanted attention.

He'd learned to fly a Piper Seminole, a five hundred-thousand-dollar twin 180 horsepower Lycoming engines with over 200 gallon fuel capacity giving it almost a 900 mile range on each refueling with a speed of 160 knots true air speed, KTAS, or three-hundred miles per hour.

He'd taken a huge chunk of his savings to have optional equipment installed prior to delivery. The Seminole had a global positioning system (GPS), XM Satellite program, WX 500 Stormscope and an Automatic Distance Finder which set him back a total of $21,000 but the package allowed him to fly from Seattle,

Washington to Limon, on Costa Rica's east coast with just four fuel stops.

He basked in the Caribbean coastal community, becoming a local quickly picking up colloquial Spanish quickly. Tourist pamphlets highlighted Limon's pirate history; he was the 21st century Canadian pirate, hiding in Central American's rain forests.

Travel to and from Costa Rica was as commonplace as travel within Canada, given the number of Canadian entrepreneurs in the Central American country.

He'd purchased a small house on the beach away from tourism, hiding the currency within the interior walls.

Enjoying his one night in an average Calgary motel, he was just stepping out of the shower when his cell buzzed indicating a text. He hadn't heard from Stan in six months, and it was a welcome sound. He flipped open the closure and read, "Meet me tonight, 11 pm at location E." a 7-11 parking lot on Calgary's outskirts.

Brian dressed quickly and headed to the meeting spot, making sure he arrived exactly at 11 knowing Stan gave him a one-minute leeway. He found Stan inside browsing the magazine rack. Not exactly original Brian thought, but it worked. No one paid them any attention. As Brian stood beside Stan, Stan said, "Can you line your boxes with lead?"

"Yes."

"Start doing it. You'll need twenty boxes with the same interior dimensions."

Stan took the magazine he was holding, pulled a Starbucks canned espresso out of the cooler and headed to the cashier, never glancing back, or acknowledging Brian.

This was Stan, thought Brian, who'd learned never to question his partner. He had made him a very rich man.

Chapter Forty-Four

Rebecca was up and running down her lane to the country road before sunrise then back to shower, dress and breakfast on scrambled eggs, bacon, and Texas toast and on the road to Radke's ranch by seven thirty.

As she pulled into the ranch she found Tom waiting for her at the round pen with the bay colt already kicking up his heels looking for a way out.

"Hi Tom, nice to meet you," Rebecca greeted as she jumped out of the truck. "Derrick told me a lot about your operation and what you want with the colt but just to be sure I have it right, can you go over it again?"

"Hi Rebecca, nice to meet you too. I asked Derrick to do this colt because I've had some problems with trainers who put in thirty days and leave out a lot of the basics. When my guys climb on expecting a sound ranch horse, they get something that spooks easily and neck reins when it wants to. I know Derrek's work and figure I'm better off paying the extra to have you come and take care of this colt. If this guy turns out right, you can do all my starters."

"Sounds good to me, I'll get on it right away. And thanks for the opportunity."

They shook hands and Tom left to get on with his day, leaving Rebecca to get acquainted with her new charge. She started by walking around inside the round pen talking quietly to the skittish colt for about twenty minutes, then went to her truck, got a bagel and coffee, and sat on the top rung of the pen eating while the colt tried to figure her out. He wasn't having anything to do with her, which was fine with Rebecca, she expected as much.

After a time, she jumped off the rail, grabbed a long-handled whip, walked into the middle of the pen, and snapped the whip over the colt's rear. He took off bucking and rearing with an indignant air, running around her. As he was about to stop, she snapped it again, keeping him moving. This was the activity; several circles one way, then forced him to change directions. The objective was to get the colt to accept her as dominant. He'd show this by coming to her when he submitted. He refused.

After nearly an hour she put the whip away, walked up to him and hooked the lead rope to his halter and walked him to cool off. She moved him from the round pen and took him over to the barn and a paddock Tom had pointed out. Once loose, the colt ran around bucking to let her know he was still in charge. Rebecca couldn't help but laugh as she'd seen it so many times working colts as a child.

Elisabeth woke to her Blackberry's vibration, entered a series of codes, and read that Jessica had assigned her data to a Washington surveillance team. The hacker pulled on sweats and headed to the kitchen for coffee, poured a mug, then moved to the monitoring room.

There were a number of emails back and forth between the subjects her system had recorded last night. All encrypted with simple vague references, but the intent was clear.

It was Rebecca's presence at the White Grizzly, not her which had stirred conversation. There was to be a meeting this morning at a prearranged location which apparently everyone knew. There was another email referring to a mole at StoneHead.

"Holy Shit," Elisabeth said out loud. "This is insane. A mole at the president's ranch?"

Elisabeth sent Jessica a message and received an immediate reply. Jessica would send one of the ranch staff to the meeting and work on locating the mole.

Jessica was on a quad when her Blackberry vibrated. She stopped to code it and read Elisabeth's message. She had no one to send to check the meeting. Dean. Unorthodox but it was her decision.

She pulled the radio off the quad's handle and keyed Dean on the isolated radio frequency that was scrambled to and from the ranch's main communication center. "Dean, I need you to check on a couple of guys for me in town. The surveillance team will be here in a couple of days, but we need to know what these two are doing. Can you meet me in front of the house?"

"On my way Jessica"

Their quads arrived about the same time. Leaving them running, they dismounted and met between them where Jessica filled Dean in on Elisabeth's problem. Dean would head to town in his own truck and find out where Elisabeth's suspects go and if they met anyone else. She had him take the distance communicator which would record conversations up to three hundred yards. Then she hit Dean with the bomb.

He went ballistic because he obviously approved the hiring of the mole. He walked around shaking his head, running his hands through his hair trying to grasp the ramifications of what he'd just heard.

He got himself together and came back to Jessica. "Let me deal with the meeting first then if it's okay with you, we can sit down and go over staffing and isolate this threat and close it quickly."

"Glad you're taking a lead on this Dean. We'll talk later. No need to share this with anyone else until we have facts."

Satisfied Dean would accomplish his task Jessica returned to planning the security system upgrade. As she drove back to where she'd left Bruce and Jason, she mused about Dean's unorthodox role at the ranch. If he wanted, he could be a Service Agent anywhere in the world, but he loved his lifestyle, sort of a big fish in a small pond. His reputation for protecting the president coupled with the skills he'd learned at Rowley made him quite unique and effective.

She empathized with him and the task ahead to find the mole. Dean would look at the problem as being his, he let the traitor in.

Elisabeth got in some stretching while waiting for her hair curler to warm, had more coffee and decided to have breakfast with Deb again. She needed to cultivate that relationship to speed her classes' acceptance process. Hair and make-up done; the agent checked the monitoring system once again. Nothing. Out the door. Beep the security system active and off to Debs.

The restaurant was quiet as Peltowski once again missed the morning rush. Deb seemed to be genuinely receptive and glad to see her. She'd experienced this previously with undercover work where she'd made her way into lives that she abandoned as quickly as she nurtured. She rationalized her callousness as part of the forest, not concentrating on the trees. *Christians for a Better America* had to be dissolved by any means possible she mused as Deb brought her scrambled eggs in a soft tortilla and two sausages. Deb was busy as the morning rush began but her smile told Elisabeth she was welcoming. Short on time, she ate quickly left another hefty tip and paid her bill, Deb being the cashier today. Deb offered her the best for her first day, and then handed her a brown paper bag.

"Your lunch, something tells me you won't have a lunch hour."

"Did you include that in my check?"

"No, this one is on me. Something tells me my kids are in for a teaching treat. Have a super day Elisabeth."

"Thank you Deb. I will. See you tomorrow."

With that, Elisabeth jogged to her car and headed to school, buoyant with the unexpected encouragement.

Rebecca spent the afternoon with the colt back in the round pen, making small moves in his direction, running him around in circles, changing directions then walking over and petting, lifting each leg checking his hooves, rubbing his face; all to gain his trust.

She packed it in around 4, put the colt in his paddock, found Tom and told him she'd be back in the morning. Tom mentioned the colt was due for a vet check and he thought it a good idea for Rebecca and the vet to get together prior to her checking the horse.

Penelope Barker.

Rebecca called Pen when she got back in the truck and found the vet very amiable and willing to meet for breakfast the next morning at 7 am prior to going out to Toms. They decided to meet at the Bread Basket on seventeenth. Rebecca headed to town, stopped for a steak, vegetables, and a six pack of coke and headed back to her cabin.

There wasn't a barbeque so she pan fried the steak and greens, made a salad, and sat on the deck with a coke enjoying the evening, wondering what information the local vet would have to offer.

She was up early, got in a run and was out the door by 6:45 heading to the Bread Basket. She found a parking spot easily just before the morning onslaught.

The vet wasn't difficult to spot, woman alone in a center booth. She walked up and introduced herself and sat facing the door, Pen fortunately having taken the seat facing away. The vet was about five-seven with long blond hair in a tight ponytail under a beat-up straw cowboy hat. She was wearing a well-worn pair of

Wrangler jeans, similarly, beat up cowboy boots and a light blue blouse.

"Great to meet you Dr. Barker, your morning going well so far?"

"Whoa, you're Rebecca. I guess I'm pretty noticeable and it's Penelope or Pen. My mornings going great, how about you?"

"Okay. Pen it is. Me too, couldn't complain on a gorgeous morning like this. You order yet?"

"Nope, been waiting for you. Just got here actually. Janis will be over in a minute with coffee. You been to the Basket before?"

"No, just got in town and started with Tom's colt yesterday. They have a specialty here I should try?"

"Actually they do. Belgian waffles and strawberries. That's what I'm having plus a couple of eggs."

"I'm game, let's make it two."

Janis arrived with the coffee pot and welcomed Pen and Rebecca and asked if they were sisters. Pen laughed and said, "No, we just shop at the same thrift store." The women laughed at slam of their attire. They ordered the waffles and eggs and Janis headed back to the front to greet two guys standing at the front door staring at Rebecca and Pen.

"How long have you been here in StoneHead Pam, you the only vet?"

"I moved here right from Washington State Vet School about fifteen years ago and took over from a long-time resident who was retiring. Been here ever since. Am originally from Alaska but when I graduated I wanted to be in a place where I could ride my horse and run my sled dogs. How about you?"

Rebecca was ready for the question and had her cover story down pat. "I graduated from Montana State with an education degree, taught elementary for a time but was quickly bored. I'd done rodeo all through high school and college, been around horses pretty much all my life, trained a lot of colts for family and friends so I asked a local trainer if I could work for him for free for two months, train a few horses and if he liked the results, he'd hire me. Been with Derrick for about the same as you've been here. Love working with horses.

Don't get the summers off and the money is peanuts but I'm happy and for me that's all that counts. I gave up on finding a guy to share my lifestyle. I found out early I wasn't the mom type and I guess I'm just too obstinate or self-centered, opinionated or whatever, for guys to get past the visual."

"I hear what you're saying. Sounds like what I went through. Guy asks you what you do, and you tell him you race dogs, and you never see them again. Even guys who race give me a wide berth not wanting to take the chance of losing to a woman. I would have thought that attitude was long gone after four-time winner Susan Butcher took Alaska's fourteen day Iditarod race from Anchorage to Nome, but it's still around."

Their breakfast arrived, Janis refilled their mugs, and they ate in silence enjoying the joy of the waffles and fresh berries bouncing around their taste buds. Rebecca came up for air and asked, "So, what do you have planned at Toms this morning?"

"Checking the colt you're working on. He needs de-worming, plus a couple of lactating mares need attention. How tight is your schedule today? I know Tom is tied up and I need help with the mares otherwise they'll kick the crap out of me when I separate them from their foals."

"I'm open. I just worked the colt a little yesterday so this will work well as my objective the first few days is just getting him used to my presence, my scent and moving him around at will. I can help."

They finished their breakfast and Pen picked up the check saying it was on her for Rebecca helping with the horses. "Thanks very much Pen. Let me leave the tip though." She reached into her back pocket for her wallet and pulled out a twenty. Rebecca smiled as Pen duplicated her actions, neither woman carrying a handbag.

They attracted the stares of the two guys who'd been drooling previously and knew they were wondering if Pen and Rebecca were a couple. She smiled at them knowing they'd shit their pants if she opened her jacket revealing the semi-automatic HK. Men, such morons she thought.

Jackson's next day was equally successful with each class squirming, anxiously waiting while he took attendance then out the door to the library. Geez he thought, maybe I made a mistake not teaching as he felt an air of lightness and joy he'd never experienced with his practicum. This day the kids had no questions and spent the entire time researching, writing, and commiserating with team mates. He shirked the librarian's attempt at chit chat, not wanting to be sidetracked and spoil what he was sure was going to be an enjoyable experience with the kids.

His confidence grew with each class, particularly the often irksome tenth graders who continued to show delight in the change of pace. Their topic choices covered several hundred years of American history.

He'd given them few restrictions, many guidelines and tremendous encouragement. One group was preparing a debate between British soldiers in the 1700s in Boston with dock workers of Boston Harbor. This is going to be good he thought. They'd already learned so much more from their internet research than they ever could with text books.

He made it to lunch and was sufficiently confident in his afternoon lesson plans to eat in the staff cafeteria. He was one of the last to arrive and there were only a couple of seats left at a table with two male teachers. A student host lead him to the far corner and introduced him to those seated. The men welcomed him. Jackson ordered the Sloppy Joe special with both a salad and fries.

"Thanks for sharing your table guys. I don't know anybody here yet and have been pretty busy the first few days getting my feet wet. What do you guys teach?"

"I teach grade ten Math and Science," said Tony Kross. "Plus I help out with the wrestling program."

"I'm strictly senior Math," offered Lloyd Merritt. "My hat is off to you guys who can teach the tenth graders. I'd go screaming out of here if I had to do it."

The men chatted about the general things people do when they first meet, local politics and sports. Jackson learned both men were married to teachers who taught at the elementary. Lloyd and Tony were taken by Jackson's comment that he'd played hockey at Northern Michigan University. The usual teacher sport interest in Wyoming was football and they had coaches coming out of the woodwork for those sports but few if any hockey coaches, particularly ones who'd played for a university team. The men mentioned the Victor Willey ice arena and the summer hockey school which was short on coaches. Jackson said he'd think about it. Everything depended on whether he could impress the administration for a job in the fall.

Jackson had enjoyed the collegiality of his fellow teachers, which was also a new experience. During his practicum, the full-time teachers with whom he'd been paired emitted an arrogance he found distasteful. It was as though they resented him entering their profession. One friendly Michigan colleague said his background scared them. These guys were a breath of fresh air.

Of course in all fairness to the others, these guys were under the assumption he came straight from university and his practi-cum. They made plans to meet at the local Parrot for drinks and dinner later that day. Jackson wasn't aware that Lloyd had later called his wife who had a single colleague she'd bring along.

Jackson finished his classes and put some notes together for next week's courses, tidied the desk, chatted with the custodians as they started their shift then headed to the Parrot around five. The local watering hole was easy to find considering the twenty-foot bird guarding the front door. He found a space in the far corner of the busy parking lot, locked the truck, and made his way behind several other TGIFers into the pub. Seating was a free-for-all with none available, and drinkers three deep at the bar vying for the bartender's attention. Jackson made his way with the crowd and found himself between two guys about his own size. It was impossible to converse with the people, noise, and the country band, so he just smiled, nodded, and kept his spot.

He'd just made his way to the bar when he heard his name being yelled. He turned and saw Lloyd and Tony with three women. They held up their fingers indicating he should order six drafts. He did and passed them overhead back to his group, paid the bartender grabbed his pint and made his way through the crowd to where Lloyd and Tony had managed to snag a large corner table within view of the band but away from the massive speakers.

It was pretty obvious what was occurring with the extra female, but Jackson played along as he'd done so many times at Northern. The very last thing he needed now was a relationship. He may as well throw away his career and that wasn't going to happen. Even one-night stands were risky considering his weapons, which he refused to relinquish for anybody or anything. Whenever he went to a woman's place for the night he had to excuse himself and hide his weapons in her bathroom, often in a laundry hamper under a pile of towels and he always had to get back to the bathroom before his date.

No hugging. No cuddling, never staying overnight. And he couldn't remember the last time he'd had a second date. His reputation among women wasn't healthy and pretty soon women shunned him figuring he was a typical womanizer.

But for tonight he was the available bachelor and played the role. He and Niki danced and chatted by themselves and with the others who were constantly watching them out of the corner of their eyes. Finally he made his excuses and exited around eleven and headed to his truck, sighting being bone tired and leaving a confused Niki with her friends.

He'd just made it to the parking lot and was heading to his truck when two guys approached from the Parrot's darkness. Oh, fuck, here we go again, thought Jackson. Where do these assholes come from? He ignored their approach and continued to the darkness of the parking lot's corner. He was just about to key the driver's side when the two approached. "Hey asshole, what the fuck did you think you were doing in there?"

"Excuse me? Are you talking to me?"

"Well there ain't nobody else asshole. I asked you a question. You come to our town and come in here and take over with our women. That can't happen."

"I don't want to cause trouble boys; I was just having a beer with friends. It won't happen again."

"You makin' fun of us because you think you're better than us? We know you're the new teacher."

"No guys, really. I understand where you're coming from and I agree, I shouldn't be dancing with Niki."

"Jake, this fucker is makin' fun of us. Hear him talk, like we was a couple of dummies. Maybe Mr. college needs some local tunin'. Whadaya think?"

"Whoa, guys, this isn't necessary."

The larger of the two had moved right in front of Jackson with a threatening air. As he pulled his arm back to hit Jackson, Jackson stepped to a forty-five to his left into the Big Guy's space, wrapped his left arm around his assailant's right arm capturing it and preventing the punch. Jackson then pivoted on his left foot and delivered a cupped palm strike under Big Guy's chin with a twisting upper body motion whipping Big Guy's head back bouncing it off the truck's hood.

Big Guy was out, so Jackson pulled him forward, so he'd collapse behind him. Now Jake came at him ready to hit with a roundhouse punch. Jackson stepped to his right and delivered a front kick with his left foot to Jake's crotch. As Jake bent over grabbing his groin, Jackson delivered a powerful snapping right fist to Jake's left temple. Jake collapsed on top of Big Guy.

Jackson looked around. No one was watching. Fifteen seconds. The physical altercation didn't faze him, didn't make him think of the damage he may have done to the two men or any ramifications of his actions.

He was Delta.

He was Secret Service.

He slipped behind the wheel and drove slowly out of the lot and headed home, parked in the garage, fobbed the system, grabbed a coke, and repeated his evening's routine-sitting in the dark listening to the coyotes. It seemed like the critters were enjoying the game as they repeated their behavior exactly the same every night. Even to the timing. He'd been home about an hour when he heard a truck enter the driveway. The coyotes stopped their chatter and stillness entered the fray.

There were no lights on in the house. The sound of two doors opening and closing, then whispers and the sound of gravel crunching. The whispers grew as two silhouettes rounded the corner of the house. They approached the back door, each man carrying what appeared to be a baseball bat. Jackson was three feet from the screen door when Big Guy reached for the door handle. Jackson was off the chair instantly and without a sound, drew his HK and had it in Big Guy's ear before either man had any idea Jackson was there. Both were drunk, that was evident by the stench and their swaying.

"This isn't a good idea my friend. This is a nine-millimeter in your ear, and I'd just as soon pull the trigger, and then kill Jake too, as fuck with you. Nod your head if you hear me?"

Big Guy did. "Jake, you hearing me too?"

"Ya, I hear you," his voice quivering. "Just don't pull that trigger. We don't mean nothin'. We was just goanna tune you up some 'cause you got the drop on us back at the Parrot."

"Not a good idea guys. You have no idea who you're fucking with. You best leave here, and forget you saw me, ran into me at the Parrot and particularly forget that I was dancing tonight. If I see you again, you'll never reach your next birthday, and no one will ever find your body. You understand fellas?"

Big Guy and Jake echoed, "Ya just don't shoot. We're outta here."

"Good decision, now fuck off."

The men walked slowly to the edge of the house, rounded the corner, and then ran back to the pick-up. Jackson heard the truck engine roar as they spun gravel all the way back to the pavement then squealed away.

Jackson returned to his corner porch chair and waited for the mellow yipping to return; his heart beat never having risen above sixty.

All in a day, he thought.

Chapter Forty-Five

"Kids are Worth It."

Barbara Coloroso

Elisabeth parked in the staff lot. No other cars. No heads to turn as she grabbed her briefcase and headed in the side door to her classroom off the main foyer. A few kids were already milling around, probably those whose parents lived out of town and dropped them off on the way to work. She had plenty of time to load her program. She keyed the door, turned on the lights and shut the door behind her. She hit the main control switch which booted all the computers simultaneously. She'd loaded a variety of popular teen computer games into the system programming them to coincide with various scores previously achieved on the keyboarding curriculum. She hoped she'd chosen ones the kids liked but didn't play regularly. She refused to use any games vilifying law enforcement, women, children or where violence was glorified.

8:55 the bell rang. Elisabeth opened the door preparing for the onslaught. She was surprised at the orderliness the eighth-grade students displayed. They took their seats; she closed the door and walked to the back of the classroom behind the computers which were separated from the desk area. Every head turned and she waved them back. "Gather around guys".

"Good morning everyone, I'm Elisabeth Peltowski and will be filling in for the rest of the term for Ms. Panigon. She left me pretty specific instructions for the next few weeks leading to your final. Her primary concern is that you do well because your acceptance to the high school advanced computer classes depends on your getting a "C" or better. Do I have that right?"

Heads bobbed up and down with considerable frowning.

"Some students find keyboarding extremely boring and consider it a form of physical punishment, just shy of having to read Shakespeare." Smiles and nods all around. "So, what I propose is that we work on polishing these skills through gaming. Just to make sure I'm on the right track, how many of you guys game, either on a PC or handheld?"

All hands raised and some smiles starting to expand.

"Great. Then this is what I've done. I've programmed each computer to acknowledge you as that computer's web master. So have a seat at any computer and I'll guide you through the opening stages."

When they were all seated, squiggled into comfortable positions she continued, "Type in your full name, it isn't case sensitive but use capitals wherever it's expected in English. Okay, now your computer should be flashing colors, banners, and such exclaiming that you are the master. Anybody not have that?"

No response.

"Good, now what I've done is divide Ms. Panigon's tasks into daily and weekly goals so by the end of the term, which is pretty close, you'll have the proof of your skill level. In just a minute I'll send the data out that will start you all off at the same level. Now this isn't a race and I've reconfigured each lesson so it isn't anywhere near what you may have already done. You'll know any mistakes immediately because the program will block your advancement. Everyone ready?"

Hearing no objections Elisabeth went to the mainframe and activated the program she'd developed. The system started with accolades and overtures directed to each student. She heard giggles coming from some of the girls as they viewed the virtual characters shopping for clothes or playing sports. The boys were greeted with similar computer characters playing a variety of sports with the individual boy's name on the back of each jersey. One of the boys yelled, "Hey Ms. Peltowski, this is so very cool. You did this? I gotta learn how to do it. I'll blow my snotty brother away with this stuff."

"Thanks, and yes, I wrote the program. Now I'm going to activate the review lessons. These would normally come across your screen in the same format as what you've done all year. These are different, but just follow the directions and remember, your objective is to relax, let your fingers do the work, not your shoulders and back. When you've completed the assigned task you will automatically go to a game where you have to use the skills you just demonstrated in the lesson to succeed. Everyone ready, okay here we go."

Elisabeth activated the program and was met with total silence save the clicking of keys. Twenty-six teenagers quiet. She smiled at herself wondering where fate might have taken her had she known these skills when she taught. But she figured she'd have a hell of a time convincing principals and supervisors this was the way to teach kids. It didn't take long for students to be successful with the basic review. She programmed for success. She heard laughs and giggles and loud woops from every kid as they each played a different game. She wandered around behind students looking over their shoulders. There was no way to cheat the program. You either got the right answer or were shuttled back to a review. Nobody needed a review. One boy was playing Pacific Rift, a course which punished ignorance, but rewarded individuality with risky jumps.

Reckless driving was also punished by crashing and having to restart. Several were playing Ultimate Band which, although designed for eight-to twelve-year-olds, was captivating none the less as it moved smoothly from simple to complex, capturing rock performance. Every student was captivated, completing the basics quickly. She glanced at her watch and was surprised how quickly the period had gone. She walked to the front of the computer section and raised her voice, "Can I get you to stop for a minute? Good, thanks. Do I assume the assignment meets with your approval?"

"You bet Ms. Peltowski. This stuff rocks," were the general comments.

"Unfortunately the period is over, but I'll tell you what we can do. How about here at lunch and after school till about four thirty unless you have a bus to catch. If a lot of you come in there won't be enough computers so if you have a laptop, bring it in and lock it here with me and just plug into the system? If you have a security problem with bringing the laptop, let me know and we can work something out. Let's everybody log out and the system will allow you to return to the same place."

Everyone did then got up almost in mass and were socializing when the bell rang. Several students turned to her with huge smiles and waved to her as they headed out the door. She'd never known the feeling of teaching successfully and damn, it felt good.

The rest of her morning classes were equally enjoyable with identical student reaction. The last for the morning was her sixth-grade keyboarding class. The district offered the course each of the three middle school years, but kids only needed to take it once. If they took it in sixth then they qualified for the advance courses in seven and eight, the latter of which prepared them for the coveted and sophisticated software development high school course. After the last class before lunch a girl stayed behind with a friend.

She looked over her shoulder to make sure all the other students were gone and came up to Elisabeth and said, "Ms. Peltowski, I'm Sandi, my mom is Deb at the restaurant, and this is my friend Shelly. We just wanted to tell you how much we think we'll enjoy your class. We've never had anything like this before.

The whole school is talking about you and calling you the Wizard. We'll run and get our lunches so we can try and get a computer."

Before Elisabeth could respond the two youngsters were running out the door while other kids were coming in, lunch bags in hand. Everyone was milling around ready to pounce on a computer. Finally Elisabeth gave them the go ahead and there was a surge with every chair being filled immediately with a number of disappointed students standing by the door. Elisabeth moved to the front of the computer section and got students' attention.

"I'm overwhelmed with your enthusiasm and interest. Actually I'm speechless. I was thinking one or two of you would take the offer. So, how about this suggestion. Those of you who have a computer now, you let others come in after school if they can. If there is anyone on a computer who is not a bus student and could change with someone at the door who is, let's do that for starters."

Several kids graciously gave up their computer to someone at the door.

"Okay, so I'm assuming everyone at a computer now is a bus student. So this afternoon those non bussers can have access. How does that work for everyone?"

Numerous head nodding, a number of arms/fists waving showing approval.

"For now, if any of you without a computer have any questions, feel free to gather around up here and we can brainstorm and share ideas."

Students around the door immediately converged on her, grabbing seats, shimmying up on desks or leaning against the wall. They were opening their lunch bags and trying to eat and ask questions. Elisabeth did a quick nose count and figured there were at least seventy kids in a room the Fire Marshall approved for twenty five. Oh, boy she thought, this could be a problem, but she figured she'd enjoy the glow and deal with any repercussions later.

She'd learned her lesson in England and wasn't going to repeat it in this lifetime.

Questions ranged from was she married, to did she have a boyfriend, to where she learned such awesome computer skills. One girl asked what courses she had to take to be like her. Elisabeth assured her that she was on the right track, outlined what she could take through high school that would prepare her for a university program. Elisabeth said that the market place was finally acknowledging female intellect. The majority of medical and veterinary school enrollment was currently female because girls are accepted in senior high school physics, chemistry, and biology classes now but weren't a number of years ago. They excelled academically and their exceptional grades placed them above men with lower grades. When she made the last comment, a loud cheer went up from all the girls, which coincidently were the majority of those gathered around her.

The lunch hour screamed by with many kids not having finished their lunch-too busy talking and enthralled by Elisabeth's commentary. The bell rang and the kids reluctantly headed to their next class. Elisabeth had a preparatory class, called a prep, right after lunch so she locked the classroom and headed to the staff room carrying Deb's brown paper bag.

The room was empty, every teacher being back in class. She sat in a corner at a long Formica table, spread her lunch out and shook her head at the contents. A tuna fish sandwich that couldn't be on the menu given the height, pickles, potato chips, two cookies, a pint of milk and napkins. Elisabeth found it impossible to understand. She'd been in town but a few days impersonating someone and this was her reception. But in her defense she thought, considering this morning, maybe she wasn't impersonating.

"Formless evil injures people. Evil with form kills people."

Mingjial, Zen Buddhist

Dean had little difficulty finding the subjects Jessica wanted shadowed. He was curious about her information source given she didn't leave the ranch, but he'd learned long ago that if he was going to be a successful team player and enjoy the Service's confidence, he didn't ask unnecessary questions.

He knew Harold Richards and his address on Rumsey was easy to find. Dean drove to the end of the block and parked three houses down and settled in to wait for Richards to leave. Over the years he'd downplayed his position with Mr. Bakus, instead, cultivating the small town good ole boy image, a retired teacher who enjoyed puttering around a big spread and rubbing shoulders with real cowboys.

The Service had obtained a concealed weapons permit for him without Dean having to present himself to the local sheriff, which helped maintain the image. He carried the Service's issued Sig in a shoulder holster, preferring this carry to a hip holster that seemed to be less accessible while on a horse or ATV. Even now he acknowledged his quick draw ability. He'd prepared for his stakeout by picking up the local paper at the Seven-Eleven along with a coffee and muffin. For any passer-by he was waiting to pick someone up.

He didn't have to wait long. He'd just finished the muffin and half the coffee when Richards came out of his house in a hurry, jumped in his compact, backed out of the driveway and sped away, obviously in a hurry. Dean threw the muffin remains onto the passenger seat, placed the coffee back in the dash carry and pulled out behind Richards.

Dean didn't have far to go before he saw the subject pull into the same Seven Eleven Dean had just left thirty minutes previously.

Richards pulled up beside another compact from which two guys exited. The first guy Dean recognized as Joe Sarkowski the local insurance broker. The second guy he didn't know.

Dean pulled into a spot two rows and several vehicles behind them, parked and set the voice-finder on the dash. The technology looked identical to a radar detector you could get from any commercial spy store. This particular device was a little more sophisticated than the public could purchase but not by much. It recorded conversations up to 30 meters/90 feet. The system included stereo headphones which Dean purposely left behind with Bruce so there could be no misunderstanding. He plugged it into the recorder which lay on the passenger floor. For all intense and purposes he was a customer enjoying his coffee and the morning paper. Dean paid little attention to the three, glancing periodically over the paper to insure their continued presence.

"The fighter has one object in view: to go straight, looking neither backward nor sideways to crush the enemy."

Dr. Forrest E. Morgan

The Martial Way

Rebecca and Pen arrived in separate vehicles and parked by the main barn. On the way down the long driveway and through the archway which read, "Colt Town", Rebecca noticed for the first time the ranch's extensiveness.

The main ranch house was visible from the highway with the barns tucked in behind and surrounded by numerous deciduous trees; Green Ash, Crab-Apple interspersed with huge evergreens; Lodge Pole pine and Douglas fir, some of which had to be hundreds of years old considering their diameter and the StoneHead short growing season at five thousand feet elevation.

The entire landscape was crisscrossed with paddocks; rails made from pine poles-and connecting lanes. She hopped out of the truck and hurried around to help Pen carry supplies from the tricked out Dodge 3500 dually with the specialized refrigerated unit that slipped into the truck's bed. They carried the equipment into the main barn and stacked it next to several large stalls all holding mares with their foals.

The mares came as one to each door and peered out, ears perked forward checking to see if the noise was friend or foe. Pen started at the first stall, raised her left hand gently to the mare, indicating the mare should back up. Once the mare was away from the door, she opened it, stepped aside to let Rebecca enter, closed the door then gave Rebecca directions to hold the foal at a distance while Pen checked the mare.

She said she would be taking teat samples for mastitis, blood for red blood count and then de-worming the mare. It would take a while with each mare as they had to move slowly and calmly, to ensure that momma didn't retaliate and kick the shit out of both of them to get to her foal.

Rebecca had been through this numerous times on various ranches, but it was nice to have someone else take the lead and certainly easier with two doing the job. One person trying to work a mare while keeping baby at bay is next to impossible, but vets do it all the time. If someone tried to separate the mare and foal, the mare would bust through hell to get her baby back and such stress was just not an option on any reputable ranch.

Pen got her samples; put them in her carrying container that looked like an old fashion milk bottle carrier. She instructed Rebecca to release the foal which immediately ran over and started nursing from the mare.

The women exited the stall, bolted the bottom section of the Dutch door, took the samples back to Pam's rig, labeled, placed them in the refrigerated unit, then returned to the barn to repeat the process with the next mare.

Considering the number of mares Pen worked on, Tom had quite an operation. She made a mental note to get more detail about the ranch.

The morning breezed by with neither woman noticing the time. Around two Pen said she was done and looked at her watch. "Wow, where did the time go? I'd never be done without your help Rebecca. Thanks. This leaves me some time to a preg check, pregnancy check on several polled Herefords down the road. What are you doing for dinner? I should be done by 5 or so. How about we hit our local dance hall, have dinner a few drinks and see if we can pick up some male action?"

Rebecca laughed at the ease with which they'd gotten on in a short time. "You're on. I'll work the colt for the remainder, hit the shower and meet you. Hope they have line dancing. Don't know if folks still do that."

"They sure do. Cassandra's is a former cat house built in 1902 with line dancing, a riding bull, and the best potato skins in the territory and the coldest long necks in town. She's on Yellowstone. You can't miss it. Casual dress but you gotta keep those boots and hat. How about six?"

"You got it. See you at six. You sure you don't need any more help?"

"Positive. Thanks again." Pen got in her Cummins Diesel and powered out of Colt Town.

Rebecca went to the colt's paddock and played games; him trying to keep away and her trying to halter. The paddock having corners, she won within a few minutes, haltered, and led him out and over to the round pen. She slid the pole across the gate and let him loose in the eight foot walled structure. The colt ran to the middle of the fifty foot diameter pen, turned, and gave Rebecca

"That" look which communicated; "you won the first round but not the game".

Rebecca walked up to him but instead of trying to pet him she got behind and waved her arms, sending the colt away. She did that a number of times sending him in circles. After about ten rounds, she picked up her six foot whip, stood in the pen's middle and cracked the whip over the colt's behind...not touching, but almost.

The colt took off running around and around. Without telegraphing her actions, Rebecca stepped in front of the colt which promoted an immediate slide stop by the colt and a spinning action on his rear legs and off in the opposite direction.

She kept that up for forty-five, stopping abruptly waiting for the colt to approach her, to accept her position in the equine hierarchy. He refused. He stared at her with, "That" look. She didn't give him an opportunity to reconsider but raised the whip and the session was back on.

She repeated the routine three times without him coming to her. She glanced at her watch and saw that it was four thirty and the colt was quite lathered. She placed the whip in a holder by the gate, grabbed the halter and lead rope and walked up to the colt approaching him at his left shoulder. He watched her intently with his left eye; feet spread one slightly in front of the other ready to bolt if necessary.

Her calm demeanor and soft words put the colt at ease. He stepped forward with the one front leg that was slightly behind, lining both front legs beside each other, telling Rebecca that he was calming. He blew snot several times, releasing any further tension while she haltered and led him around for thirty, cooling him down, then releasing him back into the paddock where he immediately ran around, stopped by his water trough, gave her one more glance and took a long drink.

Rebecca put her gear in the truck's back seat, climbed in, locked the doors, cranked the tunes, and made notes in her training diary for later referral if necessary. Back at the cabin, the trainer showered and was at Cassandra's by ten to six.

She chose to stay in her truck and wait for Pen so they could enter together, having found over the years that one woman at a bar churned the testosterone waters quicker than two women entering together. She'd asked some of her male friends why and they said guys are often intimidated by groups of women but figured they could hold their own with one.

Pen arrived in her tricked out Dodge within minutes. Rebecca got out and was by the truck's rear end as Pam exited and locked. They looked at each other and started to laugh. At first glance you'd think they had chosen their outfits contemporaneously, both had on Wranglers and the same dusty stained boots they wore that afternoon. The only difference, Pen's was yellow blouse and Rebecca blue. Both were women's oxford button downs.

Cassandra's boasted full length swinging saloon doors that had been extended to fill the doorway and were winterized. Pam led the way pushing both doors simultaneously; entering a boisterous and celebratory crowd which had started some time ago. The dance floor was full of floor pounding line dancers, the echo ricocheting from wall to wall, the reverberation competing with the country band.

They made their way to the bar standing forth in line. The loudness was the only inhibiting factor keeping males at bay. Rebecca was sure she could smell the testosterone and was pleasantly surprised to see that the vast majority of men were coupled, meaning they would be hard pressed to hit on her and Pen. This was good she thought.

They each got two Bud Long Necks and made their way to the seating area, scanning, looking for someplace to light. Pen spotted two women sitting alone. She caught their eye and they eagerly waved Rebecca and Pam to their table.

Two guys sitting with a male group jumped up, ran to the dance floor's edge, and brought two chairs, bowed, then left. Rebecca couldn't suppress a smile, nodded to the men, and sat down with Pen's friends. They were far enough away from the band's speakers that a reasonable conversation was possible.

The vet introduced Bethany and Sabrina, nurses at StoneHead Hospital. The conversation bounced around the who, what, where and when as the women drank and ate potato skins. They signaled their server for four more Long Necks and another plate of skins. After their refills arrived the band started another Line Dancing segment and all four headed for the dance floor.

The band was playing Sugarland's *Settlin'* and dancers were lining up.

Everyone started at once stepping forward one, two, three, four, five, six, seven, eight, stepping right twice then turning in unisons clapping twice then repeating the process to the left ending up facing in another direction doing a few cha-chas and hip swings, and butt jiggles. Rebecca was pleasantly surprised that all her friends knew the moves and were enjoying themselves. She loved line dancing as a social activity because you didn't have the embarrassment of asking someone to dance, of being rejected or rejecting.

Everyone danced by themselves, getting into the music, not having to deal with a partner and his or her nuances. Everyone was dressed similarly with jeans, boots, and scruffy hats. You could tell there were no *dudes* who tended to wear brand new duds trying to fit in. There were a few dancing beginners who quickly picked up the steps.

The women stayed on the floor through four sets then relinquished their space to others while they headed back to their table to work on new Long Necks. Rebecca had successfully encouraged them to down their beer before heading to the dance floor so a passerby couldn't slip GHB into their drinks.

GHB is a sedative, is odorless and colorless and can be easily dropped into any glass or bottle of liquid. The recipient feels light headed and talkative and experiences the loss of inhibitions which is why it is called the Date Rape Drug.

The band was taking a break, their music being replaced by lower decibel canned, allowing the foursome to chat. Many women have been stereotyped into a category of bland eaters, limiting their consumption to salads and low calorie dishes. Not necessarily so, particularly this group.

Bethany said, "How are you girls with jalapenos? Cassandra has a burger with chili you will die for. How about we do four?"

Everyone cheered raising their arms and motioning their server over, ordered the burgers with Joe-Joe fries and four more Long Necks. Rebecca yelled, "We came here looking for male action but I'm having too much fun to be bothered, how about you girls?"

"Hear, hear," they chimed.

Pen picked up the conversation, "Bethany and Sabrina are also mushers. Girls, why don't you tell Rebecca about your teams?"

"Love to," said Sabrina. "I have twenty dogs, mostly cross breeds, malamutes and huskies. I race either six or eight. It's a part-time thing for me, but I do have a local sponsor. It's a lot of fun, do some traveling and meet great people. Can't ask for more than that."

"I'm just about the same," said Bethany. "We don't race against each other. If one of us is doing four, the other will do six. We don't like competing against each other."

Just then their Jalapeno Burgers arrived, the French fry wedges and more Long Necks. They stopped talking to eat. Each woman had difficulty getting a mouth around the massive burger dripping with chili but there were no complaints. One bite then a swig of beer to cool the mouth.

While eating, two guys came over and asked them to dance. Between mouthfuls, Rebecca said, "Thanks fellas, but no, this is a girls night out, maybe some other time."

The men persisted, trying to coax at least one of the women to join them on the dance floor. The foursome's refusal seemed to fuel the persistent men and they kept on and on until finally Rebecca stood up. All six feet, one hundred and fifty pounds.

"Look gentlemen, what part of 'No', don't you understand?" she asserted. "We've tried to be nice but you're pissing me off. Leave us alone or we'll call the manager."

"Okay, Okay, bitch. We're just trying to have fun. Jake here said you guys looked like fun girls. Boy is he fucked," said the bigger of the two as they turned and left.

All three other women looked at Rebecca with raised eyebrows. It was Pen who broke the silence. "What was that all about, any of you guys know them?"

"Not us," said Bethany.

"Are you really as tough as you came across Rebecca?" asked Sabrina.

"Yes," said Rebecca with a smile and returned to her Jalapeño and Long Necks.

"Speaking of being tough, Rebecca, I have to do some work on a couple of stallions which got into a pissing contest at an outfitters out by Yellowstone in the morning. You wanna come along? These stallions can be a pain in the ass, and I may need to sedate both to suture."

"I'm your girl. What time?"

"How about I pick you up at seven, we do breakfast again and head out? Bethany, Sabrina, you guys want to join us?"

"No can do. Have to work ourselves, but keep us in mind for the next time," said Bethany.

"I'm in. Breakfast, then deal with an equine pissing contest, sounds good to me," said Rebecca.

"Okay girls one more dance before we head out," said Rebecca as she got up and two-stepped over to the band. Moments later she waved to the trio to get to the dance floor just as the players started with Sugarland's *Something More*, the song to which women across north America dance and celebrate their freedom and self-proclaimed destiny.

The band's lead female singer had Sugarland's Jennifer Nettles' southern twangy voice and started the set waving her arms and stomping to the beat. Every woman, including Cassandra, got on the dance floor and did three sets of Nettle's inspirational number...the guys wisely choose to remain seated.

"I'm off, I should get some sleep. I really want to do the bull next time," said Pen, referring to the mechanical riding bull.

"Me too," added Bethany.

Pen looked at the bill and said, "Eighty dollars. You guys wanna leave her, what a twenty?"

"At least," said Rebecca as she took out a twenty and a ten and placed them on the bill. Each of the women followed suit, acknowledging what each understood. The tip was crucial for the server.

Rebecca caught the server's attention, and she came over. They gave her the bill and money, thanked her for a great time. The server asked if they needed change, and Rebecca said no, the rest was hers which brought a huge smile and profuse thank you.

The women split off as they exited the bar with Bethany and Sabrina turning left and Pen and Rebecca heading straight out. They stopped by the dually and were chatting, laughing about the good time they had and planning the morning when the two guys from the bar came around from behind a canopied truck next to Pen's.

"Well, well, Jake, we're in luck, these girls are just waiting for us so we can have the dance we didn't get inside."

"I don't think so boys. It's late and we have to get going. Thanks again for the offer," said Rebecca.

"No, not late at all girls, we really are gonna have that dance, right Jake?"

As the talker spoke to Jake, he reached for Rebecca and grabbed her left shoulder, gripping her blouse tightly. Rebecca reacted instantly stepping to her left at a forty-five, wrapped her left arm around his, which broke his grasp, then with his arm trapped, she stepped to a 45 with her right leg and flipped him over her hip. He landed hitting his head on the pavement. She drove her boot heel into his groin then toed him in the ribs. The guy was out, and it took seconds.

Jake stood with his mouth open, backing away from Rebecca as she said, "We don't want to dance Jake. Is that okay with you now?"

"Ya, ya, I get it, I get it," he said nervously as he turned and ran around another truck and disappeared.

"Holly shit Rebecca, what was that all about? Should we call 911?"

"No, means No, and they didn't understand that, so I had to define it for them. And no, we don't call 911. Fuckhead is alive so we leave him. No one saw this," she smiled.

"Son-of-a-bitch, I've never seen anything like that. I thought we were going to have to run for it."

"I don't run. Let's get to gettin'. We have a fun day planned for tomorrow," finalized Rebecca.

Pen laughed, shook her head, and said, "You got it girl. See you at seven." She got in the Dodge and left while Rebecca did several three sixties making sure Jake wasn't lurking, then got in her own truck and motored out of the lot.

Chapter Forty-Six

Jake was lurking several trucks away and heard Rebecca and Pam's conversation and thought, who the fuck are these women? This was too many fight losses in too short a time for Jake. They never lost a fight. Never. He waited until he saw the big blond leave the lot and rushed over to Patty who was starting to come to.

His face was a mess, blood oozing out of his nose and mouth, his forehead was red and scratched from where it hit the pavement. He thought he must have lost a few teeth and maybe the facial cuts needed stitches. Patty tried to get up, stumbled and grabbed onto Jake. "I gotta get you to the hospital man," said Jake, "you got a couple of good face cuts there."

"No, no hospital. Just help me get home. I can't move my right arm; I think I got a broken rib, and my nuts are killin' me. I'm not goin' to no hospital and have to explain I got fucked over by some bitch."

"Okay man, your choice," said Jake as he took Patty's arm and helped him to Jake's truck. He figured he'd take Patty to his place and let him sleep it off and come back tomorrow for Patty's truck.

This is just too weird, thought Jake, getting beat up twice and once by a woman. That's not just a coincidence he told himself.

Dean waited until the three men separated then removed the dash device and returned to the ranch. He requested the guards notify Jessica that he was on his way. She was waiting for him in the parking area as he drove up. "What did you get?" she asked as he stepped out of his truck.

"Not sure, but these guys were acting suspicious yet totally oblivious to my presence. Not sure if that indicates anything."

"Let's get this to Bruce," she said as Dean grabbed the recorder and they headed into the main door, opened again by estrogen.

"Hey Bruce, Dean has the recording. Let's download the conversation and find out who these guys are."

"You got it Jessica," Bruce said as he took the device from Dean and set it up on a readied spot beside a computer. "I'll upload the conversation to the computer and save a copy on another USB." He manipulated cables until he was ready; hit the play button on the original and sat back to listen with Dean and Jessica.

"Okay Harold, what's so important?"

"I got an email from Mike here and he said there were two women in the store that gave him a funny vibe. You tell him Mike."

"I was pumping gas when this tall good looking blond drives up. She says she's a horse trainer. Has the logo of a Montana outfit on the truck. Says she's training a colt for Tom up the way. I checked and that part's correct.

"But I wasn't a cop for thirty years without developing radar for one of my own and I say she's a cop. She's big like a female cop. Must be six feet plus and one fifty. She's built too. When she put her groceries away, I could see her upper arms bulge. I'm telling you guys she's a cop."

"Okay, say you're right, what would she be doing here?" asked Sarkowski.

"What I want to know," interrupted Richards, "Is why we haven't heard from Shepherd or Marrington. Those guys check in with us weekly and we haven't heard from them in three weeks. There's been nothing in the Idaho papers, I checked. Now this cop shows up."

"Yeah, but Harold, what's a cop from Montana doing being involved with us? If it were FBI she'd be from Seattle, or Denver, not Montana," said Sarkowski.

"Okay, let's settle this right now," added Sarkowski as he pulled out his cell and dialed telephone information for Montana. "Yes, operator, I need a number for a Flathead Training Stables." He took out a pen and wrote a number on his hand. "Thank you operator. Now we find out what's what."

He keyed the number and after five rings a man answered, "Flathead Stables, Derrick here."

"Hi Derrick, my name's Todd and I'm calling from StoneHead. I saw your truck on the highway yesterday and I need some training on a couple of five year olds I just bought. They've been raised in the bush and pretty spooky. I got them halter broke but need thirty days on each by a pro. You available?"

"Thanks for calling Todd. I appreciate the business. I'm not available for a while. I've got six horses on the go here, but I have a staff member in your area training for Colt Town, fella by the name of Tom. Maybe you know him?"

"I do know Tom. What's your employee's name and I'll go out to Tom's and see if he can work me in."

"Actually it's a her. Name is Rebecca Simpson. She is an excellent trainer. Give her a chat and one of you can get back to me."

"Will do Derrick, and thanks for the information."

"Okay," said Sarkowski. "That's pretty definite. Flathead stables employs a Rebecca Simpson and that's the name the woman at the market gave you Mike."

"Good enough for me. I guess my radar is getting rusty in my retirement. Sorry to have spooked you boys. I'm pretty sure the other woman is who she says she is. Lots of positive feedback from parents and kids about her classes. Pretty obvious to everyone that she is a teacher and a hell of a good one apparently.

But I still have a concern about Shepherd and Marrington. I expect they were hit and arrested and probably in some government jail. If they kept to the plan, they've sent the FBI on a wild goose chase, and we should be okay. Other than this Simpson chick, we've not seen or heard anything that would link Idaho with us. The last pack train should be in any day but with Idaho down, I want to know what happened to their supplies. Are they sitting in the bush somewhere?

"We'll just have to wait till they get back. No use worrying about it now. There's nothing there to connect to us," said Harold.

"I'm okay with that but we need to keep on our toes. We need to have our end of the project prepped and on the road before the congressional races get going. Our units have to be in place at the designated speech sites days before Bakus arrives. Anything from our guy at StoneHead Ranch?"

"Just the usual encrypted weekly reports. The last transmission indicated there were two Secret Service agents analyzing the security system and making changes. The email didn't indicate what the changes were and when they might be in place. An agent by the name of Jessica Fukishura is in charge. Guy's name is Jason Spencer. She's Chinese or something and the email says he looks like a Crip from L.A.", said Harold.

"Okay, so we're on top of that. Doesn't really make any difference what they do at the ranch and if Bakus comes here or not. His itinerary is well documented, and we'll be wherever he is, unprotected." added Sarkowski.

"Sounds good, you guys going to Sunday services?" said Mike.

"Wouldn't miss it for anything," commented Richards.

"Me neither," said Sarkowski.

"Okay then, I'll see you guys on Sunday."

Bruce heard a door open and close but let the recorder run a few more seconds then shut it off.

Only Rebecca and Elisabeth would have noted that Mike had lost his good ole boy dialect.

"I don't know what to say here," said Jessica. "I'm dumbfounded that we have a mole. Let's deal with that first Dean. Bring me the bios of everyone on staff and you, Jason, Bruce, and I will look them over and see what we can find that doesn't fit.

"Dean looks like you really hit pay dirt here. Rebecca's cover is still intact. The surveillance team will arrive tomorrow using the cover of Wyoming Power just in case any of us see their rigs around town. They'll take over covering the guys Dean just recorded.

Bruce will get a copy to Sorento who'll forward to the surveillance team. Sorento will also update them on these guy's Sunday plans. I'll let Sorento know our suspicions of a mole and wait for him to blow. I have to convince him not to send the cavalry."

Jessica closed and locked the conference door, "Jason, you are not going to believe what Dean has uncovered. These guys are after Bakus, not at the White House but on the campaign trail. They plan to have explosive teams at every stop on the congressional re-election campaign. Sorento is going to blow...pun intended... when we tell him. And are you ready for this, we have a mole." She proceeded to fill Jason in on Dean's reconnaissance.

"I guess there's no reason to hold off any longer. I'll have Barry send the encryption. How are we doing on the security details?"

"Just finished, we can get these off to Sorento as well. Good thing the Service has equipment and supplies available; it might help to expedite the installation."

Jessica left Jason to wrap up the plans and prepare them for transmission while she headed to the security room and sent the message to Sorento. Man was the shit going to hit the fan in Washington, she thought.

Elisabeth's last two classes were delightful repeats of her morning. She stayed with a class full of kids until four thirty when she told them they had to get home, or their folks would be worried. She'd already fielded a half dozen parent calls wondering why their child wasn't home. Lots of bemoaning as students departed but with smiles and chatter as they headed down the hallway to the school's main door.

Elisabeth was tired, she'd put her all into the first day and was ready for a long bath and a glass of wine. She logged off the main frame, grabbed her coat and briefcase, locked the classroom, and headed out to her car. She stopped by the market, bought more groceries, two paperbacks and rented two movies and headed back to the house.

The substitute spent that night and Saturday preparing the next week's lesson plans, reading, watching videos, and sleeping. She checked the recorder numerous times but found nothing additional to add to the previous emails. She wondered how Jessica handled the intel. She knew neither she nor Rebecca could move on those guys. Part of the frustration of undercover, she acknowledged, not knowing the big picture. Letting the concern slip from her mind, she fell asleep on the couch.

Rebecca was waiting on the porch when Pen drove up. Rebecca got in a run and did isometrics on the porch railing using her upper body to do pull/pushups, arm curls and squats. She was ready for breakfast and hopped in the dually before it had come to a stop.

"Good morning Pen, how are you this morning?"

"Great and you?"

"Ready to take on those big boys with the attitude," Rebecca said, referring to the stallions.

"They may be docile considering the trauma of the lacerations, but I doubt it. I've seen guys like this totally unaffected by similar cuts."

They small talked covering the short distance to the diner, Rebecca asking about local happenings, politics, and the like. Neither woman brought up the incident of last night. Pen pulled in to a half full parking lot and they both jumped out, eager for coffee and breakfast.

Janis had seen them crossing the lot and had two menus ready and took them to one of the only two booths available near the back. After last night Rebecca was operating in Orange and moved past Janis to take the seat facing the front door leaving Pen to slide in across from her.

"You must be hungry," said Pen.

"Famished! Janis, you have a morning special?"

"Two eggs, sausage and toast or pancakes for four ninety-five."

"Sounds good to me, make it pancakes."

"Make it two," added Pen.

Janis filled their coffee mugs and left with their order.

"So, tell me more about these horses we're seeing this morning?'

"Okay, one is a bay and the other a sorrel, about fifteen hands each, five year olds. Not normally scrappers but of course the outfitter runs his own breeding/replacement program so with mares in heat, you know how it is."

"Yeah, I do, how do you want me to help?"

"We'll check out their disposition when we get there but I'm not in the mood to try and talk them down. I'll give them a sedative but to do that I'll want them haltered and tied to the stallion post outside the barn. That sucker won't budge. Then just stay by his head and keep him preoccupied while I give him the sedative."

"You know the outfitter very well?"

"Guys name is James Watson, and his company is Yellowstone Outfitters. Good guess huh? Anyway, the guy's been in business forever. His dad, Don, started it in the forties; just retired a couple of years back and James took over. He's really expanded the business. He has the usual fall and spring black bear hunts, photo, and fishing trips but he just seems to have more of them than his dad and bigger groups.

James has guys taking supplies to his various camps from spring break-up through till first snow fall. Bear baiting is legal in Wyoming, so hunters are pretty much guaranteed a kill. Anyway, you'll get a chance to meet him."

Janis arrived with huge platters of food and a big grin, "Sure wish I could eat like you girls. I eat a bagel and cream cheese and it goes right to my butt."

Everyone did the nervous laugh while Janis refilled the mugs and headed to the front to seat another customer. Pen and Rebecca didn't talk, just ate. Several times Rebecca pulled at her blouse around her waist making sure it was sufficiently puffy to hide the H&K.

They lingered over coffee picking up the previous conversation and Rebecca enquiring about StoneHead's political make-up. Coffee done Rebecca paid the check and both women visited the restroom then headed west to Yellowstone an hour away.

Rebecca kept a steady chatter acting touristy with questions regarding the huge reservoir just outside of town. Pen explained that it provided irrigation into the area, was completed in 1910 and provided recreation for area residents. They passed Sylvan Pass and Pen mentioned that the trail system for hikers and outfitters began in the general area.

About ten past Sylvan Lake, Pen turned off into a camp situated in a canyon's mouth by the highway, stretching north from the road. Immediately visible were huge barns...Rebecca counted five that were at least half a football field in length all interconnected with paddocks and lanes.

Pen pulled in front of a roughly built building that Rebecca assumed was the office but could have been another animal shelter given its unattractiveness. They both got out and a slight man of about forty, wearing a pair of well-worn chaps, a thirty year old big Stetson and boots came out of the office to greet them.

"Hi Pen, thanks for coming on such short notice. I appreciate it. Have no idea what got into these two 'cause they've never fought before, and I didn't think the mares were close enough to affect them."

"Glad to do it James. This is Rebecca Simpson. She's training a colt for Tom Radke."

"Hi James, nice to meet you, quite the place you've got here. Pen's been telling me about it on the trip out."

"Nice to meet you too Rebecca, I've been working this place since I was big enough to ride. Took folks out on moose and bear hunts since I was in high school. Dad retired a few years ago so been doin' it myself with some wranglers ever since."

"So, lead us to these bad boys who need some stitching", said Pen.

James led them around behind the office and over by two paddocks separated by a lane where the stallions were prancing about. The three leaned against a primary railing system constructed of pine logs while the horses ran around an interior railing system made of railroad ties. Pam did a cursory check as the bay came to the fence to check them out.

"Looks good from here, I'll drive over and get started. Thanks James, I'll let you know how I make out."

"Okay."

Rebecca stayed by the paddock while Pam returned to the dually and brought it around, backing it up to the fence. "Let's do the bay first as he's closest then we can work on the sorrel. Why don't you get him hooked up by that stud hitch over there while I get the sedative?"

Rebecca took a halter and lead rope off the fence post, climbed the railing, and dropped into the paddock. The stallion snorted, stared at her, and pawed the ground. Rebecca noted his ears were perked forward showing curiosity, but the pawing created a mixed signal.

Rebecca was acknowledging the horse's vision anatomy, approaching at an angle which allowed the stallion a chance to evaluate her intentions. She spoke quietly and stroked his shoulder, rubbing her hand slowly and gently and fitted the halter.

The trainer led the horse through two metal gates and tied him to the stud hitch with an interlocking knot which would prevent his escape. Pen waited with a syringe and a cotton ball containing disinfectant. The vet injected a mild sedative and within seconds the stallion sighed, shifted his weight once and stood mesmerized.

Removing equipment from a portable tray, she flushed the rump laceration with iodine while Rebecca stood beside the patient's head while stroking his shoulder and speaking softly. Pen sutured quickly and efficiently, was concentrating on her task and didn't see or hear the pack train enter the compound from the wide crevasse to the north.

Rebecca did.

She casually observed two wranglers and ten mules as they angled behind the farthest barn, probably two hundred yards away. She was bracing for their approach and wondered how the stallion would react to the geldings when she noticed they didn't come back into view. Strange she thought. Where'd they go?

Interrupting her thoughts Pen said, "Okay, all done with this boy. Can you put him back while I clean up and get ready for the next patient?"

"Will do," said Rebecca as she untied the stallion and guided him back through the gate system closing and latching each after her. He was still unsteady but coming out of the mild sedative quickly. She unhaltered him then stood back as he slowly walked around regaining his balance.

She hopped the fence and repeated the haltering process with the next patient. As she left the paddock, she glanced down the wide lane between barns expecting to see the packtrain, but it was nowhere in sight.

She brought the second stallion around for Pen to repeat the suturing process. She moved him to a paddock while Pen cleaned up and returned her supplies to the dually,

Simpson meandered down between the barns listening for any presence of the pack train. She realized they could have been passing through to another outfitters compound further toward Yellowstone.

She'd made her way to the end of the two barns when she overheard male conversation coming from inside the barn to her left. This was very strange Rebecca thought, why unload the packtrain inside a barn and where were the customers? Maybe this was a supply train to the various outfitter camps in the mountains, but even so, they would have unsaddled outside and released the mules into the paddocks. She decided to return that evening to see what these guys were up to.

It was midafternoon when they left the outfitters and were heading back to StoneHead. Pen said she had other patients to see before she headed home and asked Rebecca if she wanted to tag along or be dropped off home. Rebecca opted for the former.

Chapter Forty-Seven

K aren had spent the majority of her four days off with Tom. They did the usual new love dating things; opera, pizza and a movie, dinner at Tom's, but on the forth night she had to beg off to get ready for her shift. Tom told her he'd miss her, and they vowed to keep in touch when she overnighted.

The first two days were uneventful with a pleasant crew and passengers to Vancouver and then to Los Angeles but there was underlying stress with the Vancouver to LAX run as an Air Canada flight attendant strike was looming with no progress in month long negotiations.

Deplaning in L.A. she was notified that a strike had been instigated and she was grounded till further notice. She stopped at the security office to obtain firearm clearance for LAX and was surprised that the airport's chief of security had processed a carry permit valid throughout the state. He told her that he'd entered her police information into the state's law enforcement weapon's data base, so every jurisdiction had the permit information.

Wow, she thought, that sure removes a great deal of stress. When she thanked the chief, he replied that he'd known of the strike's eminence and since her reputation preceded her, he wanted to help with the extended L.A. stay.

Her normal schedule included a one overnighter which she'd planned to take at the Channel Road Inn on Santa Monica Beach. She'd texted Tom from Vancouver of her hotel and that she'd call him that night. She taxied to the beach.

As the driver came to the Pacific Coast Highway from the freeway Karen rolled down her window to absorb the abrupt air change-an actual air scent not available to Angelinos. The breeze had a moisture content that enveloped her face raising her expectations and reducing her stress level.

She was beat and ready for a nap, but it was a beautiful sunny day with a slight ocean breeze which swept in through the cab's open window with euphoria of kelp and seaweed.

The driver turned right on Channel Road then a quick left into the small parking area of the B&B. By the time the driver opened her door-they do that in S. Calif.-she'd changed her mind about a nap and planned to head to the beach immediately.

The marshal paid the driver and gave him a twenty tip, leaving him with a huge smile and profuse thank-you. She walked up to the main door, sat her bags down and the door opened by a thirty something woman, short brunette hair under a rainbow knit cap, wearing a flowing cranberry beach cover-up who introduced herself as Mary Parker, her host.

Parker took Karen's bag and allowed her to enter first. Karen stood in the foyer's coolness and let her eyes adjust to the low light. As she glanced around, her eyes picked up the quiet sitting room with stone fireplace and numerous love seats and chair arrangements.

As she panned the room, she stopped and froze, not sure her eyes were telling her what was before her.

Sitting on a cream Gardenia loveseat with one kaki pant leg over the other holding a glass of wine and wearing a terribly sexy grin was Tom.

Karen screamed and ran into the living room and threw herself at him. Fortunately he'd anticipated her actions, was up and had the wine on the coffee table when she hit him. She smothered his face with a barrage of kisses the last of which lasted into the embarrassing phase with Parker leaning against the door smiling.

"When did you get here? No, how did you get here? What are you doing here? This is crazy I just texted you this morning."

Tom threw up his arms in surrender and said, "Getting the flight was the easy part. A Toronto Police Service (TPS) helicopter had just dropped off several VIPs and I jumped in. We were at Pearson within minutes. I badged my way to the Air Canada desk and was the last one on First Class. Everyone knows you and was delighted to go out of their way.

The TPS pilot has a buddy who choppers out of LAX. He met me on the tarmac and dropped me off on the beach just down the street. I probably flew over your taxi on the freeway.

The hard part was convincing Ms. Parker that I was legit. I encouraged her to call our liaison officer at LAPD while I waited outside. I was afraid I'd be stuck outside when you arrived, but LAPD came through and identified me and here I am."

"You're unbelievable," she smiled and shook her head. "You just took off, just like that."

"Well not just like that. I called my staff sergeant from the plane. He couldn't stop laughing long enough to be upset. So, I have several days here to spend with you if you want."

"If I want, are you nuts? This is the most fantastic thing that's ever happened to me in my life.

"I guess I'd better check in Ms. Parker."

"Not necessary Ms. Winthrop, already taken care of. The afternoon is yours."

"Shall we go to the beach then?"

"Well, that's something I didn't have time to work out. I have no clothes other than what you see." he said, waving his arms.

"Not a problem Tom, we have several bathing suits that will fit you," said Ms. Parker.

"Great, let's go then," cheered Karen.

Mary showed them to their room, gave the key and highlighted the Inn's services noting evening aperitifs at four and breakfast any time after seven. Mary closed the door behind her, and Karen was the first to have her clothes off while Tom struggled with his pants. She finally pushed him back on the bed and pulled them and his boxers off.

Laying back on the bed, she nuzzled his neck and said, "I still can't believe you're here. This is so utterly fantastic, it's like a fairy tale."

Tom said nothing, but his grin spoke his quiet and emotional feelings.

They spent the afternoon body surfing, surprising each other with their skills. They lounged in the hot sand, ignoring its entry into every body fissure. By five, they were ready for a shower, a drink and dinner.

They showered at the fresh water facilities by the promenade that ran north and south by Pacific Coast Highway, agreeing they'd do a run there in the morning. They were dry by the time they'd made the five minute walk, hand in hand, to the inn.

Entering their room via the patio and facility's back door, they made love again in the shower.

Karen dressed in casual khaki slacks, Bottega Veneta Woven Flats and a pink button down Oxford blouse. She wore her light weight leather jacket to cover her shoulder holster. Tom dressed in what he'd worn all day, vowing to shop in Santa Monica the next day. They sat with other inn patrons in a sitting room which adjoined the back yard covered patio. This room had three matching Beijing Stone couches creating a social setting with a quarry cocktail table of natural slate and pine creating a balance between rustic charm and sophisticated design.

They shared a local red, hors d'oeuvres and chatted with a couple from France and another from England. They grew restless, made an exit, called a cab, and headed to the Albatross restaurant up the coast near Malibu.

The Tross faced the ocean with individual dining rooms separated from each other by dense bamboo curtains. Darkness had enveloped Malibu by the time they'd been seated and ordered drinks. Night lights spotted the incoming waves creating an eerie, almost claustrophobic but relaxing aura. They spent the evening sharing childhood ocean/water experiences laughing at each other's duffus behavior while embracing the Tross' Alberta grain fed Black Angus fillet, pan fried red potatoes and steamed asparagus.

They got back to the Channel Road by eleven and were both so exhausted they crawled into bed and slept the slumber of contentment. But only after they laughed at each other's routine of putting a chair against the doorknob and their semi-auto on the night stand; Karen's beside her Blackberry.

Karen woke the next morning with a start, opening her eyes quickly and grabbed for her Smith. Tom felt her movement and sat up immediately taking a dramatic second to orientate. Karen realized she was motivated by the CSIS device vibrating. She reached for it, glanced at the read-out; she flipped the covers and stepped out of the Queen naked and apologized to Tom saying that she had to take it.

"No apology necessary, just walk slowly."

Karen shook her head and smiled as she grabbed the complimentary Channel robe and closed herself in the bathroom. She glanced at the read-out, "Intel on weapons grade Cesium being delivered in Los Angeles. Origin unknown, advise soonest if can verify." She knew Cathy and Jessica would be receiving the same message. She acknowledged then deleted.

She went to the bathroom while there, washed up and returned to find Tom had made coffee from the complimentary set up on the dresser. He had a cup ready for her and offered no conversation regarding her behavior, knowing from personal experience it was both none of his business, classified and a relationship breaker between law enforcers.

He said, "So, what should we do today besides get me some clothes?"

"Let's start with breakfast here. Apparently it's to die for, then clothes for you. I heard there's a James's Men's Wear on Second in Santa Monica if you want to give it a try. But first how about you putting on that wet bathing suit and we head to the beach promenade for a run?"

Tom jumped into the loaner bathing suit and was standing by the door in ten seconds. "Geez, you gotta give me a few more minutes than that," laughed Karen.

Tom said he'd meet her on the front porch and took off barefoot. He borrowed a ball cap at the front desk then sat on the front stoop waiting for Karen who showed up moments later in her U of Ottawa track suit.

"Are you going to run barefoot? Aren't you afraid of stepping in something?"

"I'm tough, I can take a few glass cuts and ring worm," as he started running with Karen rushing to catch up.

They did forty five, up and back, Tom running on the balls of his feet, heels never touching the promenade's pavement. Then hit the shower, separately this time! Karen dressed in a pair of Bermuda shorts with a sleeveless chocolate blouse that she knew Tom would like since it accentuated the breasts he seemed to enjoy.

They headed for the back patio and breakfast, Tom feeling out of place in his third time around attire.

Mary and two servers had brought out platters of gumbo-style chorizo hash, scrambled eggs, pitchers of orange juice, coffee and stacks of thick country toast and jars of homemade strawberry jam.

The same guests as the previous evening were at the family style breakfast table and everyone shared their day's agenda. One couple was going to Will Rodgers State Park while the other was going to hit the Santa Monica Pier. Tom didn't tell them he was going clothes shopping although they could probably tell by his wrinkled suit.

After breakfast they called a cab which took them to Third Street, Santa Monica's famed shopping experience. They found James's easily and Tom picked out two pairs of Enderlin Striped Pants, one a tan and the other chocolate-to match Karen's blouse, the style of which he commented on several times in the cab-and co-ordinate Space Dye Yarn Polo shirts.

He bought several sets of underwear, a bathing suit, sox, two belts and a Polo shaving kit. She just sat in a courtesy chair and watched Tom fly through the store. He had his shopping done and paid for in thirty, a task Karen was positive she could never replicate.

They spent the rest of the morning window shopping then stopped off the Mucky Duck, a British Pub on Second Ave. then grabbed another cab and returned to Channel Road where they changed then spent the afternoon at the beach.

Their three days ran together and by the third evening Tom had a body burn, a new wardrobe, and a burning desire to spend more time with Karen but yielded to a call from his boss asking if he was coming back to work or taking an extended honeymoon.

He caught a cab the morning of their fourth day and took a Delta flight to Toronto while Karen stayed to wait out the labor dispute. She rebounded from the tearful goodbye, dressed and cabbed to the Santa Monica Police office on Olympic Blvd. choosing a lightweight tan Burberry Jacket to hide her Smith.

The marshal badged her way past the desk sergeant and was introduced to the department's international liaison's lieutenant. She briefly explained her problem and that she needed to communicate with the RCMP via a secure browser. She was shown to a computer station in a separate office and was left alone.

Karen quickly logged on to the force's secure system and was able to educate herself regarding David's encrypted message. It appeared David had intel regarding Cesium being stolen from Bernic Lake in Manitoba and being smuggled into the U.S.

So far, the intel was unconfirmed rumors. Her research revealed that Cesium was used in cell phone transmissions, missile guidance, and global positioning satellites. Ouch! She thought, lots of terrorist potential there, no wonder David was involved.

Staying logged onto the forces' system, she sent David an encrypted message confirming receipt of his transmission, of her current research and advising that she'd make discreet enquiries. She copied to Jessica and Cathy.

She logged off the force's system, deleted the browser history then inserted a hard drive cleaner which removed all history of her presence. She returned to the lieutenant's office, thanked him for his courtesy and left the department.

Chapter Forty-Eight

Pen dropped Rebecca off at the cabin around sixish then took off to do paperwork at the clinic. They agreed to get together again in the next couple of days. Rebecca made a quick dinner of mac and cheese, herbal tea and watched sit coms until ten then headed back to Yellowstone.

Simpson parked in a vehicle pull-out about a mile before the outfitter's turn-off. She locked the truck and walked through the bush beside the road making sure she dropped out of sight whenever a vehicle passed, which wasn't too often given the darkness and time.

The moon was like a giant spotlight as she approached the compound by circling to the right behind the office and in through the same trail as the pack train. There were no lights on anywhere and she was fortunate for nature's illumination. She moved covertly behind the long barn into which she'd seen the train enter earlier and felt her way along the barn wall to a large double stock door. Moving past that, she found the smaller people door. She ran her hand down the door jam and felt a lock. The latch wasn't excessive security and the lock felt like a standard twenty dollar keyed system.

She quietly retrieved her pick pouch from her left rear pocket and felt for the slimmest tool, inserted it into the lock and manipulated it deftly. She had it open within minutes, removed the lock, and stuck it in her pants pocket ensuring it wouldn't be lost in the dirt, then slowly opened the door, and was startled by the loud creaking blasting from the hinges. She stopped to spit on each of the three hinges. Tried it again. No squeak. She closed it quickly and waited for sounds of company.

Hearing none, she removed a hooded, high intensity pen light and began her search. She knew there was something here the wranglers were hiding, otherwise why not unsaddle outside. The mules were absent, presumably out in the paddocks.

She moved left to right past hay stacks, equipment storage, large outfitter boxes that were strapped to the mules during the trip, one on each side. She counted twenty, lifted their lids and looked inside. Empty. She stuck her head in and took a deep sniff. Holly shit, she whispered. What the fuck? She checked each of the boxes and they all had the same smell.

She moved on to her right until she found a ten by ten stack of what had to be the packages from the boxes. She moved around to the back of the stack, removed her clip knife, and cut one of the back packages and stuck her finger in, removed it and tasted. Fuck, she thought, this is a fortune in pot.

The Drug Enforcement Agency classifies marijuana as a Schedule one drug along with LSD and heroine. Although only ten states have not legalized cannabis for medical or recreational, the strength is far less than that produced illegally.

Simpson was positive she had stumbled on a massive quantity of the illegal product.

She'd just put her knife away and was running through her options when she was grabbed by the jacket and jerked back violently. She dropped the light, landed on her butt, and was kicked in the ribs with a powerful blow that sent her rolling forward.

Ignoring the pain she came up and out of the shoulder roll and stepped to her left to barely miss something being thrust in the direction she'd vacated.

She felt the body movement just to her right, brought her leg up and extended a side-kick into the darkness. It hit its target with a cry of pain and a screaming, "You fuckin' bitch, you're dead."

Knowing where her fallen assailant lay, Rebecca spun on her right foot and got behind him, pounced and with one smooth move had her Smith and Wesson HRT boot knife grasped in a slashing grip. Her superior strength and muscle mass were no contest for whomever she had underneath her. She felt his hair with her left hand, grabbed and yanked back while putting the knife to his throat.

"Okay, mother fucker, what were you saying? If you move a muscle this knife cuts your carotid. That's a death sentence if you're too fuckin' dump to know. I'm going to pull you to a sitting position. If you resist it's your carotid. Nod if you understand?"

Whomever she had nodded. Rebecca twisted her left hand and his hair, and the guy moved his legs and sat. She removed her belt and tied his hands behind him telling him she was retrieving her light but if he moved she'd shoot him. To convince him she had a gun she removed it from her shoulder holster and ran it up and down his cheek, convincing him quickly.

She found the light and scanned the area finding several sections of orange binder twin used to secure hay bales. She tied her assailant's wrists, removed her belt then tied another twine section around his neck and fastened it to his wrists pulling his neck back considerably and his tied wrists up.

Simpson found a grease rag and stuffed it in his mouth, pushed him back down to the barn floor, reached inside her jacket and pulled her mini Canon and took a series of photos of the cannabis. Next she grabbed her Blackberry and called Jessica who answered on the third ring.

"Got a little problem boss," she said without waiting for Jessica to speak. "He's hog tied and I'm bringing him back with me. Can I bring him by?'

"Blind fold him first," was all Jessica said then hung up.

Rebecca had to smile at her boss' simple but effective management style. She found a work shirt hanging on one of the six by six retaining posts. She grabbed and wrapped it around his head, using the shirt's sleeves to tie a knot then dragged him out through the same door she entered, locked it, and retraced her steps to the truck, frequently smacking his head with a backhand each time he stumbled.

Jessica had called the guard station ahead of time and the corporals opened the gate quickly, checked her ID without any conversation, nodded their approval, and opened the second gate section where the jeep patrol was also waiting. The sergeant sitting in the passenger seat nodded and waved her ahead. She moved slowly up the long driveway and into the opening parking area where two additional guards met her and took charge of the ranch hand. Jessica was standing on the ranch house porch with her arms crossed and an expression Rebecca couldn't determine was glee or pissed. She soon found out as Jessica motioned for her to come inside.

Jessica led the way up the porch and pushed the already unlocked door, stepping aside to let Rebecca enter then closed and let it automatically lock. Jessica walked along the hall through the living room glancing to the fireplace's dying embers' glow and headed into the conference room. She closed and locked the door, switched on a light and motioned Rebecca to sit.

"Give me."

"Okay here it is. This is bigger than we expected Jessica," said Rebecca as she proceeded to tell Jessica her evening's activities. "I only saw the pot before he jumped me but I'm sure there's something else in that barn. There was another large black plastic stack off to the right of the pot. I think it's worth checking out. No one is going to miss our guy so why don't I go back there and check out the rest of it. Will be faster than getting Jackson involved."

"I'll call Sorento and get Jason to interrogate your guest. We can't involve the sheriff because he'll want to take custody then the entire community will know something's up, and our guys will go underground. You go back and find out what's up. Things are happening so fast it's impossible to keep everyone in the loop.

Dean, oh, you haven't met him. He's part of the original Bakus ranch security that the Service kept on and trained. Anyway, Dean taped three locals whose emails Elisabeth had intercepted. The three met at a local coffee shop parking lot with Dean sitting a few vehicles away.

The *CFBA* are planning on attacking Bakus during the congressional re-election campaign appearances. They intend to take as many congressional members with them as they can. Sorento is going to go nuts when I send him this info on top of what I just told him, which by the way, is that we have a mole here at the ranch. Glad I don't have his job. Oh, and the surveillance guys will be here ASAP, using the power company vehicles etc. as their cover."

"Whoa, boss, back up a sec. What was that about a mole?"

"Part of what Dean recorded was that our guys have someone here at StoneHead Ranch who's been keeping the coffee shop guys informed on us. We don't know anything more at this time. Dean and I are going over the documents."

"Anyway, back to surveillance, they'll get set up then be scouring every area outside the town limits for signs of a large operation. They'll relay that to Sorento's team in Washington and if they find anything noteworthy, Sorento will let us know and either Jackson or you will do the recon.

You're up to date so go. Get back to me tonight with whatever you get. I don't care what time."

Rebecca nodded and left. As she walked through the ranch house she felt the same electricity and energy she'd experienced just a few hours ago when she dropped her attacker. Yup, you're an adrenaline junky Rebecca and you love every minute of it, she said to herself as she almost skipped to the front door.

Chapter Forty-Nine

Jessica knocked on Jason's door and heard him moving around a few seconds later. He opened the door with sweats on and a blurry expression. "Get dressed, you have an interrogation. I'll meet you in the kitchen."

She rummaged around in the kitchen and found the coffee and started a pot. Jason arrived a few minutes later a little more awake.

"What's happening?"

Jessica filled him in and told him he needed to get everything from the guest and to use the Patriot Act if necessary. She shared her reasoning to exclude the sheriff in the process. She poured them each a coffee then left to send encrypted messages to Elisabeth and Jackson and update Sorento.

Once the messages were sent, she sat back and reviewed the message from David, then the one from Karen. She immediately understood David's concern, too much bureaucracy and little real communication.

She knew about cesium and its involvement in missile guidance systems and global positioning satellites from several Berkeley classes and agreed with David and Karen regarding the potential threat. But it would appear it was more than a potential threat at this point if David's information was accurate.

Her mind raced with the information and coupled it with her knowledge of Iran's nuclear program and the latest International Atomic Energy Agency estimates of 2,227 pounds/1,010 kilograms of low-enriched uranium. Subversives could combine the refined uranium with the cesium, creating a low-level dirty bomb and the capability of knocking out North American defenses.

Iran's facility at Natanz located southwest of Tehran and in a valley at the eastern base of a 3,000 m/9,800 ft. mountain range, produced their enriched uranium. The United Nations nuclear agency claims that no material could be smuggled out of the facility and at the same time states that it is inspected once a year.

Jessica's brain was racing with the mind-boggling information. If Iran is smuggling the nuclear grade uranium out, there is a good possibility it is either coming to the states or is already here waiting for the cesium. Shit, she thought. She went back into the communication room and fired off another note to Sorento, reminding him of Jason's African experience and Jackson's time in Los Angeles with smuggled weapons. She had to leave the follow-up to Sorento and get back to her task at hand, determining the threat potential to StoneHead.

Pennington had just gotten back to his house and garaged the truck when the downpour erupted. He ran for the house in Orange due to the rain noise eliminating all other sounds. He fobbed the system, shut, and locked the back door and made his usual building recon. Finding it clear he brewed a cup of peppermint tea in the microwave, hearing his mother gasp at the thought of not using a tea kettle, grabbed the BBQ lighter, returned to the porch and ignited the grill.

Jackson sat in his customary corner while the unit heated wondering if his recent visitors would be stupid enough to talk. Word would spread quickly in this small town, and he would be SOL, shit out of luck, to continue the operation. He couldn't isolate himself and not attend staff social functions. That would generate suspicion and questions. Trying not to be too critical, he accepted life's reality that some guys just have to participate in pissing contests. He also knew Jessica would have his hide if he allowed himself to be injured.

Prepared for their return regardless, he headed to the kitchen and shelled the prawns for the grill. He gave them a good wash then doused with a mixture of cayenne, chili powder, garlic, and olive oil. While they grilled he made a Caesar salad, cut French bread, and took it all out to the deck, freshened his tea, dropped the prawns on the salad and sat back to enjoy the sultry evening's rain...with his H&K on his lap.

The day's physical exertion coupled with the relaxing meal and soothing tea brought sleep quickly. Dishes in the sink at nine, undressed throwing his clothes on the occasional chair and he was down and out; until the Blackberry screamed its need.

It took the teacher a few seconds to semi-wake then reached for the unit, entered his encryption code, and read the message. Short and sweet communiqué that drew him awake immediately with adrenalin joy.

He had no idea what the next twenty-four would bring but the message was clear, *Night recon. Stand by for details*. He walked around the bedroom pumping his arms bouncing with excitement. He had the rest of the tea, tried to relax, returned his heart rate to sixty then back to bed to recapture his slumber.

When Winthrop returned to the Channel Inn there was a message from Air Canada saying the strike was over and that she was to report the next morning for the first flight out to Toronto. "Oh well, she thought, all good things come to an end. She had the start of some facial color and felt more relaxed than she had in months, maybe longer.. She called the LAX assignment desk advising her of her morning arrival, paid her Channel Inn account, had her last meal at Albatross, packed, left a voice message for Tom that she'd be arriving tomorrow morning and was in bed by ten.

Elisabeth woke with a start, grabbed her H&K, and rolled off the couch landing in a kneeling combat position, her mind playing catch-up to the awakening sound. She shook her head to clear the cobwebs then realized it was her Blackberry vibrating that woke her.

Grabbing it off the coffee table she typed in her code and the device let out a loud ear-piercing yelp. Quickly she realized she'd entered the wrong code, entered the proper one and sighed as the noise subsided and the screen came to life with the message, "Go to the eleven o'clock service at StoneHead Evangelical Church."

She smiled at the read-out knowing of course that it was from the boss of few words. She hit 'Next' on the control panel and found a second, more detailed message advising her of Dean and Rebecca's findings and that she was to get herself invited to the Church's farm tomorrow to provide information for Jackson's recon.

Finally, she thought, I'm getting some action. She knew that several of her female students were church members by their attire, long cotton print dresses, hair in a bun and extreme introverted personalities. She hoped to strike up a conversation with some tomorrow. She decided to wear her most conservative Teacher outfit to create an aura of coalescence. She laid it out on the un-slept part of the queen and crawled back into bed, falling asleep plotting tomorrow's dialog.

Karen was up early and out the door before the Inn stirred. Santa Monica Taxi was waiting for her in the small parking area where the driver got out, placed her bag in the trunk, opened the rear door, watched her enter, smiled, re-entered the driver's side and asked, "Where to Miss?" All unusual actions for taxi drivers, thought Karen.

The morning was a blur as she forced herself to recapture her working mode. She did her LAX Security and Air Canada check-in on auto pilot, hit the loading shoot, found a jump seat, downed the Grande latte she picked up on the way in and waited for the caffeine to kick in. In fifteen she was ready to go, in hyper Yellow.

The flight was uneventful, the norm for the early bird special, in contrast to the dinner or late night flight. She landed at Pearson and called Tom while she walked to the taxi zone but had to leave him another message. She called his office, was informed of his anti-terrorism conference, and decided not to try and call again but texted instead, advising him of her landing and asking him if he was free for dinner. She'd no sooner put her personal Blackberry away when it rang a text. She stopped again and read the message, "Jessie Kennedy Wine Bar at 6?" She quickly replied "Yes" and skipped out to grab a cab; home to get in a run, shower and choose an impressive outfit.

Karen arrived at the wine bar at 5:45 and found her timing impeccable; she snagged a table just as another couple was getting up. The hostess came over and told her she would have to check with the reservation kiosk. Karen felt somewhat smug advising the nineteen something that she was Tom Hortonn's guest.

The young woman responded with an apology, cleaned the table, and brought a bottle of chardonnay and two long stem wine glasses that Tom had obviously ordered. Mm Karen wondered, we've only been dating a few weeks and I can already anticipate his actions. That's good, isn't it? Or is it? She asked herself.

She sipped her wine and watched the door seeing Tom saunter in a few minutes later. He spotted her instantly and skirted bussers, servers, and customers to greet her with a huge bear hug then hands on each side of her face and bent to kiss her gently, "Oh, it is so good to see you Karen and such a great surprise. I expected you to be on an extended force paid holiday."

"The delight is mine as well and yes, I expected to be stuck in that terrible environment for weeks," she laughed.

Karen poured Tom a glass of chardonnay, refilled hers and they clinked, welcoming each home. Their server arrived shortly with a platter of their favorite appetizer; parmesan and artichoke stuffed potato skins with Olive Tapenade-anchovy, sun dried tomatoes and black olive dip.

Jessie's was an upscale party place for the inner-city professionals most of whom lived within walking distance. Sundays were often the time to visit your neighbors and co-workers in a pleasant social setting.

Tom and Karen were reliving their Santa Monica time when Tom noticed a guy sitting solo at the bar who caught Tom's eye. Tom raised his hand and waved him over. Karen turned and saw the fellow advancing on their table and glanced back to Tom with a raised eyebrow. Tom smiled in response just as Del Richey came up behind Karen. "Del, welcome to Jessie's, how did you hear about it?" asked Tom.

"The staff at the Strathcona suggested it. Close to the hotel and good food. I didn't realize it was such a neighborhood gathering place."

"Del, this is Karen Winthrop, RCMP Air Marshal. Karen, Del Richey, with the Calgary Police."

"Nice to meet you Del, can you join us for a little?"

"I don't want to intrude on your date, but sure for a couple of minutes." He signaled a server asking for another MGD, pulled a nearby chair over and sat beside Tom.

"Were you at the anti-terrorism gathering with Tom?" asked Karen.

"I was. Tom organized a hell of a learning experience. I've only been with Calgary for about five years and just starting to branch out. I heard about the conference and got the time off with the proviso that I pay my own expenses.

I guess you're involved in this all the time Karen, as is Tom. Sometimes I think the problem is almost overwhelming, but Tom's experts put so much of the problem into perspective, and I think they sold the majority of attendees on the co-operative investigative approach. I know my boss will be on board and with the federal economic stimulus money available, we will be front and center being on line with the new software."

"That's excellent Del. I'm often in Calgary on a stop over to Vancouver. Always fascinated with the city's financial energy and approaching the airport with the Rockies in the distance is breathtaking. How did you get hooked up with Calgary Police if you don't mind my asking?"

"Not at all Karen, I apprenticed out of high school in auto mechanics and loved it until oil prices dropped and I got caught up in the oil field lay-offs. The federal government had a career overview program of which I took advantage. After hours of testing they said I indicated a problem solving penchant. That didn't mean a thing to me until they told me Calgary was looking to hire mature people.

I laughed at the time, never thinking of myself as mature, but it worked. I sailed through their screening, pre-hiring program and then their training. I just took the corporal exam and am on the waiting list. I'm planning on being one of the 40 to 45 members of Alberta's integrated counter-terrorism squad Suderman talked about today.

As Tom probably told you, Suderman is the assistant commissioner with the RCMP's Ottawa-based Integrated National Security and Enforcement Team. This new team will guard against Al Qaeda et al, as well as home-grown radicals like those who bombed the British Columbia pipeline. This is going to be huge and I'm going to be part of it.

"I've overstayed my welcome. Nice to have met you Karen and Tom, thanks again for the great experience. I hope we can keep in touch." Del excused himself and made his way back to the bar where he ordered another Miller Genuine Draft and dinner, planning to get back to the hotel early for a decent night's sleep and head home in the morning. He counted the last fifteen as a trip bonus, meeting Karen who was obviously Tom's girlfriend, and networking like he did. Fabulous career moves he thought.

"Oh, the exuberance of youth," said Tom.

Karen laughed and nodded but knew Del was on the right career track. She so much wanted to share with Tom and Del her recent research created by David's message, but knew it wasn't her place.

Chapter Fifty

Jason made his way through the multi-car garage, the corner of which had been converted where two military guards stood in front of a steel door. They saluted him, which Jason found interesting given his last experience with the Service's armed guards. He smiled at the two M-16 carrying men, snapped off a quick, respectful salute and entered the cell where he met another guard standing behind Rebecca's guest whose head jacket had been exchanged for a red bandana across his eyes and one in his mouth.

The guard stepped to the side and Jason activated a tape recorder sitting on a small table beside the prisoner then slid in to stand behind him.

"Well cowboy you've created quite a shit storm for yourself but I'm here to help you put this all behind you.

This is how it's going to work. I'm going to remove the gags and ask you some questions. You give me the right answers and the rather large gentleman standing next to me will not hit you. Give me the wrong answers and you will begin to hurt.

Now, the first thing you need to know is you are not getting a lawyer. If I'm satisfied with your answers you will spend a few years in prison. If you lie to me, then you are going to the new Guantanamo. I know you've heard of the old one that the U.S. is shutting down, but you see America couldn't be without a Gitmo for traitors like you.

The country wasn't about to let all those terrorists go back to their country of origin to wage war on us all over again, so we made a new prison. It is far, far away from civilization. In fact, the only way you get there is by air. All prisoners are in isolation twenty-four seven. They never hear another human speaking, and they are never spoken to. It's like living in a vacuum with the lights on all day and all night. Those who go nuts spend the rest of their lives in a drug induced coma.

We don't need water boarding, we just make you an offer you can't refuse, that is if you have any smarts. So, cowboy, you decide. If you think you can give me the answers I want, nod your head."

The unkempt wrangler quickly nodded up and down numerous times bringing a smile to Jason and the guard. Jason reached over and removed the gags and gave the prisoner a small plastic cup of water.

"Smart move cowboy. Now the first question, where did you get the dope? Remember, you're making monumental decisions here. You either end your life as you know it or have a chance at a resemblance of a future."

"I bring it here from Idaho," he gasped. "We do a six day pack train trip through Yellowstone: been doing it for years. I bring the mules into the reservation and a bunch of guys load the train and I come back. That's it. I got nothin' more to do with it than that. I get paid wrangler wages and a bonus for coming in on time. I get no cut of this shit so why should I have to pay for gettin' caught?"

"Well partner, that's called gettin' fucked. But let's continue. You bring anything else back besides the buds?"

"Sometimes we bring back meth, I swear I have no idea where it comes from."

"What do you take over the mountains? And don't tell me nothing."

"Explosives. I don't know what they are exactly, and I have no idea what they're used for, and I don't want to know.

Part of the way to the reservation I met a couple of guys with pick-ups on a forestry road. They unload the train and I continue on my way. I don't say nothin' to them, and they don't talk to me. The last trip I came back with the same stuff I carried over. I'd planned to leave the explosives with the Indians but there was a bunch of shit happening there with cops all over the place, so we just turned around and made our way back.

The stuff is still in the barn where that chick attacked me. Who is she anyway? She's a fuckin' Amazon. I thought for sure she broke something she hit me so hard." The wrangler had thought out his options quickly and knew he had little if any bargaining chips with his captors. He also figured that trying to be a smart ass would get him nowhere with these two hardcore, so he buckled to their pressure and took his chances.

"She's someone you never want to meet again partner. So, now, tell me how the explosives get to the barn."

"I have no idea about that either. I come to work, and the stuff is stacked ready for me to load."

"What about the outfit's owner, James. How does he fit into this?"

"Fit into it? You fuckin' crazy? He runs the operation. After his dad retired James had to pay him for the outfitting business and wasn't going to settle for the peanuts his old man lived on for years. I think he has big plans for himself in a couple of years. But I have no idea what. I mind my own business and am happy to get the extra money."

"Any idea who supplies the explosives?" Jason tried again.

"If I had to bet I'd say it was a rancher because it smells like some kinda fertilizer, but I really have no idea. Never met anyone in the barn, like I said, it was always just there."

"How do you know its explosives then?"

"Come on man, I may be stupid but I'm not that stupid. I'm hauling all this shit over the mountains for months and there's more than just fertilizer. Every other trip I took gallons of stuff that smelled like what dry cleaners use. Then another trip I'd take a bunch of other shit, but I didn't look in the boxes. I got the message really quick from James that I could either get some easy money or be out of a job, permanently. He acts like a good old boy, but I wouldn't want to cross him. So I just do as I'm told, get a wad of cash and keep my mouth shut."

"Okay, we're done here partner. We're going to check this information and get back to you. My friend here will show you to your accommodations. If you think of being an asshole, remember he has two buddies outside the door and remember the new Gitmo."

"Ya, I get it. Do I get to know where I am or who you are? I figure you're American but what are you man? You're no cop that I've ever seen. No offence man but that hair."

Jason smiled, turned, and exited the room to bring Jessica current.

Rebecca had no difficulty retracing her steps to the Yellow-stone Outfitter's barn. She was pissed at herself for allowing the prick to get her previously, so she was working in heightened Orange. Using her lock picking tools in half the previous time, she was in the barn, had her penlight on and was walking through the enclosure, past the pot when she stopped abruptly.

In the corner furthest from her earlier discovery was another section of pallets stacked with eighteen-inch-tall oblong metal cans. She counted each layer and came up with about two hundred. Reaching behind the stack she retrieved one from the middle, swung it out and onto the floor. Unscrewing the top she turned to keep her back covered and bent to get a whiff. She reeled at the pungent odor, not needing an analysis to recognize it as Nitromethane. No photos this time, that was probably what caught their attention, the flash.

She screwed on the cap, tucked the can under her arm and finished checking the barn. She found boxes of dynamite, blasting caps, timers, and assorted electronics. She backtracked, relocked the barn door and back to the pick-up parked as previously in a pull-out east of Yellowstone. She booted it back to StoneHead Ranch with her prize.

Jackson woke and found himself unmotivated after the previous day's exertion. He got in a long early morning run, prepared a full bacon and egg breakfast while wandering around the house working at keeping his composure waiting to hear from Jessica.

Around noon he decided to work on the garage, fixing the work bench and upgrading the garage door's security. By mid-afternoon he'd just about given up on hearing from Jessica when his Blackberry vibrated. Checking the screen he found her orders for the next night and smiled at the anticipation of action. Excited at the prospects, he spent the remainder of the afternoon completing his task, increasing the market value of his rental then had an early dinner watched the early sit-coms, checked his lesson plans for his classes and went to bed, sleeping more soundly than he had in days.

Fukishura had just come out of Bruce's domain when she saw Rebecca in one of the monitors carrying a can and wearing a huge smile. Bruce said, "My doesn't she look like a Cheshire cat? What's she been up to?"

"I sent her back to the barn to do a complete finding. Looks like she's got something. I hope it isn't what I think it is, or maybe I should hope it is, then we know we're on the right track."

She left the security room and met Rebecca at the front door and raised her eyebrows as Rebecca entered. The tracker replied with a nod and brilliant smile then followed Jessica through the kitchen and the back hall to the conference room.

Rebecca entered first as Jessica secured the door behind her. Rebecca walked over to where Jason was sitting and plunked the can on the table.

"You gotta be shittin' me Rebecca. This is unbelievable, an exact duplicate of what Jackson found at their Idaho compound. What's our next move?" commented Jason.

"I'll update Sorento, I'm sure he's as overwhelmed with what we're finding as are we. I told Jackson to stand-by for a night recon at this farm that we believe is connected to the StoneHead Evangelical Church. Elisabeth is getting herself invited there today after church. Tomorrow, or I mean later today, I'll contact the Idaho FBI SAC and get them involved from their end to see if they can locate the source of the drugs. Let's keep this group as small as we can. No Wyoming SAC yet and maybe not necessary at all. We all know what happens when we get too many hands in the pot and we definitely know what the FBI is like regarding territory, right Rebecca?"

"Oh ya, let's keep those guys at arm's length if not further. You remember Jackson telling us the run-in he had with the Nez Perce County Sheriff when he was in Lewiston? The guy may be an asshole, but we can't work that end by ourselves, how about we consider bringing those guys in first and the FBI second?"

"I like the idea Rebecca, but we already have the reservation connection with our cowboy's confession, so we'd be in deep shit by keeping them out. Also we don't want to lower ourselves to their level by being territorial too. So how about we all get some sleep and I'll fill you in when I hear back from the Idaho SAC and Sorento?

Rebecca, you keep your cover. We have to move fast here because even though the outfitter will probably think the wrangler took off on his own, it's not a guarantee. We need warrants for the outfitter and whatever we find at the church farm. I'll have Sorento handle that.

We also have to be prepared for a confrontation at the farm. Dean's information told us they are hyper alert and expecting something from the FBI since the Idaho cell went down, plus they have that stockpile at the outfitters to move on and whatever they may have at the church farm. I suspect they are in the process of moving the latter to deeper cover.

I'm concerned that the group is forcing the government's hand and we're without the necessary legal documentation. All we have so far is the chemicals and illegally obtained conversations that could be construed as hyperbole. We're between a rock and a hard place. If we wait for Sorento to come back with warrants, which I question he can get, these guys will rabbit, and we will have no way of knowing where they will turn up against the president and legislators. I think I can make a case for our actions so leave that to me.

Okay, let's go. I'll be in touch. Jason, you'll supervise our guest. And I want that confession signed."

Jessica left Jason and Rebecca, sent off a quick transmission to Sorento then went to bed setting her watch alarm for eight and crashed.

Chapter Fifty-One

Peltowski woke jazzed with the thought of action. She realized quickly that the euphoria she'd experienced at school was short lived and that she needed the energy of action. She checked her monitoring system, finding the three *CFBA* members chatting about this morning's church service with the preacher speaking on *Covenant Keepers* and their collective need to make decisions regarding the farm given the colleagues they spoke about recently not being in touch.

What is that all about, thought Elisabeth?

Elisabeth began the morning relaxing with coffee, watched Fox News then did some stretching on the floor, observed the perfectly coiffured news readers, shook her head thinking the adage, there for the grace...

Finished coffee, laced runners, put in forty-five on the trails alongside the dirt road in front of her house, then yogurt, English muffin, orange juice, shower, dressed in church mixer outfit, hair back sans make-up...a farm invitation.

The hacker pulled into the church parking lot at nine-forty-five and joined about thirty other vehicles discharging women and children. She found a spot and joined the trail of worshipers feeling eyes questioning her presence. She had just about made it to the front steps when she spotted a man of about fifty dressed in black and white vestments greeting members when out of nowhere, Shelly ran up and wrapped her arms around her waist.

"Miss Peltowski come with me I want you to meet my parents," she said, pulling Elisabeth by the hand.

Elisabeth was prepared for the reception but still, Shelly's familiarity took her aback. Shelly held her hand and guided her up the steps and into the church foyer where a startled couple were staring at them. Shelly dragged and pulled Elisabeth over to the forties couple; the mom wearing a carbon copy of Shelly's and the dad, a disciplinarian in his black suit, white shirt, and black bowtie. "Father, Mother, this is Miss Peltowski, our new keyboarding teacher."

Elisabeth extended her hand gently to the parents with the mother reciprocating and the father nodding but refusing his hand. "Welcome to our church Miss Peltowski," offered the mother." The father remained silent but cut her to the quick with a stern look as though she were an errant child.

"Thank you, it is a pleasure to be a guest this morning. In traveling to my new job I've missed the comfort of my church family."

"And what family would that be Miss?" criticized the father.

"Dumfries Fundamentalist Congregation in Omaha sir," replied Elisabeth, who, having anticipated the question sent an encrypted message to Jessica earlier and hoped Sorento's connections were able to set the cover quickly; she expected Father to check her out considering she was encroaching on his domain and receiving accolades from his daughter.

Father didn't reply other than to nod his head. The congregation was fully seated, and Mother gestured that they join the other worshipers. She invited Elisabeth to join them in their customary front pew. Elisabeth figured this was the first time she'd attended church in Yellow as she settled herself primly beside Shelly.

The service began with an opening prayer from Robe staring down with lightning intensity. That was followed by several hymns, all of which spoke of the congregation's sinful lives and their need to redeem themselves to the Almighty.

Robe sat off to the side as the singing subsided and a regally clad male entered from a sliding side door and stepped to the front of the congregation. He was a duplicate of Father and just about every other man present with his stern demeanor. Resplendent in royal blue and red vestments he led the group in another prayer, asked the Lord to open their hearts so all could repent and cleanse their souls.

He began his sermon by walking back and forth across the raised platform then descended to do likewise up and down the aisles speaking directly to each and every worshiper, many of whom cringed at his glaring accusatory stare. He recited many biblical passages which Elisabeth recognized from her childhood bible studies but with considerably altered interpretation.

What she recalled were words of encouragement and support, but this pastor changed the wording to criticize and lambaste the men and women to whom he spoke. He praised an organization called *Covenant Keepers* of which Elisabeth had never heard but suspected the congregation an intimate history with them.

The pastor's delivery appeared directed to women in general and mothers specifically that they were to submit themselves to their fathers' and husbands' superior intellect and world knowledge and do their bidding less the Lord find them blasphemous and punish them.

Elisabeth had anticipated the sermon but not its forcefulness. She knew this was her opportunity and she took it. Sitting with her back forced against the pew, her feet flat on the floor and her eyes facing ahead, she didn't look at the preacher as he passed by her row and looked directly at her, challenging her to meet his glare. She forced herself to relax emitting an aura of compliance; the acceptance and joy of doing so.

The preacher reached the front pew, turned, and began a new assault, this time against the federal government and bureaucrats in general. He lambasted Bakus' administration, claiming Bakus' political philosophy was a direct violation of Gods' will and that it was the congregation's task, in fact their obligation to rid the nation of the blasphemous leader at all costs.

Elisabeth estimated the rampage lasted the greater part of fifteen minutes, putting the sermon over the hour mark. As though sensing the time frame, the preacher sighed, took the two steps up to the platform, turned and blessed the congregation, offered the service over to Robe: the two men changing positions.

Robe led worshipers in a number of hymns then ordered ushers to pass the offering, suggesting members check their tithing to ensure they're on track. Just before the benediction, Robe reminded the congregation that they were expected to attend the pot-luck lunch at the farm at noon.

Ninety minutes from start to finish and Elisabeth wondered if she'd made sufficient impression to be asked to lunch. Shelly took her hand and Elisabeth walked between Mother and Shelly into the church's foyer where the preacher was greeting the exodus.

Mother stopped to thank him for a lovely service and introduced Elisabeth who curtsied and thanked the preacher for allowing her to attend and bask in his wisdom and guidance. She'd counted on Shelly making the lunch offer and was surprised when it came from the preacher, whose offer was part religious leader and part lecher, Elisabeth not knowing the percentage of each.

Father had taken his direction from the preacher and seemed less hostile as he told her to follow them in her car out to the farm, saying that his family had chores to do there and didn't know when they'd be returning to town. Once in her car, Elisabeth felt around for the device, pushed the activation button once, heard it beep and then started the car and took her position in the caravan of worshippers heading to the farm.

As she drove she made mental notes of the various landscape changes but relied mostly on her concealed GPS, global positioning system strapped to her stomach under her blouse.

The stream of vehicles continued at a steady forty mph on gravel roads in a north-westerly fashion following the valleys leading away from StoneHead.

After about forty minutes they dropped down into a lush valley dotted with hay fields and pastures with grazing black and white Holstein milk cows. Vehicles found parking spots in the oversized lot beside an oblong barn and disgorged their occupants. Scores of men, women and children descended upon the caravan with hugs and handshakes; friends not seen for a while Elisabeth concluded.

Shelly and Mother came up to Elisabeth's car as she opened her door and shut off the GPS. They began introducing her to the numerous women curious about the visitor. Elisabeth's demeanor won her over to the locals and within minutes they were leading her into the barn, which in fact had been converted into living/eating quarters. Long tables had been set out to accommodate the various dishes the visitors now placed in sections according to meats, salads, and desserts. Shelly took Elisabeth's hand as several of the women gestured that they were to be the first to follow the men in the food line.

It was an awkward moment when Elisabeth moved to sit with the women-men were seated separately-and Shelly wanted to join her. Mother chastised Shelly and told her to keep her place and eat with the other children. Elisabeth's heart went out to Shelly but kept her composure, ignored the exchange, and sat with Mother.

Elisabeth fielded dozens of questions about her family, church, and work which Elisabeth answered with calm replies, keeping her head somewhat at a downward angle showing submissiveness to the group. Her actions brought quick acceptance by the others; many asking her to join them again the next Sunday.

After lunch Elisabeth offered to join in the clean-up but her hostess would have none of it and called Shelly over to show Elisabeth around the farm.

They started with the vegetable garden which appeared to be about an acre of fertile soil, then moved to the milking barn, loafing sheds for newborn calves then out the back and along a dirt road that led to the hay fields. On the return trip, Elisabeth asked about a side road that led through bush. Shelly said she didn't know where it went but was excited to go on an adventure. The two wandered down the little used dirt road sidestepping tall weeds, around various bends and turns coming to a dead-end at another large barn that was built into the base of a formable hill.

Shelly skipped ahead to find out what their treasure held. Elisabeth had other motives and she too rushed toward the well-kept structure. The main vehicle doors were barred from inside, so they walked around to the people door which was ajar. Shelly pulled it open, entered, and waved Elisabeth forward.

Elisabeth closed the door behind them only to find they were in total darkness. She felt along the inside door jam and found a light switch which struck light in a dozen overhead five hundred watt light fixtures. As the darkness was overcome, Elisabeth stood motionless as the vastness of the materials stacked on pallets. Her nose told her what the bags contained, and experience was her clue to the metal cans.

"What is this stuff Miss Peltowski? I've never seen it around the farm before."

"I don't know either Shelly, probably material for the farm. But there doesn't seem to be anything exciting like bunnies or lambs so let's keep exploring the outside."

Elisabeth took Shelly's hand and opened the door and found herself face to face with a mountain of a man. The guy had to be six five and two fifty and he just stood blocking her exit. "You shouldn't be here lady."

"I'm so sorry, we were just out for a walk and Shelly thought there might be lambs in the barn, so we took a look. There aren't so we're heading back."

"Lambs? You lookin' for lambs? We got lots of lambs over in the other barn. I can show you later but now I have to go fix a tractor, " Mountain replied in a manner that indicated he might be a bit slow.

"Are you sure Father won't be mad? I don't want to get into trouble. They won't allow me to come to the farm again for a long time and I'll have to stay home by myself."

"No, they won't get mad, will they sir?" asked Elisabeth.

"You shouldn't be here lady, but I won't tell anyone you was lookin' for lambs," was all Mountain could get out.

"No, Shelly, they won't get mad. Let's leave this nice man and get back to the others. There's no need to say anything to your Father. No harm done."

They retraced their steps and were back at the main housing area in twenty. Elisabeth made her apologies that she had to prepare for class the next day and had to get home. One of the men offered to guide her back to the main road so she hugged Shelly telling her she'd see her in class, thanked Mother and drove off.

Chapter Fifty-Two

Cathy was in a staff meeting when her coded Blackberry vibrated. She excused herself and returned to her office, shut, and locked the door, took a seat behind a massive oak desk, and decoded the text.

David.

She was taken aback by the content and was glad she was sitting down. Her worst fears were unfolding before her eyes. She had to meet with David to get all the particulars; any suspects, where was the cesium headed and then formulate a plan? She sent him a coded message and asked for a face to face immediately so they could formulate plans to get to the bottom of this potential catastrophe.

Rebecca slept till almost noon and rose groggily staggering into the kitchen to make coffee, drink two glasses of water and jogged around the living room to put life back into her system. Two coffees later she started to feel somewhat human, went for a twenty run, showered, and dressed in sweats. She glanced at her watch and cringed at the two on the dial. What the hell she thought, the day's almost gone. She grabbed a couple of granola bars and headed to Tom's to put in a few hours with the colt.

She didn't spend too much time schmoozing him in the paddock but rather haltered him quickly and moved to the round pen, making this the third time around. Rebecca started immediately, forced the colt to circle her for six laps, then changed directions.

After ten minutes she reduced the number of laps and forced him to change directions after every lap. After twenty minutes she stopped, put the whip on the ground and turned her back on the colt, watched him over her shoulder. Within seconds he was at her shoulder, blowing hot air through his flared nostrils.

She slowly turned and stroked his neck and shoulder running her fingers through his black mane, speaking softly. She started to walk away, and he followed her within about two feet; close enough to be "hooking-up" but at a sufficient distance to not invade her space.

The colt was now hers. She walked over to the rails with the colt right behind her. She lifted the saddle blanket off the rail, turned and showed it to the colt, told him not to be fearful. Rebecca was convincing the colt that although he was by nature a flight animal, one who ran first and questioned potential danger later, he could suspend that DNA trait with her. To do so required tremendous trust by the colt. But she had him now and would proceed slowly over the next few sessions and get him saddled, bridled, and ridden, then depending on Tom's instructions, work on advanced skills the colt would need around the ranch. She packed it in around six, satisfied that she'd had an incredibly successful day.

Simpson stopped at the Grizzly for a steak, a large russet and salad fixings and headed back to the cabin. Evening was upon her little corner of the valley when she pulled up the long driveway and parked. She brought her groceries in, locked the door, set the system, and spent the remainder of the evening fixing a meal, drinking herbal tea, and generally enjoying what she anticipated would be the last of her solitude for some time.

Elisabeth made it to the main highway and waved her appreciation to the parishioner in the red pick-up who had guided her, then made it for home as fast as the speed limit would allow; wouldn't do the operation much good for the school marm to get a speeding ticket, she thought. Once in the house she activated the system and sent an encrypted message to Jessica outlining her discovery, asking directions for handing off the GPS to Jackson. That done, she tried to relax with a cold Pepsi and ice, putting her feet up and watching mind-numbing television.

Two Pepsis later she was in the mood to fix dinner; a chicken breast with parmesan, garlic and rosemary and a large salad. While the breast was cooking she took her drink into the monitoring room and checked the emails flashing through StoneHead and was surprised to see one from the preacher to Mike.

"One of the town families brought a guest to the farm today, the new substitute at the middle. She says she's from Omaha's Dumfries Fundamentalist Congregation. Check it out and confirm. If she's what appears from today's appearances, we can go from there. The kids seem to like her, saying they call her the Wizard at school. Seems a rather independent career choice for someone purporting to be a fundamentalist."

Wow, that is surprising, thought Elisabeth. She'd been preparing for an onslaught from the church board. This was good news. She immediately sent a message to Jessica advising her of the email content and elaborated on her farm visit including her run in with Mountain then went wearily to bed.

Kate, Andy, Dean and Lela had continued management chores from their own ranch houses after Marc's arrival, coming over to the main house every few days to socialize. Marc had slid smoothly into his role with incredibly healthy and satisfying staff meals, regaling everyone with his healthy living and physical fitness philosophy.

Marc hadn't saved breakfast for Jessica and Jason so when they rose from their cocoons around ten, he told the duo he'd make them whatever they wanted when they were ready. Jessica admonished herself for oversleeping, but not too much, knowing Bruce would have gotten her up in an emergency.

She and Jason felt refreshed and decided to get in a long run before brunch. By the time they'd returned, showered, and dressed it was noon. They returned to the kitchen to find Marc's skillet hot, and pancake mix ready to go. He poured them orange juice and coffee, removed bacon from the oven and set about making them several stacks of pancakes.

They were in the middle of the first stack smothered in butter and Vermont maple syrup when Bruce stepped into the kitchen and laid two transmissions beside Jessica, grabbed a plate and cup then helped himself to cakes and coffee. Jessica took a moment to peruse the documents then said, "Change of plans. Sorento says Rebecca's findings won't get us the federal warrant. We need photos. Shit. Since when didn't a federal agent's word suffice? Nothing we can do about it. I'll send Rebecca back to the outfitters and Jackson to the farm tonight and they can get the photos."

She then read the second one and after a few seconds yelled, "Yes!" She yelled. "We got them. Elisabeth found the identical supplies at the church farm that Rebecca did at the outfitters. Geez these guys have enough explosives to wage a small war. But we still need visual proof. Possession of the explosives will get them a little prison time but will do nothing to cut the head off the dragon, their plans will continue without these locals. In the meantime, I'll have Elisabeth drop the GPS off here today at the front gate where Jackson can retrieve on his way to the farm. Since we won't arrest on possession alone, Jackson can get some photos of the farm supplies which, hopefully, will get us wiretap warrants while we work on getting proof of their intent. Too bad the President won't use the Patriot Act so we can do this the Bush way without the legalities.

"In the meantime Jason you work with our guest again and see if there's anything more you can wring from him. I'll check to see when the security installation guys are scheduled, hopefully tomorrow, otherwise let's keep ourselves primed."

Elisabeth woke around six, glanced at her watch and jumped out of bed. She pulled on sweats and wandered into the kitchen, made coffee, and immediately checked her encrypted Blackberry for messages and read Jessica's instructions to get the GPS to the ranch ASAP.

She walked around the living room cursing for oversleeping. She'd planned to be up early and prepare for her classes, now she had to forget that and get out to the Ranch with the GPS. She wolfed down a couple of pieces of toast and coffee while heading to shower and to dress.

Elisabeth drove up to the Ranch's gate's speaker phone and announced her arrival to the guards showing her ID to the CCTV. She was instructed to exit her vehicle and bring the device to the gate. She was met by two guards, one of which stood at an angle with an M-16 leveled at the car, given a person or persons could be hiding there.

She opened her jacket slowly revealing her Sig then carefully extended her left hand holding the ID. One guard reached through the gate's bars, took it from her, read it, returned it then asked her for her package.

Package she thought, what's this guy think I did gift wrap it? She reached into her side pocket and retrieved the small device and passed it through the bars. The guards thanked her and returned to the security house while Elisabeth got in her car and motored back to town and her classes wondering all the time what reception Shelly would have for her today.

Winthrop had just entered her condo when she grabbed the phone on the first ring. She put the receiver to her ear, "Meet me nine tomorrow Starbucks." Then the line went dead. She made a mental note of the appointment then put the call out of her mind and busied herself getting ready for bed wondering when she'd have the time to tackle her laundry and condo cleaning.

She was waiting for David at the back of Starbucks commanding a seat facing the street when David arrived at eight forty-five looking his spookiest in a London Fog trench coat with the collar up. Had it not been a blistery day she figured he'd gotten caught up in the theatrics of spook-dom. He stopped to order a double vanilla latte, waited for its preparation then joined Karen, scooting in beside her forcing Karen to slide further into the corner.

"Thanks for coming on such short notice Karen," David said as he sipped his latte. "You know about the recent anti-terrorism conference that just wound up here. One of the components was the creation of a joint Alberta anti-terrorism task force consisting of nationwide police departments, the RCMP and CSIS. Have you followed the government's changing policies over the years since 9/11?"

"Yes."

"Glad to hear it because that's why I asked you here. We have the cesium to track down, and deal with whatever fall-out that generates. Your Secret Service connection plus your numerous airport security networking made you our choice. You wouldn't leave the force but be sequestered to us for an indefinite time frame. You would make Corporal. The Force will jump your income to the max for your new position. That will bring you well above seventy thousand plus the various perks. You interested?"

"I'm flattered and yes, I'll take it. What do I have to do to make it happen?"

"Nothing, you just did. With that he got up and walked out leaving Karen with her mouth a gap, a combination of shock and pleasure.

Chapter Fifty-Three

Jackson's eyes jolted open at his usual internal alarm, grabbed the H&K, rolled out of bed taking aim at the bedroom door. Nano seconds later his brain acknowledged the lack of threat, rose slowly, laid the semi-auto on the bed, and wondered if he would ever wake up like a normal person.

He checked the Blackberry and was convinced it was malfunctioning. Nope, good to go but no Jessica message. Shit. He'd wound himself tight with anticipation and now nothing. He accepted reality and proceeded with his morning routine; coffee, stretching, isometrics and a forty-five run.

Pennington put the reconnaissance out of his mind by the time he hit the shower, knowing he'd have to be focused for today's classes, the presentations. He dressed in his conservative best; charcoal pants, black tassel loafers, pale pink button down shirt, filled a travel mug, grabbed two muffins from the bread drawer and headed to school.

Arriving ahead of the student masses and other teachers, he stopped by the staff lounge for another coffee and found Tony Kross marking papers. Jackson greeted him cordially not wanting to interrupt his concentration but as Jackson poured the coffee Tony commented, "Good morning Jackson, you should have stuck around the other night, lots of excitement. Apparently two guys jumped a third dude in the parking lot and the third guy beat the crap out of the two attackers.

Cops arrived doing routine bar checks and found two unconscious men in the parking lot. Story goes that they claimed to be victims who got beat up, but the deputy wasn't buying it given these guys' reputation.

Didn't get arrested them though, I guess because there was no victim unless you believed Jake and Patty."

Jackson took his coffee and followed Tony out the door then headed on his own down the hall, smiling to himself in spite of his attempts to remain professional. It did feel good to drop those assholes, he mused.

He spent a few minutes fine tuning his lesson plans then went into the hallway and meandered among the students, greeting those whose names he'd memorized, asking them about their weekend.

By the time the bell rang his first class had congregated around the classroom door. Even though the door was open, it seemed no one wanted to be the first to leave Jackson's impromptu social gathering. After all the other doors closed, he led the way into his classroom with everyone following. He smiled to himself acknowledging that kids were kids regardless of their geographical location and all wanted recognition as a young adult.

He quickly took roll and asked which group wanted to shine first. Every hand reached for the ceiling, so he made a random selection and immediately the first group bounded out of their seats and rushed forward.

Jackson was so absorbed in their speeches he momentarily forgot his own evaluation process. The first group acted as reporters airing live from the Gaza Strip during the Israeli attacks. As a presenter stepped forward, they would address another member of their group who would portray a Palestinian. Jackson was astounded by the depth and complexity of the questions and even more blown away by the emotion of the answers. Years of conflict were exposed, and extreme hatreds were voiced with such reality and forcefulness, several students in the audience could be heard gasping.

The next group took the Israeli position, and the presenter explained the political and military reason for the attacks. The next two presenters of the same group assumed the roles of Tel Aviv University students chatting about their hopes for a successful campaign against their country's primary physical threat. They went so far as to create a pub setting with empty beer bottles and candles on Jackson's desk, having removed all his papers and books.

Each successive group offered their own historical interpretation of recent and ancient events, amazing Jackson with their command of dialects, their sentence structure and most of all their lack of apprehension to public speaking. After the final group completed their task he walked to the front of the classroom shaking his head then turned to the class and said, "I applaud each and every one of you for an amazing presentation and performance. You've blown me away to the point of speechlessness. Well, almost. Have you guys done a lot of speeches in English or other classes?"

A fellow from the back of the class whom Jackson would have previously pegged as introverted, stood, and said, "No sir Mr. Pennington, none of us have ever done any public speaking or prepared speeches for any class, either here or at the junior high. We talked about this in the library, all of us, and I volunteered to tell you thanks from all of us. None of us can remember when we've had so much fun learning or learned so much having fun. You rock Mr. Pennington."

As the student finished all the others rose and clapped causing Jackson to blush with more emotion than he thought he had in him. Finally the students sat, and Jackson leaned his seat against his desk, smiled and said, "Thank you for the warm comments but you guys deserve all the credit, all I did was make the opportunity available. I'm sure you'll agree that this experience will be with you forever and is applicable to every aspect of your life. Wow, there goes the bell. I'll have your grades for next period. Have a great day, and thanks."

The students were all smiles as they walked up to Jackson, shook his hand then filed into the hallway.

Elisabeth started the day with considerable trepidation. If Shelly decided to chat with her about the events at the farm within hearing distance of any curious ears, her cover might be blown, and the reverberations and ramifications would be devastating to the mission....referring to her confrontation with the big guy at the farm.

It never happened. Shelly was in her first class, greeted her as though nothing adverse had occurred during the weekend. Elisabeth sighed relief and carried on with her lesson plans of the previous week, allowed students to advance at their own pace and enjoy the fruits of their accomplishments with the games.

A number of students advanced at a more rapid pace than she'd anticipated so during the lunch period she uploaded several more complex games and tweaked the system reducing the frequency of advancement requiring them to complete more assignments successfully before winning the game reward.

Her day went quickly, and her thoughts were directed to the students and their accomplishments and not the Service's objectives. By four the busses arrived, and her classroom emptied quickly as students ran to catch their transportation home. She checked her lesson plans for the next day then left the classroom and headed home to wait to hear from Jessica.

The rest of Jackson's day was equally successful as were his students who excelled with their presentations. He tried to leave the classroom for lunch, but the classroom filled with students right after the lunch bell and he couldn't get away. They brought their lunches and sat around debating the assignment they'd just presented. The student from the Maveric joined the group and Jackson found his input interesting. Jackson hadn't had an opportunity to meet any parents yet nor had he chatted extensively with the Maveric staff, so he didn't have a handle on adult input to these teen lives.

Kevin expressed a moderate approach to the Middle Eastern political debate in general but felt Washington spent too much time kowtowing to Israel which contributed to the area's imbalance of power.

At one point in a conversation he felt his Blackberry vibrating but he couldn't excuse himself without being rude and that was something he refused to do to the kids.

After his last class of the day, the routine was the same with his afternoon students stayed behind to chat about their assignment and History in general. Many asked him personal questions about where he was from and if he would apply for a permanent position for the fall. He assured them he was here to stay and would indeed be trying for a job...feeling somewhat remorseful for his deception.

After the last student left for the day Jackson snuck a peek at his Blackberry and noted Jessica's message that his recon was on for tonight and that he was to stop by the Ranch guard house for a GPS which would give him directions to the church farm.

He'd just returned the device to his pocket when Tony stuck his head in the door and offered, "Seems like you're the talk of StoneHead Jackson. Whatever you did, the kids loved it and are asking for more. Congratulations. Hey, you have time for a beer after school?"

"Thanks Tony but I'll have to take a raincheck for later in the week, maybe Friday night. I want to get this marking done for tomorrow."

"Friday it is. I'll organize the foursome again and we can pick up where we left off."

"Sounds good. See you then", added Jackson as felt the discomfort begin in the pit of his stomach at the thought of a repeat performance at the Parrot.

Simpson woke feeling more luxurious than she had in months, contributing the feeling to the anticipation of an adrenaline rush. She dressed in sweats and runners, strapped on her H&K, and put in sixty minutes up and down the gravel road alternating between pounding the ditch, running the barbed wire line or on the road itself.

Back at the cabin she prepared a modest breakfast of OJ, scrambled eggs, thick toast, and coffee, showered and headed to Tom's to put more time on the colt, hoping she'd have a few more days here to at least get a saddle on him.

Brian was putting the final touches on the underground grow-house after Stan's orders to increase production 24/7 because of the demand and soaring prices. His previous procedure was to take a little down time after loading the crop on the train cars, head to the city for a day or two of R&R. He decided to get the new seeds planted and on their way, take two days off, then come back and clean up the refuse from the processed crop.

Brian was trimming the small pot plants to increase their lower stem growth when his phone vibrated. Activating the screen he read Stan's message regarding the murder of a Nez Perce deputy, advised Brian to ship the next batch to Vancouver rather than Idaho. Stan expected the murder investigation to stall within a month and everything would return to normal. He also advised Brian to prepare to retrieve dangerous goods from the Calgary storage garage and ship to Los Angeles via the lead lined containers he'd built.

Brian replied that he'd received the text, understood, and would comply, deleted the data, and then returned the device to his cargo pants and continued trimming, wondering what this new operation would mean to him financially..

Chapter Fifty-Four

After the last student left Pennington glanced at his watch, saw that it was already six, locked his files in the desk, locked the classroom door and walked quickly to his truck. He stopped by the market and bought a package of chicken breasts, a bottle of cumin and red chili powder, Tibetan tea, potatoes, and carrots then headed home for a decent meal before nightfall.

Once in the house, the truck garaged and the system on, he relaxed, brewed the Tibetan, and prepared his dinner, browning the breast then adding the vegetables and spices and letting it all simmer while he prepared the evening's action plan.

Once he had the plan memorized he retrieved the H&K MP5SD automatic rifle, night scope, night goggles, spare magazines and miniature digital camera from a floorboard cavity then changed into a black T, black cargo pants, Magnum boots and dark windbreaker. He put everything in a black backpack and laid the supplies by the back door, set the table, served his meal on a China dinner plate, then sat and ate with a combination of hyper enthusiasm and calm he'd learned in Delta. The system had served him well through many missions as it would tonight.

Jackson washed, dried, and put his dishes away, gathered his gear, locked the house, fobbed the system, and put his supplies on the passenger seat. He backed out of the garage, returned to shut, and locked it then drove to StoneHead Ranch where he was able to obtain the GPS system with little effort once he showed his ID.

He followed the GPS directions northeast out of town winding through the various valleys until the system beeped that he was within a mile of his destination. He pulled to the side of the one lane gravel road, cut the lights, backed into the bush, grabbed his gear, slipped on his protective vest with ceramic plates capable of stopping rifle bullets and set off through the terrain of saplings and the odd mature tree…a remnant of logging years ago.

The terrain rose slightly over the next few miles finally cresting at the lip of a large valley. He dropped to the ground just as it slanted downward and retrieved his night goggles from the pack. He could make out dark structures about three hundred yards into the valley. There were no lights visible, not even yard illumination. The goggles picked up what appeared to be either cows or horses in the fields and other animals that were viewed as spots through the glasses. No humans. He returned the glasses to the backpack, slipped the automatic rifle across his chest, and descended into the valley.

He skirted the main barn that Elisabeth had noted was their primary sleeping quarters and came upon the dirt lane by jumping several barbed fences, which started the Holsteins.

The agent headed away from the buildings guided by a shimmering light from a half-moon and found the barn within fifteen yards, the people door unlocked.

Jackson opened the door with both hands, putting pressure on the hinges to prevent a squeak. Once inside he repeated his opening process to close and latch the door. He waited several seconds while his eyes adjusted to the total blackness, then turned on the pen light with a narrow hooded beam and began his search.

He'd just swung the light across the back of the barn picking up reflections of the materials Elisabeth had noted, when he heard voices coming from the lane he'd just traveled. He quickly retrieved his camera and started clicking photos of the entire area, stopped to pry boxes open and photograph the contents then moving to another stack. The voices were getting louder as they grew closer and Pennington could make out part of the conversation, "What did Louise say she saw again?" said a male voice.

"Getting me out of a good night's sleep this better be good," replied another.

Jackson heard at least a dozen different voices question each other and whatever Louise had seen that caused her to alarm and arm the men. He didn't want to be caught in the barn, so he put the camera away and ran for the door, not bothering to worry about the hinges. Mistake. "Fuck", said Jackson as he heard the loud screech as he opened the door.

The noise was obvious to anyone within a hundred yards and the church men responded instantly shouting as they closed the distance to the barn, "Someone is there; you guys circle around back and see if we can cut them off."

Jackson took off to the back of the barn and scurried up the hill and around the peak and stopped where he'd have a side view of the barn. He laid prone, swung the automatic rifle, flipped the bipods, uncapped the night scope covers and sighted in those just coming around the barn.

The teacher hoped they'd figure their ears played games and conclude a false alarm when one of the men yelled, "He came through here. Look, you can see the dirt scuffed going up the hill. You guys go around the back of the hill and come up from the rear, you other guys go back around the barn and circle in from the left and we'll follow his trail up here. Yell if you see him and shoot if you have to, we have too much to lose here."

Jackson figured that just about covered all possibilities. He was stuck, no out and he couldn't afford to be captured. The ramifications of a secret service agent captured by a domestic terrorist group was too devastating to consider, so he opened fire, strafing the treetops of each of the groups forcing them to retreat to the barn for cover.

The rifle's popping created no echo and couldn't be heard beyond the barn's perimeter. They scattered like mice, dropping to the ground, crouching and duck walking back to cover. He was sure he'd counted correctly and saw the same number of attackers return as had advanced but decided to alter his location as a tactical measure in case one was able to come up behind him.

He could see the light reflection coming from the buildings in the distance. It was only a matter of time before reinforcements arrived with who the hell knew what kind of arsenal. He removed his Blackberry and sent out Jessica's chosen distress signal that would reach all four agents then returned fire with accuracy this time. His placement was within one inch of the cross hairs hitting his targets' knees and watched them flop and scream on the grass. He'd dropped three when the gun fire stopped abruptly. His night scope revealed an increasing number of recruitments scurrying through the bushes approaching his location. He sent another automatic burst over their heads forcing them flat, but that held them only momentarily then they were up advancing on him again.

Rebecca was preparing dinner when her Blackberry's screen flashed rapid RED advising her Jessica was calling action code. Before she could react, the device rang. She pushed Talk and listened to Jessica say Jackson was in trouble at the church farm and to meet her, Jason and Elisabeth at Belfry Highway and the county dump road.

NOW.

Rebecca stuffed the Blackberry into her pants, grabbed the tactical bag of automatic rifle, spare clips, and other assault gear, stuffed her feet into her Magnums ran out the door, locked, fobbed and was on her way down the lane within two minutes, truck blowing gravel in high plumes.

Rebecca screeched to a stop almost sliding into the dumpsters, slammed the shift into Park, jumped out swinging her long awkward bag, fobbed the truck and jumped into the back of the waiting Suburban barely getting the door closed as the vehicle gained speed and spun on to the highway.

Jessica filled her in on Jackson's situation, "He's pinned on a ridge above the barn you found Elisabeth. He counted twenty shooters, and it would seem they're going for broke giving it everything they've got.

I contacted the Billings, Montana SAC Special Agent in Charge and their SWAT-Special Weapons and Tactical team is en-route, ETA thirty. We'll direct them from the ground as they approach from the northeast. She laid out her tactical advance plans as Jason manipulated brake and accelerator around the gravel turns keeping all four wheels grounded and preventing them from flying into the continuous abyss on his left.

The agents struggled into their tactical vests as the SUV swayed back and forth around curves.

No flashing lights, no sirens. They gained air as the huge SUV cleared the ridge leading into the valley. They could see the compound lighted to its maximum with a number of residents scurrying to shutter the main barn's windows. Elisabeth directed Jason through the parking area, around the milking barns and out the back to the storage barn.

Jessica's plan was to bail from the Suburban one hundred yards from the assault rear guard then fan out two on each side of Jackson's attackers, approaching the insurgents one on one with their silenced automatic rifles, keeping in touch with their throat mikes.

As Jason came close to their demarcation locale, they all donned balaclavas and night goggles while Jessica sent a nano second Blackberry burst to Jackson telling him of their arrival. Their coordinated advantage was the four agents were wearing jackets marked with Secret Service in bold luminescent lettering visible only through night vision technology.

Jackson picked out the four immediately and was able to maintain his barrage while the agents converged from each side. Jackson was dropping his attackers by shooting their legs, an easy target given the short distance and night scope.

The four agents advanced on the barn. As each Church dropped, the shooting agent would disarm and plastic cuff him... wrists and ankles...before moving on to the next.

Fukishura and Peltowski exited to the left of the Suburban, kept each other in sight and converged on the attackers. Jessica approached the first from behind without his knowledge, raised the rifle and dropped him with a blow to the back of his head. Cuffed and unloaded his rifle. She watched Elisabeth take her first with a side kick to the back of his legs, dropped him immediately, then a rifle butt to his ribs, cuffed and gagged. Jessica moved ahead and was about to repeat the last process when the attacker turned and leveled his 30.06 at her mid-section. She immediately kicked her legs out in front and while dropping down on her butt she set off a short burst that cut the guy in two. She rolled sideways, rose on one knee, and took out his partner with another short burst. Fuck this prisoner shit, she thought. She continued her pursuit checking each downed assailant looking for Harold Richards and the other leaders.

Jessica and her team were ten into their counter assault when they heard the whoop, whoop of the Air Force's EC 725 Cougar chopper carrying the FBI's SWAT team of twenty agents. The entire area for one hundred plus yards was illuminated by the chopper's high intensity undercarriage spot lights blinding the shooters and causing them to scurry for cover. The gun ship's firearm's officers manned the two 7.62mm machine guns sweeping the area awaiting firing orders. Jessica directed the chopper, through her tactical headset, to an open area directly west of their location.

"Tact One to Tact two, three, four," Jessica called over her headset.

"Go Tact One, replied Rebecca."

"Any of you have Richards and the other leaders?"

"I have Sarkowski," replied Jason. "No sign of Richards."

"I have Mike," added Elisabeth.

"Okay keep looking. We need all these guys," said Jessica.

The chopper landed abruptly disgorging ten agents per side. Once empty, the chopper rose again and hovered over the fire fight position illuminating it completely. SWAT spread out surrounding the Church members ordering them to the ground then disarming and plastic cuffing them.

The counter assault was over in minutes with the landscape cluttered with prone bodies. Ten SWAT members took off at a run to secure the main buildings while Jessica and her team joined the other ten to round up the *Christians for a Better America* members, dragged them into the barn and secure the perimeter.

Once inside the agents double checked each prisoner for weapons and found a number of concealed handguns, knives, and box cutters. FBI and Secret Service agents kept their balaclavas in place heightening the mystery as to their identity. All prisoners were gagged and blindfolded with hands cuffed behind and legs extended and cuffed.

Jessica stepped outside, messaged Jackson to secure his position, keep his head cover and reconnoiter at the barn. Within minutes she could see Jackson drop out of the bushes and approach her on the run. He was somewhat hesitative given that his actions had been what prompted the full scale counterattack; would his actions be approved or was he in the shit... ran through his mind as he approached.

As he walked up to Jessica she gave him a smile that he could see in her eyes which told him he was okay, "Nice work Delta, come inside and see what you reigned in."

Jackson smiled and followed her into the barn where he was greeted with similar supportive comments from SWAT members.

They were debriefing him in hushed voices when he caught site of his colleagues standing to the side watching. He excused himself and jogged over receiving congratulations and hidden smiles from all three.

Jessica waved her agents to the barn's far corner for a quick debriefing.

"Okay guys, great work here but we have a problem. No Richards and without him we know the other cells are going underground or at the very least be on hyper alert. And we have no name for our mole. I think we've been able to maintain your covers. There's no way these guys could ID any of you, so keep the covers.

The suspects are going to claim self-defense of their compound, their farm and be totally within their rights. The bureau has had these guys on their radar for some time so the attorney general can deal with the fall-out.

Chapter Fifty-Five

The SWAT commander approached Jessica and said, "Agent Fukishura, we've secured this area and my other team is doing likewise at the main compound. Several additional choppers are en route from Billings and Great Falls and will be here within twenty to transport the prisoners back to the Air Force Base in Great Falls. Denver's SAC, Dominique Cooper is sending agents to secure the scene and will be handling the investigation for the FBI since Wyoming is their jurisdiction.

That does it for us. Your Agent Pennington is some kinda, kinda I tell you. His reputation from busting the cell in Idaho was already legend and now this. You'd best keep an eye on him because I think Cooper might want him for her SWAT team, I know I'm going to try and get him."

"Thank you sir, I'll keep Pennington close, so he doesn't wander. We'd best be getting back so we can debrief Washington."

The team helped carry Jackson's gear as they walked to the Suburban, packed and headed back to where they'd picked up Rebecca. En-route Jessica said, "Well done you guys. We proved our ability to infiltrate and complete a mission. We're going to reconnoiter at the Ranch later so grab your ride Rebecca and head home. Elisabeth, we'll drop you by your car as well and you can get some sleep too."

Rebecca bailed, grabbed her gear from the SUV's rear storage area and jogged to her truck as the Suburban hit the road.

"Elisabeth and Jackson, you guys get back to work; your cover is intact. Here we are Jackson," she said as they pulled up to his bushed truck. "I don't want the press to get wind of this and by sunrise they will be out in force looking for answers."

Last stop was for Elisabeth who exited quickly and was in her car and headed home immediately.

Back at the ranch, Fukishura said, "Okay, let's get this thing written up the best we can while were waiting for the others. I'll send what we've got to Sorento then provide him an addendum later. Maybe we can catch some sleep."

They spent the next few hours doing just that. Satisfied that they'd provided as much information as possible and noting further data was coming, Jessica had Barry send the encryption then she and Jason went to bed. Didn't set an alarm. She'd check with Dean later that day about the mole, but for now she needed sleep before she fell flat on her face.

Winthrop was mystified by her conversation with David. First to stir the confusion was a couriered package the next morning with a Visa chipped Gold Card requiring no signature, a CSIS identification card with her name, photo, index fingerprint and a small icon that indicated her iris scan was on record, notification that her direct bank deposited salary had been increased substantially and a note, presumably from David, to shred the envelop.

Later the same day she received an encrypted text from David instructing her to go to Edmonton for her first in a series of meetings regarding their last conversation, to whom she was to report and that she would be directed after the meeting to a debriefing location.

It all seemed so overwhelming and happening so quickly that she had to stop thinking, relax, and tell herself that this is what she wanted. Having done that she was able to move on and quickly felt the excitement and adrenaline rush of the clandestine world.

Karen had a relaxing dinner with Tom at her place and tried to explain in as vague terms as possible her new assignment. Tom stopped her mid-sentence and said no explanation was necessary and they would see each other when and where they could, reiterating that he really wanted the relationship to continue.

With that assurance under her belt, she headed to Edmonton on the next WestJet flight, deciding to forgo Air Canada, feeling it would be too difficult to explain why she was not riding shotgun.

Jackson and Elisabeth arrived later the next day, parked their vehicles by the Ranch's front door and were met by Dean and Andy waiting on the porch. Armed. Never being at the Ranch previously, albeit Rebecca at night, they were all taken aback at the sight.

All three agents stopped instantly as they exited their vehicles, not sure what to do or whom to do it to. Dean and Andy waited a few seconds relishing in the newcomers uncertainty. Finally Dean said, "Welcome to StoneHead folks, I'm Dean Jamieson and this is Andy Gardner. We work for the President here at StoneHead. Jessica will explain our roll."

The agents lifted their hands from their weapons as Dean said with a grin, "Sorry about that agents, couldn't be avoided given the short time frame. Please follow us."

"Thanks guys," said Jackson, "Your gear gave us a bit of a start. We've never seen non Secret Service guarding the President."

Dean replied as he walked around their vehicles, "We don't actually guard Mr. Bakus the way you do. We were with him before the election and have been armed from day one. A lot of Wyoming folks are, gun laws being somewhat liberal here compared to other states like New York or Washington, D.C. Anyway, Jessica will fill you in. We've both been trained at Rowley by the way."

Dean and Andy walked through the front door and the others followed. They showed them into the living room where a tea set was placed on the long coffee table. "Help yourselves to tea agents and I'll let Jessica know you're here," said Andy.

It was after four when Jessica and Jason met in the living room, to find the others seated in front of the fire, each cradling a cuppa. "You guys look pretty good, must have had a good rest," Jessica said as she entered the living room.

All three raised their tea mugs as Jessica walked to the kitchen stuck her head in and said hello to Marc who replied, "Hi Jessica, can I get you some tea and snacks?"

"Sounds great Marc thanks." She headed to the security office wondering if they'd heard back from Sorento. Bruce was in his usual spot watching the numerous screens that monitored the entire Ranch and glanced up as she entered, "Hey Jessica, I heard you guys done good huh? Sorento thinks so too but with a major caveat. Here's his reply to your transmission." He handed the papers to Jessica who leaned against the door jam and began reading.

After a few minutes she said, "I'll be damned. This is totally crazy. But holy crap!"

Bruce looked at her with arms raised questioning. Jessica asked him for an encrypted line, entered the soundproof cubicle and got Sorento on the phone. Listened for fifteen, hung up and left without clarifying for Bruce.

Bruce located Dean who joined the living room group just as Jessica said, "I just got a reply from our partial debriefing transmission from Sorento and you're not going to believe this."

Jessica started, "Before I begin, a toast to us for an unbelievable job." They clinked mugs and she continued, "The SAC, Dominique Cooper did the initial interrogating starting with Elisabeth's student Shelly's, Mom. The group is claiming religious freedom with none talking. We'll wait and see what happens, and you will see in a moment, the Christians for a Better America has created an almost impenetrable religious freedom cocoon.

"We need to pick up the trail of the drug supply coming from Idaho. Sorento said Rebecca's experience in Arizona is reason for us to handle that end of the investigation. The FBI arrested James, so as of now Rebecca, he needs to be replaced and his business operational. I'll leave that to you. We can create a cover that you bought the place with Derrick your partner. Something to that effect. You also need to keep your relationship with Pen current and active.

"Dean, what have you found about our mole?"

"Didn't have to do much Jessica, Len Thiessen was gone this morning. Andy was making his rounds and Thiessen's animals were bellowing for food and water. When Andy told me, I checked out Thiessen's room and found he'd cleared out.

He must have been early this morning after you guys got back. I checked with the front gate, and they said he passed through right after sun-up saying he was heading to the feed store for antibiotics for a colt. The guards had no reason to suspect him. I apologize Jessica, Thiessen was vetted as closely as the rest of us, approved by Washington and none of us suspected he would turn."

"I suspect he joined Richards somewhere and they are both in the wind. We can get out a BOLO, be on the lookout, through the state police from Sorento but I wouldn't count on any success. They'll hook up with another cell. No apology necessary Dean, shit happens, and we'll deal with the fall-out.

"Sorento isn't as pissed as I had expected. He acknowledged that we had to do what we did, and he will work with the FBI and attorney general, just as we speculated, and leave us out of it.

He's contacted the Canadian RCMP's assistant commissioner and the National Security Enforcement unit and their Canadian Security Intelligence Service (CSIS). His intelligence is the cannabis Rebecca located is coming from either Alberta or British Columbia. The drugs are of such high quality; the price has skyrocketed and lining the producers' pockets big time.

I don't know what the spooks have to do with this, but we'll find out. The Mounties will be working with the FBI on that end, but we have to deal with the explosives.

CSIS is following leads on missing cesium from Manitoba, and they believe this stuff is going to be used in conjunction with enriched Iranian uranium smuggled out of Iran and either headed here or already in place.

There is a down side though and I'm sorry to have to be the messenger. Shepherd, Marrington, their wives and children have been released from federal custody."

Multiple moans around the room and heads shaking in disgust. Jackson and the team had put together an excellent operation and to have it taken apart by the federal attorneys can be disappointing. In one door and out the other that law enforcers across the nation find frustrating.

"I know, I know," she said with a combination of sorrow and anger. "This is a major setback for the FBI, the attorney general and justice. We know what they had there, but the group declared religious freedom as their defense and have high powered attorneys prepared to fight the charges and shout "persecution" for years.

"On another up note, while back in DC, I had a beckoning from on high to meet with a White House representative. I was prepared for another political hack but found out she is a Bakus anointed law enforcer who has put together a nationwide crime aggregate system that, in theory at least, has all crime data from every jurisdiction in the country, from small towns to megalopolises. I plan accessing the data base shortly and plug in our information and see what we get back. I'll brief you when that happens.

"But for us, here is the weird part, are you ready for this? We're to remain here at StoneHead and supervise the security installation while waiting new orders for...our own unit. Can you believe it? We are a new unit that will deal exclusively with domestic and foreign threats against the President. What do you guys think, you in?"

Jason was the first to speak, "All right! Stability at last. I'm in Jessica."

"Count me in," chimed Rebecca and Elisabeth simultaneously.

Jackson wondered aloud, "I'm in, although Jessica, so thank you."

"Mine as well Jessica. I thought teaching was boring until this assignment where I created my own lessons. I thank you as well."

Jessica replied, "You're both welcome. Should we have a name for the unit?"

Rebecca offered, "How about 'The J Team'?"

"Perfect," said Jason.

The agents raised their cups and said in unisons, "To the J Team."

Jackson added, "Now, where is the wine and appetizers," standing and walking toward the kitchen.

Acknowledgements

This work was the suggestion and encouragement of writer, educator, and friend Les Wiseman who shaped my writing style through numerous classes, The Province newspaper experience and successive column years.

The inspiration for Jessica Fukishura is my martial arts student Jessica Fukushima, who epitomizes the "J" Team's will, determination, and superior martial arts skills.

Fashion expertise goes to Elise Laina, who educated me on fashions which would catch your eye and in which shoes/boots the characters could fight. Elise deserves special recognition and appreciation for her incredible Italian cuisine expertise and her continuous flow of support, information, suggestions, and encouragement.

What would be attractive on Jessica, Karen and Shelia is Heather McCormick's contribution and for steering me through Holt's mind-blowing fashion offerings.

My martial arts expertise has to be credited to the many law enforcers, both civilian and military, with whom I've trained and taught combat martial arts, a style in which I hold a 6th Degree Black Belt. Also to my first martial arts karate instructors, Eighth Degree Black Belt Sukwinder Manhas, Black Belt Paul Manhas and Tenth Degree Combat Martial Artist Brad Steiner.

My appreciation to law enforcer Jack Ross for his expertise with the intricacies of pack trains and his criminal behavior anecdotes garnished from years with the RCMP and West Vancouver Police Department.

Medical expertise is heaped upon Kasteen Beltowski with her many years in emergency room trauma centers who shared her anatomy knowledge.

Dr. Barrie Bennett's teaching methods are highlighted in several chapters with the same success as I have experienced while implementing them in classrooms. Dr. Bennett's Cooperative Learning takes students to new heights of learning.

I had the honor of attending Lt. Col. Dave Grossman, U.S. Army (Ret) law enforcement seminars. He has had a huge impact on my life so a "Hoorah" to Dave for his contributions and for the use of his motivational quotes.

Special thanks go to Lisa Samuel for her Southwest interior design, Channel Road Inn and their relaxing and romantic hospitality...thanks Heather and Dominique for all the support and encouragement, Richard Brown for permission to use his "Legend" Series, David Crighton and his ink impressions of the Toronto skyline, and the staff at New Mexico Pinon coffee, copious quantities of which were consumed by the White House Secret Service crew, Kicking Horse coffee from the greatest of places, the Canadian Rockies, for their supplying the incredibly impressive flavor at the Toronto Police Academy, Taser International for suspect control tactics and Jim Gregg, master shooter and his "Hole in One" concept and shooting advice.

All things criminal and prosecutorial are credited to law enforcers Kim Babala, Roy Davidson, Loren Wood, and Rick Drought with their many years of investigations both internation- ally and domestically.

The intricacies of the international railroad system couldn't have been successful without the assistance of Shawna Phillips at CP Rail. Thanks for all the guidance.

Glenn's Japanese cuisine expertise is credited to Joe and Elsie Komori for their recipe and preparation of the various dishes presented.

Chef Marc Stucki lent his rise to fame for the StoneHead compound and his many gourmet presentations.

Jacket art critiquing goes to Anne MacDonald and Elise Laina for their choice of Andy Cook's impressive photograph.

Boordy Vineyards were kind to offer their name for the wine selection at the Secret Service Training center. And, yes, there really is a Craig Stevenson and all that is written about him is true and not embellished by me in any way.

Special appreciation goes to my spouse Judy who put up with hours of my isolation, my constant jotting the plot on scrap paper, getting up in the middle of the night to write, a sundry of weird behavior over the course of this work and for her editing expertise.

30,000 Secrets

Jonathan McCormick

Prologue

L en Thiessen was blasting east out of StoneHead, Wyoming trying to maintain the speed limit, but anxious to put time and distance between him and StoneHead Ranch where he had wrangled for the last five years, albeit more as a mole for the Christians for a Better America, CFBA, than working cows.

He had a good thing going for a very long time; better than average wages, a spacious bunkhouse with meals prepared by a renowned chef, his own ranch gelding...a good future, but not as good as what he had been promised by Harold Richards. Thiessen just had to report anything out of the ordinary at the president's ranch on the throwaway cell Richards had given him, in exchange for monthly cash deposits in a storage locker in a nearby town.

Over the past few months, he had connected with Richards almost daily due to the increased activity at the ranch, beginning with the arrival of two Secret Service agents who seemed to be all over the property at any given time. He had run into agent Jason Spencer while bringing injured cows down to the main compound.

Thiessen was shocked, to say the least, when the man he saw had no resemblance to his preconceived notion of a Secret Service Agent; long dark brown dreads, dark complexion, six-foot or so, 190 pounds, baggy jeans and a short-sleeve, bright yellow Tommy Bahama Academy shirt hanging out over his pants. The way the guy carried himself, it was obvious to Thiessen that this was no run of the mill agent; this guy was in shape and operated as though he was ready to do battle in a Nano second. He did not believe the guy was an agent at first meeting and had his hand on his .44 while the guy reached for and showed him his identification.

Then the guy started jive talking as though rapping with homeboys, not protecting the president of the United States. It was a very uncanny experience that didn't sit well with Thiessen. It was as though Spencer knew Thiessen was not what he purported to be and that could be dangerous not knowing if at any time his message passing side-line would get him fired...or worse.

Thiessen had no idea who or what Richards was or that he, Thiessen, was on the edge of a looming catastrophe that would put him on the run for the rest of his life.

On several occasions, Thiessen found he was calling Richards several times daily, after he spotted Spencer taking measurements and photographs around the chain link fence which ran as a perimeter encompassing the main ranch house and the adjacent ranch bungalows, creating a tight secure compound.

Thiessen thought of photographing the agent and maybe con a bonus from Richards but reconsidered given the huge closed-circuit television system integrated throughout the 3,000 acres. He knew he could be on camera at any time and didn't want to have to explain himself to the military security detail or ranch managers.

Thiessen had no idea that the ranch managers would soon be fired for hiring him or the intense efforts the agents would expend to find the mole...him. To the managers' credit, Thiessen's resume was totally legitimate; it wasn't until much later that he threw away a lifetime opportunity and jumped into bed with President Bakus' enemies.

Thiessen had finished his evening chores the previous night, had dinner and settled into the television room for a few hours of sitcoms and maybe Tom Selleck in *Blue Bloods* when his burner cell vibrated in his Levi's back pocket. He excused himself from the other wranglers and headed to the restroom and read the text. It was from Richards. Very short. Not encrypted. "Get out now and hide."

This was unusual behavior for Richards, often a man of many words, mostly superfluous and droning, so Thiessen accepted the warning; not having a clue as to the why, or where he would go.

He headed back to the bunkhouse, packed a quick duffle, jammed in a couple of handguns, and took off in his beater pick-up. It was still early enough that the gate guards didn't question his comment that he had to head to town for colt medication before the feed store closed.

Now Thiessen was burning pavement, furtively scanning the side mirrors every few seconds looking for any sign of a state trooper. With every mile, his heart rate slowed, and his shoulder muscles began to relax, knowing that the Secret Service wouldn't be coming after him even if they knew he was the mole.

Chapter One

Captain Michelle "Bam-Bam" Nicholodian, her co-pilot Lieutenant Keely O'Reilly and shooter Second Lieutenant Billy Rae Boyanton were chowing in the ready-room, keeping their blood pressure and heart rates low while they woofed today's special of Mongolian BBQ Stir Fry.

Because they were on duty in their flight suits with helmet and gloves at the ready and required to be visual on their Cougar, their food was brought to them by officers' mess stewards who had set the round table beforehand with cutlery, cloth napkins and glasses of ice water...milk or milk products were not consumed while on duty as the crew might develop phlegm during a flight causing difficulty with their face masks and air supply flow.

Conversations were limited or non-existent during these times per protocol and experience...this might be the last meal they have for some time if the horn blasts. Speed and anxiety aside, they did have numerous discussion topics in common.

This base being in Great Falls, Montana they had become skiers, not accomplished, although Bam-Bam considered herself a black run flier, but days off fun kinda boarders. They were all getting four off at the end of this duty round so today the conversation hovered around the weather and if the clear Montana skies would continue into their leave days.

Billy Rae had just taken a bite of his Mongolian, the spicy sauce dripping down his chin when the adrenalin gong show blasted from the four mega speakers above their heads..."Gonnnnnnng! Gonnnnnnng!.."

The crew ran napkins over their faces, chugged a mouth of ice water, grabbed their helmets, gloves, and ran for their Cougar, plugged in within twenty yards of the exit door. Bam-Bam was through the chopper's door first and scrambled to her command seat while Keely jumped into the side bench and Billy Rae pounced into his ordinance control center, each with a personalized Beretta Submachine clipped to the fuselage next to them. Bam-Bam had the five-blade, fifty-three-inch diameter composite main rotor in motion within seconds of her butt hitting the energy absorbing body seat as the deck hand simultaneously unplugged the battery charger and gave her a two handed over the head whirling motion with both arms.

After lighting his control panel, Billy Rae bounced over to the starboard 7.62 mm FN MAG-60/30 machine gun and swung it outward, chambered a round and sat. He breathed consciously and slowed his heart rate to 60 while Bam-Bam lifted fifteen thousand pounds of metal grace one foot off the tarmac and throttled to maximum, paralleling the tarmac south bound.

Keely meanwhile was processing their orders received through the onboard computer system and relaying the coordinates to Bam-Bam with Billy Rae following the conversation through his own headset, knowing action was moments away...target unknown.

"Target is a '92 Chevy pick-up, light blue, no canopy, heading presumably east out of StoneHead. No plate number yet. Intel from The Ranch and Secret Service supervisor Fukishura, the driver is a Len Thiessen, a ranch hand believed to be a mole for the Christians for a Better America, which Fukishura and her team just took down. Fukishura is confident Thiessen will not head west into the national forest, as there are no side roads onto which he can escape.

Bam-Bam was scanning the skies doing a VFR, visual flight rules, for any small aircraft, which might not have noticed Malmstrom's traffic controller's flight advisory. "Copy that

Lieutenant Keely. On your toes Lieutenant Billy Rae as we are only going to be able to take one pass at this guy when we find him…we will be maxed on fuel by the time we spot him given his lead."

"Copy that Bam-Bam, I'm on it", replied Billy Rae, the craft's 7.62 moving back and forth rhythmically with his head braced against the scope.

Bam-Bam moved her control stick slightly to bring the Cougar up to five hundred feet and maxed out the two Turboméca Makila 2A1 Turbo shaft engines to 201 mph while Keely followed the computer chatter from Malmstrom Air Force Base as their air traffic controllers provided approved altitude and cleared the airways for their pursuit. Malmstrom had recently made international headlines with the revelation that many of the Air Force's nuclear arsenal personnel had cheated on a proficiency exam. Thirty-four officers responsible for the launching configuration of the missiles were suspended and eleven more were investigated for illegal drugs.

Jonathan McCormick

McCormick holds a Sixth Degree Black Belt in Combat Martial Arts. He is a U.S Marine (inactive) and trained with famed CIA operative Rex Applegate and Royce Gracie of the infamous Gracie family and the Ultimate Fighter Challenges.

He is a former member of the American Society of Law Enforcement Trainers instructing Seattle, Washington Police officers and King County Sheriff's deputies & has trained with the Canadian Military Police, RCMP and Victoria, British Columbia Police Department.

McCormick is an associate member of the British Columbia Women in Law Enforcement-BCWLE. He has written for law enforcement magazines Blue Line and Twenty-Four-Seven and has been a guest writer for the Vancouver Province.

McCormick was the personal security columnist for the British Columbia newspaper The Province.

He wrote personal security articles for the Canadian Association of Retired Persons, B.C. Woman and Maturity. He has written women's self-defense pieces for Full Contact and Black Belt magazines.

Contact McCormick at jonathanmccormick.com

Manufactured by Amazon.ca
Bolton, ON

43582939R00267